UnderLife

Jocelyn Romero

DEDICATION

Mom. Dad. Grandma.

Thank you for raising me to believe in my dreams and create a happy life. I don't know where I'd be without your support.

CONTENTS

ACKNOWLEDGMENTS

Evan Sandman
Thank you introducing me to I Ching, being my friend,
and lending your genius to edit UnderLife.
You're one of the best kept secrets in Hollywood.

Friends and Family – You're the reasons life is worth living in every incarnation. Our relationships are timeless. More adventure awaits.

CHAPTER ONE
THE FOOL

New Orleans, Louisiana
Fifteen Years Ago

Walking with her luggage rattling along beside her, August Cannon crossed the automatic glass door threshold of New Orleans International Airport. She left the air conditioned sanctuary of baggage claim, entering the immense steam room which is the South during summertime.

August's blouse was giving its best instant saran wrap impersonation on her flesh. She resisted the impulse to take off her suit coat because it would expose the Beretta nine millimeter pistol resting in her shoulder holster.

August closed her mind to her sweaty discomfort, and looked around for the person they said would be there to greet her. Standing six feet and one inch, with a runner's build, and only twenty-one years spent on the planet, August looked more like a successful young model than a woman armed with a concealed weapon.

A uniformed policeman was leaning against one of the concrete pillars thirty feet to August's left. At first she dismissed him as one of the traffic cops with the tedious task of making sure vehicles kept flowing through the pick-up area of the airport. August's opinion shifted as he gave her a beaming smile. He seemed unconcerned with the continuous hubbub of auto activity. They stood staring at each other for a few moments before August marched up to him.

"Are you my ride?" she asked.

He responded in the kind of Cajun drawl that makes words feel like they've been smothered in honey. "Only if you've been naughty, darlin'."

"Excuse me? Aren't you here to pick me up?"

"Aggressive. I like that. Well, I can't play right now, gotta pick up some old stiff from Washington, DC for a big case we're working on. Maybe later we can get togeth-"

August pulled out her wallet and showed him FBI credentials.

"Well, I'll be a gator's cousin. You're August Cannon? I thought you'd be some old man in a boring suit and not the future mother of my children."

"Don't flatter yourself," her eyes drifted to his name badge, "Officer Drake."

"Please, call me Gareth."

"What would please me most is if you kept your remarks to me in a professional context. Can we get going? I have work to do."

"Alright, alright, my apologies, ma'am," Gareth straightened his posture and gave her a short bow like an Old World gentleman. He picked up her suitcase. "Right this way."

Gareth walked ahead of her with a graceful stride to his illegally parked car. Gareth opened the car door for August, flashing his brilliant teeth into another welcoming smile. August gave him a withering look, but said nothing as she accepted his embarrassing chivalry and got into the police cruiser.

While circling to the other side of the car Gareth radioed dispatch and reported in Special Agent Cannon's arrival.

August sized him up at about five feet nine inches, with the stocky build of a football player. His face still possessed a boyish exuberance which only age or experience would erase. She put him at maybe a year or two older than she was. He probably joined The Force out of college. If Officer Gareth Drake had as much athletic talent as he did charisma and confidence, August imagined that whatever university he got his undergraduate degree from paid for his education. His smile and swagger spoke of a man who scored as well off the field as on. She looked at his hands. Encircling his right ring finger was a gold band with Greek letters on the front. Yep, a fraternity ring, that confirmed it. Only a man a few years out of college, or someone really obsessed with their early adult years, would still wear one of those rings.

Gareth slid into the driver's seat and fired up the engine. "Now, Sunshine, do you wanna get settled in at your hotel, or if you're hungry I know a place we can g-"

"Take me directly to the Martel home, Officer Drake."

"Yes Special Agent Cannon, right away." He gave another eye-twinkling gaze, put the car in gear, and hit the gas.

Soon they were exiting the airport and getting onto Interstate Highway – Sixty-One, heading east towards the heart of New Orleans.

The air conditioning provided a much needed respite from the summer heat. For just a moment August took in the cloudy skies and how the tropical climate habitually transformed any receptive surface into a botanical bonanza. Then she extracted a large manila folder out of her briefcase.

August scanned the police report which had been faxed to the FBI's D.C. office. They were traveling towards 1205 Philip St., located in the Garden District.

Reading the case file and New Orleans dossier her handler prepared, August got excited about every detail. No matter how minute, every tidbit seemed like a precious piece of information critical to her investigation. The Big Easy was an intimidating place for an inaugural solo field mission.

Gareth was having a hard time driving because his eyes kept straying to gaze upon his passenger. After a few swerves and one particular hard slam on the brakes, Gareth redoubled his efforts to navigate the vehicle properly. The woman sitting next to him was more intoxicating than a late night in the Quarter. It felt as compulsory to hit on her as it did to breathe.

"If you don't mind my asking, aren't you a little young to be a Special Agent? I thought the minimum age was twenty-three?"

"They made an exception for me," said August. "I got my B.S. in Criminal Justice at seventeen years old."

"Oh you're some kind of kid genius, is that it?"

August flashed to being six years old and the astonished look on her parent's faces when they walked in on the middle of an interrogation session. She was grilling Teddy Bear about the repeated burglaries at Barbie's Dream House. Before her parents could react young August sternly ushered them out of her bedroom, whispering, "The Bear is about to break."

August quickly shoved the memory as far away as she could, for fear it'd make her laugh. It was already proving difficult to get this guy to be serious and focus on the case instead of wondering how she tasted.

Gareth saw a smile tugging at the corners of August's mouth. "Why does a beautiful young woman like you want to chase after the scary bad guys?"

"What did I say about being professional?" snapped August. "I think you need to be more concerned with your driving than my motivations for law enforcement."

"Sorry ma'am."

"Officer Drake, you were the first person on the scene, correct?"

"Yes ma'am, that's why the brass sent me to get you. The Lieutenant said the incident sparked the Feds interest, and I was to collect the Special Agent they were sending at the airport. I am ordered to assist you in any way I can. So, why is the Federal Government so concerned with a suicide victim?"

"Alleged suicide. We still have not ruled out other possibilities."

"I can see that. Dispatch had me thinkin' I was walkin' into a murder scene, but when I got there-" he broke off. The memory of walking into the master bedroom of the Martel house haunted him.

"What is it?" August asked.

Gareth sighed, "Someone would have to be completely nuts to slit their own throat like that."

"It says here Morgan Martel, the seven year old daughter, was a possible witness?"

He looked over at August before turning his attention back to the road. If she was disturbed by their conversation, he could not see it on her face. Special Agent Cannon either had ice water running through her veins, or the best game face he'd ever seen.

"Yes ma'am. However, it was Edison Martel, the father, who found Morgan hugging her mother's corpse. He says she was whispering to her mother, but when he pulled her away from the body, Morgan clammed up."

"What was Morgan whispering?"

"Mr. Martel said he couldn't understand what she was saying. He got irate with me for even questioning him. He yelled for a bit, burst into tears, then started apologizing up a storm."

"The body is still untouched at the morgue, correct?"

"Yes ma'am, we've got her on ice. The family wants to cremate it once we finish our investigation."

Officer Drake took the Carondelet exit off of the highway, and turned on St. Charles Avenue.

August paused to take in a bit of the mysterious city. The whole area seethed with lush green vegetation, like an Urban Arboretum. Two one way roads flanked the tracks and overhead electrical lines. Every block was populated by down home cookin' restaurants, ivy entangled houses, and alternately, a liquor store or a bar. A trolley rumbled by their squad car as they slowed for mid-day traffic. It was dark green with rust colored trim, and filled with all sorts of people. She could smell the distinctive ozone odor of the trolley's electrical juice.

They traveled about half a mile west on St. Charles Avenue before taking a left on Josephine Street. August took a deep slow breath and focused on the task at hand. Less than seventy-two hours ago Gwendolyn Martel had allegedly taken her own life, possibly in front of her daughter.

Gareth's gravelly drawl interrupted her musings, "Now I don't know how much experience you've had with grieving families, and all due respect to you out ranking me and all, but I don't know how kindly Mr. Martel or the folks helpin' him out are gonna feel about us waltzing in on their grief. If I knew why the big boys at the Bureau were so interested in an artist's crazy wife, I could give you the answers you're lookin' for. Then we wouldn't have to bother these nice people."

"I appreciate your sensitivity to the trauma this family is experiencing and your willingness to assist me, Officer Drake. Rest assured it is imperative I conduct my own investigation, the details of which I am not at liberty to discuss with you at this time."

August wrote a note in her case file and inquired quietly, "Are you always so protective of witnesses being interviewed?"

"Yes I am when they are young girls who have lost their mother. Look, I'm a team player, and the more I know, the more I can help out. If a crime other than the taking of one's own life has been committed here, I want to know."

They pulled up in front of the Martel home. A clutch of large trees obscured the house until they were practically on top of it. The style was Italianate Victorian, popular a century before. The home was gorgeous and well maintained. Half a dozen white pillars stood as imposing sentries on the front of the three story structure. The white mammoths supported a balcony on the second floor and a relaxing porch on the first. A fresh looking coat of white paint with neutral colored accents, a generous lawn, and flower beds dressed up the exterior of the building.

On the right side of the house a driveway led to an unattached two car garage covered in ivy. In the driveway rested a beat up old blue Chevrolet pickup truck next to a flawless late 70's burgundy BMW 733i. They looked like the prom queen and the auto shop kid out on a date together.

Gareth cut the engine, still waiting for a reply from this beautiful, enigmatic, and not a little frustrating woman. He watched her study the house for a few moments. August turned and gazed at Gareth in such a penetrating way he blushed.

Then August smiled at Gareth, and his breath caught. He forgot about the little political power struggle he was pulling with her. His stomach did a flip-flop.

Gareth's initial flirting with August stemmed from a lengthy lothario lifestyle and a sincere love of women, plural, not singular. In an instant everything got serious, much to his shock, like a switch he didn't even know was there flipped inside his heart. He almost didn't hear her when she said, "Shall we?" while opening the passenger side door to get out of his cruiser. Gareth made sure the volume was off on his radio, not wanting it to squawk inappropriately.

As they approached the large white double front doors they heard and felt the drum, bass, and guitar crescendo from the end of a bluesy song. Once August reached the front door, she paused, cocking her head to one side, and listened. The next song came on, a slow deep bass line. Barely three notes in, August said, "Huh… appropriate."

"What?" Gareth said. He recognized the song as familiar, but didn't immediately place it, until the guitar line wound in and Robert Plant's muffled voice could be heard singing, "Been dazed and confused for so long it's not true..."

"I'd get the Led out too, if I were them." August murmured, as she rang the doorbell. Gareth would have laughed, but he was too surprised to respond. He didn't know what surprised him more, August's quick identification of the song or her cracking a joke right before entering into an awkward situation.

They waited a few moments. No one answered the door. August rang the bell again. They could hear the two-note ding-dong over the music, but apparently, no one else could. Gareth knocked loudly on the door. "Hello? Mr. Martel?"

No response. Gareth was about to bang away again, but before he could let loose, August grabbed and turned the door handle. It opened, and they were met with an unleashed cacophony of Led Zeppelin.

Their shoulders collided as each attempted to take the initiative in entering the Martel house. August shot Gareth an authoritative look and he yielded.

Amber afternoon sun filled the foyer. High ceilings with crown molding, bright bay windows, and the dark mahogany staircase were all typical to ornate New Orleans architectural style. A six foot marble statue of a muscular man doing a one-armed hand stand dominated the room. Natural and track lighting lit the piece up. It was framed by the staircase winding up to the second floor. A feat of balance in itself the artwork required its weight to be perfectly proportioned like the man it embodied, or else it would not be able to stay upright.

"Hello?" They could barely hear their own voices over the music coming from the back of the house.

August walked around the statue. She marveled how the sculptor captured the look of intense concentration on his model's face. The plaque at the bottom of it read:

Upside Down Eddie
Remy LeTour

August found an unoccupied den in the front room off the foyer. It was a tidy sitting room with red velvet couches facing each other, a mahogany coffee table in between, and a fireplace with a large antique mirror hanging over the mantle.

Following the music into the hallway, a row of wall mounted gargoyle masks leered at them. They passed a small bathroom, and arrived at two fifteen foot dark wooden doors left ajar. The Led Zeppelin concert was coming from inside the room.

August peered inside, and pushed the door open. It led into a spacious studio which looked like a renovated greenhouse, with more windows than walls. Inside they saw two handsome men, each with dark hair and powerful physiques. They looked like they were brothers in facial bone structure and skin tone. One of the men was about a head taller and much more broadly built than the other. They were both covered with paint and clay. Each wore shorts which must have been khaki at some point, but now were too dirty to discern.

Neither of them noticed August and Gareth's entrance. They were too busy dancing around a six foot block of wet clay, taking turns punching, kicking, or hurling themselves into it for a big bear hug.

August saw two ten foot work benches littered with beer, Southern Comfort, and wine bottles, all covered with clay hand prints. Paint tubes, chisels, palettes, hammers, paint brushes, empty Chinese food containers, pizza boxes and a multitude of other debris were scattered about the room in a haphazard fashion. August had a compulsive desire to find a garbage bag and clean up the whole mess.

A giant ten foot by fifteen foot canvas was mounted at the back of the workshop/studio. August smelled wet paint underneath the earthy moist clay odor permeating the room, and saw fresh paint strokes still glistening in the light as they dried. It must have been an earlier violent artistic venture by the two men. The canvas was an explosion of sadness, rage, and passion. Jackson Pollock would have approved.

In the back right corner of the studio there was a ten foot sculpture covered with pillows and cushions. August's inner child grew jealous when she realized what it was: A kid-scale enormous pillow fort complete with a bead curtain front door. Perched in the second level window of the fort was a young girl with a mop of curly red hair, clutching a blanket, watching the scene with rapt attention.

The little girl, who August guessed was Morgan, made brief eye contact with August, and dropped her eyes to a patch of well-worn fabric clutched in her small left hand. It looked like a threadbare piece of her baby blanket. Morgan slid back, her face disappearing deeper into her pillow fort, until only her tiny fist full of plaid fabric was still in sight.

The larger of the two men noticed them first. The smile on his face evaporated. He got the attention of his companion, who went to the record player and turned down the music.

August stepped forward, extending her hand to the shorter man. "Sorry for barging in. I'm Special Agent August Cannon and this is Officer Gareth Drake, whom I believe you've met before. Edison Martel?"

"Please, call me Eddie." He made a move to shake her hand, realized his own was filthy, and withdrew it with a sheepish smile.

Meanwhile the much taller man, who August guessed must be the sculptor and best friend, Remy LeTour, did not come over to greet them. Instead, he opted to forage for a beverage in the cooler underneath the work bench furthest away.

"My sincerest condolences for your loss. I can't begin to fathom what you and your loved ones are going through right now. I wouldn't be here unless it was imperative I speak with you for a few minutes privately."

"He's not going anywhere with you today, lady. If you want to question the grieving husband you're going to have to wait until tomorrow." The sculptor friend barked, cracked open an ice cold beer, and took a deep slug from it.

"It's okay, Remy, I can handle this. They look like nice enough people. Forgive my manners, would you like a drink?"

"No, thank you," August said.

"Hey Eddie, we were working, remember?"

Eddie looked at him and shrugged helplessly.

"At least help me wrap this up," grumbled Remy.

Remy traded his beer for a couple of sponges from a nearby water bucket. Eddie joined his creative partner in slathering water on the large sculpture. Then they covered it in Saran Wrap and heavy plastic sheets.

August and Gareth stood off to the side and watched. The low voices of the two artists could be heard in escalating whispers. Eddie's welcoming attitude aggravated Remy's disdain for their unwanted guests. "Why are these pigs even here? They should respect our privacy. How can they possibly help us now?"

When they finished watering the clay, Remy reunited with his beer. He walked by and shoulder checked Gareth, smearing a variety of art supplies from his bare skin to the Peace Officer's uniform.

"What the hell, man? Why don't you lighten up?" Gareth said.

"Why didn't you call before busting in here, uninvited, into a house of mourning, asshole?"

Both men threw menacing stares. Before they could square off with each other, August stepped in.

"Gentlemen, please. Calm yourselves." Remy didn't even look at August. He sulked over to his cooler, finishing off his beer en route.

August glared at Gareth, and addressed Mr. Martel, "Gentlemen, please forgive our intrusion at this dark time. Mr. Martel, Eddie, I flew in from D.C. specifically to speak with you and your daughter but I'm sure we can-"

"C'mon, baby shots, Eddie. Baby shot? I think it's time." Remy held up the bottle of Southern Comfort enticingly. He scooped up a couple of shot glasses and filled them halfway, beckoning Eddie to join him.

Eddie giggled at Remy's offer, and August realized how hammered these guys were. At least all the alcohol fueled a creative frenzy, which was probably the best coping method anyone could hope for under the circumstances.

Eddie took the shot, clinked glasses with Remy, and knocked it back. Gareth gave August a pointed I-told-you-so look on his face, which Eddie caught as he rejoined them.

"Gareth is right. I'm in no shape to have a coherent conversation with you right now. We started early. Can you come back tomorrow?"

"Yes, sir, we can. How about we-" August's speech broke off as the little girl from the pillow fort tower appeared at her father's side.

Eddie noticed his daughter when August did, and crouched down to gather her into his arms. He picked her up during the hug. "Hi honey, are you okay? Can Daddy get anything for you?"

Eddie stroked Morgan's hair, his eyebrows wrinkling into a concerned frown. Morgan stared at him with wide eyes. She held up the green plaid scrap of fabric clutched in her hand, offering it to her father.

"Thanks honey, but you hold on to your Blankie."

Eddie sighed and rested his forehead on her little shoulder as a heart stopping tide of grief crashed in. He felt her little arms wrap around his head. Tears burned down Eddie's face. Eddie pulled himself together, put Morgan down, and held her hand.

Remy walked up to Eddie, and put a hand on his shoulder. Eddie looked over at him, grimaced, and dropped his head.

Morgan looked at August with eyes more suited for an old wise woman. The girl held her gaze steadily, stoically. August got a sinking feeling in her stomach like she'd hit the first drop on a roller coaster. A wave of nausea followed, her knees weakened, and darkness clouded her vision. August lost consciousness before she even hit the ground.

CHAPTER TWO
WELCOME TO UNDERLIFE

The sound of crashing waves filled August's ears. She opened her eyes to a bright blue sky. Bewildered and a bit panicked, August sat up. She found herself at a beach she did not recognize, sitting on a green plaid blanket with Morgan. They looked at each other in mutual shock.

August scrambled to her feet, hand going to her gun, but it wasn't there. She was no longer dressed in her Prada power suit, but instead in a purple patterned one piece swim suit. August checked her body for wounds, marks, or abrasions. Maybe she had been drugged and taken here? No, there didn't seem to be any evidence of an attack or rough handling.

One second they were at the greenhouse studio in the Martel home and the next, a beach? Wearing different clothing? What the hell was going on?

August surveyed the area around them. She and Morgan were sitting on a strip of land in front of a fifty foot cliff face. The cliff formed a crescent alcove for the secluded beach. The tree-topped cliff edge obscured the view of any landscape beyond the rocks. Late afternoon sun saturated everything in warm colors.

Morgan's eyes were fixed on August. Morgan was wearing a blue tank top with matching shorts. August kneeled down, and did a cursory examination of Morgan. The girl seemed fine.

"Morgan, what happened?"

"You can see me?"

"What? Yes, of course. What happened? Where is your Dad?"

"You can do it too?"

"Do what? Where are we? How did we get here? Who brought us here?"

Morgan shrugged, and uttered a gasp of delight when she noticed their blanket. The girl gleefully fell back. Morgan stretched out, took the edge of the blanket, and rolled herself into it like she was wrapping herself into a cocoon.

August had a moment of confusion and then it struck her. Their green plaid blanket looked like a much larger, whole version of Morgan's precious Blankie. She patted Morgan's side to get her attention. The kid giggled in response.

"Huh," August grunted. Unfortunately the small revelation did nothing to solve any of the overall, 'Where are we?' and 'How did we get here?' questions.

Well, at least it was a gorgeous day, wherever they were. August knew she should be searching for someone who could tell them where they were, but she was so stunned by their arrival that she felt no motivation to explore their surroundings.

Between the bright sunlight and the cool breeze playing through her hair, this place was relaxing. August sat back down onto her side of Blankie, and contemplated their next move.

About thirty yards away, the ocean was busy doing its perpetual courtship with the earth. August figured it must be low tide since most of the beach in front of them had a hard packed, I'm-underwater-most-of-the-time look to it. An abundance of sea shells and driftwood were strewn about like hastily discarded clothing.

High or low tide, the muddy ritual never changed. A wave crashed in, the water surged upon the terra firma, commencing a slippery dance with the sand before luring it back to its watery domain. Then the elemental lovers parted only to be reunited moments later by the next wave.

A loud siren cried out in alarm. Startled, August sat up. The piercing wail was coming from further down the beach. Its exact source was obscured by the cliffs. The siren persisted for five full seconds, and then ceased, the remnant sounds echoing around them. August examined their section of the beach for other people. They seemed to be alone.

August looked at the water and a woeful, "Holy shit," escaped her lips. The awesome horror of a rapidly approaching set of tsunami sized waves could be seen miles out off shore.

August's jaw gaped open. Not only did they just teleport to some God-only-knows-where sunny beach, but now about a million gallons of salt water was on its way to drown them. August turned to the only familiar thing there.

Morgan smiled up at her, reaching over to take August's right hand in both of hers. Then the little girl said, "I don't know how to swim."

August's survival training took over. She jumped up, pulling Morgan to her feet. "Run!" August said. Morgan complied, and they took off down the beach. Somehow they needed to get around the rock wall. It would be their deaths if they waited for the deluge to dash them against it.

Morgan did her best to keep up with August, but in her haste, she tripped and fell into the sand. In one fluid motion August threw Morgan's small body over her right shoulder.

Morgan gave a yelp of surprise when tossed around like a sack of potatoes. Her protests stopped there. Morgan did her best to hold on to August without impeding her movement or hurting her by gripping too tightly.

It amazed Morgan that the pretty lady was present, but she was grateful for her help. Morgan didn't know why the ocean was going to attack them, and she wished her mother was there to hold her.

August barreled over the sand with the ease of a professional athlete. Despite the added seventy pounds of cargo, August moved quickly. Her mind whirled, trying to figure out where they could go to survive the devastating wall of water.

They needed to get to higher ground, and were running out of time. August's muscles burned as they got closer to clearing the rock wall. She prayed for some kind of building or easy access to higher ground once they got around the earthen obstacle.

Her heart leapt when she saw a one story building about two hundred yards in the distance. Getting to the roof was their best hope. August pushed harder. Her limbs and lungs protested with pain as she strained to get them to safety. Luckily her cargo did a great job molding herself to August's body, making it easier for them to move together.

The water heading towards them roared in its frothy fury. August knew in her gut they would not make it to the building. She scanned for something else useful. A cluster of about a half a dozen oak trees stood about forty yards away, the largest of the bunch about fifty feet tall. August thought it might hold up through at least the first wave. She risked a glance over her shoulder. There were no other options.

After twenty more yards, the sand gave way to more hardened earth. Panting, August swung Morgan down to her feet and with a gasp said, "Morgan, the trees!"

Morgan ran the last twenty yards, which gave August a chance to recover her upper body strength. Once they reached the largest tree, Morgan turned to August, putting her arms up in the air for a boost. August was impressed by how cooperative and coordinated this kid was. She grabbed Morgan, and lifted her as high up as possible. Morgan planted her feet on August's shoulders and clutched at the lowest branch. She tried to pull herself up but couldn't.

August put her hands underneath Morgan's feet. Morgan's skinny legs wobbled, but stabilized when she became more accustomed to the support.

The extra inches got Morgan high enough to get a full arm and then a leg over the branch.

August inhaled sharply as cool water washed over her feet. She crouched and jumped as high as she could. Her hand caught the base of the branch Morgan was sitting on. The branch shook violently, forcing Morgan to cling to it and hold on for dear life. As the wobbling subsided, Morgan became mesmerized at the sight of the water rising on the trunk below.

The branch would not hold both of them for long, so August used it to get her legs wrapped around the tree while her bare feet searched for a place to grip. August's right big toe found a knobby perch. She took a few deep steadying breaths, and searched for the proper path of perches needed to ascend the sturdy oak.

On the other side of the tree there was another branch. August realized that getting to it was a precarious endeavor at best. She needed to find another way quickly.

August jammed her left hand into a make shift hold on the bark of the tree and winced when she felt the middle fingernail break. Gritting her teeth through the pain, August got a foothold and kicked off, clutching at another branch a couple of feet up. August dangled from her left arm before getting her right hand on the branch above. Then, she did a gymnast kip maneuver which gave her enough momentum to get a leg anchored securely. August wrestled her body onto the bough.

The tree groaned and creaked as five feet of flood water bullied the base of the oak. The sound of rustling leaves could be heard over the liquid roar of the waves. The water continued to rise fast.

"Are you okay, Morgan?"

"I'm scared."

"Me too sweetie… Hey, can you see me?"

August observed Morgan's knuckles go white as she gripped her branch. It took Morgan a considerable amount of strain to force her head to turn and glance up at August.

"Yes."

"Okay, we need to get you up here. Can you stand up near the base of your branch?"

Morgan's stomach somersaulted at this idea, and she was forced to look away from August. The landscape liquefied, and she felt dizzy. Adrenaline brimmed, and her limbs didn't feel attached anymore.

"I don't know how to. I'll fall."

"Listen to me, Morgan. We are going to do this step by step. Take a deep breath, and let it out slowly."

"Um, okay."

"Now, when you are ready, scoot your body backwards until you can feel the tree trunk behind you."

Sweat dripped off of August's face as she watched Morgan gathering energy to move. August wanted to yell at Morgan to hurry up, they had no time to wait, but she was afraid to startle the girl.

August hazarded a look to the ocean, and every ounce of moisture evaporated in her throat. They had seen the least of what was coming. It was only a handful of minutes before the next one hit, and it promised to be bigger than the first.

"C'mon, Morgan, you can do this."

Finally, the girl gained control over her extremities and was able to get herself to the trunk of the tree.

"Good job, honey. Now I need you to sit up with your legs on either side of branch, like you are on a horse." Morgan pushed herself up to a sitting position, feet dangling.

"Great. You are doing so well, Morgan. Okay, turn yourself around until you are facing the tree." Morgan twisted her torso to the left, and hugged the tree.

"Yes. Carefully, swing your right leg over the branch. Keep holding on to the tree and breathe. Get your left foot up on the branch, then your right one. Awesome, Morgan! You're almost there. One more deep breath and stand up."

Morgan slowly stood, scraping her body across the bark. The groaning sways of the tree did not help the process any, nor did her shaking hands. She shimmied to a standing position.

While waiting for Morgan, August straddled her bough, facing the trunk of the tree.

White froth crested the peak of the second wave, its momentum building, gobbling up everything in its path, obliterating the earth.

"Morgan, reach for my hand. We're going to swing you up here." August leaned over, covering as much distance as she could between them while still retaining her balance. Morgan reached her small hand up, got on her tip-toes, and stretched out to meet August.

Their fingers grazed then finally grasped each other at the exact moment when the second wave hit. The whole tree rocked hard, bending to absorb the watery onslaught. August didn't have the hold she needed, and Morgan slipped off. August watched Morgan's terror filled eyes as the girl plummeted into the dark waves below.

"Nooo...!" August said. She swung her leg over the branch and shoved herself off, landing about five feet away from where Morgan slipped in. August remembered to bend her knees once her feet touched the water to dampen the blow of hitting the ground. The water broke her fall a bit, but she still came down hard on packed earth. The force of the landing knocked the air out of August.

Morgan broke the surface before August did. Both flailed their limbs about, coughing while gulping fresh air into their lungs.

They grasped and held on to each other tightly. The strengthening current already swept them past their tree. They could fight to get back to it, but August doubted their chances.

A smaller tree in the grove split with a loud snap. The bulk of the leafy mass came down right on top of them.

August enveloped Morgan's body with her own to protect her. She grunted, taking the brunt of the hit on her back from a branch in the upper canopy. It left a gash across her shoulder blades. August ignored the burning pain.

The fallen tree's branches dug into the earth beneath, creating an anchor point as well as a temporary barrier from the tidal onslaught. August moved closer to the tree, hoping it could offer a safer place on top of its trunk.

"Morgan, are you okay?"

"I- I think so." Her eyes welled up with tears, and she hugged August while they floated. August had one arm around Morgan, and was holding onto the fallen tree with the other. She patted Morgan's body down, finding no wounds or breaks. Morgan was shaken up, but it did not seem like she was in shock from internal injuries.

August's feet sunk into the drenched earth, aware of how vulnerable her bare legs felt in the muddy cauldron. Some unknown object scraped against her left calf. This spurred her back into action. After a labyrinth in logistics of watery branch negotiation, August got Morgan onto the trunk of the tree.

While they were climbing onto their makeshift raft, another oak near them fell. Creaking turned into groaning, then loud snapping, and finally a thunderous collapse, as the water overpowered another of nature's leafy sentinels. August was so focused on getting the girl to safety she didn't notice the third tree go down. A harpoon shaped branch javelined towards them from the newly fallen oak. There was a sickening crunch as the sharp wood collided with the back of August's head. A gasp of air escaped August's lungs before her mouth went slack, her azure eyes glazed over, and her face pitched forward into the water. Morgan saw large splinters penetrating the back of August's skull. Blood oozed everywhere. August's limp body sunk underneath the murky water.

Morgan screamed.

CHAPTER THREE
A-A-AND WE'RE BACK

August regained consciousness, sputtering and heaving air into her lungs. Body jerking, she whipped her head around, scanning the room. August was back at the Martel house lying on a couch in the living room with half a dozen people around her. Gareth Drake's handsome, concerned features filled August's field of vision.

"August, relax. You fainted." Gareth put a hand on her shoulder.

"What? I-" August rubbed her eyes. Was all that just a hideous nightmare? She felt a close kinship to Dorothy and her Oz experience.

A tap on the back of her hands interrupted August's thoughts. Uncovering her face, August discovered Morgan, dry and healthy. Morgan's ancient eyes were in contrast with her prepubescent body. She gazed at August. A goofy grin spread on the girl's face. To everyone's astonishment, Morgan barreled towards August and threw her arms around her.

They hugged for a few moments. Morgan pulled back, took August's right hand in both of hers just like at the hellish beach trip, and asked, "Will you teach me how to swim?"

Well, at least I know I'm not completely crazy, was August's first thought. She managed to stammer out, "Y-Yes."

August couldn't believe how steady her voice sounded. She wanted to grab Morgan by the shoulders and scream, 'What the fuck just happened?' Lucky for everyone's frayed nerves, she didn't.

"Woo Hoo! Thank God almighty, Little Bear speaks!" Remy said, lumbering over to scoop Morgan into his muscular, clay-paint-and-alcohol-splattered arms. "Morgan, my darlin', it's good to hear that beautiful voice of yours. You gave us all a scare."

Eddie sat on the opposite couch facing August. His composure melted when his precious daughter broke her silence, tears of relief streaming down his face. An attractive, dark-haired woman August did not recognize was sitting next to Eddie. The woman turned to him, opening her arms. He slumped into them. She kissed the side of his head, whispering comforting words of love and support. He wept openly on her shoulder.

Remy gave the revived federal agent an appraising eye, and then said, "Glad to have you back with us, August."

Remy shifted his attention to the perky package in his filthy arms that now needed a bath. "You hungry, Little Bear?"

Morgan nodded.

"Good. I am, too." Remy said. "Eddie, let's get cleaned up and cook some dinner. Gareth, August, join us when you're ready. Honey, could you wrangle Dorcha for me?"

At first the unidentified woman did not move a muscle to release Eddie, but then they slowly pulled apart. As far as August's foggy mind could deduce, the woman embracing Eddie was perhaps Remy's wife or girlfriend. She cared deeply for Eddie, that much was certain. She did not even flinch or hesitate to embrace a man sitting on a towel-draped couch with most of his skin covered in art supplies. August made a mental note to interview the mystery woman. Odds were she was an intimate friend of the recently deceased.

Eddie rose from the couch, his head down, eyes cloudy and swollen from crying.

The dark haired woman got up, and went over to the corner of the room where another young girl, about four years old, was playing with laminated Montessori three part reading cards. The girl said "Fiyah Tuck!" when picked up, pointing to the cluster of cards.

This must be Dorcha, August thought. Remy's daughter?

"Yes baby," the dark-haired woman said.

The sound of Dorcha's voice snapped Eddie out of his gloom, and he intercepted the woman before she left the den. "I've got her, Marin."

"Are you sure?"

"It brings me great comfort to be close to the girls right now, if you don't mind? Don't worry. I'll make sure she gets a bath before dinner."

Marin handed the girl to Eddie, and exited the room. Dorcha gave Eddie a sleepy smile, nestling into his embrace for a quick nap.

August tried to sit up, but Gareth barred her from doing so by sitting at the edge of the couch. "Easy there, Special-Agent-who-abruptly-passed-out. No need to jump up quite yet." He leaned into August, keeping her lying down.

"I'm okay, really."

"I'll be the judge of that. I was about to call in the medics if you'd been out any longer. I wouldn't have pegged you for a fainter. How very delicate of you, Miss Cannon."

She pushed his warm body away from hers and sat up. "I am not a fainter. I've got nerves of steel. I don't faint. What just happened doesn't count."

"Why not? What happened?"

August opened her mouth to speak, but paused, her jaw slack. How could she possibly explain the experience? He would think she was crazy, or winding him up. Despite herself, in the short time she'd known Gareth, August cared about his opinion.

"Hello, August? Want to explain why you got weak kneed and unconscious? Don't say it's my ravishing good looks, because I'll believe you."

"How long was I out?"

"About fifteen minutes. Now, answer my question."

"I don't know. One second I was in their greenhouse studio, and the next, I'm coming to on this couch." August went to stand up, but changed her mind when an explosion of pain rocked her head. "Did I hit my head when I fell? The back of my skull is pounding."

"No, I caught you before you crumpled to the floor. You really don't know why? Have you ever fainted before?"

"No and no. Actually, I'm more embarrassed than anything else."

"Even unconscious you're charming."

August glared.

Gareth smiled, "Morgan certainly believes so. Three days of not talking until you came along. Why do you think she asked you to teach her how to swim?"

"Okay, Officer Drake, quit it with the third degree."

"Alright, alright… at least admit it's all a bit strange."

"Hey, could you get me some aspirin? I don't want this headache to get any worse," August said.

"I think I've got some."

Gareth opened a pouch in his police utility belt and pulled out a sample packet of pain medication.

"One thing I've learned livin' in the Big Easy is to carry aspirin. You never know when a hangover or a head wound might occur. Want some water?"

"No." She ripped open the packet and knocked back the pills. "How long have you been living in New Orleans?"

"I reckon it's been about six years now. Graduated from Tulane and decided to stay. No place quite like this city. I love it."

"Tell me about it," August said while lying down on the couch and closing her eyes.

Gareth spun a yarn to his new federal friend about the glory days of football, the birth and growth of his interest in law enforcement, and what it was like being reared by a big Irish Catholic family in Washington, D.C.

Gareth divulged his southern accent wasn't native but had seeped in over time, and he loved how it sounded even if his family teased him mercilessly during the holidays.

At first Gareth didn't know if August was listening or asleep. Then he heard a low chuckle when he was telling her about his grandmother, who lived with Gareth's family when Gareth was young, and who used to take sick glee in torturing Gareth's father by flushing wooden Q-Tips down the toilet.

* * *

Glancing around to see if she was alone, Marin took a detour on her way to the kitchen, venturing into the men's workshop.

Heading straight for the giant painting in the back, Marin got close to the canvas, noting they used acrylic paint. She paced up and down the length of the piece, thoroughly inspecting it. Finally, she planted herself directly in front of it. The dramatic behemoth looked like how she felt. Marin stood there for a long time, her mind paralyzed by shock. Everything had changed.

Marin kept expecting to hear the musical lilt of Gwenny's soft voice. This had been one of their favorite activities, secret communion with their husband's freshly born work. Gwenny's giddy anticipation whenever they snuck into the workshop caused infectious giggling. The memory of it reverberated in Marin's ears. Only in her absence did Marin realize how much Gwenny's innocent enthusiasm heightened the experience of discovery.

Emerging from her reverie, Marin focused on the disastrous clutter in the room, revolted by the chaos surrounding her. She made a mental note to call Consuela the maid the following day before the debris started to crawl around on its own.

Marin wanted to take a peek at the sculpture, but didn't dare disturb the plastic sheets wrapped around it. A shameful pang of jealousy hit the pit of her stomach. Even during such tragic times, the partnership between Eddie and Remy flourished. As much as she adored their collective work, it always made her feel separate from them, isolated. Marin had to accept she envied their creative intimacy. She felt guilty for being so possessive, but she knew that over many years her resentment for their tight bond had festered.

Marin's throat tightened and her chest felt heavy. The muscles around her left eye began to twitch. Marin forced herself to take deep breaths, but the tears were still flowing. She massaged the area around her eye, trying to get it to calm down.

* * *

August listened to Gareth yammer on in his low pitched, sexy voice for about half an hour. The pounding in her head receded. August sat up, went into the hallway bathroom, splashed some water on her face, fixed her hair, slapped some lipstick on, and pulled herself together.

August and Gareth went into the expansive and well-lit kitchen. A clean Remy LeTour was in full chef mode. Eddie was playing Remy's sous-chef. Remy merrily barked orders to Eddie. It became apparent that this was being done for show, because Eddie was anticipating each cooking command. They worked together with the same blissful, explosive harmony as they did in their studio. These men were artists, through and through.

Marin sat in between the girls at the kitchen table. Dorcha was in a booster seat, a coloring book in front of her. Marin was monitoring Dorcha's activity, because Dorcha was carrying on quite a love affair with her crayons. Dorcha was alternating between scribbling in her Sesame Street book and attempting to ingest her favorite colors. Usually Marin was able to intervene before Dorcha could test just how non-toxic Crayola's crayons were. Despite steady vigilance, there was a slobbered on Brick Red drying on a napkin next to Marin, and a Periwinkle Blue had a nice chunk taken out of it.

Morgan needed very little supervision. August watched her staring at the men preparing the meal like she had with the grief sculpture in progress at the greenhouse studio.

Remy looked up from stirring something in a sauce pan, and said, "Well if it isn't the darling drowsy detective."

Eddie elbowed Remy in the ribs while brushing by, and continued on to the refrigerator.

"Sorry for being rude in the studio. I hate being interrupted when we're working," Remy said. His initial boorish attitude had mellowed out considerably.

"You two are welcome to stay and eat with us," Remy said.

"Thank you, that's very kind, but I don't want to impose. We can come back tomorrow." August felt awkward and vulnerable after passing out in front of them.

"Nonsense, we insist. We will talk afterwards, that's why you're here, isn't it?" Eddie said.

Gareth whispered to August, "Don't be rude."

"Yeah, I thought it was imperative you speak to Eddie?" Remy said.

"Yes, you're right. We'll stay. Thank you," August said.

"Excellent," Eddie said. "Please, help yourself to anything from the bar in the dining room."

"Twenty minutes until dinner," Remy said.

August and Gareth wandered into the "dining room", although banquet hall was a more fitting title. It was easy to imagine the lavish parties these walls must have witnessed over the years. August and Gareth helped themselves to glasses of ice water. The second they sat down at the table, Eddie came into the room as if on cue. He carried bowls of the classic New Orleans staple, Red Beans and Rice with Homemade Sausage.

Gareth smiled broadly. "Aw'right. Thank you, Eddie. Much appreciated."

Eddie grinned at them and went back into the kitchen.

Gareth grabbed the Tabasco sauce from a collection of bottles at the center of the table. He sprinkled it into his bowl, stirred, and dug in.

Marin came into the dining room with the girls shortly after. August rose from the table to greet her, and Gareth followed suit.

August said, "I didn't get a chance to introduce myself before. Special Agent August Cannon."

"Marin LeTour."

Gareth said, "Officer Gareth Drake."

"You were here the other day," Marin said to Gareth.

"Yes ma'am. I'm so sorry for your loss."

"Thank you."

Marin's voice was distant, drained. August thought the pretty woman looked exhausted, but her pitiful appearance and silky southern accent were oddly charming. Marin shook each of their hands with a feathery grip.

"So you're Remy's wife?" August said.

"Yes." Marin's eyes glazed over a bit, and she nodded.

August stifled any further questions, feeling it was wiser to wait. Marin wasn't in any shape to be interviewed, and August preferred to speak with her alone.

The three of them stood there for a moment before August and Gareth returned to their seats.

Marin redirected her attention to getting a shy Dorcha prepped for dinner. The preschooler stared at the guests like this was the first time she really saw them.

Morgan got herself a booster seat and sat down next to August. They gave each other conspiratorial smiles and August leaned over and nudged Morgan's shoulder a bit with her elbow. Morgan laughed and pushed back.

Gareth loved watching the exchange between the two, but couldn't figure out why they were behaving like old pals.

"What is it with you two?" he asked.

"Officer Drake, can you climb trees?" Morgan said.

August chuckled, shaking her head.

"Morgan, I am a great tree climber," Gareth said.

"You are?"

"Oh, yes."

"Show me!"

"Well, uh," Gareth looked to August for direction.

"Honey, it's too late for that today," August said to Morgan.

"Tomorrow, come back, please?"

"I believe that's up to your Dad."

Moments later Eddie re-entered the dining room carrying a stack of plates, silverware, and napkins.

"Daddy, can August and Gareth come play tomorrow? They show me swimming and trees. Please, please, please?"

"Of course they can, Little Bear. As long as they aren't too busy working for the law."

"It would be our pleasure. Right, Officer Drake?" August said.

"Yes ma'am," Gareth said.

Morgan squealed while hopping up and down in her seat.

August gave Morgan a warm smile. It felt good to watch her getting some relief and excitement.

Meanwhile, Marin wandered over to open the windows, lighting tapers throughout the room along the way, bathing them in soft candlelight as the sun set. August heard cicadas outside, singing their low pitched mating song. While everyone talked, Marin stood removed from the conversation, smoking a cigarette.

The meal was terrific. It was a blur of soft shelled crawfish with Creole mustard, fresh cornbread, seafood gumbo, stuffed bell peppers, and bread pudding with whiskey sauce for dessert. August's appreciation for authentic Southern cooking soared. The food was so delicious that August couldn't help eating until she felt bloated. There were a few harrowing moments when things got too spicy, but after copious amounts of water, and later at Remy's suggestion, milk, the fire behind her lips settled down to a manageable roar.

Surprisingly, no alcohol got consumed with dinner, except for the heavenly whiskey sauce on the bread pudding. Eddie and Remy decided to postpone their sorrow drowning until after talking with August and Gareth. The appearance of the fainting federal agent snapped the men into a silent decision. Postponing sorrow drowning until after the law officers got what they wanted from them.

Mellow, subdued conversation flowed during dinner. Gareth guided the chatter with funny random tidbits he'd heard around the station. The men got excited when the subject of football came up. By the time Gareth finished pontificating about the Saints and the NFL overall, it felt as if Remy and Eddie had adopted him as a brother.

After dinner, all pitched in to clear the table. Then Remy, Marin, Morgan and Dorcha went into the family room to watch some television and relax. Gareth excused himself, went to the squad car, and checked in with dispatch. August moved into the kitchen where Eddie was washing dishes, humming to himself.

"Can I give you a hand with those?" August said.

"No, don't want your pretty suit to get dirty. I can manage. Thank you, though."

"Are you sure? I don't mind."

"No, think nothing of it. You can help by keeping me company while I do this."

"I can do that."

August watched him clean for a while, considering her approach.

"Eddie, do you know why I flew to New Orleans?"

"I don't have a clue why the Feds would send you all the way out here."

"Does the name Pablo Escobar ring any bells?"

"Escobar... that does sound familiar. Wait, isn't he a Columbian drug lord? What does he have to do with me or my family?"

"Have you ever had contact with anyone affiliated with him?"

"Please don't arrest me for saying this, but I did a couple of lines of coke a few years ago during Mardi Gras. I thought my heart was going to explode. As far as I know, it's as close as I've ever gotten to that scumbag."

"We busted one of his cells operating out of Miami, and found a couple of your paintings at their warehouse."

"So some bad guy likes my art. What does this have to do with me?"

"I don't know how much they appreciated your work, but they were definitely enamored with the large canvas size and sturdy frame construction you seem to favor. The frames had several kilos of cocaine taped inside them."

"Oh."

"How good is your bookkeeping?"

"Marin handles all of the books for Remy and me. You'll have to talk to her. I'm great with colors, but I suck with numbers."

August took a steadying breath and plunged onward with her questioning. "Do you have any reason to believe your wife's death was not a suicide?"

Eddie's hands stopped moving. He stood frozen for a moment, soapy suds dripping off a scrubbed skillet.

"No."

All ambition to clean drained out of him. He put down the pan, grabbed a towel, and sat down at the kitchen table.

August joined him. She knew Eddie was barely maintaining basic functionality, the wound in his heart, so fresh and raw, bled anew from the slightest stimulus. Eddie's sobs of grief flowed. August fetched him a napkin from the holder on the counter, waiting while he regained composure.

"I can't believe she's really gone."

"I know, Eddie. I am so sorry."

"I thought we were happy. I had no idea she was even capable of doing that to herself. Gwendolyn abhorred violence. She couldn't even kill a cockroach, filthy bastar-"

He broke off. This time August reached over to hold his hand. When he seemed able to speak, August asked, "Had she been exhibiting any bizarre behavior recently?"

"Well, she always had a delicate temperament to start with. It's one of the things I love about her, how sensitive she is- was." Eddie pulled away from August, burying his face in his hands for a while. Then he detached from the abyss long enough to finish responding to August's inquiry.

"Lately, it seemed like she got overwhelmed too easily. Gwendolyn had panic attacks over nothing, start talking like she was someone else, and not remember it later. Whenever I'd suggest seeing a doctor about it, she would refuse. Gwenny hated doctors. I never knew why. She'd insist she was fine, just having a rough day, and needed to relax. After taking a long hot bath my Gwenny would be back, loving as ever. I have no idea what kept troubling her. I- Oh, and poor Morgan. My Little Bear." He dissolved into tears again.

"The police report says you found Morgan with your wife?"

"Yes. Oh God- So much blood, I'll never get the image out of my head."

"I know this is difficult, but please, I need you to describe what happened."

"There isn't a whole lot to tell. We had our usual family dinner, and Gwenny was quiet, although she seemed to be in good spirits. Remy and I went into the studio to continue working. We'd both been on fire that day and wanted to capitalize on the inspiration. Marin had gone home because Dorcha wasn't feeling well."

"They don't live here with you?" August asked.

"A lot of times they stay here, which I don't mind at all. I love them. However, the LeTours do have their own place. It's from Marin's side of the family, not too far from here. Anyway, they left, and Gwenny said she was going to put Morgan to bed then take a bath, as was her custom at night. I never heard anything. We blast music in the studio, as you know. After a few hours of intense work, Remy and I closed up for the night, and he went home. I went upstairs to find- I mean they were-"

Eddie's breathing got heavy and irregular. Tears flooded his face. Then his features formed into a look of terror. All of the hair on August's body stood up.

"There were pieces of mirror everywhere and blood, so much blood. My two babies, wrapped into each other- At first I thought it was Morgan who- who was hurt. Then I got closer- Oh, Gwenny! Why?" Eddie's voice cracked. It took considerable effort for him to continue. "The shard of glass was still in her hand. She'd lodged it into her palm when she grabbed it, her grip was so fierce. Little Bear held onto her, rocking them both gently, oblivious to the blood, and whispered in that soft voice of hers. Oh God- I can't keep going. Please, don't make me talk about this anymore. I can't. I don't- I don't understand. What did I do wrong? Why would she want to leave us? There was no note, no warning, no reason, nothing."

Eddie looked at August rabidly, like she could answer these questions. Unfortunately for all of them, August was as confused as Eddie about Gwendolyn's motive for suicide. August knew her lack of experience was showing, but she couldn't help feeling heartbroken by their loss.

"Eddie thank you for speaking with me. I can't begin to fathom what you're facing. I am sorry, truly. No one should have to deal with this."

"Thanks, I guess. I wish I knew why on earth Gwenny would do something this horribly final. Was it my fault? Should I have forced her to go to the doctor? Why wouldn't she be able to tell me about whatever was going on before it got so bad she had to hurt herself like that?"

"I don't know. If you'll allow me, I'll do my best to find out."

"You would? Why? Aren't you only here because of Escobar?"

"Technically I am here to investigate any connection to Pablo Escobar's organization, and determine whether or not there was any evidence of foul play in your wife's death. I intend to examine all of the evidence. Unless you object, I am going to have an autopsy performed on your wife's body."

"Okay, if you think it will help."

"I also need to speak to Morgan, alone."

"That's up to her," Eddie said.

"Fair enough. Thank you."

"Thank you, August. I know you don't have to do this. Anything you can find out might help. I don't get it. It makes no sense. My love-" Eddie dropped his eyes, and the next words were uttered in a defeated whisper, "is gone."

* * *

August found Gareth looking stuffed and relaxed in front of the house. Gareth lounged on the porch swing, working a toothpick through the crevasses of his choppers.

"Radio dispatch and tell them to contact the medical examiner. I want a full autopsy performed on Gwendolyn Martel immediately."

"August, I think we know the cause of death." Gareth conveyed a dark look, running a finger across his neck.

"That's an order, Officer Drake."

"Wh-" Gareth's jaw muscles clenched as he swallowed his glib retort.

Apparently his candor was not appreciated, Gareth thought. So much for thinking he had melted the frosty façade and had gotten friendly with his stunning co-worker. Gareth got up and straightened his uniform.

"Yes ma'am," he said.

Man, she could be intimidating, he thought.

* * *

While Gareth handled things with dispatch, August tried to rest for a minute, even though a thousand details were flooding her mind. She imagined a brilliant white sheet of paper to get her brain into neutral. August decided it would do at that moment to analyze all of the information she'd been exposed to. It would hinder further receptivity. After successfully putting away the sewing circle of hens in her mind, August went back into the Martel home.

Moonlight was spilling through the windows, bathing the front rooms in ghostly ambiance. In the dim light, the Upside Down Eddie statue gave off a spooky energy, as if it could come to life at any moment. August heard crickets, cicadas, and who-knows-what other bugs deep into their opening sets of nighttime serenading.

August went into the family room at the back of the house. The room had wood paneling, a sectional couch, and a big television. There was a sliding glass door leading to the back yard. The television was tuned to a baseball game in progress. Remy lay sprawled out on the couch, flat on his back, fast asleep. Dorcha, cozy in her jammies, was similarly unconscious and belly-to-belly with Remy. Dorcha's head rested on her father's chest.

August wondered where Marin was. She looked outside. On the back porch there was a concrete patio between the family room and the greenhouse studio, with four big rough-hewn wooden lounge chairs facing away from the house. The moonlight illuminated lazy puffs of smoke drifting up toward the stars from one of the wooden thrones.

August, careful not to disturb anyone, found another staircase at the back of the house. It took her to the far end of the second floor's main hallway. August heard a deep, muffled voice, followed by an unmistakable high pitched giggle through a closed door further down the corridor.

On her way towards the voices, August couldn't help noting one gorgeous painting after another on the walls around her. Like the main floor the art upstairs was also lit beautifully.

Eddie's work upstairs seemed like a cross between Monet, Renoir, and John Waterhouse. It was very different in style from the madness of the more recent work downstairs.

The subject matter varied greatly from piece to piece. One painting showed a sinister looking fog filled swamp at nighttime, and another right next to it showed a raucous party scene.

August leaned in to read the small title plaque next the first piece, appropriately titled:

Bayou
Edison Martel

Both works were done with oil on canvas. The second one, entitled "Holidays", was set in the downstairs banquet room. For that painting, Eddie used vibrant colors, illustrating his guests with exquisite detail. He possessed a wonderful ability to give his subject matter a sense of life and motion, making the frame feel like it was a gateway to another world. August could hear the music and laughter inside the room that day.

August reached the centerpiece of the hallway collection. This work depicted two beautiful ladies dressed to the hilt in Victorian style dresses, complete with corsets and fans. They sat on a bench in an alcove cut from the stone wall of a courtyard garden. The depiction of the plant life and ivy surrounding the women was intricate and precise.

The woman on the left was wearing a deep purple, velvet gown. She stared out at the viewer with an unsettling intensity. On her lips were the beginnings of a smile which could only be described as feral. It took August a beat to realize she was looking at a glamorous version of Marin LeTour. The pale wraith of a woman she'd met today a shadow of Marin's painted self.

On the right was the recently departed Gwendolyn Martel, dressed in a gauzy whisper pink gown. The gown seemed to flow around Gwendolyn's lithe frame as if stirred by a light breeze. In the picture, Gwendolyn's focus was on Marin. Leaning in close, her lips were almost brushing Marin's ear. Gwendolyn held her fan up like it could give the women full privacy to gossip behind it.

The painting was called "The Secrets of Women". August could see it revealed the intimate dynamics of two families. August lingered, thinking of how this art was connected to the mystery of these people.

These grand canvases were near some smaller, sober, and technically precise portraits of family members. It looked to August like several different artists had created these portraits, but there was a neatly etched EM on the bottom right corner of every canvas.

August reached the door where the sounds were coming from. She paused, waiting for a moment of quiet before knocking.

"Come in!" Morgan said.

August opened the door, and saw another precious, cavity-inducing, father/daughter moment. Edison was on the floor with his legs in the air, and Morgan's body was balanced on the soles of his feet for a good old fashioned game of Airplane.

Morgan enjoyed a moment or two of airtime. Then Eddie said, "It's a bird. It's a plane." and Morgan giggled and began to lose her balance. Eddie held Morgan's hands to stabilize her. Then Morgan let go, striking a Superman flying pose. Morgan kept it up for a few seconds before laughter took over, and Eddie put her back down to the ground.

"August!"

"Hi, Morgan. Eddie, I wanted to know if we're still on for swimming lessons tomorrow."

"Morgan, do you really want August to show you how to swim?"

"Yes Daddy. It's okay, right?"

"Sure it is."

"Do you have a swimsuit?" August asked.

"Yes!" Morgan squealed, ran to her dresser, and pulled it out.

Eddie smiled. "How about three in the afternoon? There's a YMCA and a park within walking distance from here. We can all go together."

"Will Officer Gareth be coming, too? He promised to help me climb trees."

"Yes, ma'am, I will make sure of it." August turned to Eddie, and said "I know it's late, and you've already been such gracious hosts. Do you think Morgan and I can talk for a bit on our own?"

"Up to you, Morgan. You don't have to if you don't want to."

"I want to, Daddy. August is my friend."

"Okay, I'll read you a bedtime story and tuck you in when you're done."

August walked Eddie to the bedroom door while Morgan rearranged the gang of stuffed animals on her bed, making room for August to sit. "Thanks, Eddie. We won't be long," August said in a low voice.

"Be gentle with her. She's a survivor, but I don't want to make anything harder on her than it already is."

"I understand."

Eddie left the room, and August closed the door behind him.

August joined Morgan on her furry animal laden bedspread. August kicked off her shoes, pulled her legs up, and sat cross-legged. Morgan smiled, and mimicked her pose.

"Hi."

"Hi," Morgan said.

"I gotta say, Morgan, you're one unique and brave young woman. I've never met anyone like you."

"Thank you," Morgan said.

"Do you remember our trip to the beach?"

Morgan broke eye contact, a sly grin on her face, and spoke slowly, "Yes. You saved me. Thank you."

"What happened, Morgan? Where were we? How did we get there?"

"No one has ever come with me before and remembered."

"Come with you? Where? Where were we?" August said.

"I don't know, at the beach?"

"Have you ever been there before?"

"No."

"Have you seen that beach before? Like at school, on TV, or in a magazine?"

Morgan shook her head. "No, the place was new."

"Has that happened before? One second you're with your family, and the next, somewhere completely different?"

"Oh yes! Sometimes it takes a long time to get back, but when I do it's like I just left. Daddy says I have a real big imagination." She stretched her arms out for emphasis. "He thinks I make the stories up. You know it's real, right?"

"Real? That was terrifying! I don't know if I'll ever let my guard down near the ocean again. What happened at the end? Last thing I remember is we got you onto the big fallen tree trunk. Then I woke up on your couch."

"You- a big piece of wood hit you on the back of your head and-" Morgan said, tears threatening to spill down her cheeks.

"Oh honey," August said, pulling Morgan in for a hug. Morgan's small fingers snaked into August's hair. Morgan was feeling the back of August's head, to make sure it was intact. August said, "I'm okay. I woke up with a headache, but it went away. Everything's all right. Shh."

Morgan sobbed harder. "It's my fault she's gone."

"What?"

"I couldn't keep the people out."

"What do you mean? What people?"

"Strangers kept coming in and upsetting Mommy."

"There were strangers here, in this house?"

Morgan shook her head. 'No'.

"I don't quite understand what you mean, sweetie. You know it wasn't your fault. Please remember this. She took her own life. There was nothing you could have done."

"Not true! In UnderLife, I help her. I failed. I couldn't stop them!"

"UnderLife?"

"It's what Mommy called the places where I go that only I remember going to. She used to think I was making a joke, like Daddy and Uncle Remy do when I talk about my trips. When the people wouldn't stop coming into her Inside House, she listened better."

"Where is her Inside House?"

Morgan contemplated the question, and with some hesitation, tapped her heart. Color rose in her cheeks. Morgan shrugged her shoulders while looking away, like she was embarrassed to suggest a house could be inside a heart.

Once again, it struck August how thoughtful, mature, and articulate this girl was. Most seven year olds were more concerned with ponies, Cabbage Patch Kids, and sticker collections. August couldn't believe Morgan was trying to claim responsibility for her mother's suicide.

"What did her Inside House look like?"

"Exactly like our house, except the longer I was there, the darker it got. Then Daddy's paintings started to talk." Morgan said.

"What did the paintings say?" August said.

"They wanted to break out of their frame prisons and come inside. At first I was able to convince them to stay put. I told them 'No! You are not allowed here! You stay! Stay in your frames!' and they did. I was allowed to come back to Waking Life, but only for a little while. I kept getting pulled back into the scary, talking, painting house over and over, and then," her voice dropped to a whisper, like the paintings populating the house could overhear their conversation. "One of them found a way to break out, and he must have told the others how he did it, cause then they were all escaping from their frames and getting inside. I fight them. No good. They win, bigger and stronger than me."

"People came into her Inside House, not this house?"

"Yes, I already tell you."

"What happened to your Mom once they got into her Inside House?"

Morgan's eyes sank. She pursed her lips, trying to hold back the flood of tears. "She, she, lost who she was, thought she was the other people, and then would get confused and big time angry. It was only sometimes at first, for a small time, and no one noticed. Then it got to be too much, and Mommy got real scared, And I,"

That was it. Morgan finally crashed. Tears turned to sobs, wracking her petite body so hard she began to hyperventilate.

Eddie burst into the room. "What are you asking her? I was afraid this was going to happen."

He picked up Morgan, who buried her face into his chest, breathing heavily and still crying. He cuddled her for a moment, then looked up, daggers in his eyes, "August, could you please leave? We are done for today."

"Yes, I'm sorry sir, I-"

"Not now, Special Agent Cannon."

August gave an odd shallow bow, and she hurried out of the Martel home.

Gareth was waiting for her by his car.

"Dr. Bombrau is working graveyard at the morgue. He's our best man, and he'll do the full workup on Mrs. Martel. The Doc's report will be ready by eleven in the morning at the latest."

August nodded and averted her eyes. Every nerve ending burned with embarrassment. She had gotten carried away with Morgan and had pushed her too hard. Morgan had been excited about their adventure, and she had wanted to please August. August had taken advantage of Morgan's enthusiasm, and she felt ashamed because of it.

Gareth and August got into the police cruiser. August gave a heavy sigh and leaned forward, resting her forehead on the dashboard for a moment.

"What happened, August?"

"Take me to my hotel," she said, her voice muffled by the door of the glove box.

"Are you sure? Don't you want to get a drink to-"

"Officer Drake," she said with authority, lifting her head up.

"Yes ma'am, your hotel, right away. Where are you staying?"

"Hotel Provincial, the address is-"

"I know where it is." Gareth let out a low whistle as he started up the car and pulled away from the curb. "That's one swanky place in the Quarter. Sure nice of the Feds to take such good care of you."

"I'm covering the upgrade, Officer Drake. If it were up to my bosses I'd be staying in some rat trap, roach infested Petri dish of a room."

Gareth wracked his brain to come up with something insightful or disarming to say. All of his wits abandoned him.

They were quiet for the rest of the ride to the hotel.

Gareth was confused. How did an unfortunate but routine suicide, turn into some kind of subtle mystery? He felt inept. Gareth had to admit to himself that he had no clue what was really going on. Gareth didn't see any evidence of criminal activity. The case needed a team of psychiatrists rather than criminal investigators.

Then there was the woman next to him. She looked like a Sports Illustrated cover girl, but carried herself like a hard-assed pro. Yet, out of nowhere, she fainted dead away like a delicate lady stuffed in a corset. Her features were unreadable. August's poker face would give even the shrewdest of card sharks pause.

August felt Gareth churning next to her. The inner teenage girl with a big crush on the hunky guy wanted to let him in on everything that was going on, but that would be a mistake. August needed to focus, to sift through everything while it was still fresh, get some notes down, and report to her handler. Besides, their easy rapport was dangerous. She did not need to be feeding the flame. Gareth Drake could make this investigation a lot more complicated if he got more involved. The mission was too important to get distracted by a selfish attraction.

They arrived at the Hotel Provincial. Gareth pulled the car up to the front curb. They sat there for a few moments until August broke the silence.

"Thank you for your assistance today. We're supposed to give Morgan her surf and turf lesson tomorrow at fifteen hundred. Are you still up for it, Officer Drake?"

"I am at your command, Special Agent Cannon. Do you need a ride to the coroner's office in the morning?"

"You don't have to do that. I can get a cab."

"It's my duty, ma'am."

"Very well, pick me up at oh-eight hundred. I want to see the late Mrs. Martel and expedite the autopsy."

"Yes ma'am."

Gareth didn't bother reminding August that the autopsy wouldn't be available until eleven. Gareth wanted to spend as much time with August as possible. Never in his life had anyone had such an enticing yet soothing effect upon him. It was maddening and wonderful.

Gareth felt foolish for not being able to figure out what was going on with August? Maybe she was incredibly ambitious, wanting to prove her capabilities as a field agent. A reasonable explanation, but something didn't add up. A big piece of the puzzle eluded him, and August wasn't about to explain.

Dr. Bombrau would have a fit if they showed up at his office earlier than expected unexpectedly, but looking at August's face, Gareth knew there was no use mentioning this. A sick part of Gareth wanted to see the stodgy old coot try to give August a hard time. The coroner wouldn't know what had hit him.

Gareth smiled and dashed out of the car, intending to open August's door for her. She beat him to the punch. He changed direction, retrieving August's suitcase from the trunk.

"Thank you."

"My pleasure," Gareth said.

"Good night."

"C'est une honte que j'ai partir," (It's a shame I have to leave.) Gareth said.

August tilted her head, eyebrows raising slightly, and turned away, walking towards the hotel lobby door. The steward opened it for her. While entering the building, August said over her shoulder, "Monsieur, vous voyagez une ligne mince." (Sir, you travel a fine line.)

'Quoi?!' (What?!) She speaks French? He clutched his heart. Now Gareth knew why he had such a hard time staying interested in the women he dated. He decided to either marry someone as exceptional as this, or forever remain a bachelor.

Gareth never felt so excited and terrified in his life. Fifty thousand screaming football fans were nothing compared to the thrill of August. He almost skipped back to his car. Gareth fired up the engine, heading to the station to sign out before going home.

* * *

August liked the elegant interior design of the Hotel Provincial. She checked in, and asked if the concierge could procure two pairs of swimming goggles, one adult and one child sized. August tipped him one hundred dollars. He promised to have them by the morning.

She entered her lavish hotel room, complete with a four- poster bed, fireplace, table, chairs, an antique desk, and a balcony. The art deco style bathroom was outfitted with a modern shower alongside a large claw foot tub.

August spent the next two hours writing down every observation from her day, including her thrilling ride through UnderLife.

August used the coffee maker in the bathroom to boil water for some chamomile tea. While it steeped, she opened the French doors leading to her small balcony, letting in the sounds of the Quarter. August fetched a towel from the bathroom, spread it on the floor next to the small wrought iron table outside, and sat down.

August straightened her posture, imagining her head was suspended from a string. She put her hands on knees, palms up with fingertips touching, closed her eyes, and took deep breaths, in through her nose, out through her mouth.

A whirlpool of thoughts spun around August's mind. She let them flow without fixating on anything specific, trusting all relevant details were included in her report. August concentrated on keeping her breathing steady and full. Once her intellect calmed to a manageable roar, it was easy for her to slip into a meditative state. August relaxed and allowed the environment to penetrate her consciousness.

A breeze drifted in from the French Quarter. The air was thick with moisture. Music from several sources rang through the night. The loudest was a throbbing electronic beat from a nearby dance club. August also heard the brassy notes of a classic zydeco band in full jam, and a street saxophonist playing the blues.

At night, August could feel New Orleans's whispering seduction. The city pulsed with passion. August understood why so many people came here to party themselves into oblivion. The city offered an ever present, sultry dare. It devoured all sensible judgment, bending its occupants toward ecstatic and obscene experiences.

The laughter and clinking glasses from the open doors of bars lured August to go do some night life investigation, but she resisted the temptation. August had a job to do.

August stood up, took a big swallow of her tea, gave her notes one final review, and picked up the phone to dial her handler's number.

"Hello?"

"Hi Louise."

"August, how is the case going?"

"You sent me to investigate the paintings found in Miami and the recent suicide of Gwendolyn Martel. My task was to see if any connection existed between her death and Pablo Escobar."

"Yes."

"But that's not what this is really about, is it?"

"No, not entirely."

"The little girl, Morgan Martel, she…"

"…has a rare gift, yes. What do you recommend we do?"

"Help her heal and grow."

"Tell me what happened."

CHAPTER FOUR
LINES OF THOUGHT

August's sleep was plagued by a rerun of the tsunami nightmare. She woke with a start, her body curled into a tight fetal position, pajamas drenched with sweat. The glow from the first rays of morning light filled the hotel room. August had left her window shades open so the sun could stir her from sleep. She preferred this method to an alarm clock or a wake-up call, and she needed to get a jump on the day.

August unfurled her body, extended her limbs to a more comfortable position, and lay still on her back. She kept her eyes closed and took deep breaths, processing the ideas racing through her brain.

August had many questions. She was having a hard time believing her UnderLife experience had even happened. If someone else had described that story to her, and insisted it was real, she'd believe they were deranged. Did Morgan actually pull her into her own subconscious? Science would say that was impossible. Yet, August's vivid memories of the experience could not be ignored.

Where did they go? Why a beach? Was it a real place, or a shared delusion? Were they in some other dimension? Why was there a tsunami siren? Why give them warning in a doomed scenario?

How did Morgan bring August into UnderLife with her? They just looked at each other. August blinked. Then they're at a beach, poised to be ambushed by the ocean.

August reflected on her conversation with Morgan. Morgan had known something was wrong with her Mom before anyone else did. Morgan also seemed to think that by going into Gwendolyn's UnderLife, maybe she could have saved her. Was something like that possible? Could Morgan be trained to harness her UnderLife ability? How?

August got out of bed and padded over to the bathroom. She splashed cold water on her face, and then flossed and brushed her teeth. August put on jogging clothes and went downstairs to look for some food. August found a continental breakfast spread already laid out in a banquet room near the lobby. The establishment was used to having hungry guests at all hours. August drank a glass of orange juice and grabbed a banana.

She cruised through the lobby and paused outside, peeling her fast fuel fruit in front of the building. The concierge from the night before, now in street clothes, exited the lobby and approached her.

"The items you asked for shall be here within the hour."

"Thank you. Getting off of work?"

"Yes. Good morning."

"Good morning," August smiled.

He nodded and walked away.

August stretched while devouring her meager kick start breakfast. She couldn't stop mulling over the last twenty-four hours of her life.

A picture of the eye-twinkling Gareth kept popping into August's head, which she would squash each time. It'd do her no good to dwell on him right now. Way too distracting.

August ran, at first loping along to warm up, and gradually jogging into a steady pace. She memorized the major landmarks and streets of the French Quarter as she was running.

The air was earthy and crisp. A light fog burned off and the sun continued its march into the heavens. An ethereal quality permeated the city. August could only describe it as an energetic potency of possibility. She explored the infamous French Quarter, loving the lush vegetation on and around the buildings, glistening with morning dew. August ran alongside the Mississippi River west on Decatur for a while before plunging back into the neighborhood comprised of venerable buildings.

August knew New Orleans was below sea level and it unnerved her a bit. Only an ingenious series of levies kept the Mississippi delta from swallowing the land. It felt curious to be in a place existing through the will and effort of its inhabitants.

No matter how many times August reviewed her UnderLife trip she didn't have any further insights. She wondered if she had handled the situation properly. August decided, given the same scenario, she would not have changed any of her actions.

August ran north by the French Market and Jackson Square. She looped around the Louisiana Supreme Court building, staying on Royal Street.

On her way back, August located a large newsstand. She bought The New York Times, and scanned through copies of London's Daily Telegraph, Melbourne's The Age, and Tokyo's Asahi Shimbum. She found no mention of a tsunami anywhere in the world yesterday.

August returned to her hotel. August was so immersed with reading she didn't notice Gareth standing in the lobby, a half an hour early, to pick her up. She slammed right into him.

Gareth's left arm snaked around August's waist, steadying her, while his right hand shot out as far away as it could get. The coffee cup Gareth held splashed a bit of its contents harmlessly to the tiled floor.

Gareth looked handsome wearing a light weight white linen suit, with a powder blue button down shirt, and the faint outline of a white tank top underneath. He had begged the Lieutenant to let him work in plain clothes today while continuing to assist the FBI. It was worth it to see the approving eye August gave him.

"Nice suit," August said, slipping out of his embrace and continuing through the lobby.

"Thank you, kindly." Gareth's posture puffed up with pride. It took him a few quick strides to fall into step with her. A musky smell of sweat lingered around August, intensifying the impulse to ravish her body with pleasure. Gareth restrained his desire. "Did you enjoy your run?"

"Yes, I love this city."

"I brought you a local favorite, chicory laced coffee." Gareth presented it to her.

August ignored his gallantry and kept moving. "Sorry, I don't drink coffee." She hit the button for the elevator, and handed Gareth The New York Times. "Wait here, I'll be down in thirty minutes."

"Take your time."

* * *

A damp haired August returned in exactly half an hour. She wore a tailored light beige pantsuit. She carried her briefcase in one arm and a small black duffel bag in the other.

August got the swim gear from the front desk.

Gareth returned August's newspaper, "I know this great breakfast place we can-"

"I'd rather go see the results," August said.

"At the Coroner's? They said they'd be ready for us by eleven. We've got a few hours."

"That's so the day shift can read the report. The night shift has already done the work. Let's check it out. I don't need my hand held by the medical examiner. Besides, it'll give us time to get lunch before we're due at the Martel's."

"You're the boss, and I know just the place," Gareth said, eager to have some private time with August.

"Then let's get a move on," August said.

* * *

They arrived at the police station. Gareth took August downstairs, into the heart of the New Orleans Sixth District Coroner's office. They went down a long deserted hallway. Gareth opened one of the examination room doors. It was vacant of any personnel, living or dead.

Incessant buzzing emanated from the florescent lights above. The mostly stainless steel room and concrete floor gave the impression the entire place could be cleaned with a fire hose. Gareth and August walked through the room to Dr. Bombrau's office in the back.

The office was small, or maybe it just seemed that way. The desk and floors were cluttered with box upon box of case files. If any kind of organization existed to the jumble of paper surrounding them, it was not discernable.

Gareth moved a stack of books and sat down in one of the chairs. August strolled over to the desk, peeking at the papers on it. The pack rat haven was making August feel claustrophobic, and she didn't want anyone to see that. August's jaw clenched. She hated any environment which made her feel closed in. The oppressive veil of death shrouded the whole office and examination room.

Dr. Bombrau entered the room. He was a portly man in his early fifties, with shaggy dark brown hair peppered with grey, and he stood five foot five on a tall day. The doctor wore a work apron covered in blood, chemicals and unrecognizable debris. He had a couple of medical charts tucked under his elbow. Dr. Bombrau was so intent upon scraping the last bits of strawberry yogurt from its container that he didn't notice his guests until he was almost on top of them.

"Oh, hello. Can I help you?" Dr. Bombrau said.

"I'm Special Agent August Cannon here to pick up the results from the Martel autopsy."

Dr. Bombrau nodded and grumbled, "Um-hmm," in response. He focused on August, his eyes flitting around, soaking all of her in. His piercing scrutiny made August uncomfortable, yet she did nothing to hinder his examination. August would bet that if someone blindfolded Dr. Bombrau, he'd be able to recall every last detail of her appearance. Good thing Louise gave me a head's up about this guy, thought August.

She'd mentioned to Louise the night before that Dr. Bombrau planned to perform the autopsy. Louise had known all about the eccentric medical examiner, which shocked August. According to Louise, Dr. Bombrau was one of the best in the corpse business. His ability to extrapolate the cause of death from the evidence provided was excellent. He specialized in solving bizarre cases that had baffled his colleagues. Every government agency had consulted with him at one time or another. If Dr. Bombrau hadn't been so loyal to the Orleans Parish he could've made a lot more money cutting up and examining the dead at Quantico or with any Ivy League research team, but the man refused to travel. He wouldn't leave the borders of the Crescent City and never told anybody why.

Dr. Bombrau's medical talents did not translate into any measure of social skill. He was considered very difficult to be around, as he had no sense of tact.

Dr. Bombrau sized August up, "Well groomed, symmetrical facial bone structure, athletic physical build, clothes too expensive for the salary you are earning, quite young for a Special Agent to be alone on an investigation. Is this your first solo case? Is that why you're so early?"

August smiled at him, unfazed.

He gave a closed mouth smile back. "You have a disarming countenance, underneath dwells many secrets. Follow me, I'll show you what I found with Mrs. Martel."

Gareth couldn't believe it. He'd known the man for years and never saw someone get along with him. Gareth asked Dr. Bombrau, "Doctor, how come I've never gotten such a thorough examination from you?"

"Too easy, you're a walking gonad."

August couldn't stifle a snicker. Gareth wanted to give her a tough-guy glare. He ended up winking at her instead.

Dr. Bombrau led them to another examination room at the end of the hallway. He drew back a curtain, exposing Gwendolyn Martel.

The autopsy had been completed. There was a large Y incision on the torso. The skull cap was off, and as they got closer, August noticed Gwendolyn's brain not inside.

August saw the jagged self-inflicted laceration on Gwendolyn's neck. A deep cut. She'd sliced right into the carotid artery. Gwendolyn must have bled-out in minutes.

August sighed, such a sad sight to see.

Dr. Bombrau ignored the body, going straight to the back of the room to a large workstation with all manner of instruments and vials, including a hefty sized microscope. The medical examiner opened a refrigerator, revealing Mrs. Martel's brain.

Unseen by the medical examiner, Gareth gently put a hand on August's lower back.

The audacity, he just won't quit, she thought. August wanted to step away from him or wheel around and tell him off. Yet she didn't move a muscle. It was difficult to deny the shiver through her spine or the flutter in her stomach. August excused it away. It's just that he started me, she thought, which is why my body reacted like that. It's nothing. It would be inappropriate to think of anything but the case. Stop being so selfish August.

August didn't know that Gareth's touch had been an unconscious gesture for his own comfort. Gareth had seen a few dozen dead bodies in his short career, but his stomach still turned every time. Once Gareth felt the supple muscles of August's lower back on his palm, his simmering desire melted away the nausea.

Dr. Bombrau put Gwendolyn's brain on the counter. August could tell he had found something interesting. His attention was riveted. The doctor picked up forceps from a nearby surgical tray, and used them to expose and point out a dark mass of tissue.

"Subject possessed Grade IV glioblastoma multiforme," reported Dr. Bombrau.

"You're saying she had an inoperable brain tumor?" August said.

The coroner smiled broadly, showing his jacked up teeth. Dental care was not one of the man's top priorities.

"Subject had two of them, one located in the orbitofrontal cortex of the left hemisphere, the other in the primary auditory cortex." Dr. Bombrau showed August both lesions.

"What functions do those areas of the brain control?" Gareth said.

"Decision making and sensory input, especially hearing in the case of the second tumor," Dr. Bombrau said.

"You mean like resolving those tough judgment calls of whether or not it's a good idea to slash one's neck with a glass shard?" Gareth said.

"Possibly," Dr. Bombrau said.

August thought of Morgan's description of the people breaking into her Mother's Inside House, Gareth was closer to the truth than he realized.

Gareth worried that August had been offended by the question. He backpedaled, "All due respect to the deceased. I've been havin' a hard time figurin' out how anyone could do that to themselves."

"People suffering from this type of tumor have been known to exhibit a wide array of erratic behavior. The tumors were in advanced stages of growth, as you can see from the size." Dr. Bombrau said.

"Any evidence of defensive wounds, or signs of a struggle?" August said.

"Her right knee has a quarter-sized bruise on it. Not a conclusive injury. The cut on her right hand was made presumably by her grip on the mirror shard that she opened her neck with."

"Have you finished the paper work on Mrs. Martel?"

"Yes, give me a few minutes to copy it." Dr. Bombrau left the examination room.

Gareth watched August inspect the remains of Gwendolyn Martel. Her focus was mesmerizing. He stayed quiet. The adrenaline dump from their close proximity to the dead and the electrifying presence of August started to wear off. Gareth was left feeling a bit squeamish. Dr. Bombrau couldn't return soon enough.

The Coroner shuffled in before too long, and handed the autopsy file to August.

"Thank you, Doctor. You've been most helpful," August said.

Dr. Bombrau nodded.

Gareth and August left the Medical Examiner's lair.

A few minutes later they were in the police station's parking lot. Gareth felt rejuvenated by the fresh air. He said to August, "I wanted to give you fair warning that I will be filing a sexual harassment complaint with my Lieutenant about you."

"On me? You can't be serious."

"I am, and although I am flattered by your obvious attraction towards me, I do not think this is an appropriate time or place to explore matters of the personal variety."

August couldn't help but laugh, and she decided to play along. August appreciated the distraction from the fresh images of Gwendolyn's dissected corpse.

"I see. Officer Drake, I apologize if you feel I have objectified you in any way. Could you please communicate to me exactly what I did to offend your delicate sensibilities, so I do not transgress in the future?"

"No disrespect intended, ma'am, but your beauty has been taunting me since my eyes had the good sense to gaze upon you. My sole ambition is to get my work done. It keeps distracting me."

"Right, all you want to do is work," August said.

"There have been multiple violations upon my person. Every breath I take is an assault by your lovely scent. Against my will, I have been forced to be fondled by your charm. Well, I won't stand for it. Who is your commanding officer at the Bureau? They need to hear about your conduct while in the field. It's atrocious how you treat a perfectly innocent young man who feels like he's from the South."

"Hey, let's not fly off the handle here. Why don't we go to your favorite restaurant, and maybe we can work something out?"

"I don't know. I feel like I have to say yes or you are going to undermine my career aspirations. I'm going to pretend to mull this over." Gareth gave it a full three seconds, "Alright, I'll go. You drive a hard bargain, Special Agent Cannon."

"I know. I can be a real bitch."

* * *

Gareth took her to the northwestern edge of the French Quarter. He parked his car in a nondescript lot at the mouth of a dark alley. They exited the vehicle. Gareth shot August a mischievous look, daring her to inquire about the unsavory place they ended up for lunch. He strode into the sinister passage like he owned the place. August followed with more confidence than she felt. Gareth approached a modest metal door. He rang a waist-high doorbell. It was located on the side of the doorjamb facing away from where they entered, hidden from general view.

August examined the area. She noticed surveillance cameras in discreet lofty positions throughout the alley.

A few seconds later the door opened, and they were blasted by a breeze of frosty air-conditioning. The doorman was in his late fifties, wearing a tuxedo and a welcoming smile. He ushered them indoors, recognizing and expecting Gareth.

August snagged a card and a couple of mints when they passed the host stand. The business card was royal purple with silver lettering and it said, "Discretion," along with a phone number.

The Maitre d' led them into a twisted narrow hallway with the occasional door. Soft conversation and muffled laughter drifted into August's ears as they moved through the building. They continued up a staircase and onto a balcony. It overlooked a lush courtyard dominated by a crepe-myrtle tree blooming with pink flowers. A pair of robins' chirped and bounced around on the branches.

August heard bubbling water tinkling from a fountain beneath them. A bumble bee buzzed around nearby, working amongst the violet flowers of the wisteria vines clinging to the outer wall and wrapping around the thick wooden banister.

They were seated in a secluded booth with a view of the garden. August settled in and detected a sweet smell. She saw honeysuckle blooming on the wooden lattice-work of their booth.

"I love this place. Thank you for taking me here."

"It's my pleasure, beautiful."

August let the compliment slide by without comment.

Lunch was delectable, and the conversation flowed like they had known each other for years. August revealed no details about herself or her assessment of Gwendolyn Martel's death. She evaded direct questions by being opinionated on a variety of topics, and when all else failed, a flirty look or a slight touch would make Gareth forget what he was talking about. Then August would retreat into a benign subject, and continue to eat her meal.

August knew she couldn't explain her real theory about Gwendolyn Martel without raising suspicions about her cover. Federal Agents weren't known for going with psychic drowning as a cause of death unless it was on some kind of science fiction show.

Gareth insisted on paying. The server told them they needed to depart by way of Discretion's front entrance.

Gareth and August walked out the door of the restaurant into a long outer hallway with ornate scones and lit with red Christmas lights with another door on the other side. The door to the restaurant closed behind them, pushing them out into the alluring atmosphere. Gareth led the way with the same self-assured familiarity as he did walking into the restaurant's back alley entryway. There was a sweet smell of jasmine coming from a brazier filled with smoldering incense.

Gareth stopped. His broad frame blocked August's view. She thought maybe something was wrong up ahead. Gareth turned to face August, his face troubled. It looked like he was trying to say something urgent, but no words came out. He exhaled a puff of air, and did the only thing he had fantasized about since they met. Gareth leaned in fast, kissing August so fiercely, that her body responded before August's brain could suppress the action. The rule-following task-master in her mind raged and railed at how improper this behavior was, chastising her for not putting a stop to it immediately, but her body and consciousness only registered the task-master as white noise, because all she could focus on was how soft and full Gareth's lips were, how delicious it felt to have his strong hands all over her. Her mind yielded as her body melted into his.

It was a whirlwind of kissing. Then he pulled back and stroked her cheek. Gareth ran his hand down her neck and over her breasts. August saw his wristwatch. It was two-fifty pm. They only had ten minutes until they were due at the Martel's.

He observed her noticing the time and planted another searing kiss upon her. August matched his vigor then pulled away.

"Damn it!" Gareth said.

They were both panting with enflamed lust.

"We have to go," she said.

"Just a few more minutes," he said.

"Can't keep them waiting."

August stepped close to him. Her mouth was less than an inch away from his. Her breasts grazed his chest teasingly. "You're going to have to suffer."

Gareth leaned towards August for a final kiss. She dodged his advance by stepping away from him, straightening her disheveled suit.

"Let's go," she said.

"Aw'right, you cruel and sexy woman," Gareth said. His hand cupped the obvious and proud erection straining against his slacks. "I'll meet you at the car. I can't even look at you right now."

As she walked away, August heard Gareth grumble, "Settle down, boys."

She giggled, opened the door to the street, and the hall filled with bright sunlight. August stepped out onto the sidewalk. She emerged from a black metal door with no handle on the outside. Once the door was closed behind her, it blended into the dark brick wall around it. There were no markings or signs alerting the random passer-by to its presence. The door to Discretion was sandwiched between a liquor store and a shop sporting wall to wall dispensers of every flavor of the highly intoxicating Hurricanes. Unlike the pleasant smelling sexy red hallway, the sidewalk had a permanent stinky-vomit-mixed-with-stale-beer-after-party odor. It spurred August on to go find the car.

They arrived ten minutes late at the Martel home. Gareth retrieved a blue gym bag from the trunk of his car.

Gareth rang the doorbell while staring at his companion, wishing he had August all to himself. An older Cuban woman, a feather duster in her hand, answered the door.

"Help you?" she said with a prominent accent.

"Hello, Special Agent Cannon and Officer Drake to see-"

"August!" Morgan said. They heard the thump, thump, thump, of short-legged, full tilt running. A blur of pigtails whizzed by. Morgan barreled into August for a big bear hug.

"No love for me?" Gareth said.

Morgan responded by throwing herself at him. Gareth picked Morgan up, twirled her around, and got rewarded with an onslaught of laughter.

August greeted the woman who answered the door, "Hi, what's your name?" August asked, offering her hand.

This perplexed the woman, not expecting August to address her. She hesitated to shake August's hand.

"That's Conseula," Morgan said.

"Hi Consuela, nice to meet you," August said.

Consuela, looking uncomfortable from the attention, said, "The Misters in shop and Misses in la oficina."

"Thank you. Please, don't let us disturb whatever you were doing."

"Sí," answered the housekeeper, retreating.

August made eye contact with Gareth. He smiled.

"C'mon Morgan, let's go outside and do some climbing," Gareth said.

"Okay," Morgan said.

"Give me a minute to change." Gareth went into the bathroom. He got out of his suit and into some black shorts.

Gareth came back to the living room, and found Morgan and August whispering to each other. August looked up. Gareth saw her luscious lips part as August's jaw relaxed. He had left his shirt off, giving August a wonderful view of his chiseled torso. August blushed. Gareth wanted to tackle her.

Gareth took Morgan to the backyard. August heard him begin his tutorial.

"Now, Morgan, climbing is a full body exercise. It takes a lot of strength and balance. I am going to teach you some simple drills. They'll help you with climbing and with any sport you want to play. It's time to meet your new best friends: sit-ups, lunges, push-ups, and jumping rope."

August went up the front staircase to look for Marin's office. She paused outside a closed door, listening. August heard the muffled rattle of fingers tapping on a keyboard and the hum of a printer. August knocked on the door.

A female voice with a Southern drawl answered, "Come on in."

Marin's office was very different from the disorganized artists' studio. It was an obsessive-compulsive organizational masterpiece. Nothing in the room was out of place. August saw that the full bookcases were arranged with library call numbers labeled on the spines, the Dewey Decimal System. August was impressed.

Marin was reading pages from a print out. Her face was still drawn and pale, but compared to yesterday, August thought it looked like Marin had gotten some rest.

Marin glanced up. "Eddie told me you had Gwendolyn autopsied. What did you find out?"

"Let's get Remy and Eddie. It'll be easier if I tell you all at once."

"Give me a minute to finish this," Marin said.

"Sure, take your time." August sat down. "Oh, one thing, my supervisor is a stickler for details. Do you have a copy of Gwendolyn's birth certificate?" August said.

"Yes," Marin said. She leaned over to open the bottom drawer of her workstation and produced a folder. August looked through the file. It contained all of the family members' birth certificates. August jotted down Gwendolyn, Eddie, Remy, Marin, Dorcha, and Morgan's dates, times, and places of birth into her notebook.

Marin said, "Eddie also said you needed some information about our customers. Is there any particular painting or sculpture I can help you with?"

"Yes, a very large piece called 'Swamp Sunset'. Who did you sell it to?

Marin clicked the mouse several times.

"Swamp Sunset, I remember it, wonderful use of rich colors, excellent shading. Eddie spent ten solid weeks working on that enormous painting. Here it is, sold to Diego Mitchell, interior designer." Marin turned the computer screen for August to see the ledger entry.

"Thank you." August wrote down the customer's information, and closed her notebook. "How are you coping?" August asked.

Marin cringed. "Not well. I can't believe it happened, poor Eddie and

Morgan. They are such lovely people. It's not supposed to be like this. I should have seen it coming. Gwenny and I used to be inseparable. I'm her best friend, for God's sake."

August guessed that Marin hadn't really talked to anyone about Gwendolyn's death yet. Marin seemed relieved to find a friendly female ear.

Her words gushed forth in her delicate accent. "I feel responsible. I'd been blowing her off lately, thinking her paranoia and neediness were the usual Gwenny getting freaked out by nothing. She was always skittish, even as a teenager. I had no idea things had gotten so bad for her. My new law practice keeps me busy, and I have been putting in many hours on the job. I guess I felt like Gwenny needed to grow up too, since the only real work she did, if you could call it that, was modeling for Eddie."

"What about raising Morgan? Kids are a full time job," August said.

"You're right, but I figured if I could manage it, so could she."

August was going to disagree with Marin, but seeing how guilty Marin looked, she decided not to add to Marin's misery. August said, "Understandable. Shall we round up the gentlemen downstairs?"

Marin LeTour nodded and stood. They walked into the hallway. Marin said, "I'm sure you've noticed how close those boys are. They've been that way since they were knee-high. Nearest to brothers as you can get. Bless their hearts."

They went downstairs. Marin got the men while August used the bathroom. Everyone congregated in the living room. Remy sat between Marin and Eddie on the couch. August remained standing.

"Alright, don't dress it up, August, just give it to us straight," Remy said.

"There is no evidence of foul play. The wounds were self-inflicted. During the autopsy, the medical examiner found two aggressive brain tumors."

Remy, Eddie and Marin were stunned.

"Brain tumors?" Remy asked.

"Yes, in the frontal lobe and another one pressing against the primary auditory cortex. The Medical Examiner said it could have caused her erratic and violent behavior. They were fast growing and inoperable. It was a freak occurrence. Nothing you could have done."

"Why didn't I make her go to the doctors? Could we have caught this? Gotten her some kind of treatment?" Eddie asked.

"Typically people don't get random MRIs as a preemptive tumor check. Gwendolyn probably misunderstood any symptoms she experienced as a temporary bad mood or an off day." August said.

"How long would she have had if she…" Remy said.

"Six months, a few years, it's hard to tell in these cases."

The men seemed comforted by the information, but Marin broke down, sobbing. Marin collapsed into her husband's waiting arms. Remy held Marin and stroked her hair. Eddie reached over and held Marin's hand for comfort.

August sat down, watching them, wishing she didn't have to be the messenger of grim tidings.

"I need a drink," Eddie said.

"Me too," Marin said.

"I'll join you," Remy said. "August?"

"No, thank you. I'll go see how Gareth is doing with Morgan."

The three mourners retreated to the dining room.

August found Gareth in the backyard with Morgan. Gareth and Morgan had discovered a couple of water guns, and had abandoned the climbing lesson. They were running around the yard squirting each other and laughing.

A sweaty Gareth ran over to August, gun leveled to shoot her.

"Oh no," August said.

Morgan ambushed Gareth in defense of August.

"Ready to go swimming?" August asked.

"Yes!" Morgan and Gareth said in unison.

"I get my stuff," Morgan said, entering the house.

"Can't wait to see you in a bathing suit, darlin'," Gareth said to August as he walked by.

Gareth gave August an eyeful of lust. It made her feel naked. Gareth smelled like a mixture of sweat, cologne, and sweet, spicy pheromones. August fought the urge to touch his slick, heated skin.

"We should check and see if any of the others are planning to join us," August said, forcing her body to turn away.

"Lead the way sexy," Gareth said.

They went inside and headed for the dining room. Someone had put on Nina Simone's record, "I Put a Spell on You". The blues wafted through the house.

August found Remy, Eddie, and Marin at the dining table, camped around a pitcher of mojitos. Eddie was telling them he wanted to move away from New Orleans and start over. Remy was saying that he had no desire to leave, but hated the idea of not having his best friend and business partner around. Marin thought the family should all stick together, wherever they were.

"How are you doing?" August said.

Eddie, defeated and drained, said "I don't think I'm up for the park today. Do you mind taking Morgan on your own?"

The LeTours didn't seem much better off. Remy refilled their glasses.

Consuela, purse hanging off of her shoulder, guided Dorcha into the dining room. August guessed the housekeeper was ready to get out of there.

"Consuela, could you stay another couple of hours to baby sit?" Marin used a tone expecting agreement.

When the housekeeper hesitated, Gareth interrupted. "We can take Dorcha along with us. I come from a huge family. I'm great with the little ones."

Dorcha cooed happily. Her saucer eyes fixed on Gareth.

"You don't mind?" Marin said.

"Not at all, the more the merrier," Gareth said.

August, Gareth, Morgan and Dorcha slathered on copious amounts of sun block and then walked several blocks north to the YMCA. They took a stroller along with them just in case Dorcha got tired.

Morgan's first swimming lesson was a resounding success. It was clear that Morgan trusted August, and was eager to learn. August put water wings on Morgan, and they began at the shallow end.

August had Morgan holding the wall of the pool to practice kicking. Then they worked on Morgan holding her breath and closing her eyes underwater. This earned Morgan the goggles August had purchased for her earlier. Once Morgan had picked up the freestyle arm movement, she swam the length of the pool with August. August felt Morgan getting nervous when they reached the deep end, but Morgan soldiered on through her fear.

Gareth was being handsome playing in the shallow end, Dorcha cackling in his arms. They didn't stay in the water too long, because Gareth was worried about Dorcha's sensitive toddler skin. They settled down on a blanket underneath a maple tree. Gareth read to Dorcha while she stared at the sun drenched leaves. Every so often, Gareth glanced toward August and Morgan in the pool.

After the swim lesson, August and Morgan were lying on a blow-up raft together, floating around, relaxing.

"Can we talk about the UnderLife?"

Morgan bobbed her head up and down. "You mad cause I cry last time?"

"Of course not. I'm so sorry about that, Morgan. You know if at any time you feel like you don't want to talk anymore, or if you want to change the subject, please tell me. I won't be angry, I promise."

"Okay."

"I believe your gift is some kind of astral projection ability. Where you go, or how, or why, I haven't quite figured out yet."

"Ast-" her face got a cute focused look of concentration.

"Astral projection."

"Yeah, what is that?"

"Your physical body stays in the same place, but your consciousness travels somewhere else."

"Oh yes! Kids do this, right?"

"Actually no. If there are any other kids who can, nobody knows about them. Morgan, do you know how you do it? How you travel to UnderLife?"

Morgan shrugged, "No."

"Do you see where you're going in your head first and concentrate on the image?"

"No, it happens just like you said. One time I here, and the next, UnderLife. Sometimes I don't know I've gone there right away because the place looks the same like where I am. You the first to come with me. Thank you."

"I'd say my pleasure, but that was pretty scary." August brushed some errant strands of hair out of Morgan's face. "You need to be very careful when telling other people about what you can do. Most people won't understand. Others will want proof. Maybe it will be better to wait until you're older before you start sharing, Morgan.

"Okay, I be careful... I wish Mommy was alive. Glad she sent me a new friend."

"Yes, wherever we are in the world, I will always be your friend."

"Me too, August."

They hugged each other tight. The sudden movement caused them to lose balance on the raft, and they rolled into the water, laughing.

Gareth watched Morgan and August interacting at the park. Professionally he was jealous and wanted to be in the know the way August was. He felt that something significant was happening here, but he had no idea how to articulate it. It appeared to Gareth like August and Morgan had known each other their entire lives.

The sky was brilliant pinks and purples as the sun slipped towards the horizon.

On the way back, Morgan pushed the stroller with Dorcha crashed out inside of it, and August and Gareth walked behind them.

Gareth spoke low, so only August could hear. "You're going to be a fantastic mother someday."

"Where did that come from?" she said.

"Seeing you with Morgan at the park, you were both so serene. I almost forgot you and she just met yesterday."

"Yeah, well, so did you and I."

Gareth asked, "Who are you? Why are you really here?"

August smiled at him as they turned the corner onto Philip Street. August was about to reply when she saw something in the distance. Gareth followed the direction of her gaze and saw an older man in a dark suit and sunglasses waiting beside a black Lincoln town car. The man tilted his head in a subtle nod at August.

August turned to Gareth, "Something has come up. I have to go."

"What? Why?" he said.

August continued to walk towards the Martel house. "Sorry for the abrupt exit. It was wonderful spending such a beautiful day with you."

"You're leaving?" Morgan asked.

August entered the house to give quick good-byes to everyone.

Morgan opened her arms and raised them over her head, demanding a hug.

August obeyed with a big bear grasp, and picked Morgan up, who squealed with delight. August embraced Morgan for a few moments, and then set her down.

"Take care of yourself, young lady."

"Next time we go to the beach."

August snorted with laughter, "Oh-ho, funny, you smart aleck." She stroked Morgan's hair and whispered, "I believe you could grow up to be an amazing Healer if you want to." Morgan smiled back at her and nodded. August kissed Morgan on the top of the head and gave her another squeeze.

Eddie gave August a quick hug. "Thank you for everything."

"Listen to your daughter, Eddie. She has wisdom way beyond her years and she speaks the truth," August said in a low pitch so only he could hear.

"I will," he said. Eddie got choked up, and retreated, embarrassed by his frayed emotions. Any further loss right now, even of a new friend, was too much for the sensitive painter to cope with.

Finally August got to Gareth Drake.

"Officer Drake, thank you for all of your hard work. It has been a pleasure and honor to be handled by such a professional." She shook his hand, bringing up her left hand to cup Gareth's hand in both of hers. August's touch paralyzed Gareth. He felt compelled to follow August's lead, to keep everything brief and official.

"Th-Thank you Special Agent..." Gareth stared at August as he trailed off. It took a couple of beats for him to recover. Gareth bowed his head. "Ma'am."

Neither of them turned away. Several moments passed. It took every ounce of self-control Gareth possessed not take this wondrous woman into his arms, and plant such a dashing kiss it would take her breath away. Instead, August saw Gareth's jaw clench and heard his breath quicken.

"Look at you being all serious," August said. She flashed a sexy smile, turned on her heel, walked to the town car, and got in without looking back.

Gareth watched August leave. The look on his face was a sad sight.

* * *

While they were driving away, August interrogated the Man in the Dark Suit.

"Why are you here? What's going on?"

"We're needed elsewhere," he said.

"Can't you take care of it? Why do I have to leave? I wasn't finished with my investigation."

"You got everything you need."

"How do you know?" She thought for a moment. "Have you been following me?"

Silence. She peered at the rear view mirror, trying to read the expression on his face. He gave nothing away. The man's face was as blank and stoic as ever.

"Tell me about what happened with Morgan Martel," the man said. His eyes met August's in the mirror, a smile tugging at the corners of his mouth.

August glared back at him.

* * *

Gareth tried to catch up with August at her hotel, but the front desk clerk said she had checked out a couple hours before. When Gareth flashed his badge, the young man admitted it was August's driver who had closed the account.

The lovelorn cop chased August all the way to the airport. Once again Gareth used his credentials to get information, but there was not an August Cannon listed on any flights.

Gareth wondered, was August using an alias? But why would an FBI agent need to use a false name? If she didn't come to the airport, where did she go? Gareth couldn't wrap his brain around it. It was frustrating the hell out of him. Gareth paced around the airport, holding the tiniest sliver of hope he'd run into August. He tried to sort out his despair over someone who he had been blissfully unaware of two days before.

Gareth spent an hour roaming around every inch of the airport. He almost gave up. Then it dawned on Gareth to ask for the manifests from private flights.

There were a few private jets which had flown out during the day. One stood out in particular, Palomino Air. It had no passenger list. The plane was a Bombardier Challenger 601. The attendant helping Gareth said it had transatlantic range and could hold at least fifteen people. It was bound for JFK Airport in New York.

Something important must have come up for her to fly her out in a private jet, Gareth speculated.

Later, he tried to trace the chartered jet, but he hit a dead end with Palomino Air. He couldn't find a listing anywhere with that name. If it was a legitimate company, they had the worst marketing team ever.

August was a rookie agent, Gareth speculated, getting her feet wet on a case with a minimal amount of danger. The man was probably her trainer. August was not on the books yet because she hadn't finished her training. But why did they need to leave on a private jet? Why all the secrecy?'

It's enough to drive a man to drink, Gareth reckoned, and decided it was an excellent suggestion. Gareth grabbed his wallet, and locked up his apartment. He walked down to Snake and Jakes Christmas Club Lounge for some liquefied sedation and random socialization.

A journal entry written by Gareth about the hunt for August Cannon: "Infernal woman! Here I've created a nice life in my beloved New Orleans, serving and protecting, and out of nowhere the tranquility is dashed away by August Cannon, if that's even her real name. She made me feel like I don't have a clue about what is really going on around me. So secretive and fascinating. How can the Bureau have no record of Special Agent Cannon? Who is this woman? Is she a spy? A mercenary? Why would any company or country be interested in the suicide of a woman with no great wealth or political connections? What did Morgan Martel have to do with anything? Why did August faint when she saw her and the next thing you know they are best friends?"

CHAPTER FIVE
REND ASUNDER

Berkeley, California
Three Years Later
Martel/LeTour Family

The first six months after Gwendolyn's death were the hardest. Everyone just did their best to get through the day's tasks at hand. In typical New Orlean's fashion, there was a considerable amount of self-medicating from bottles of spirits.

Eddie and the LeTours sold their homes and left New Orleans before the year ended. Everyone needed the change. It took a massive effort to move, but the work was a welcomed distraction. They moved west to Berkeley, California. Over the next couple of years their solidarity helped them survive. They picked up the pieces and learned how to live without their beloved Gwendolyn.

They bought a big Victorian house with four bedrooms not far from Berkeley's campus, and they leased a studio with a gallery storefront a few blocks away. Marin suggested that the men create some small, signature art pieces which could be cheaply replicated. They sold a few designs to large corporations like Target, Pier 1 Imports, and Cost Plus World Market. It was a smart decision, providing them with a base survival income. The financial cushion gave them the freedom to focus on larger, more personal work.

Over the years, August called Morgan every so often to check in. The adults thought it was a little weird that the two had developed such a lasting friendship during the family's darkest hour, but they couldn't deny how much Morgan lit up when August called. Morgan would talk about August for weeks after one of their marathon phone conversations. After a while, everyone got used to Morgan hearing from Auntie August.

Time passed. They settled into routines. Marin worked part-time as a contract lawyer. Eddie and Remy would work until they had enough pieces for a show, and at the show they would sell what they could. Then the family would take a vacation, and when they got back Eddie and Remy would go right back to work. The LeTour/Martel Gallery did three or four exhibitions a year.

One evening Eddie came home after a big spring art presentation. He had told Remy and Marin he wanted to check in with Morgan and Dorcha before the party got into full swing around 9 pm. Also, he had spilled some red wine on his shirt, and he wanted to change it before he got too drunk to care.

Morgan, now ten years old, was at the tail end of a massive Uno tournament with Kelly, the teenage babysitter. Dorcha had already been knocked out of the finals, so she was sitting next to them, engrossed in her color touch pad Simon game.

"Having fun, girls?" Eddie said.

"Yes Daddy, Kelly taught me Uno, I love it!" Morgan said in a rush, absorbed in her game.

"That's great, honey," Eddie said, kissing his daughter on the top of her head.

"How did the art show go, Mr. Martel?" Kelly said.

"Wonderfully, thank you for asking," Eddie said, disappearing into the bedroom hallway, already unbuttoning his soiled shirt.

He returned after few minutes, tucking in a black button down dress shirt. "Kelly, make sure the girls don't go to bed too late."

"I will. After this game it's bedtime," Kelly said through brace laden teeth.

"Aww," Morgan said with Dorcha joining in a beat later.

"Listen to her, young ladies," Eddie said. "Kelly, you know the routine, help yourself to anything in the kitchen. We probably won't be back until very late." Eddie handed Kelly envelope, "Here's for tonight in case you get up earlier than I do. Thank you for staying over, I appreciate it."

"No problem, they're fun to hang out with."

"Glad to hear it. Okay, my little women, give me a squeeze."

Eddie hugged Morgan and Dorcha, waved good-bye to the babysitter, and left.

A short time later, Morgan nestled in her bed, blankets firmly tucked under her chin. She calmly laid there with her eyes closed, relaxing.

* * *

There was a bright blinding light. Morgan tried to cover her eyes, but she couldn't move her hands. Her legs were stuck too.

Morgan blinked furiously, trying to adjust her vision. Flutters of panic needled Morgan's gut, and she prayed for her sight to return.

It was lucky that her other senses seemed to be working fine, because Morgan heard a snorting sound and smelled something disgusting close by.

"Clop, clop…"

Horses, she thought? It would certainly explain the shit smell. Morgan's vision seemed to be clearing. Unfortunately, her limbs were still of no use. Struggling was only causing pain in her ankles and wrists. She was definitely tied down.

Morgan tried to bolster her morale. Calm down, Morgan, she thought to herself. I'm in the UnderLife with some horsies. I love horses, remember? Yeah, in theory. I don't actually have any experience with horses other than watching them on TV.

Morgan tried to dispel the rising sense of dread by reassuring herself this wasn't Waking Life. Whatever happened, she would be fine. Panicking wasn't the wisest of actions. Morgan needed to find a way to solve the puzzle. She tried to assess the situation rationally. Okay, she thought, I've been pinned down pretty good from the start of the situation. I can now see shapes, but my vision's still blurry. Morgan chastised herself for watching Return of the Jedi so many times. Now she knew how Han Solo felt when Jabba tried to have him chucked into the Sarlacc. The joints in Morgan's arms and shoulders were aching from being splayed out on the ground.

Morgan couldn't fathom where this scary episode was coming from. Was she being punished for some reason?

One of the horses neighed, pulling Morgan out of her speculations. They seemed to be all around her. Morgan hoped she wasn't going to get trampled. That would hurt like hell.

"Hey! Hello out there? Please help?"

She was answered with pain.

"Bad idea, bad idea, Ow, OW!"

Morgan clammed up, realizing her voice only made the ropes tighter.

Morgan concentrated on not moving. She needed more time to get her vision back. The bindings seemed to go slack and taut arbitrarily. It dawned on Morgan that she was bound to the horses themselves. Morgan's skin began to crawl with fear. She was in much more trouble than she had thought. Morgan knew she might be in for a world of pain before being allowed back into Waking Life and out of this nightmare. Morgan had been in dangerous situations before and had gotten out of them. She trusted that there must be a way to get through this.

Morgan heard footsteps coming closer and a soothing "Shh" sound. Morgan didn't know if it was meant to sooth her or the horses. Either way it worked, because the ropes went slack. Morgan rubbed her eyes, grateful to relax strained limbs.

"Thanks," she said. Morgan sat up and faced the general direction of the unidentified approaching figure. Whoever it was, they wore a cloak with a big hood, their face lost in shadow. The figure held some kind of rod with a glowing tip.

Morgan blinked rapidly, trying to speed up the recovery of her eyes.

The figure made a low clicking sound, which brought the horses to attention. Morgan was flung into a spread eagle position on the dirt. She felt searing pain ripping through her arms. Every joint in Morgan's body screamed.

The figure approached Morgan, and the red glow came closer to her face. "What are you...? No! NO!"

The cloaked figure jammed the hot iron poker into Morgan's right eye. The poker flayed her eyelid before plunging into the soft orb. An explosion of agony rocked Morgan to the soul. Morgan screamed until her throat was raw. Her voice cracked from the strain. Blood oozed down her cheek and jawline, dripping into her mouth. She spat it away, her limbs helplessly stretched out.

"Please. Please," Morgan said.

No reply.

Morgan smelled the ugly stench of her own burnt flesh. Why was this happening? she wondered. What did I do to deserve this torture?

Morgan hoped that that was the end of it, but she was wrong. The cloaked figure stabbed Morgan in the other eye. Morgan's blood curdling screams began to spook the horses. They did their best to run away from the disturbance. Morgan's pain was ratcheted up to an unbearable degree.

Morgan prayed for relief, unconsciousness, even death. Her right shoulder made a horrific crunching and popping noise as it dislocated from the socket. A new blossom of agony swept through her body. It was not long before her left shoulder joined the right, but it seemed endurable compared to her hyper extended knees straining to keep her hip joints intact. It was to no avail. The joints in her knees, elbows, hips, and wrists were pulverized. Morgan Martel was being ripped apart.

Morgan was experiencing new levels of pain she never thought possible. The torture was perpetual. Morgan begged for mercy with every thought and cry. This was the only activity keeping Morgan's sanity from unravelling.

Then there was an awful tearing sound. Morgan's beleaguered senses told her the ripping was coming from her own skin.

Finally, the horses quartered Morgan. Her arms and legs were torn from her torso, mangling Morgan's innocent, prepubescent body.

Morgan's limbless torso clung to life. Mercifully, the unfathomable agony overloaded her nervous system, slamming her into shock. Morgan labored to breathe pathetic, ragged breaths, keeping herself alive.

Through an ocean of pain, Morgan heard a crackling sound. There was a blast of heat, and a low roar of greedy flames. Morgan consoled herself that it wasn't real. I am just a kid, she thought, having a nightmare, asleep in my bed.

Morgan wanted to wake up. She needed to wake up. Her nerve endings were frayed, butchered by the punishment she was enduring.

The shrouded figure picked up what was left of Morgan's body and chucked it onto the blazing bonfire.

Morgan's spirit sprung from her mutilated body. She had a momentary bird's-eye view of the scene, but she was too stunned to retain any details.

* * *

Morgan awoke with a start just before dawn. Everything was fine. No more pain. Morgan felt relieved to be back in Waking Life, but the horror from the recent experience lingered.

Morgan was startled by a sudden noise. She sat up and realized her father was in her room, retrieving suitcases from the closet. Eddie was wearing a rumpled version of his clothes from the night before. His were slacks wrinkled, and his shirt was half unbuttoned with the sleeves rolled up.

"Daddy?"

"Baby, get up and pack your things. We have to leave." Eddie kept his head down. He placed two large suitcases next to the door and held on to a medium sized one.

"Where are we going?" Morgan said.

"Away. Now get up," Eddie said.

Morgan got out of her bed. "Why are we going Daddy?"

Eddie put the suitcase he was holding onto Morgan's bed. "Honey, don't question me. Get changed." Eddie went to Morgan's dresser, opened it, and began transferring clothes into the suitcase.

"What about Dorcha, Remy, and Momma M?" Morgan asked.

When Eddie didn't respond, she pressed him. "They coming with us? Why not coming with us?"

"Morgan!" Eddie yelled, making eye contact with her. Morgan gasped. Eddie's tear-stricken face reminded Morgan of when her mother died. Eddie kneeled down, taking Morgan by the shoulders. His grip and tone were fierce. "What did I say? No questions. Now get ready. We're leaving."

For the first time in her life, Morgan feared her father. Her eyes welled up with tears.

Eddie saw Morgan's reaction, and he softened. "Baby, I'm sorry, we have to go. It's time for a change. We have to do it alone. Get dressed and gather your favorite toys."

Morgan did as she was told.

Within the hour they were on the road in Eddie's hastily packed van, heading towards Los Angeles.

CHAPTER SIX
HIEROPHANT

They arrived in Los Angeles in the afternoon.

Eddie's unusual outburst had freaked Morgan out. She didn't want to be separated from Dorcha, Remy, or Marin, but her relationship with her father was the most important. Thoughts of losing him were more terrifying than anything.

They spent their first week in Hollywood at a Super Eight Motel. Eddie searched for and rented a loft downtown for them to move to.

Morgan tried to talk about the LeTours, but Eddie was unreceptive. Eddie pleaded with Morgan to promise never to ask him about them again. Morgan agreed, though it broke her heart to do so.

A month later, a pre-paid moving truck arrived with the rest of Eddie and Morgan's belongings and furniture. Morgan hadn't heard her father communicate with the LeTours, nor did Eddie explain how he orchestrated the shipment.

By the following week they had settled in at their new loft home.

Eddie partitioned off a work area, enclosing it for privacy. He put on a Walkman and got engrossed in his latest painting.

Morgan was reading Nancy Drew: The Mystery of the Fire Dragon when the phone rang.

Morgan picked up, "Hello?"

"Morgan, there you are," said the voice on the other end.

"August! How did you find us?"

"You're listed. We've got a computer here which searches all of the telephone directories in the country at once."

"Cool," Morgan said.

"How are you? Do you like Los Angeles?"

"Yeah, it's alright." Morgan's voice dropped to a whisper, "I miss the LeTours. Daddy won't say why we left Berkeley. I'm so glad you called."

Morgan glanced over at the calamander screen her father was working behind. Morgan told August everything regarding her Waking and Under Lives. August listened to Morgan's story, and said, "Hang in there, buddy, do your best to adjust to the new city, and be nice to your Dad. I'm sure he's having a rough time."

"I'll be good," Morgan said. "Whatever happened to Officer Gareth? Do you still talk to him?"

"No, I haven't seen him since the last time I saw you. I heard he joined the United States Marshals Service."

"Have you ever run into him while working?"

"No, can't say I have," August said.

"When can I see you?" the girl said.

"I'm not sure, sweetie. I promise to call you when I can."

Morgan heard loud voices in the background. They were yelling in a harsh language she did not understand.

August's voice tensed and she spoke quickly, "Take care, we'll talk soon."

"Ok" August hung up with Morgan in mid-sentence.

* * *

Many weeks passed before August contacted Morgan again. Meanwhile, Eddie had enrolled Morgan in school and life was marching on.

After the first six months in Los Angeles, Eddie began dating Yvette Rutherford, an art dealer who adored him and his work. Yvette got Eddie's career rolling again. Within the year Eddie had enough money to make a down payment on a spacious three bedroom house in Echo Park.

Morgan - Age Thirteen

It was an early Sunday afternoon in the Martel household. Morgan was cooped up in her bedroom doing homework, when the phone rang. "Hello?" Morgan said.

"Sweetheart, I've been thinking about you all morning. How are you?" August asked.

"August please help me I don't know what's going on. UnderLife adventures are way more frequent and dangerous. They seem to begin and end at random. Half of the time I have no idea why it's happening, where I am in that psychic realm, or how to complete the journey without getting killed.

"Hm," August said. "Have you started getting your period yet?"

"Uh- Yeah, last month," Morgan said.

"Congratulations. It's nothing to be ashamed of, or embarrassed about."

"I know, it's just odd. Thank God my Dad's new girlfriend Julie was here and told me how to use a tampon. Pads are gross."

"Yeah, I don't like them either. Right, I think I know what's going on here with your increased UnderLife activity," August said.

"What? Please tell me. The kids at school think I'm a big weirdo because I've passed out a few times during the day. Dad hasn't found out yet, but when he does he's going to freak out and make me go to the doctor's."

"What's happening in the UnderLife before you pass out? Do you end up unconscious after every episode?"

"No, sometimes I can get through whatever happens and I don't die and then I just shift back. It happens when I have a Game-Over."

It took a beat for August to understand what Morgan meant. "You faint in Waking Life if you die in the UnderLife?"

"Yes, like you did. Why is this happening so much? Do you know what's going on?"

"You've hit puberty, my dear. Your gift seems to be reacting to the influx of hormones by sparking many shifts into the collective unconscious," August said.

"What do I do? How do I stop it?"

"I'm not sure you can or are supposed to. In the meantime, ride it out, and tell people you're narcoleptic."

"Does that mean that I'm on drugs?" Morgan said.

"No, honey. Narcolepsy is a neurological sleep disorder. People who suffer from it can't help falling asleep. At other times they aren't able to rest properly. The episodes are sometimes accompanied by vivid hallucinations. If I hadn't personally experienced UnderLife with you, I would've thought that's what your condition was."

"I have narcolepsy?" Morgan said.

"Sort of. It's just the technical term for the fainting side effect of your fatal UnderLife encounters. Let your Dad take you to the doctor. They'll confirm this diagnosis. Try to make it seem like a minor case, so they don't make you undergo a lot of tests or give you any medication. If they insist on medication, pretend to take it, but hide it under your tongue or in your cheek. Then flush it when you have a chance," August said.

"Narcolepsy, okay. At least now I can give a reason. Dad will be relieved there's an official medical explanation. He worries. I get why, with Mom and all, but it's a little much."

"I thought Eddie knew about UnderLife. Don't you two discuss it?"

"Oh no, it's one of the subjects Dad would rather avoid. If I can't make it happen at will, or bring him in, it's not a real thing to him. It's okay though. At least I can talk about it with you."

"Maybe in time he will be able to," August said.

"Why do you think I can do this whole UnderLife thing?"

"There are cultures who consider what you do a variant of a shaman spirit walk."

"What's a shaman?" Morgan said.

"Someone who is powerful and acts as an intermediary between the natural and spirit worlds. They often take on the roles of healer and metaphysical guide for their people. When a shaman goes on a spirit walk, he or she leaves his or her own body to travel to other planes of existence. Shamans use many different methods to initiate their trances, depending on the culture: Singing, meditation, dancing, consuming entheogens such as peyote, marijuana, ayahuasca, or datura, drumming, near death experiences, or even pain. But you seem to be able to trigger your spirit walks all on your own."

"So science knows about this?"

"Many spiritual books and belief systems talk about experiences like these. However, as far as the scientific community is concerned, what you can do is about as explainable and credible as magic, faeries, or unicorns."

"Am I shaman?" Morgan asked.

"You've got a tremendous amount of raw talent and you could become quite an influential one, if it's what you want. It's a dangerous and difficult path of service, filled with many challenges and responsibilities. Don't worry, though. This is not something you need to decide now. Let yourself grow up first. When you're older we'll talk about it again."

"I want to help people," Morgan said.

"Then you will have the chance when the opportunity presents itself."

"How?"

"I'm not quite sure yet, but I have faith you'll it figure it out." August changed the subject. "How's your father doing?"

"Pretty good, I guess. He's been dating Julie for about a month."

"Oh yeah? Do you like her?"

"Sure, Julie's nice. She's an art student, has her tongue pierced."

"What happened to Kate? I thought your father really liked her."

"I'm not sure," Morgan said. "Last time I saw Kate she was here modeling for a portrait."

"How did it turn out?" August said.

"I don't know. I never saw it or her again."

Morgan – Age Fifteen

Eddie saw Morgan off to school. He was in the kitchen making a caramel chocolate birthday cake for Morgan with his girlfriend Kim, when the phone rang.

Kim answered for Eddie while he wiped off his hands, and then handed the phone over to him.

"Hello?" he said.

"Eddie? It's August."

"August, how are you?"

"Very well. You?"

"Good. You just missed Morgan. She won't be back until this evening."

"I know. I wanted to talk with you privately," August said.

"Oh? About what?" he said.

"I was so moved by Morgan when I first met her."

"Well, you did faint," Eddie said.

"Walking into your studio overwhelmed me. Your art reflected such immense sorrow and loss. Then seeing the two of you hold on to each other with love. My emotions got the best of me. I know I'm trained to be detached, but I was a lot younger when that happened, and it captured my heart."

"That's touching, thank you," Eddie said.

"Be warned, you might think this is crazy. When I left New Orleans I started a college trust fund for Morgan. It has been steadily maturing all these years."

"You did? How, how astounding! I must say I'm a bit stunned. Why would you do such a thing?"

"We both know how special she is. Morgan is like the sister I never had. I want her to have every resource available, so she can build a happy life."

"I know you do," Eddie said.

"Thank you. I can't express how much it means to me that you will let her take my gift."

"How much are we talking here?" Eddie said.

"At this point, it is at about a hundred and fifty thousand dollars."

"What? August, that's too generous. We can't accept it."

"Of course you can. Besides, it's already in her name."

"I, I don't know how to respond."

"Please take in the spirit of generosity in which it is offered. I would prefer it if you don't tell Morgan about this until after she's decided what she wants to do after high school."

"Morgan is very excited for college. High school has been difficult for her socially. It's been hard for Morgan to feel comfortable in her own skin. I think she'll have a lot more fun in a collegiate environment," Eddie said.

"The awkwardness is not too surprising. It's a tough age, all those raging hormones. If you don't mind, let's keep this conversation between us. I'll call back later on to wish Morgan a happy birthday."

"I understand. Thank you, August, you're an exceptional woman."

Eddie was relieved to have the help. Money slipped through his fingers like water. For years, Remy and Marin had handled the budgeting. Eddie's business skills were grossly underdeveloped. He took great comfort in knowing Morgan would be provided with the opportunity for a higher education.

Morgan – Age Seventeen

"August, I'm so glad you called. I have wonderful news!"

"Do tell."

"I got accepted into UCLA!"

"Morgan, how wonderful! Well done!"

"I also got into Duke and Northwestern, but UCLA has always been my first choice. I don't want to be too far from Dad."

"It's quite an accomplishment, regardless. Those are all fine schools."

"Dad told me what you did," Morgan said.

"Whatever do you mean?"

"The trust fund, I can't believe it. All this time that's been there? You are my guardian angel. I wondered why Dad never seemed to sweat how much the schools' tuitions were. He just kept saying, 'Don't worry about it. Your job is to get accepted. We'll figure something out.' Thank you from the bottom of my heart. I promise to work hard and make you proud."

"I am proud of you, Morgan. Do you know what you want to study?" August said.

"Psychology, I think, and some kind of Anthropology," Morgan said.

"Really?"

"What? You sound disappointed."

"It's just... Psychology? It seems so general, boring."

"Not when subconscious interactions are actual events. The possibility of encountering my or someone else's worst nightmare makes me want to learn as much as I can about how the human psyche operates. I've also been reading about Transpersonal Psychology. They're all about spiritual experiences. I think those scholars would be fascinated by what I can do. I could get some excellent insight about my theoretical psychic ability," Morgan said.

"All good arguments, I stand corrected. You've already got a lot going for you as a student. You know how to take a position and defend it, point for point."

"Thank you," Morgan said. "The other thing I've been dying to tell you about is I had another tidal wave experience in the UnderLife."

"What triggered it? Were you with anyone? What happened?" August laughed. "Maybe I should let you tell the story."

Morgan giggled. "I have a new band I'm in love with, called Virtuoso. Victoria Shine is the female vocalist. Remember, she was on that variety show with Darian Vihzor as a kid? She's so sexy, and has an awesome voice. The lead guitarist Cuneo and Victoria are dating. They're all over the gossip magazines. In their first video they play out a whole gothic vampire fantasy. He brings her into the fold as his bride."

"Oh yes, I've seen their pictures before," August said.

"Well, I was listening to their self-titled first album when the shift occurred. Suddenly I was working as a planter on a terraced rice paddy. It was daytime, the weather was muggy and overcast. There was a river below feeding the ocean. The ocean was less than a quarter mile away. There were other people toiling in the fields with me. I'm not sure how I knew about planting rice, but I seemed to be on automatic pilot. I was so absorbed in my task of seeding the flooded field, that I didn't even see the tidal wave coming. It hit. I swam my ass off and survived. Then the physics of UnderLife bent and a riptide pulled me out to the sea. I found myself with a few other survivors. We were treading water in the canal entrance of a floating shantytown filled with pirates. I started to swim back, but the ship's quartermaster said the tides were too strong and I would never make it alive. He said the only way to gain my passage back home was to work on the ship."

"What was that like?" August said.

"The UnderLife episode ended when I agreed to indentured servitude."

"What song was playing when this maritime expedition began?"

"Actually, the album had just ended," Morgan said.

Nine Months Later

"I tried getting a hold of you through the Bureau, but they don't have any record of you," Morgan said.

"I'm off the grid right now, doing undercover work. They're not allowed to acknowledge me. That's also why I can't give you my number. What's going on? Did something happen to your Dad?" August said.

"No, he's fine. Now I feel silly getting so worked up."

"How's college life?"

"Good, I love it. I met someone, but I totally blew it."

* * *

UCLA Freshman Year

After Morgan's first cultural anthropology class, she went to the school's swimming pool to get some exercise. Morgan sat in the Jacuzzi, boiling herself into a cheap warm-up before doing laps. She checked out all of the half-naked eye-candy cruising around. Morgan's mouth gaped open when she saw the six foot plus body of a sculpted man emerging from the pool in his snug Speedo. It was quite an impressive instant for Morgan. Standing several feet away was her masculine ideal in the flesh.

Fucking adorable! I am going to be so happy in college if these are the kind of guys roaming around, she thought.

She was terrified by the notion of approaching him. His beauty was so intimidating Morgan had to remind herself to breathe. Morgan's limited experiences with effective flirting had left her dumbfounded and self-conscious. The old schoolyard method of punching someone you liked and running away was making total sense. Morgan wanted to talk to him but chickened out.

A week later, Morgan and Anne, her roommate, went to the first big bash of the year at Rick's Bar. They had gotten some fake IDs from Karl, a sleazy guy living on the second floor of their building. The IDs were successful on their maiden voyage.

Rick's had an extensive video jukebox with screens positioned throughout the establishment. Morgan kept putting on blocks of Virtuoso videos.

Her favorite video, "Lure", was the one with the vampire fantasy. Morgan was so enraptured by the video that she didn't notice the man leaning against the wall observing the crowd. The man was watching Morgan, entertained by her fixation on the video.

Morgan took a swig of Corona, still trying to shake the taste of the Jaeger shot she and her roommate had taken. Morgan knew she was officially buzzed when she lifted her beer in salute to Victoria and Cuneo on the television screen yelling, "Sexy!" The video got to the part with the core vampire biting scene between Cuneo and Victoria. Victoria moaned as blood flowed down her neck.

A man's voice near Morgan spoke, "Yeah, that looks like a healthy relationship."

Morgan glanced over.

Oh my God, it's the beefcake from the pool, she thought.

Morgan tried to act cool and not gape at him. "It's therapeutic. They're working it out with their art."

Morgan looked away from the TV and focused on him. She'd already seen the video a hundred times at least, so it kept playing on in her mind. The next shot on the screen was of Victoria as the trickster God Pan. She was dressed in goat leggings complete with shiny black hooves, horns, fu-man-chu, and a brown furry bra. Victoria took a long drink from a goblet of wine, staring directly into the camera with a devilish and dangerous gleam in her eyes.

"More like acting out," the guy said, drinking a Heineken. The man beamed at Morgan.

"Yes, she sure is. Victoria Shine has quite a raucous and ostrobogulous sense of humor," Morgan said with a smile.

"That's got to be word-of-the-day calendar, which means you have Professor Derr for English Lit."

"Good call. We got an assignment to work these ridiculous words into everyday speech." Morgan stuck out her hand. "I'm Morgan."

"Balthazar."

They shook hands. He continued, "Professor Derr always makes freshmen do the obscure mission. Okay, now I know you're diligent about your studies and attracted to the dark musician type."

"Not exclusively," Morgan said.

Balthazar laughed.

Morgan grinned back. They looked at each other. She saw his eyes flitting around a bit, taking in all of the details of her face, hair, and body. Balthazar's handsome features mesmerized Morgan. His presence felt so yummy that Morgan could barely resist the desire to sabotage the distance between their bodies. At this point Morgan was clearly flirting. There seemed to be an unspoken agreement between them. If they had sex it would be magnificent.

He drank it in, enjoying the attention, but then he sighed, "I can't."

"Oh."

Of course, he has a girlfriend, Morgan thought. What was I thinking? Men this hot always have girlfriends. On the off chance they become single there's a pack of women lurking in the wings, ready to pounce at the earliest opportunity. Morgan berated herself for getting her hopes up.

Morgan did her best to look nonchalant and kept up some inane chatter about adjusting to college. They ordered more drinks, and continued to keep a respectful distance. Morgan's Ego wanted her to go find someone available, since this heartthrob was already taken, but they had such an easy chemistry that Morgan couldn't bear to tear herself away. She could also tell Balthazar enjoyed her company, and was experiencing some self-conflict about his previous commitment.

Balthazar kept looking over her shoulder, his guilty conscience freezing the conversation. Morgan followed his gaze. Standing near them was an athletic looking guy with a strained smile. This must be Balthazar's babysitting friend, Morgan thought, making sure Balthazar wasn't going to forget his loyalties.

A different friend of Balthazar's approached with a couple of women he'd met. Balthazar took the opportunity to guide Morgan away from the guy who was watching them.

They slid into a booth, with Balthazar next to the wall, to Morgan's left. Morgan was on the aisle. There wasn't much clearance between the seat and the table, and the surface hid their laps.

Morgan and Balthazar talked with the other people in the booth. Eventually the others fell into a conversation with each other and Morgan and Balthazar just listened.

Balthazar nudged Morgan's shoulder with his. She turned to him. To Morgan's utter surprise and delight, Balthazar had unzipped his fly and taken out his stiff cock.

The expression on Balthazar's face said please don't be disappointed we can't date. See how hard you make me?

His cock was gorgeous. Ideal. It was long, thick, and ready for action. Balthazar's bold concession of lust made her want to fuck him even more. Morgan wasn't about to let this opportunity of naughty provocation pass her by. Without hesitation, she discreetly reached over with her left hand to caress the tender skin of his dick.

The conversation shifted again. Morgan tried to sound casual while exploring Balthazar's cock and balls with feathery touches. She took him in her hand and began stroking softly. Balthazar did his best to put on an impassive face and mask the pleasure Morgan was giving him.

The fact that this was all going down in a crowded bar only made it sexier for both of them. Since they were doing it in public, Morgan and Balthazar could pretend that Balthazar wasn't betraying his girlfriend. Morgan didn't know if anyone else knew what was going on, but if they did, she was none the wiser.

She quickened the pace, and his dick throbbed. Balthazar's hands covered hers to stop him from coming. Morgan withdrew, realizing she had almost made Balthazar shoot his load.

Balthazar regained his composure while Morgan chatted with his friends. Then Morgan turned, smiled at Balthazar, and pitched her voice low for his ears only. "I've got my dorm room all to myself tonight."

That was a lie. She didn't. Morgan saw her roommate Anne out of the corner of her eye. Morgan knew it would take very little bribery to get Anne to stay over at her on-again-off-again boyfriend's place.

Balthazar leaned in and whispered, "Okay, but my friends can't know."

They made plans to meet back at Morgan's place in half an hour. Morgan excused herself to go to the bathroom. On the way she grabbed her roommate. Unfortunately, Anne and her temperamental dude, Roger, were in the middle of some drama. Anne wasn't receptive to Morgan's request. Morgan begged and promised to do Anne's laundry for a month. Anne agreed to figure something out for the night.

Morgan rushed back to the dorms. She was turned on, ready to engulf Balthazar with all of her passion. Then it happened. At the bottom of the stairwell Morgan slipped into UnderLife.

* * *

Morgan found herself in a non-descript office building. Morgan's first thought was about Balthazar. She felt that he was near. Morgan searched for Balthazar. She went up a flight of stairs and discovered him standing in the center of the hallway.

"Balthazar, there you are. Sorry for the delay," Morgan said.

Balthazar did not respond. He seemed to have no awareness of Morgan's presence. Morgan waved her hand in front of his face and pushed his shoulder. Nothing. Balthazar appeared to be in a catatonic state, or under some kind of spell.

Morgan focused her will on Balthazar. She was convinced that she could dispel whatever was holding him in frozen stasis. Just as Morgan seemed to be making some headway in diffusing the fogginess around Balthazar, and he beginning to respond to her, Balthazar vanished.

The scene shifted. Morgan sensed an impending attack. She looked around for Balthazar so she could help him survive the battle.

Morgan found herself on a steep ramp about sixty feet wide and a hundred feet long, held up by a network of wooden scaffolding. The scaffolding resembled a jungle gym, extending fifteen feet up on either side of the ramp. Morgan had no feeling or picture of anything else.

All of the sudden Morgan saw two female foes marching towards her. The first had spiky blond hair, perfect make-up, and was dressed like a militant go-go dancer. Her companion was taller and was wearing a pink track suit, with her straight brown hair up in a ponytail. Both were brandishing large black bull whips. The two women charged forward to attack.

Morgan had weathered enough UnderLife battles to know the consequences of defeat: another sleepy time incident. She knew that in Waking Life she was standing at the bottom of the stairwell in her dormitory, about to meet up with one of the hottest guys she'd ever seen. Morgan's thrilling dream of transcendent sex was hanging in the balance. Passing out was not an option.

The situation pissed Morgan off.

Of course she would be detoured by the fucking UnderLife now, of all Goddamn times. Morgan wondered if there was there some kind of cosmic orgasm embargo on her. She was determined to successfully solve this unexpected problem. Morgan was due for an important naked rendezvous, and was not about to give it up without a fight.

Well, wherever Balthazar is, he's going to have to fend for himself, Morgan thought.

Morgan turned to face the immediate threat.

Blondie was obviously the leader and the more capable fighter of the two. Morgan did her best to stay mobile, keeping the brunette between herself and the blonde.

The brunette in the pink track suit accidentally nailed the blonde with the back swing of her whip. The blonde yelped at the unintended attack, forcing the brunette to drop her focus on Morgan. Pinky looked over her shoulder and stammered, "Sorry."

In the confusion, Morgan tackled the clumsy brunette. Pinky took the brunt of the fall when they hit the ground. Morgan landed on top of her. Morgan kneed Pinky in the stomach. Pinky curled up, wheezing. This allowed Morgan to wrestle away Pinky's whip. Pinky started to fight back, but Morgan shoved her hard and stood up. She kicked Pinky in the face, stunning her. This gave Morgan a chance to square off with Blondie.

71

Morgan felt confident she could use the bull whip. It took several attempts for her to get a feel for the weapon. The first few strikes missed Blondie completely. Blondie had more success with her whip, opening a gash on Morgan's forearm when Morgan blocked a shot aimed at her head.

Morgan recalled a saying about whips, that it was all in the wrist. She focused on isolating her movement. In exchange for Morgan's lapse in defensive vigilance, she got hit with another glancing blow on her left shoulder.

The pain from the lashes focused Morgan's resolve. She finally cracked her whip just right, wrapping it around Blondie's waist.

UnderLife's bizarre physics changed again. The whip Morgan was holding became impossibly long. Keeping Blondie secure with one hand, Morgan threw the whip handle over one of the wooden beams hanging next to the side of the ramp above her. She caught the whip handle, and before Blondie could disentangle herself, Morgan kicked her over the side of the ramp. Morgan snaked the whip around her arm and braced herself, as the bullwhip went taught on the beam and then in her grip. This left Blondie dangling over a fifty foot drop. With her principle attacker at her mercy, Morgan scanned the area for the other combatant.

Pinky had moved a safe distance away at the bottom of the ramp, conceding her defeat. Pinkie was joined by a man. Somehow, this man communicated to Morgan telepathically that he was on Pinky's team, and that he was gay. Morgan did not know why his sexual orientation was relevant.

Morgan scrutinized Faggy, expecting him to surrender on behalf of his teammate. Rather than concede Blondie's defeat, Faggy yelled at Morgan in a language she couldn't understand. It gradually dawned on Morgan that Faggy was stalling for time.

Morgan checked on Blondie, only to discover her climbing back up the scaffolding, with the whip still around her waist. Morgan jerked on the whip to dislodge Blondie from her perch. Blondie managed to hold on to the scaffolding, just barely. Morgan followed up by pulling on the whip with her full weight. This caused Blondie to lose her grip, and she screamed in terror while plummeting out of sight.

Morgan looked down at her arm with the leather whip wrapped around it. As soon as the whip became taut with Blondie full weight, the whip began to unravel itself from Morgan's arm rapidly. She made sure it would not snag anywhere. Once loose the bullwhip disappeared over the side of the ramp. Morgan heard Blondie's screaming end in a sickening thud.

Morgan turned on her heel and headed towards Faggy. He had sabotaged Blondie from being able to give an honorable surrender. Faggy had purposely delayed Morgan. This action compelled Blondie to continue fighting, and it had forced a deadly response from Morgan.

Morgan got into Faggy's face and yelled, "That was your fault! Her death is on your head!"

A horn sounded. Morgan started walking down off the ramp like there was a scheduled break in the battle. A huge warrior with a jagged scar on his cheek who Morgan hadn't seen before joined her as she descended the ramp. Morgan figured the warrior was a teammate of her opponents. Morgan acknowledged the scarred warrior with a nod and said, "She was a fine warrior who died honorably."

The warrior graciously accepted Morgan's words of respect. Morgan walked away from him.

Suddenly, the whole scenario became clear to Morgan. This was the UnderLife version of competing with rival suitors for a lover. It was combat on a raked battleground. All-out force was allowed, but death strikes were only to be used as a last resort. If a warrior knew he or she was defeated it was best that they surrender rather than die.

Morgan's confidence swelled. She was sure that since she had fulfilled her mission, she would return to Waking Life any moment. However, the scarred warrior had snuck up behind Morgan. Morgan was unaware of the blade heading towards her back until the tip pierced through her chest. As she was about to die, Morgan realized the real lesson of this UnderLife visit: Never let your guard down on the battlefield.

* * *

Morgan woke up at the bottom of the stairwell hours later. Her head throbbed with pain, and she saw a few droplets of blood on the stairs beneath her. She touched her forehead and winced when she felt a small cut on the right side. Morgan realized she must have hit her head on the hand rail or the stairs when she passed out. By the time Morgan made it back to her dorm room, Balthazar had already come and gone.

Morgan discussed her latest UnderLife experience with August on the phone a few days later. "If the UnderLife adventure hadn't ended yet, why did you turn your back on any possible threats?" August asked.

"A dumb mistake, I know. I assumed I'd completed the puzzle, and I wanted to get naked with Balthazar. I'm so familiar with UnderLife, I forget how serious and specific each lesson is," Morgan said.

"How do you know if you've learned the lesson?"

"I shift back into Waking Life like nothing ever happened. Although sometimes I'm a bit disoriented while I jog my memory to remember what I was doing before the episode occurred. The last disastrous UnderLife performance left me passed out in the stairwell for hours." Morgan said.

"How unfortunate," August said.

"You're telling me. I was so mad at myself for missing such a wonderful sexual opportunity. The next day, I got Balthazar's number from the student directory and called him to apologize."

"Good idea. How did he respond?"

"Well, I left a contrite and suggestive message on his voicemail. He called me back the next day when he knew I would be in English class."

"Oh."

"Yeah, on his message, Balthazar lamented about how much he'd drunk, and despite a sincere attraction towards me, he was committed to someone else."

"I'm sorry, Morgan, that's rough," August said.

"The real knife twist was when I saw him shortly after with some petite blond chick hanging all over him, which I assume is his girlfriend."

"It's his loss, Morgan. I'm sure he's not the only good-looking person who would love to have all kinds of fun with you."

"I know, you're right, it's just so frustrating. I keep obsessing about the whole thing."

"Understandable. Don't let it get in the way of taking care of yourself or your responsibilities."

"Yes, Auntie August," Morgan said with a sing-song penitent kid voice.

* * *

Morgan was forced to write Balthazar off as taken. She tried to pretend it didn't matter to her. Morgan submitted herself to a quiet self-flagellation over the whole ordeal. Thoughts of Balthazar fueled many a sexual fantasy.

Morgan ignored Balthazar the whole next year whenever she saw him around campus. It was Balthazar's senior year. Morgan figured he'd forgotten all about her and would be leaving soon for his compelling post-college life.

Morgan – Age Twenty-One – Three Years Later

Over the next few years, Morgan's desire to be of service of to humanity got stronger. However, she was fuzzy on the specifics of how she could be of the greatest help. Morgan had faith that the path would reveal itself.

Meanwhile, she had massive amounts of school work to deal with. UCLA was a four year blur of lectures, experiments, films, papers, tests, and endless hours of homework.

One balmy afternoon in late September, Morgan was studying in her favorite café near campus. Morgan wasn't getting much school work done that day. Instead, she was immersed in a Vanity Fair article about the one year anniversary of Cuneo's accidental drug overdose during Virtuoso's second world tour. The reporter had tried reaching Victoria Shine for comment, but had gotten stonewalled.

One month after his death, Victoria had released a memorial song about Cuneo called "Left". The surface meaning of the title was obvious. It was also a reference to how Cuneo had restrung his guitar to accommodate his left handed playing, like his hero Jimi Hendrix.

"Left" had topped the charts for a season, despite Victoria's refusal to appear in public to promote the song. She had let the song out into the world, and then had disappeared into seclusion to continue mourning. The music video for "Left" was a highlight reel of Cuneo and Victoria footage.

Morgan was still upset over the whole tragedy. Morgan had cared for Cuneo, loved his music, but it had been obvious from Virtuoso's first music video that Cuneo harbored a troubled soul. Morgan had hoped that Cuneo would find a way to heal whatever was causing him such pain. Morgan thought Cuneo had been a fool for not relishing Victoria Shine's love while he had had the chance. Victoria's sex should have been the only drug Cuneo indulged in. Unfortunately, Cuneo had focused more on getting high than on digging into the real labor of personal growth.

Morgan finished the article, disappointed to find no news about

Victoria's current whereabouts and activities. Then, out of the blue, Balthazar Bennington walked into the café.

Balthazar saw her. He paused for few moments, considering. Then Balthazar strode towards Morgan's table with a big smile on his face. Morgan acted like she didn't notice him approaching.

"Hello."

"Hi," Morgan said, looking up.

"Hi, it's Balthazar. You don't remember me, do you?"

"Oh hey, yeah, of course I do. How ya doin', Balthazar?"

"I'm good," he said.

They gazed at each other for a few moments. Morgan seemed relaxed and calm. Balthazar shifted from foot to foot. "I'm sorry about how things went down before," Balthazar said.

"No it's fine. I barely noticed." Morgan smiled wryly at him.

Balthazar laughed and took the liberty of sitting down at her table. Morgan felt a tinge of relief Balthazar knew she was kidding.

"Are you hungry?" he said.

"Yes," she said.

"Will you let me buy you dinner?"

They went to the bistro across the street and got a table. Slipping into conversation, Balthazar avalanched into the story about the blond woman Morgan had seen him with years before:

"The woman with me after the night at the bar, Connie, we met on the swim team. We'd been seeing each other on and off since our sophomore year. For years she'd been elusive and controlling, keeping me at arm's length so I would chase after her. Connie's parents got divorced during the summer before our senior year. It was a vicious break-up. Connie's priorities must have changed, because when school got back in session in the fall, she was all over me. A few days before I met you at Rick's, Connie had decided that we were going to be exclusive. I'd been after Connie for a long time and I was stoked to get to explore a relationship with her. The guy monitoring us that night was one of Connie's best friends. You were such an unexpected jolt of temptation, so easy to be around. I was really pissed at you when you didn't show up at your dorm room. I felt like I was the one making the big sacrifice and you were playing with my loyalties and emotions. About a year later I randomly found out about your narcolepsy."

"Yeah, I totally passed out in the stairwell," Morgan said.

"Why did I take the elevator? I would have found you," Balthazar said.

"As embarrassed as I was that I stood you up, I would have been more humiliated if you had found me."

Morgan appreciated Balthazar's honesty, but she felt it was unnecessary for him to explain. All it took was one smile from Balthazar to erase whatever pain Morgan had felt so long ago. It had been thirty-seven months since that night.

Lunch turned into dinner. Drinks and many hours flowed by. Over a sundae Balthazar looked at Morgan and said, "I can't find anything wrong with you."

"Stop searching, focus on my good points, it's happier there."

"It's happy everywhere. I feel so lucky to have found you again. You don't know how much I kicked myself for how I handled things when we first met."

"As I recall, I was the one doing the handling," Morgan said, deadpan.

"Yes, what a wonderful touch you have."

"Keep it up and you're going to get fucked."

Balthazar leaned in and kissed Morgan.

Eight Months Later

Morgan graduated with a B.S. in Psychology with a minor in Socio-Cultural Anthropology. On graduation day, Morgan stood in her cap and gown, overjoyed about completing her degree, and ecstatic to share her joy with her boyfriend Balthazar, her father, and his new girlfriend Sheryl.

They climbed the steps of the stadium, heading towards the exit, and standing there at the top of the staircase, just like they had seen each other yesterday, was August Cannon. Morgan did a double take. It took Morgan a beat to overcome the shock, even though she had envisioned a reunion for years. August looked sharp in a tailored midnight blue pant suit.

August was everything Morgan remembered her to be. She was a statuesque blond beauty with an adamantine will. Time had been wonderful to her. It had weathered away the hint of nervous uncertainty the younger August had carried, leaving a mature woman whose presence felt like a force of nature. August had a strong buzz of experience and awareness about her, and an infectious joy for the moment.

In Morgan's world August had always been a super hero. August had entered Morgan's life at its darkest moment, giving her strength, acceptance, and understanding during a pivotal stage of her development. No one could reverse the horror of what had happened with Gwendolyn, but it was a tremendous blessing when August got pulled into the UnderLife.

Morgan knew that the tsunami she and August went through together had represented the overwhelming emotions surrounding her mother's death. August's actions during their doomed adventure proved to Morgan there were people out who wanted to help. August didn't hesitate to risk her own life to rescue a stranger. "August! I can't believe it's really you!" Morgan said.

August hugged Morgan so tight that Morgan felt vertebrae pop back into alignment.

"Congratulations, Morgan! What a wonderful accomplishment," August said.

"Thank you. I can't tell you how relieved I am to be done. August, I'm sure you remember my father, Eddie. This is his girlfriend Sheryl and my boyfriend Balthazar."

Eddie moved forward and hugged August. "You look lovely as ever. It's great to see you."

August extended her hand to Balthazar. He ignored it and went in for an embrace. "Auntie August! Morgan sure told me a lot about you."

They all walked to a nearby restaurant for a celebratory dinner. Morgan felt a bit dazed and overwhelmed. Everyone was enjoying each other's company. Balthazar adored Eddie. He found him to be warm, congenial, and encouraging, completely the opposite from his own father.

August put an arm around her, steering Morgan away from the rest of their party. "How are you doing?" August asked.

"Great, very emotional. It's so weird to see you today. I dreamt of my mother last night."

"Gwendolyn is always with you. I know she's proud of the woman you've become."

Putting his arms around each of the women, Balthazar cut in. "So, Auntie August, Morgan tells me you work for the FBI. That must be an exciting job."

"It has its moments. There's a ton of paperwork, though."

During dinner Morgan was giddy beyond belief and exceedingly affectionate with Balthazar.

August announced Morgan's graduation present: a weekend away for herself and Morgan to get pampered at a health spa. August had scheduled the weekend for two weeks from that date.

August was very interested to learn more about Balthazar. "Balthazar, what is it like to be a paramedic?" August asked.

"Sometimes it seems like all we're there to do is to sort through the carnage, or to revive the destitute so they can suffer further. Then there are those days when we save a life. Those times I was able to make a difference because I showed up, did my job, and we all got lucky. It makes everything else worth it. I don't know if this is the job I want to do forever. Right now it's compelling work."

Morgan rested her palm on Balthazar's thigh. August asked Eddie about how his art work was going.

Morgan squeezed Balthazar's leg muscle and slid her hand up his thigh.

Balthazar coughed into his drink, startled.

"Just kidding," Morgan said, patting his leg.

Balthazar blushed, "You're going to pay for that."

"Oh really? I'm looking forward to it."

After dinner Balthazar and Morgan went back to his apartment. When they were outside the front door he gave her a card. Balthazar unlocked the door while Morgan read it. Balthazar had hand-made the card with construction paper and crayons. The front of the card said, "Congratulations Morgan!" Inside there were two boxes, one labeled "Yes" and the other labeled "No". The question written below was, "Do you want to move in with me?"

Morgan fished a pen out of her purse, marked yes, closed the card, handed it back to him, and entered their apartment.

CHAPTER SEVEN
COMMUNION

Two weeks later, August picked up Morgan at eleven in the morning for their spa weekend.

"Wow, after almost fifteen years of not seeing each other, what a treat to get a weekend away with you!" Morgan said.

"I wish I could have come sooner. Everything does have its proper timing," August said.

"Well that's nice and cryptic."

"True. Don't think a day has gone by when I haven't thought about you or about our beach trip from hell."

"It feels like it happened eons ago. Even after all of this time, my memory of it is vivid. I was excited you were in the UnderLife with me, horribly sad from the loss of my mother, and terrified because we were almost drowned by a tsunami."

"Instead you got to see my head impaled by an errant branch," chuckled August good-naturedly.

The sickening thud of the woody spear echoed in Morgan's mind. Her body shivered in revolt.

"That was a major collision of emotions for anyone, especially a seven year old," August said.

"Enough about my drama, what have you been doing all of this time? Who are you working for these days?"

"You'll find out soon enough," August said.

"Oh c'mon! No fair! The suspense is killing me."

"That's a bit of an exaggeration."

"You know you can trust me."

"Trusting you is not the issue."

"What is?" Morgan said.

"All in due time, Red."

"By the way, where are we going?"

"There is someone I want you to meet," August said

"No spa vacation?"

"We'll hit Willow Spa tomorrow."

"Who are you taking me to?"

"The person I work for."

"Your FBI supervisor?"

"I don't work for the FBI."

"Who do you work for?"

"You'll see."

"You're being mysterious again," Morgan said.

"A great habit for my line of work, certainly frustrating to be around, I'm sure. Everyone thinks we're holing up a few days in Santa Monica for some well-earned pampering?"

"Yes," Morgan said.

"Good."

"But instead we're going to-"

"-find out when we get there."

"Aahh!" Morgan said, "You're a dirty whore."

August laughed. "From time to time."

August drove them to a private landing strip adjacent to Burbank Airport. A well-worn Sikorsky HH-60G Pave Hawk helicopter was waiting for them. On the side of the chopper was a sign which read, "Pegasus Helicopter Tours".

"Oh cool, we're going on a tour?" Morgan said.

"Sort of," August said.

Morgan approached the helicopter. It was big: at least fifty feet wide, sixty feet long, and fifteen feet high. She looked through one of the windows into a cargo hold filled with crates lashed down by a camouflaged tarp. Without cargo, a dozen people could fit inside the helicopter.

"Where's the pilot?" Morgan said.

"I'm flying us," August said.

"You can fly this thing? That's awesome!"

August pulled out a thick black scarf. "I'm sorry I have to do this."

"Do what?"

The older woman moved to place the cloth over Morgan's eyes.

"You're not serious, are you?" Morgan said, stepping back.

"I'm afraid so," August said.

"Oh c'mon, I've never been in a helicopter before, and now I won't even get to see the awesome view?" complained Morgan.

"Hey, if it were up to me you wouldn't have to do this. It's the protocol."

"Who is it up to?"

August answered her with a blank stare.

Morgan relented, "Alright, this is going to be weird. Good thing I trust you so much."

August blindfolded Morgan and guided her into the helicopter. August secured Morgan into one of the seats with a five-point safety harness. She finished by putting noise canceling headphones on Morgan.

After a few minutes Morgan felt the engines roar to life.

August's voice crackled on the headphones, "Hey Morgan, you have a microphone on your headset. Let me know if you have any problems."

"Ten-Four, all systems go," Morgan said with more confidence than she felt.

"Roger that. Put your tray tables in their upright and locked position."

"Whoa," Morgan muttered, her stomach flipping when they lifted off.

"Hang on kid," chuckled August. "This should help."

Music swelled inside Morgan's headphones. She recognized it as Victoria Shine's first Virtuoso album within two notes.

"Thank you." Morgan breathed, relaxing into the song.

The trip felt like she was at Disneyland's Space Mountain with a Virtuoso soundtrack. The blackout coupled with the jarring, unpredictable movements of the flight made for a pretty wild ride.

Morgan did her best to stay quiet, not wanting to disturb August while she was piloting the craft.

They cruised along for over an hour before Morgan sensed their forward motion ebb. The chopper hovered for a bit and descended.

Once they landed, August powered down the helicopter and opened the door. Morgan felt goose bumps rise on her flesh as cold air hit her face and exposed skin.

Morgan's gut dropped again. Whatever they had landed on was lowering.

The breeze slowed down and the air got warmer. Morgan was tempted to pull off the blindfold to see what was going on. She decided not to, out of respect for August.

August took off Morgan's headphones and unbuckled her safety restraints. She guided Morgan out of the helicopter. They walked for several minutes with August guiding the still blindfolded Morgan along.

August stopped. "Wait for a second," she said, and let go of Morgan.

Morgan heard the sound of elevator doors opening. August led Morgan inside.

August released the blindfold. Morgan opened her eyes slowly so the light wouldn't be too much of a shock. She saw that the elevator didn't have any buttons or an electronic read-out of the floor number.

"Elevator: Office," August said.

The elevator sprang to life, plunging them deeper into wherever they were.

When the doors opened, August led Morgan into an opulent office. "Make yourself comfortable. My supervisor will be with you shortly," August said.

"Can do," Morgan said, peering around the room. Other than the elevator, there were two closed doors leading out of the room. The room had no windows. There were full bookshelves, a desk, leather couches, various chairs, paintings, a large antique mirror, and a coffee table with a few current periodicals on top of it. The newest copies of the New York Times, National Geographic, Psychology Today, and a variety of other publications were available. Morgan found the newest copy of Entertainment Weekly with Victoria Shine and Darian Vihzor on the cover doing press for the television show "Love In Motion".

"Yes!" Morgan scooped it up and got comfortable on a leather-backed reading chair.

* * *

Behind a two-way mirror, August joined a small pale woman with sharp eyes. They stood watching Morgan devour film and celebrity news.

The shorter woman was sixty years old, but due to her diet and exercise regimens, Louise looked decades younger.

"I would have thought she would be more fit," Louise said, her posh British lilt enunciating Ts crisply.

August said, "The perils of learning how to party. Don't worry, I'll get Morgan started on a training routine."

"She's going to need it. Her path will become more difficult and demanding."

* * *

Morgan plowed through the magazine from cover to cover. Then she flipped back to the Victoria Shine/Darian Vihzor article to read it again. Morgan was beside herself with excitement. Victoria had signed a one year contract to join the cast of "Love In Motion".

Morgan realized she'd been sitting and reading in the office for a while.

Curious, Morgan got up and poked around the room. On one of the walls there was a framed quote from an unknown author on black paper with silver ink. It read:

How does God get to know itself?
By fragmenting into infinite pieces
Setting loose the illusionary structure of Time
Sparking Life and giving it optimal conditions to grow
Letting each individ-u-will consciousness
Find their way home
To the Light
Without Judgment about the length of any path
Time does not exist in the spiritual realm
It's a construct for the density brain
It's how we keep track so it's easier to cut together the
Lifetime Highlight Reels

There is no duality, only drama.

"Huh." Morgan wasn't sure what to make of it. The quote felt profound and silly at the same time, like a cosmic tongue-in-cheek joke. It reminded Morgan of Mr. Name Long Forgotten math teacher had who had dropped the bomb that subtracting numbers was an illusionary act, being merely addition with negative numbers. This had thrown young Morgan for a loop. Why didn't they tell her from the beginning that that's how it worked?

Morgan heard a door open behind her and turned to find a short lady, probably in her mid to late forties. The lady exuded vibrant warmth. Morgan liked her at once.

"Morgan, I'm Louise, August's supervisor."

Louise took Morgan's hand with both of hers.

"Hello," Morgan said.

"It's exciting to speak with you in person finally." Louise said.

"I wish I could say the same. I only recently learned you exist. As far as I knew, August worked for the FBI this whole time. What exactly is it y'all do around here?"

"I shall tell you. First I wanted to inquire about a few things."

Morgan said, "Sounds like therapy to me. I guess an undergraduate degree in psychology should be celebrated by talking about my feelings. Although I guess it's better to have it feel like analysis rather than an interrogation."

Louise laughed. "Interrogation? That sounds a bit sinister, don't you think?"

"Well, y'all are a bit shady with all of the cloak and dagger secrecy stuff."

"Appearances are generally misleading. The work done here is benign, yet rather delicate. Until we get past these fragile stages of growth, any attention from the world at large would do more harm than good."

"You seem sincere and August vouches for you, which is good enough for me. What do you want to know? Believe me, I have no reservations about being as open, candid, and honest as you want me to. There aren't many people I feel comfortable discussing UnderLife with. It is a relief to be around someone who already knows about it. UnderLife is normal for me, but it's crazy talk for just about everyone else."

"Oh I don't think you are crazy, quite the contrary. You're an exceptional young woman with a gift capable of helping a lot of people. That is, if you're willing to do the work it will take to develop it."

"Please don't hesitate to tell me how great I am. I love hearing it,"

Morgan said with a big smile.

"Spoken like a true Moon in Leo."

"Huh? I don't know what that means. I thought I was a Libra."

"You are. Libra is your Sun sign. We'll get into astrology later. First I want to hear your life story."

"I'm only twenty-one. This won't be a long tale."

"No, but with your ability a lot can occur in only a few moments," Louise said.

"Okay, you asked for it. Where do you want me to start?"

"Tell me about growing up in Los Angeles."

"When we moved there I was still reeling from the UnderLife episode where I got drawn and quartered." Morgan recounted the tale.

When Morgan had finished, Louise said, "Bloody hell! What a traumatic experience for anyone. Scarring for a child, even with all the trials you've endured."

"It was rough, no doubt about it," Morgan said, "I only have dim memories of moving from New Orleans to Berkeley. The second move to LA is much more vivid. Dad worked his ass off to get us on our feet, and we're lucky he's a gifted salesman. Once Dad sold a few paintings, the stress level relaxed considerably. Then my father started dating, a lot. Every time I turn around there seems to be a new woman on his arm. Once the romance is in full bloom, he'll ask if they will sit for him. He draws them in pencil, then moves on to charcoal or pastels. When Dad is convinced the woman before him is the source of his inspiration, the paint gushes forth. What Dad hasn't told them is that by the time he's finished all of these portraits have morphed into an image of my Mom."

"Oh, I see." Louise said.

"Yes. Awkward. He's got sketchpads filled with lovely women, and dozens of Gwendolyn Martel canvases. The affairs rarely last for more than a couple of months, eight tops."

"Is your Dad aware of this pattern? Do you talk about it?"

"Yes and no. Dad's not big on self-reflection, and is great at changing the subject or disengaging. When he does open up, I remember every word. Part of the reason why I studied psychology was to understand him. I love him, he's been a great Dad, and I wish he was happier. Mom would have wanted that."

"What about you? Since you've been a student for the majority of your life, please share your thoughts on what school was like for you. August told me you have a medical explanation masking your periodic tendency to fall unconscious."

Morgan nodded. "Yes, August suggested it years ago. As far as everyone is concerned, I'm narcoleptic. I'm happy to have a legitimate neurological disorder hiding my UnderLife losses. It's taken a long time for me to work through my social awkwardness. For many years I focused on how my ability made me different. I didn't feel like it was safe to tell anyone about it. I'm afraid people will think I'm crazy. I spent most of my early school years as a wallflower, craving to be included, but always feeling like the odd one out. People in school thought I was arrogant, or shy, or just disinterested. Not attractive first impressions. My narcolepsy reached its peak sophomore year in high school. The jocks and the cheerleaders started a betting pool about where and when I would pass out during the day. It made me oddly popular. Lucky for them, I was going through a sick suicidal UnderLife phase at the time. I would invariably crumple to the ground, or on my desk, or in the field, or on the homecoming float. My best moments of high school glory were when I was unconscious and unable to enjoy it. I felt like a circus act, and when I stopped passing out so much, they lost interest in me."

"Adolescence is one the harshest times in anyone's life, UnderLife or not. Coping is difficult, but all seems well now." Louise said.

"The more I get to know myself and I'm comfortable with who I am, life flows much more smoothly. Everything got a lot more interesting once I learned that partying was a wonderful lubricant to exploring sex. In college I was known to have periodic bouts of brazen sluttiness."

"August says you have quite a charming boyfriend."

"Yes, Balthazar Bennington. He's great, so much fun to be around. We've been living together for a couple of weeks now. We spend all our free time together and haven't slept apart in months, so it seemed natural to move in," Morgan said.

"Have you told him about UnderLife?" Louise asked.

"No, not yet. I don't think it's going to go over too well. At first I didn't tell him because I didn't want to scare him away. I doubted he would stick around. Balthazar always has women catapulting their pussies at him, giving him lots of options for girlfriends, and he's quite a flirt. I've been hoping I'll somehow take him into UnderLife, and go from there."

"Why don't you think he will be receptive to it?"

"He grew up in a hard-core conservative Roman Catholic family. They tend to frown on my brand of mysticism, since it's not all about Jesus. His parents were scandalized when his little brother announced he was gay. I don't know how they could have been the least bit shocked, Gregory is gay from space. Balthazar told me it has taken years for them to settle down about Gregory's homosexuality. Balthazar refuses to let his parents alienate Gregory because of his sexual orientation. Gregory is a charmer and a sweetheart, it's impossible not to love him." Pride rang in Morgan's voice over her boyfriend's unconditional love, acceptance, and defense of his younger brother.

"Balthazar handled that exceptionally well, Morgan. You might want to reevaluate his open-mindedness with the people he loves."

"I know. You're right. I just need more time. Things have been amazing. He's someone I've wanted to be with for almost four years. I don't want to jinx it or have Balthazar run for the hills when I tell him my narcolepsy is just a side effect from getting killed while adventuring in the collective unconscious. I feel insane saying that, and I've lived with it my whole life. Okay now that I've meow-meow-meowed my head off, please tell me what you do around here."

"Morgan, are you happy?"

"I sure am. I have my bad days, but so does everyone."

"How about the people you feel close to in your life, are they happy?"

"Yes, I'd say so. I don't find clinical depression or a pessimistic attitude to be attractive qualities in people."

"What about the world at large? How happy overall is the human family we're all a part of?"

"Oh, well, not so great from what I can gather. I don't even like watching the news because it's so negative. I'd say we've got a ton of gnarly issues in sore need of attention around the world. But I'm a hardline optimist who believes we are somehow working towards a brighter future."

"I share your positive outlook. I am also realistic about how much must be done to realize this dream. Real happiness is something which must be achieved through consistent effort and self-correction. Tell me about your close friends. How did you meet them? Do they know about UnderLife?"

"No, I haven't told anyone. It's kind of hard to bring up a subject no one even realizes exists. Oh sure, most people have heard of the collective unconscious. However, it's one thing to have an abstract idea in your head and another to be running away in stark terror from your inner snarling boogeyman. They'll either think I'm a lunatic or scary if I say I have uncontrollable access to our inner universes and landscapes." Morgan looked down and cocked her head to one side. "I just realized something. Pretty much everyone I hang out with I got to know through Balthazar. What a classic maneuver. To get so sucked in by a lover, other friendships wither from malnourishment. Even my best friend, Draven Powers, I met while he was dating Balthazar's little brother Gregory." Morgan erupted into laughter, recalling her first meeting with Draven.

"What's so funny?"

* * *

How Morgan Met Draven

A few months into dating, Balthazar invited Morgan to his family's Christmas party at Bennington Manor. The only family Morgan had met so far was Gregory, and they had gotten along wonderfully.

Morgan and Balthazar were running late for the event. They rarely got dressed up. After seeing each other decked out in their best clothes, it was difficult not to start fucking right then and there. The car ride over almost turned into porn. They were only able to disengage because they promised to start up again immediately after dinner.

The family had cocktails and appetizers in the spacious backyard. Morgan greeted Balthazar's parents, Thomas and Holly Bennington, and then excused herself to use the bathroom. The downstairs bathroom was occupied, and Morgan couldn't wait. Morgan was forced to go upstairs. She was walking down the hallway when she heard a noise coming from one of the bedrooms ahead of her. The door was half open. Morgan peered in as she walked by, and was stopped dead in her tracks.

Inside the room, a strikingly good looking man with stylized black hair was leaning against an antique desk. Bobbing up and down in front of his waist was the curly chestnut-haired head of a kneeling Gregory Bennington.

Draven and Morgan saw each other at the same time.

Gregory was oblivious. He would have been too busy to notice the house burning down.

Morgan was too surprised to react. Draven smiled at her like the Cheshire cat. This jolted Morgan into action. She left the room and continued on to the lavatory.

Later, Draven joined Morgan while she was grazing at the hors d'œuvre table.

"What a lovely home they've created here," Draven said, pretending he had just come from a tour of the Manor.

Morgan hesitated. "Yes."

"Are you having a good time at the party?"

"Hardly as much as you are," Morgan said, warming to his friendly demeanor.

"Ah, Gregory, what an excellent host," Draven said.

In the ten minutes it took the brothers to rejoin their dates, Morgan and Draven were enjoying each other thoroughly. They tossed witticisms back and forth like they were in a fantastic sit-com. The instant friends discovered that they shared the unfortunate distinction of knowing what it's like to lose a parent and to grow up as an only child. Draven's father had died of a heart attack a few years before. He had never known his mother.

"Have you two met before tonight?" Gregory asked.

"I wish," Draven said. "Your brother's girlfriend is awesome."

This made Morgan laugh even harder. In the short time talking, they had divulged personal details and cracked jokes ranging from benign observations to savagely wicked barbs. Yet, neither of them had bothered to learn the other's name.

"Hi, I'm Morgan," she said, shaking his hand.

"Draven. It's an absolute pleasure to meet you Morgan," Draven said.

"Likewise Draven," Morgan said.

Holly Bennington came out of the house and announced, "Dinner is served." Holly's tone implied she'd gone to great lengths to create the meal. It was a draining task ordering Sam, the Benningtons' gourmet chef, to make a five course dinner for ten people.

Once everyone was seated in the dining room, the chef sent out a delightful amuse-bouche.

"How's work going, honey?" Holly asked her eldest son.

"Great. We saved three lives this week! I resuscitated Mr. Robert Bradford all on my own with the paddles. He was suffering from cardiac arrest. When we got there his heart had just stopped. We got to work.

Next thing you know he's breathing again. Praise Jesus," Balthazar said.

"Awesome," Gregory said.

"Good job, son," Thomas Bennington said. "I still don't understand why you didn't want to go to medical school to become a doctor."

"Standing for twelve hours in surgery, up to my elbows in someone's guts is not something I want to do every day. As paramedics we're the first on the scene. It's exciting, kinetic. We help on the spot if we can, then we get them transported to a team who will do their best to put them back together."

By the time the fish course arrived, Grandmother Betty Bennington was already sloshed and eyeing everyone with contempt. Nanna was a vitriolic woman, barely tolerable sober, insufferable while drunk, and she preferred to live in the pickled state. Age had only energized Betty's contemptuous nature.

Morgan couldn't imagine, and prayed she would never find out, what Betty's hellish UnderLife was like.

Betty watched Draven and Gregory. She couldn't decide what disgusted her more, having two good looking men wasted on the world, or how damned their souls were for the revolting acts they did together.

As far as she was concerned, her grandson must be possessed by the Devil to be able to commit such sins against God. Why couldn't he be a good boy like Balthazar?

However, Balthazar did seem to have pedestrian taste in companionship. Betty didn't like the looks of the filly with him. The girl's easy smile made Betty nervous. Condescending, gold digging whore, Betty thought. Balthazar will soon tire of you. This is only a phase. You're not good enough to be his wife.

All night Betty had been subdued. Holly Bennington thought she might get through an evening with her mother-in-law without embarrassment. Those hopes were dashed during the fourth course.

"At least you can't get married in this state," Betty barked out, interrupting a hilarious anecdote Draven was delivering.

Gregory's first instinct was to diffuse the situation. Gregory felt more flustered by the talk of commitment than by Grandmother Bennington's disdain for his romantic preference. "Nanna, I think it's a bit soon to talk about mar-"

Draven decided to go a different way with it. He said to Gregory, "Oh don't be shy honey. You said you wanted to be a spring bride. I know you already have your heart set on a Royal Albert china pattern."

Sensing she was being made fun of, Nanna said, "Thank God you can't have children with each other."

"Mother! Enough," Holly said, once again mortified by Betty's behavior.

"I'm sure he got his fruitiness from your side of the family," Betty said.

Draven addressed Nanna's earlier comment. "Au contraire, my thirsty woman, we plan on having loads of kids and shall raise them all to be exactly like us."

Enjoying the reaction this statement produced, Draven continued, "I can tell what you're thinking. Gregory and I are just sitting around being gay and agreeing with each other, but there are a few fundamental differences between us about parenthood which have been tricky to reconcile."

"Such as?" Morgan said, unable to restrain herself from egging him on.

"I want to raise the children in the Church of Scientology, but he doesn't. I think children should be adopted in six-packs, so we can pit them against each other tournament style to prove themselves for our love and attention."

"You're right, honey. This is a sticky issue for us," Gregory said, "We need to bring the children up as born-again Mormons. Instead of adoption, we need to impregnate a dozen or so women. We choose the two babies who are the cutest and easiest to accessorize with."

Morgan guffawed in the middle of their repartee. She looked around at the shocked expressions of the other family members, and had a hard time controlling herself.

There was silence in the room. Draven's easy grin did not falter. He winked at Morgan.

Then Holly Bennington did the most unexpected thing. She snorted before chortling, glad someone had finally put that awful woman in her place. The deep baritone voice of Thomas Bennington joined her. Soon the whole table boomed with merriment.

Alexander Bennington, Balthazar and Gregory's eight year old brother, did not get why everything was so funny, but he was delighted that everyone else having so much fun. Alexander accidentally squirted milk out of his nose when a fit of giggles hit him mid gulp.

Grandmother Betty guzzled the rest of her scotch, slammed the glass back on the table, and tried to storm out of the room in a dramatic huff. Unfortunately for her pride, she was far too inebriated to get herself standing easily. After one feeble attempt, she gave up, and snarled at Draven, "Get me another drink!"

"Yes ma'am," he said.

Morgan gazed at Draven with amazement. It took a lot of courage to do what he did. She admired how his daring sense of humor had dispelled any family tension surrounding Gregory being gay.

Draven and Morgan exchanged numbers before leaving that night. They played together regularly.

* * *

"Okay, it's your turn. You tell me something," Morgan said.

"Alright." Louise got up, went to the desk, picked up the phone, and hit a couple of buttons on the keypad. "Will you join us, please?" she asked into the receiver, and hung up.

While waiting, Louise opened a mini refrigerator disguised as a three foot metal filing cabinet. She pulled out a couple bottles of water and handed one to Morgan. Louise unscrewed the cap of her water and drank.

The door near the mirror opened. August entered. She grinned at Morgan, moved a chair to triangulate with the seats of the other two women, and sat down.

Louise began, "I have been given the gift of Oracular Sight. One of the many methods I use for divination is a form of stichomancy. I take newspapers from all around the world, go into a meditative trance, and allow the Creative to guide my path. It was no coincidence August entered your life when she did. Using this approach years ago, we found an advertisement for an upcoming LeTour/Martel exhibition. While checking out the gallery, August scanned the police reports and found out about Gwendolyn's death. I sent August immediately to discover what she could."

August nodded, "Initially Louise had me thinking I was investigating a possible murder and drug cartel connection."

"Wait, if you aren't affiliated with the FBI, how did you have access to

New Orleans police reports?" Morgan asked.

"We have resources," Louise said with a tone which did not invite further questioning. "Funny that's the detail you focus in on."

"You thought I would have asked about how it's possible to locate someone using extra sensory perception abilities? After what I've seen, anything is possible. What I want to know is what were you looking for in the first place?"

Morgan tried to read Louise's calm expression. Wow, Morgan thought, for a woman who so easy to talk to, it was like trying to decipher a Sphinx to get a read on what Louise was thinking.

Morgan sighed. "You're not going to tell me, are you?"

"Not yet," Louise said. "Psychics come in as many varieties as athletes do. I am an Oracle Finder and Handler. August here is an Empathic Gatherer.

"More like a Wrangler," August said. "People often come with as many difficulties as they do gifts."

"What am I?" Morgan asked.

"The only UnderLife Traveler we know of so far. You have the potential to be a special kind of Mediator or Shaman, depending on how you choose to grow. I believe you have the potential to assist people in resolving their imbalances on a fundamental spiritual level. I have a theory that UnderLife occurs in the Astral Plane, which is a precursor to the Causal Plane. In philosophical mysticism, these planes are generally considered the next steps of soul evolution beyond this physical and material realm."

"Oh here we go," August said.

"You're right, August, it's a metaphysical conversation for another time," Louise said.

"No, please continue. This is all fascinating," Morgan said.

"Next time, my young friend. When you visit again, that is, if you want to?" Louise asked.

"Yes, of course! Do you have some kind of graduate school I can join?"

"Funny you should say that. We were going to ask you to study with us," August said.

"Yes," Morgan said.

"Morgan, you don't even know what we want from you. Why would you agree so readily?" Louise asked.

"First of all, as far as I'm concerned, August is family. I know she would never want to hurt me. Every time I slip into the UnderLife, I don't really know what I'm getting into. I've learned to enjoy surprises. This reeks of an adventure I'm sure the standard education system is not currently capable of providing. I know so little about my UnderLife ability. My intuition says you're the ones who can help me. Where do we start?"

Louise smiled and dove right in, "The revolution begins within. The first step is the Sacred Inner Marriage: your relationship with yourself. This personal union becomes possible only when you see that lasting happiness comes from following the path of truth and goodness."

Louise took a sip of water and continued. "It took many years for me to realize the beauty and power of neutrality. Many people are conditioned to believe being neutral is a static position. Quite the contrary, a state of balance and neutrality is active and dynamic, and ever vulnerable to disruption. The requirements are self-awareness, diligent Ego-maintenance, and a positive attitude regarding the tasks at hand. There must be a commitment to communication and action from Universal Truth."

"Sacred Inner Marriage? How do I do that?"

"There are an infinite number of ways to pledge oneself to the Truth of Life, which is Love."

"Which sounds fantastic, but esoteric. How do I manifest this on a practical level?"

"I want to do a chakra balancing with you, beginning with a series of guided meditations. Our first priority is to make sure everything is flowing unimpeded." Louise said.

"Chakra balancing?" Morgan asked.

"Chakra is Sanskrit for wheel. It's an ancient Indian concept describing the seven primary energy fields flowing in and around our bodies. Together these forces make up our personal aura. There are those who can sense or even see other people's auras. Illnesses show up in a person's energy field before manifesting physically. If the chakra can be unblocked in time, the malady will be avoided. Some people suffer from extreme imbalances in their chakras. This can be the result of traumatic experiences or actions in this lifetime. More often it stems from a previous incarnation."

Morgan nodded. This made sense to her. There were plenty of times Morgan felt the imbalance in people who seemed unsettled even in the most serene atmospheres.

Louise continued, "Balance is not a simple task. It is a journey to the most frightening neighborhoods of the soul. Deep in the cellar or graveyard of anyone's UnderLife is a personal nightmare. Understanding one's shadow side is a necessary prelude to a fully integrated Sacred Inner Marriage. It takes a courageous or naïve person to want to go into those realms of their own free will."

"Okay, sounds cool to me," Morgan said.

Louise chuckled, "I guess I shouldn't be surprised you wouldn't bat an eyelash about making this decision."

"Are you kidding? Receiving help to achieve a more dynamic balance? What a fantastic idea. The work will surely improve my UnderLife abilities," Morgan said.

"Maybe you will even attain a measure of control over your abrupt entrances and exits," August said.

"I don't know about that, but it sure would be great if I could."

"Something I want you to think about until the next time we meet," Louise said. "For almost everyone, the greatest enemy lies within. The vampiric Ego is a monster of unquenchable thirst. It's your inner maniac carrying a loaded weapon, with a mighty itchy trigger finger. When the Superior Self is operating at full strength it can keep the worst elements of the Ego at bay and harness its volcanic energy for healing, fuel, and balance. But the adaptable Ego always wants to usurp control, and it has no sense of responsibility or limits. It cannot handle the power it hungers for."

"That's for sure," Morgan said.

Louise continued. "When someone internalizes a lie, the deception is henceforth taken as truth. For instance, this happens when people start believing they are better than others because of factors such as skin pigmentation, mystical beliefs, or socioeconomic status. Once established, a lie, much like the Ego itself, influences a person's behavior with its falsehood. If the Ego is kept unchecked it will work itself up into a lather, unleashing a killing spree in the crystalline garden of self-esteem. Every shot it fires shatters something the Superior Self worked hard to build. The Ego is a viral agent bent on an apocalyptic world view. It lives in a place where some bloke named Murphy is an omnipotent lawmaker," Louise said with a wry smile.

"That was awesome!" Morgan said. "Do you have a lecture series I can purchase?"

"Not at present, no. Thank you for enduring the discomfort in transport. It's been my sincerest pleasure to meet you. I shall see you again soon." Louise stood. Morgan and August followed her lead.

"Yes, definitely," Morgan said.

Louise exited through the door on the left.

August went to the desk, opened a drawer, and took out a pad of paper, pen, and a tape measure. She turned to Morgan. "If you don't mind, I need to take your measurements."

"Knock yourself out," Morgan said.

August began to take readings of Morgan's dimensions.

"What's this for, anyway?" Morgan asked.

"Your crystal wand," August said. "It's the primary tool we're using for your energy work. It's custom-made."

"Cool. When do I get to see it?"

"It will take about a month to create. In the meantime, your first assignment is to learn about energetic interconnectivity. This will improve the conductivity of your physical being."

"Uh-oh," Morgan said.

"Your task is to exercise your body as hard as you can, at a minimum of an hour a day, five times a week."

Morgan sighed, "Of course, the perfect mission for my lazy ass."

"Swim for at least one of those sessions. Concentrate on being as fluid as the water around you. Then push the pace. Contemplate this fact: energetically we are all swimming in the same pool. Remember, psychically you can fly. Write about your experiences."

"I shall give it my full attention," Morgan said.

"Good. Now, are you ready for some well-deserved pampering?"

Morgan nodded.

August pulled the black scarf from her pocket.

"Oh, c'mon," Morgan said.

"Sorry, Doll."

Morgan let her put the blindfold back on.

August guided Morgan through a disorienting maze of corridors and elevators. Then August secured Morgan in a vehicle for the drive back into town.

"Can I put on an audio book for your headphones? It feels weird trying to make casual conversation with a scarf tied around your face," August said.

"Yeah, this is a bit of a weird way to travel. Go ahead. I've never listened to an audio book before."

Morgan laughed when she heard the opening credits. August had put on Harry Potter and the Sorcerer's Stone. Soon they were engrossed by J.K. Rowling's storytelling spoken by Jim Dale, and the hours back to Los Angeles flew by.

They spent the night at a luxurious hotel in Santa Monica. The next day involved eating, drinking, talking, and getting expert massages and a variety of spa treatments.

While they were at dinner that night, August got serious for a moment and said, "You know, Morgan, neither Louise nor I are saying you have to keep UnderLife, or your impending chakra balancing secret from Balthazar. The only things we do not want you to discuss are the helicopter ride, or where we went, or any real details about me," August said.

"Don't worry, I'll be quiet. Can't I just tell Balthazar I'm doing some work with you?" Morgan said.

"If you want, but I need you to be clear it's your choice to keep the real truth about UnderLife from him."

"I'd rather show Balthazar than tell him about the UnderLife. I'll think about it," Morgan said.

* * *

During the next month, Morgan followed her orders. She joined the Hollywood-Wilshire YMCA, and went there five times a week for swimming, weight lifting, Pilates, basketball, volleyball, cardio machines, racquetball, or whatever activity Morgan felt like sweating for that day. It wasn't an easy commitment to keep, especially at first. Muscles Morgan didn't even know she possessed were sore. Morgan had considered herself pretty active before, but she realized that her lame, once or twice a week, half-hour workouts were more about perpetuating a delusion of fitness than anything else.

Balthazar adored Morgan's dedication to getting into better shape. He often went with her to work out when his schedule permitted.

Morgan procrastinated in telling Balthazar about the chakra balancing until the day before August was due to pick her up to start the work.

"August hooked me up with a research gig," Morgan said over Sunday brunch.

"Really? What kind of research? What are you doing?" Balthazar said.

"I'm participating as a subject in a long term, privately funded study on sleeping disorders and dream analysis. I signed a non-disclosure agreement. I won't be able to discuss what goes on during the sessions."

"When does it start?"

"Tomorrow. August is picking me up."

"Oh. How long have you known about this?"

"A while. You know, I think I could get a stipend for my time," Morgan said, fabricating the detail to divert his attention.

"How much would they pay you? What do you have to do to get it?"

"I'm not sure."

"You didn't ask?" Balthazar said. "For all you know this could be an internship." He sneered. "Typical. You know your trust fund isn't going to last forever."

"That's my problem, Balthazar," Morgan turned away, attempting to retreat before her temper flared. Too late. Morgan wheeled back around, defiant. "Thanks a lot. Here I am excited about a new job opportunity in a field I actually care about and all you can think of is money."

"The finances are both of our problems. Who do you think is going to have to pay the bills when your money is gone? The rent on this place is high enough, let alone if I have to cover the whole thing."

"How did my career excitement turn into your financial anxieties? It's always about you, isn't it?"

"Career? What career? You need at least a Master's degree in Psychology if you going to get any kind of respectable job in that field. I thought you wanted to be a therapist? You don't even seem to have any interest in going to graduate school anymore."

"I'm going to ignore your awful tone and keep this civilized. I want to help people, and I don't think traditional psychotherapy will be the best use of my talents. Just because things are clear for you right now with being a paramedic, it doesn't mean I have to be set on a well-defined career path. We need to cool down before we get into another stupid fight about money. I'm going to the gym and seeing a movie. We'll meet up for dinner?" Morgan said.

Balthazar, his face flush with emotion, nodded.

* * *

August arrived at Morgan and Balthazar's apartment late the next afternoon in a black convertible Saab. She gave Morgan an approving eye after they hugged, already seeing positive changes in Morgan's physique.

August drove west to a thirty story building located in Century City. August waved a key card past the security box at the entrance to the underground parking structure. The large metal barrier swung open.

After parking the car, August led them to a bank of elevators. Once inside the elevator, August pulled out her keys, and inserted one into a slot on the elevator console. Their transport sped them up to the twenty-second floor.

They entered a small room with security doors on the north and south walls. August went to the northern door to negotiate another security check-point. This one involved a retinal scan of August's left eye.

The twenty-second floor was partitioned in half, with walls blocking any view of the southern side of the floor. Near the door to the elevator room, there was a bathroom and a small kitchen. These were the only enclosed areas. The spacious setting had an area in the middle of the room with a hardwood floor. The view of Los Angeles was tremendous. A clear day revealed a panoramic view of the Pacific Ocean, Beverly Hills, Westwood, Hollywood, and Downtown.

At the far end of the wooden floor space, there was a low table with several candles. The table was flanked by two large steamer trunks. In the northwest corner of the space was a sitting area with couches, stuffed chairs, and a coffee table. In the northeast corner there was a large telescope. There were plants everywhere, positioned to create natural pathways. These included hanging ferns, potted trees, shrubs, flowers, and herbs. The room looked like it had been engineered by an avant-garde interior designer. The place was an oasis. Morgan loved it.

Louise was waiting for them in the living room section, watching the glorious sunset.

On the coffee table there was a rectangular shaped black box.

"Hello," Morgan said.

"Good evening," Louise replied, gesturing towards the box, about one foot in length.

"For me?" asked Morgan, hands already at the lid.

"Yes, but you can't take it home until we're done."

Morgan nodded, opening it.

Inside the box was a purple velvet bag. Morgan opened the bag and pulled out a crystal wand.

"It's beautiful," Morgan said, sitting down next to Louise to examine it.

The base rod of the wand was made out of glass. On one end of the wand there was a roughly-cut clear quartz crystal, and on the other end there was a purple amethyst. On the top part of the wand, evenly-spaced down its length, were seven precious vibrational crystals. The crystals were held in place by a molded gold band which wound around the wand, snaking from end to end.

"What are these stones?" Morgan asked.

"Crystals," Louise corrected. "Onyx, carnelian, citrine, rose-quartz, blue lace agate, green moss agate, and amethyst. Each represents a different chakra. I'll go into more detail about them as we do the work. Right now the wand is a blank template. Once we harmonize it to your energy signature, it will only work properly for you. After the balancing is completed, the wand will possess a blueprint of your spiritual self. It will assist you in maintaining balance by draining negative energy or built up stress. You'll have to clean it once a month with sea salt and water. The wand has a myriad of uses. It can also be utilized to focus your energy during meditation, or to accelerate healing," said Louise.

"Is this real gold?"

"Yes. It acts as a conductor for the energy passing through the wand. The whole thing would be pretty, but useless, if the gold wasn't connecting everything."

"How does it work?"

"You're about to find out," said Louise. She stood and moved to the hardwood floor meditation area.

Morgan followed Louise. August remained seated on the couch. August took a book out of her bag, flipped to her page marker, and settled in to read.

Louise lit several sticks of rose incense. She opened the left steamer trunk and extracted a folded white down comforter. She unfurled it to let some air puff up the feathers. Then Louise doubled it up, placing the blanket on the floor a couple feet away from the candle table in a north-south orientation.

Morgan looked at the candles on the low table. There were seven of them, each about three inches cubed, in seven different colors: red, orange, yellow, green, blue, purple and white. The candles sat on a gold, oval-shaped tray with a two-and-a-half inch metal lip. Morgan guessed the lip on the tray must be there to prevent the candle wax from spilling on to the table.

"These are special chakra candles," Louise said. "I'll light them at the beginning of our meditation. I'm able to do additional divination based on how intensely the flames burn and what wax patterns are left behind. Everyone's chakra balancing differs. Often I can only see one or two steps ahead in the work. For our first meditation my goal is to get an overview of what we're dealing with in your case. We will be starting with the Crown chakra, located on the top of your head. In Sanskrit this chakra is known as Sahasrara, the thousand-petal lotus. It corresponds to the purple amethyst stone. It vibrates with your Oneness with God, invoking feelings of universal love and truth. Amethyst gives protection, strength, and focuses psychic abilities."

Louise continued, "Take your shoes off, Morgan. Get on the comforter. Lay down on your back. Settle in, relax. Put the wand on top of your chest. Rest the tip of the clear quartz on the middle of your breastbone, with the amethyst end at your belly button."

"It fits perfectly," Morgan said.

"It better with all the measurements August took. Rest your hands on the wand, with your fingers touching every stone. The right hand should be on the upper portion of the wand. Now close your eyes. Take a deep breath. Inhale." Louise breathed in audibly. Morgan followed her example. "Hold it… and slowly exhale. Take another. Imagine the air reaching every part of your body. Relax. Let your mind's activity flow unimpeded. Don't fixate on any one thing. Imagine a blank white piece of paper or cloth to dislodge any stubborn thoughts. Let it flow."

While Louise was speaking she lit the seven chakra candles.

The experience fascinated Morgan. She marveled at how little attention she usually paid to her breathing, except when working out and laboring for it. As the tension in her body eased, Morgan became aware of a subtle buzzing around her hands. It felt like something big was being ignited beneath the surface of her consciousness. Morgan was calm, peaceful. Morgan knew in her heart this was exactly the work she needed to be doing.

In her mind's eye, Morgan saw brief flashes of a large underground cavern. The cavern was humming.

Morgan heard the candles crackling. The flames were turbulent, even with no breeze in the room. Morgan wanted to peek at the candles, but she kept her eyes closed.

After some time, Louise's soothing British lilted voice floated into Morgan's ears, bringing her out of the meditative trance.

"How was that for you?" Louise asked. "Did you see anything?"

Morgan described everything as best she could. When she mentioned the humming cavern, Morgan noticed Louise's demeanor brighten.

The green, yellow, and red candles were burning much brighter than the others. The blaze mesmerized Morgan.

"Your throat, heart, and root chakras have minor blockages. I'm going to let the candles burn down. Once the wax cools I'll be able to scan it better," Louise informed her. Louise retrieved Morgan's wand, and put it back into its purple velvet sleeve.

Louise continued, "I'll look into your wand for a more detailed reading. I feel like your balancing is going to be delicate and complex. I should have known this would be the case. There are many past life connections wrapped around you, positive and negative. It's going to take a significant amount of time to unwind the karma, to give you more spiritual maneuverability. I couldn't pin-point any specific past incarnation in this meditation. The quicksilver blur of them streaming by was too overwhelming to engage. All in all, an excellent beginning. Well done, Morgan."

CHAPTER EIGHT
THE TAROT READER

Hollywood, California

The meditations continued twice a month for the next year. After the spectacular first session, progress seemed to slow to a crawl. Louise counseled Morgan to be patient. The only way for the process to be safe was if it didn't arouse Morgan's Ego. Morgan wasn't too sure what Louise meant by that, but she trusted Louise's sense of caution. Regular exercise had taught Morgan that any great achievement was built on thousands of difficult single steps. Each meditation session felt like a spiritual massage, which galvanized Morgan's attitude, will, and focus.

Meanwhile, Morgan engaged in a series of jobs, none of which lasted long. She came home to Balthazar freshly unemployed more times than either of them wanted to count. Morgan didn't tell Balthazar that the reason she didn't stay long at any of these jobs was that she was very sensitive to the negative attitudes at these workplaces, often causing her to drop into a horrible UnderLife experience, which would cause her to pass out in the middle of the day.

Morgan got hired to drive a van into the desert for a new mini-mansion home development. Her job involved setting up an inflatable advertisement at the construction site on the roof of her van and then baby-sit it for six hours. Morgan was glad to have a job which left her alone to entertain herself. One day, Morgan was engrossed in Queen of the Damned by Anne Rice when an UnderLife shift occurred.

Morgan found herself in the bedroom of one of the homes she was advertising. Everything felt familiar, like she was living there. All of a sudden, an earthquake struck, overwhelming the shoddy construction of the house. Morgan was buried in staggering amounts of rubble.

Morgan woke to the tapping of keys on the glass of the driver's side window. Unfortunately, her unconscious face had been pressed against the other side of that window, drool dribbling from her lips. Startled, Morgan looked around to discover a very stern-faced client who had driven by to see how the sign looked. He was not impressed with his slumbering employee.

Morgan rolled down the window. "Sorry, I'm narcoleptic," she explained sheepishly.

"Then you shouldn't even be allowed to drive!" he yelled, storming back to his car.

* * *

Morgan was holed up in the waiting room at Pho-Siam, her favorite Thai massage parlor. Balthazar was running late from work. A big car accident had occurred minutes before his shift was supposed to end. He was racking up some overtime getting the victims to the hospital. Morgan didn't mind one bit. She loved Balthazar's membership in the modern-day medical cavalry.

An episode of Entertainment Tonight was playing on the television screen hanging on the wall. Victoria Shine's libido was once again breaking news in the realm of celebrity gossip.

"After a long hiatus, Victoria has reemerged from her seclusion, back into the full gaze of the public eye. Her premiere episode on the hit nighttime drama Love In Motion gave the show its highest ratings to date." reported Entertainment Tonight's Mary Hart.

"Industry insiders say Victoria Shine's childhood friend, Darian Vihzor, was instrumental in persuading Victoria to play her trouble-making Australian half-sister rival, Harmony Moore, on the series. Victoria Shine has been romantically linked to Love In Motion heartthrob Billy Slater. Their publicists will only confirm that the two are close friends. However, photographers caught Victoria Shine leaving Billy Slater's Malibu beach house at the crack of dawn a few days ago."

The camera cut to a series of still shots starring Victoria. She appeared to have been up all night, still dressed to the nines in a hot crimson cocktail dress. The pictures showed Victoria getting into the backseat of a black Lincoln Town Car.

Morgan almost jumped out of her skin when she felt a hand on her shoulder.

"Oh, Balthazar! You startled me," Morgan said.

"Sorry. I said your name. You didn't hear me," Balthazar smiled at her. She stood up. They kissed.

"How was work?" Morgan asked as they walked to the front desk.

"Rough. I'll tell you about it later. Right now I just want to relax."

Balthazar and Morgan got ready to get their Thai massages together in the same room. As was the parlor custom, traditional loose Thai-style shorts had been provided. Balthazar and Morgan donned the outfits after stripping down to their underwear. Morgan winked at Balthazar while taking off her bra, teasing him, knowing full well their masseuses were waiting for nearby. She lay down on her stomach. Balthazar begrudgingly followed suit, suddenly more interested in giving pleasure than receiving it.

Two skilled Thai ladies entered the room and merrily pummeled and stretched the couple out for an hour and a half.

When they left the massage parlor, Balthazar and Morgan walked by the Corner Café across the street on the way to their car. A woman with long black wavy hair was sitting at the inside table in front of the window. She was shuffling Tarot cards, laying them out for a grey haired man in a disheveled suit.

Morgan did a double take when she saw the woman in the café.

"She looks familiar. I'm not sure, TV or life?"

Balthazar squinted, trying to place the face. "I don't recognize her from anything."

"How would I know her?" Morgan said then shrugged. "Oh well, I'm probably just delirious from that awesome massage."

"Do you want to get a Tarot card reading?" inquired Balthazar, curious.

"Are you sure Jesus won't mind?"

"Hey, that's not cool. I'm trying to be open minded here. No slammin' the Savior."

"You're right, I'm sorry. I appreciate your sense of adventure and in theory I'd love to, but my brain is mush from the massage. I don't think I'd remember anything she'd say to me right now." Morgan laced her arm through his, pulling him closer for a quick kiss. "Thank you for getting us massages. I love getting beaten by diminutive magical Thai ladies. Gift and Noi are the two best masseuses in the shop."

"They are the best kept secrets in town. Who knew elbows and knees could be so healing?" Balthazar said.

"I want to take them away from all of this," Morgan said.

"How much do you think it would cost to have them on call 24/7?"

"Speaking of, when is your next shift?" Morgan asked.

"Not until tomorrow night," Balthazar said.

"Excellent, I get to have you all to myself until then."

"Want to go get a beer?"

"Sure," Morgan said.

The couple walked to their favorite neighborhood haunt, owned by an old friend. It was also where a lot of Balthazar's buddies loved to hang out, and they ran into several friends.

A few beers later, Morgan and Balthazar excused themselves and met up outside the business office in the back hallway of the bar. Balthazar had worked at the bar during college, and he still had his keys to the office. He used them to open the office door. Morgan and Balthazar stumbled inside and proceeded to make out, getting more hot and heavy with every passing moment. Balthazar locked the door behind him and unbuttoned his pants, setting free his massive erection.

Morgan, unfastening her own jeans, wanted nothing more than to get on his cock.

"Do you have a-?"

"I thought you had them," Balthazar said.

More kissing. She bit his lower lip.

"No. Damn it. I'm so ready for you," Morgan said.

His hand snuck into her pants while they kissed. Balthazar groaned when he felt her soft wet folds. He twirled his finger at the entrance to heaven and then teased her engorged clit, causing Morgan to moan.

She stroked his dick with her hand in response. It pulsed eagerly, ready to fuck.

Balthazar's hips thrust forward. Morgan's body wanted to respond, but she held back and stopped his hips before he could get any closer to penetrating her.

"No," she said.

Balthazar sighed, pouting.

Morgan kissed him forcefully. Then she dropped to her knees, taking the tip of his glistening member into her mouth. Morgan quickly found the rhythm which pleasured Balthazar the most. She held his dick in one hand, while cupping and caressing his furry balls with the other. A chill breeze from the air conditioner wafted across Balthazar's shaft when it wasn't in Morgan's warm mouth. It wasn't long before Balthazar came. A grunt escaped his lips.

Afterwards they rejoined their friends at the bar.

The owner, Gabe, gave them an appraising eye. "Did you two do it in my office again?"

They both shrugged, feigning innocence.

"Yes, yes you did. If I wasn't such a sick fuck I'd be offended. Mitch, get another round for my horny friends."

The couple had a great time with everyone for the remainder of the evening. After closing the bar, Balthazar and Morgan walked home, fondling and kissing each other the entire way.

"I propose we make love in the morning, or else it's going to be some sloppy drunk sex," Balthazar said.

"Deal," Morgan said.

They went through nightly rituals of flossing, brushing, and moisturizing. Balthazar slathered lotion on to his face and neck. Morgan thought this proved Balthazar was as taken with his good looks as everyone else. She was glad that he took care of his skin.

Once in bed, their naked bodies curled up together. Balthazar spooned Morgan.

"That was so sexy earlier. I love seeing your lips sucking my cock." Balthazar rubbed his left hand slowly up and down Morgan's torso, lingering at her breasts.

"Mmm. Me too."

"But I hate having to use condoms all of the time. I really wanted to bend you over the desk and fuck you."

"I know."

"My love, I want to penetrate you fully, be inside of you, with no barriers. Feel your hot wet-"

Balthazar ground his hips into Morgan, his awakening penis pressed against her buttocks. Morgan couldn't help but move with him, her body craving Balthazar's touch.

"I do to." Morgan said.

"It would be so easy." Morgan felt him rubbing another mighty hard-on against her moistening sex.

Balthazar was right. Of course it would be so easy, and Morgan couldn't deny that he felt wonderful. There was also no fear of contracting any sexually transmitted diseases. They had each been tested several times.

However, Morgan was not ready to be pregnant.

"Don't," Morgan said.

Balthazar stopped and rolled away, defeated and a bit annoyed.

"Will you at least go to the doctor and discuss all of the contraceptive options?" he asked.

Morgan laid on her back, joining Balthazar in staring at the ceiling. "You know how I feel about artificial hormones. I don't want to upset the tenuous balance in my body. I've got enough on my hands with the narcolepsy."

"What if you got a diaphragm?" Balthazar asked.

"I'd have to leave it in for eight hours after sex. With how much we fuck that thing would be in me all of the time."

"I'm sure we could compromise. Use condoms some of the time and the diaphragm only once in a while." He turned on his side and pulled her closer. Morgan felt a pleasant heat radiating from Balthazar's skin. He kissed her on the lips. "Please?"

Morgan surrendered to his loving embrace. "Okay, okay, I'll make an appointment."

They made out for a bit, snuggled, and fell asleep.

While drifting off, Balthazar couldn't help wondering if there was some other reason for Morgan's reticence to have sex without a condom.

* * *

The next weekend, Balthazar was alone. Morgan was away having dinner with August and doing a session for the sleep disorder study. One of Balthazar's paramedic buddies had begged Balthazar to let go of his night shift so he could get some much needed overtime. Balthazar had agreed, relieved to have the break. His head wasn't really in the saving game that day anyway.

Balthazar went to Corner Café late in the afternoon under the guise of wanting coffee, curious to see if the Tarot card reader was working.

There she stood, holding down the fort behind the counter.

"How can I help you?" the dark-haired woman asked.

"Um," Balthazar felt surprised by the standard question and looked up at the menu on the wall for safety. "Yeah, uh, could I get a large latte?"

"Sure," She started making it, blushing because she felt him staring at her. She was thrilled, thinking he was going to hit on her, until…

"My girlfriend and I saw you working with your cards the other night," Balthazar said.

"Oh, yeah, sometimes the manager lets me do Tarot here."

"Is there any way I could get a reading tonight?"

"I'm in the middle of a double shift today. How about we do it tomorrow?"

"I could really use some insight now," Balthazar said.

Balthazar didn't know why he felt such urgency to get something he didn't even really believe in. Maybe it was because Balthazar was at his wits end about the mystery surrounding Morgan? Maybe Balthazar just wasn't used to having someone turn him down.

Many a vain soul had paid doctors to sculpt their faces for the kind of bone structure Balthazar possessed. Balthazar was aware of the effect his handsome features had on almost everyone, and he also knew there were many ways to get people to do what you wanted them to.

"Look, how much do you charge?" he asked.

Usually the woman worked for tips, but she wished to be paid a regular fee for her talents. The prospect of another year behind the Corner Café counter tending to the masses sounded like a sentence in hell, but she didn't know what else she wanted to do. Reading Tarot seemed like one of the few things which she both excelled at and which she enjoyed.

"Twenty dollars," she said.

"I'll give you forty if you read me after you get off of work," Balthazar said.

"It won't be for a few hours, but if it's that urgent, come back at ten and I'll give you a reading."

"Great, I'll go see a movie and be back."

"Okay, see you later… Hey, what's your name?"

"Balthazar," he reached out to shake her hand.

She clasped his hand in a firm grip. "Dorcha. Nice to meet you."

* * *

Balthazar returned to the café while Dorcha was finishing tidying up and shutting down for the night. He handed her the forty dollars, wanting to get the financial transaction out of the way. Dorcha thanked him, pocketing the cash.

Balthazar helped her put the chairs up on the tables for the cleaning crew, except for the two chairs Dorcha was going to use for the reading.

Balthazar sat down, curious and nervous about getting his first reading.

Dorcha settled in. She opened up her backpack, extracted three smaller bags, and pulled out a different Tarot deck from each of them. She shuffled the first deck.

"What would you like a reading on?"

"Well, umm-"

"You said you have a girlfriend?"

"Yeah, we've been together for almost five years. Morgan's great, but…"

"What is it?" Dorcha asked.

"I don't know. There's something going on with her. I'm afraid she might be cheating on me. Although that seems absurd, because we have so much fun together. I don't know how she would have the energy to be with someone else after what we do. Wow, I can't believe I just said that. I'm sorry. This is embarrassing. I normally don't talk about personal stuff so candidly. It's weird, I feel like I can trust you."

"Thank you. You can, and don't worry about offending me. The more I know, the more assistance I can offer. Let's start with a relationship spread on the two of you and we'll go from there."

"Okay, sounds good. What do I do?"

Dorcha smiled as she absent-mindedly shuffled the first deck. She placed it in front of him. "This is the Druid Craft deck. Cut the cards three times with your left hand."

"Why the left hand?"

"It's ruled by the right side of the brain, the side that controls spatial relationships. The feminine side. The cards will still work if you do it the other way, but it doesn't hurt."

"Like this?" Balthazar asked.

Dorcha smiled. "There is no wrong way to do it."

"Do I have to focus on anything?"

"No. The cards know what to do."

"Okay."

"Now stack them back up," instructed Dorcha.

He did. While Balthazar was stacking the first deck, Dorcha shuffled the second of three decks. When Balthazar finished, Dorcha traded decks with him. "Do the same thing with the Faeries' Oracle deck."

"These are creepy looking. Three times?"

"Yes. This deck was created by Brian Froud, the conceptual designer for Labyrinth and The Dark Crystal."

"Oh yeah, I can see that now. I loved those movies when I was a kid. Some of those creatures scared the hell out of me."

They repeated the ritual with the third deck which Dorcha told Balthazar was called the Lover's Path. Balthazar cut the final deck and handed it back to Dorcha. Dorcha took the first deck and laid out a nice-card Tarot spread. She laid the first four cards in a vertical line, from bottom to top. To the right of this vertical line, she laid the next four cards in a horizontal line. Finally, Dorcha laid the ninth card in the upper right corner of the spread. Then Dorcha took the second deck and laid nine cards in the same pattern, almost on top of the first spread, but with enough space so she could still see the cards from the first deck underneath. Dorcha then did the same thing with the third deck. She was now reading a three-layer spread.

Here are the cards which came up:

@ indicates a card in a reversed (upside-down) position.

Position 1 represents **how Balthazar sees Morgan**:
   Druid Craft: 10 of Cups @
   Faeries' Oracle: #56 – Gloominous Doom @
   Lover's Path: Princess of Disks @
Position 2 represents **how Morgan sees Balthazar**:
   Druid Craft: #17 – The Star @
   Faeries' Oracle: #64 – Gawtcha
   Lover's Path: #1 - Magic
Position 3 represents **Balthazar's focal point in the relationship**:
   Druid Craft: 8 of Cups
   Faeries' Oracle: #40 – Honesty
   Lover's Path: Princess of Swords
Position 4 represents **Morgan's focal point in the relationship**:
   Druid Craft: 5 of Pentacles
   Faeries' Oracle: #16 – The Bright Mother @

Lover's Path: 9 of Coins
Position 5 represents **where the relationship is now**:
    Druid Craft: Princess of Wands
    Faeries' Oracle: #32 – Iris of the Rainbows
    Lover's Path: 8 of Cups @
Position 6 represents **where Balthazar wants the relationship to go**:
    Druid Craft: #3 – The Lady @
    Faeries' Oracle: #34 – Sylvanius
    Lover's Path: #6 – Love @
Position 7 represents **where Morgan wants to relationship to go**:
    Druid Craft: 3 of Wands
    Faeries' Oracle: #24 – The Piper
    Lover's Path: 3 of Cups
Position 8 represents **something to consider in the relàtionship**:
    Druid Craft: King of Cups @
    Faeries' Oracle: #57 – Luathas the Wild
    Lover's Path: #14 – Balance @
Position 9 represents the **overall lesson each of you are learning in the relationship right now**:
    Druid Craft: #8 – Strength @
    Faeries' Oracle: #2 – Ekstasis @
    Lover's Path: King of Arrows

Dorcha dove into analysis mode. "Here's something that pops up when I look at this spread. Your girlfriend genuinely wants this relationship to work out. She finds it shocking that things aren't flowing as well as she thinks they should be. It's your negative attitude about her which is causing the issue right now. Like you think she's lazy or something…"

"Well, she doesn't have a job!" interrupted Balthazar. "Or can't keep one anyway. I know she's got some money from her family. It's not going to last forever. Especially with how much pot she smokes."

"Do you two fight about her sporadic lack of employment?"

"All the time. She always tells me not to worry. Trust her, she'll figure it out. But it does worry me. How can it not? We live under the same roof. What happens if we get married? I'm a paramedic. We can't live off of my salary, let alone afford to raise a family."

"Does she pay half of the rent and expenses?" Dorcha asked.

"Yes, but like I said, how long is her trust fund going to last? She's got to work or go back to school. Graduate school would be the next logical step if she's going to want to get any required credentials. A Bachelor's degree in Psychology is not an impressive accomplishment for that field."

"The advice for you in the relationship is to be honest and communicate."

"We talk about our issues so much I feel like a chick," sighed Balthazar.

"But like you said, you argue about the same subject."

"Only because she still hasn't found a real job."

"Okay, however, she's asking you to trust her. When you keep chewing on the same issue, it makes her feel clenched, oppressed, and she withdraws from you. You have to be honest about what kind of space you're willing to give her. If you say you're going to let something go, that's exactly what you have to do. According to the cards, you are projecting your insecurities about the relationship onto her. Your search to unearth her possible betrayal makes her defensive. She senses the imbalance and retreats. Those actions exacerbate whatever doubts both of you have about the relationship."

Dorcha shifted gears by asking, "How's the sex?"

Balthazar smiled in response. Dorcha swore she saw color rise on his cheeks. "Amazing," he said. "I've never felt so loved by anyone. But-"

"What is it?"

Balthazar thought for a moment, "I don't know. It's weird. No matter how much time we spend together I always feel like she's got this whole other life going on. Sometimes she looks at me like a stranger and has a hard time remembering what we were just talking about, or doing. I'm afraid she has early Alzheimer's or something. Every time I suggest she get checked out by a doctor, she laughs at me. Says I'm sweet for caring, and reassures me that she's perfectly fine. I mean, Morgan does have narcolepsy. Other than the rare episodes of falling asleep suddenly, it doesn't seem to affect her too much. Sometimes I believe she'd rather fuck me than talk to me. Not that I really mind. I just never thought I would empathize with women who want to talk about their emotions, and all the guy wants to do is feel them up. Can you see what's going to happen with us? Is she the woman I'm going to marry?"

Dorcha shrugged. "I'm not a long-range oracle. I'm more like a trail-guide psychic. One thing I can see from here is that any imbalances or secrets between you two are going to continue to be sources of sorrow unless you can learn to deal with them. Keep in mind, though, as I said before, she wants it to work between you two. She wants to build a harmonious, fun-filled life together. You need to work on your negative attitude in regards to her shortcomings if you want her to relax and be more open with you."

Dorcha fell silent, a faint smile on her lips.

"Well, that's certainly a lot to think about," Balthazar said. "Thank you. I can't believe you know what every single one of those cards mean. How many of them are there?"

"As you can see I use three decks concurrently. Druid Craft has seventy-eight, Faeries' Oracle – sixty-six, and Lover's Path – seventy-eight, for a grand total of two hundred and twenty-two cards. I consider them all brutally honest friends who only want to help. To me they are a physical manifestation of faith."

"How so?" asked Balthazar, surprised that a pagan had made a correlation between the cards and faith.

"If the Tarot cards are always correct, and the only mistakes made in a reading are mistakes of misinterpretation, then we really are all connected on a spiritual level. Every time I make a call and it doesn't come true, I look back at my notes. There is always a factor I didn't take into proper consideration. I call it the Ego Smack Down. Don't worry. This typically only happens when I read for myself. With others it's much easier to give an accurate card analysis, because my emotions don't cloud my reason."

"Can you do another reading on just me?"

"Certainly," Dorcha said.

"And then if it's not too much trouble, could we dig a little more into what's going on with my girlfriend?"

"Yes, I've got just the spread."

Celtic Cross reading on Balthazar using Druid Craft, Faeries' Oracle, and Lover's Path Tarot decks.
Position 1 represents **Balthazar with no influences**:
> Druid: Queen of Cups
> Faeries: #7 - The Singer of Intuition @
> Lovers: King of Staves @
Position 2 represents **Balthazar's cross to bear, the conflict which is spurring him on**:
> Druid: #1 - The Magician @
> Faeries: #56 Gloomious Doom
> Lovers: #21 – Triumph @
Position 3 represents **Balthazar's conscious goals and aspirations**:
> Druid: #11 - Justice
> Faeries: #10 – The Singer of Healing
> Lovers: 4 of Arrows @
Position 4 represents **Balthazar's unconscious influences**:
> Druid: 10 of Swords @
> Faeries: #5 – She of the Cruach
> Lovers: Princess of Arrows
Position 5 represents **influences from Balthazar's past**:
> Druid: #15 – Cernunnos
> Faeries: #27 – Nelys the Alchemyst @
> Lovers: #13 - Transformation
Position 6 represents **influences from Balthazar's future**:

Druid: King of Wands
Faeries: #45 - Taitin the Sylph
Lovers: #11 – Justice @

Position 7 represents **how Balthazar sees himself**:
Druid: King of Cups
Faeries: #64 – Gawtcha @
Lovers: 3 of Arrows @

Position 8 represents **Balthazar's environment and how others see Balthazar**:
Druid: Ace of Pentacles @
Faeries: #41 – Ilbe the Retriever
Lovers: 2 of Cups

Position 9 represents **how Balthazar solves problems and faces obstacles**:
Druid: Queen of Pentacles
Faeries: #22 The Master Maker @
Lovers: 10 of Arrows

Position 10 represents **Balthazar's current overall lesson**:
Druid: 3 of Wands
Faeries: #39 Losgunna @
Lovers: Princess of Staves

"You seek a more detached, balanced, healing viewpoint. Maybe you need this for the work you do," Dorcha said.

"Yes, I'm a paramedic. Detachment is a key trait to surviving the job," Balthazar said.

"Indeed. However, this mentality leads to a white knight complex in your personal relationships. This shifts the dynamic with your girlfriend. You should be teammates and partners, but instead you become the doctor and she becomes the patient.

Dorcha continued. "In the past I can see you've been learning the lesson of how to get out of your own way. Sexually, I mean. In your relationship, you two have matured together sexually. In the future, your thoughts will be fiery. You're going to want to take action, grab the bull by its horns and impose your will. The cards are counseling you to be patient. You see yourself as a healer, but don't try to deny that the job is taking its toll on you. The disturbing things you see when you have someone's life in your hands, these are difficult experiences to leave at work. Your conscious goal cards show that you yearn for a more buffered perspective, like the veteran paramedics you work with. Am I going in the right direction here, Balthazar? I don't know what the expression on your face means."

"What? Oh, no, yes. Sorry. You're nailing it. I'm floored. How do you know this?"

Dorcha grinned, "Like I said, the cards are always right. Ok, here's a spread that will help me see a little deeper."

Position 1 represents **how Morgan thinks Balthazar sees her**:
> Druid: 2 of Pentacles
> Faeries: #26 – O! That Gnome
> Lovers: #19 – Awakening @

Position 2 represents **Morgan's plan for her relationship with Balthazar**:
> Druid: 3 of Pentacles @
> Faeries: #61 – G. Hobyah
> Lovers: 4 of Pentacles @

Position 3 represents **how Morgan sees her behavior with Balthazar**:
> Druid: 5 of Pentacles
> Faeries: #4 – He of the Fiery Sword
> Lovers: Prince of Arrows

Position 4 represents **what Morgan is not telling Balthazar about herself**:
> Druid: 9 of Pentacles
> Faeries: #42 – Myk the Myomancer
> Lovers: #8 – Strength @

Position 5 represents **the best job for Morgan to have**:
> Druid: #11 – Justice @
> Faeries: #8 – The Singer of Courage
> Lovers: 7 of Staves

Position 6 represents **what Morgan wants from Balthazar**:
> Druid: #12 – The Hanged Man @
> Faeries: #13 – Solus
> Lovers: 10 of Arrows @

Position 7 represents **how Morgan sees herself**:
> Druid: Prince of Pentacles @
> Faeries: #9 The Singer of Initiation @
> Lovers: 4 of Arrows

Position 8 represents **how Morgan sees her sex life with Balthazar**:
> Druid: Prince of Swords @
> Faeries: #38 – Laiste, Moon's Daughter @
> Lovers: Prince of Staves @

"Your girlfriend believes you have an issue with her unwillingness to accept something. I don't know, it's either something to do with creativity, or even with having children. Another indicator that kids might be the issue is the anxiety surrounding how she sees your sex life. Maybe she's still troubled by an argument you had about something sexual. The power of your connection can be overwhelming."

"Tell me about it," Balthazar said.

"She's still very sensitive about her career, and she feels like she's enduring an unexpected initiation. Maybe she's anxious about kids because she knows they aren't an option for her until she's made her way professionally. Your girlfriend thinks you get envious of her freedom while you have to work full time. This makes her defensive. There's a fundamental detail which she's afraid of, or which she's too insecure to tell you about. It's something she's not ready to reveal to you yet," advised Dorcha.

"Insecure? That doesn't sound like Morgan," Balthazar said.

"The best job for Morgan would involve courageously fighting against imbalances, lies, and injustices."

"Hey, do you do house calls?" Balthazar asked.

"What?" Dorcha asked.

"It's Morgan's birthday in a couple of weeks and I think she'd get a real kick out of you. How much do you charge to work a party?"

"It depends on how long you want me there," reasoned Dorcha.

"I'll give you three hundred dollars for the evening, from six pm to midnight," offered Balthazar.

"When is this?"

"October Twelfth."

Dorcha opened up her laptop and clicked on the calendar. She looked up and offered her hand. "Deal."

Balthazar took Dorcha's hand in his and smiled, "Excellent."

After Balthazar left, Dorcha did the relationship spread again with herself and Balthazar as the subjects. She felt silly, weird, and a bit guilty for doing so. Balthazar had a girlfriend he loved very much. They had spent the last two hours discussing how he could strengthen his relationship with her. Yet, Balthazar was so charming, Dorcha's attraction to him made her curious.

She mulled it over for a bit, deciding there was no harm or foul. Dorcha excused it away as customer service feedback. It was no secret Balthazar was a gorgeous and kind man. Dorcha needed to know if she had a snowball's chance in hell to be with him.

Position 1 represents **how Dorcha sees Balthazar**:
      Druid: #5 – The High Priest
      Faeries: #7 – The Singer of Intuition @
      Lovers: 3 of Cups
Position 2 represents **how Balthazar sees Dorcha**:
      Druid: Prince of Swords
      Faeries: #19 – The Sage
      Lovers: Princess of Pentacles

Position 3 represents **Dorcha's focal point in the relationship**:
   Druid: 9 of Swords
      Faeries: #57 – Luathas the Wild
      Lovers: 9 of Arrows @
Position 4 represents **Balthazar's focal point in the relationship**:
   Druid: 2 of Cups
      Faeries: #29 – Ta'Om the Poet
      Lovers: #14 - Balance
Position 5 represents **where the relationship is now**:
   Druid: Ace of Swords @
      Faeries: #3 – The Guardian at the Gate @
      Lovers: Queen of Pentacles
Position 6 represents **where Dorcha wants the relationship to go**:
   Druid: 9 of Pentacles
      Faeries: #42 – Myk the Myomancer @
      Lovers: Queen of Cups @
Position 7 represents **where Balthazar wants to relationship to go**:
   Druid: 5 of Staves
      Faeries: #22 - The Master Maker
      Lovers: 6 of Arrows
Position 8 represents **something to consider in the relationship**:
   Druid: 8 of Cups @
      Faeries: #56 – Gloominous Doom @
      Lovers: #4 - Power
Position 9 represents **the overall lesson each of you are learning in the relationship right now**:
   Druid: Princess of Cups @
      Faeries: #60 – The Pook
      Lovers: #11 - Justice

   Dorcha scanned the layout of the cards. Dorcha had made quite a good impression with Balthazar. He felt like she was a woman who could find the answers. It was no wonder Balthazar hired Dorcha for his girlfriend's birthday party.
   Balthazar's high regard for Dorcha only fueled her desire to make sure that all interactions with him would be honorable and above board.
   Dorcha knew she'd linger in his thoughts. This made Dorcha's stomach turn with excitement and a sense of dread, like she was walking into an emotional trap. It would be madness to nurture romantic fantasies about this man. Unfortunately, Dorcha's fertile imagination wasn't likely to listen to reason. Lovely lusty thoughts burst through her mind's eye. They were difficult to ignore.
   Dorcha sighed, frustrated. Balthazar's earnest love and devotion for

his girlfriend made him even more alluring. One consoling thought was that at least Dorcha knew there really were great men out there. Maybe the next one Dorcha would meet would be more receptive to her lustful attention.

It wore on Dorcha's positive attitude that the men she burned for always managed to be in the most difficult situations for her to traverse. The unlikely possibility of a relationship with these men, rather than being a deterrent, only fed the flame. Dorcha would try to reconcile what her brain and her heart were telling her, but more often than not it would only turn her fanciful lust into full-blown obsession. Maybe the continued episodes were an on-going lesson in emotional arrogance. Dorcha always felt so proud of her passionate feelings. She always did her best to communicate her affection in a positive, non-destructive way.

Dorcha's Tarot investigations helped her to keep the desire for any shady activity. While doing readings on guys she had crushes on, Dorcha did not spy on their other relationships. Instead, Dorcha kept her inquiries centered on how her crush related to her, and what she could do to contribute to the best outcome for everyone.

Dorcha believed that any trespassing on the privacy of these relationships would only come back to haunt her. She considered herself a woman of integrity and did not want to insult anyone, especially someone she cared deeply for.

Obsession is such an ugly word, Dorcha mused. She preferred the term Loving Focus. Yes, much more apt.

No wonder vampire stories had fascinated Dorcha when she was growing up. The gnawing thirst for blood was akin to the hormonal stimulus for ecstatic sexual expression. Dorcha longed to experience the rush of awe, wonder, and fear that the thrill of the hunt provided. Desires were like gazelles, loping through the grasslands, and our Ego was like a ravenous lion.

* * *

Morgan felt Balthazar wake up and get out of bed. She stirred, feeling him leave, turned over, and laid her head on his pillow. Morgan loved the smell of Balthazar's scent all over where he slept. She drifted off listening to the coffee maker gurgle to life.

Twenty minutes later Morgan woke with a start. The bedroom shared a wall with the living room, which barely muffled the loud sounds from a gory monster movie Balthazar was watching. Morgan thought Balthazar saw enough carnage at work, but apparently not. Morgan felt boredom and disdain for the entire horror genre. For her, it was all just fodder for UnderLife horrors.

Morgan got up and went to the bathroom. She peed, brushed her teeth, and splashed some water on her face.

Balthazar smiled when Morgan entered the living room. "Happy Birthday, Morgan! I'm starving. Want me to go pick up some breakfast?"

"Thank you. Yes. Oh God, what are you watching?"

"A classic, Night of the Living Dead. It's good, give it a chance."

Glancing at the screen, Morgan shook her head. "No way, what a nightmare! Mine are creative enough, thank you very much. I don't want to encourage them."

Balthazar called ahead to their favorite breakfast place. He went to get the food, while Morgan made a cup of English Breakfast tea and rattled the sleepy cobwebs out of her head with some bong hits.

They ate while watching a re-run of Strangers with Candy. Balthazar wanted to talk about the issues which had come up during the Tarot readings. He mentioned the idea of Morgan getting a job.

Morgan bristled, "Not this again."

"No, I'm not... you interrupted me. I wanted to say that whatever career path you choose, I trust you. Sure, I get jealous when I'm busting my ass running around town at least forty hours a week while you do whatever it is you do when you're on your own." Balthazar felt Morgan tensing up, but couldn't help himself from continuing. "You know, maybe you should reconsider going back to school? I know you would make a great counselor. You could help people resolve their injustices and imbalances."

"Honey, let's not talk about my career right now. I'm sorting it out."

"How?"

"C'mon, give me break. This subject is a birthday downer." Morgan lifted up his t-shirt, bending to give a flurry of kisses on his taut stomach.

"Sometimes I think you only keep me around because of my stunning good looks, kick ass body, and massive sexual skills."

"No, it's your modesty which really gets me wet. Are you feeling objectified, honey?" Morgan chuckled softly, continuing her loving attention to his torso.

Morgan got the sense that Balthazar wasn't sharing her mirth. She looked up. He stared down at her with an odd expression on his face. Morgan's smile faded with the realization that Balthazar was being serious.

"Yes, I do feel objectified. Well, a little, anyway. You always seem a bit distracted. Like there's this joke you love, and you're not including me in on it. Are you seeing someone else, is that it? Please don't spare my feelings. I would rather know the truth."

"No, it's not that, it's just..."

"Who is he? Or is it a she?

"What?"

"Oh please, I know you're attracted to women. I pay attention, and you're not subtle. I never said anything before because you have the sexual appetite of a teenage boy. You seem to have no problem fucking me senseless with mind boggling frequency. I figured you had some bisexual tendencies, and weren't feeling comfortable talking about it."

Morgan nodded. She had wanted to tell him, yet she'd been afraid he'd suggest they have a threesome. For Morgan, bisexuality had never equaled promiscuity. In fact, quite the opposite, Morgan fixated on whomever she was into, generally to the exclusion of all else. Also, despite a few dalliances, Morgan had never actually had sex with a woman. She didn't want the first time to be a group event.

Since listening to Victoria's first album, Morgan had been having sexual fantasies about Victoria Shine. Morgan had chalked it up to hero worship. It's not like they really knew each other or anything.

Balthazar mistook Morgan's silence as embarrassment for calling her out. He said, "Hey look, I think it's kinda hot, but cheating is cheating. So-"

"Balthazar, I'm not cheating on you. There isn't anybody else," Morgan said.

"Well, then, what is it?"

"Sweetie, where is all of this coming from? I thought we've been having an amazing time together."

"We are. It's just... I don't know. It feels like you're keeping something important from me and I can't understand why."

Morgan leaned in and kissed him. Balthazar responded, but he didn't let the kiss deepen. Morgan stared into Balthazar's eyes and gave him a devilish grin. Balthazar always felt like a co-conspirator in a slutty scandal when Morgan smiled at him like that. He was charmed, but still confused. Balthazar didn't know if Morgan's silence meant there was no secret. Maybe, Balthazar thought, he just liked women who seemed mysterious. Or maybe she did harbor a secret so deep and sick that the only way to live with it was never to speak of it. the monstrosity was to never speak of it? Was she right not to tell him because she knew he wouldn't handle it well? What could be so bad? Balthazar wondered.

Balthazar said, "You're not going to say anything? See, this is what drove me to get a Tarot card reading the other day."

"What? You did? From who? What did he say?" Morgan was shocked.

It was Balthazar's turn to smile and kiss her. Morgan tackled him. "You bastard, I can't believe conservative you got a reading and didn't tell me. What did he say about us?"

"Oh now you want to talk. Well, you can ask her yourself. I hired her to come over and give readings all night."

"You got me a Tarot card reader for my birthday?"

"Yeah, she's great. I told her to come at six so you could get a reading before everyone starts coming over."

"Everyone?"

"For the party, my love, we've got to have a party for your birthday."

"Well, well, well, look who is full of surprises. Alright handsome, sounds good to me, guess I'll start getting ready. Care to join me in the shower?"

"But it's only noon."

"I plan on taking my time. I'm feeling pretty dirty." Morgan cupped her hand and stroked his crotch, feeling his cock. She plucked loose the bow-knotted string at the waistband of Balthazar's Adidas workout pants, and hooked her thumbs into his underwear, pulling both off at the same time. Balthazar's generous member twitched, responding to the attention.

Balthazar drew Morgan in for a kiss while untying the belt of her terrycloth robe. He handled her breasts for a moment and gave each nipple a little pinch. Caressing Morgan's sides, and then her back, Balthazar pulled her into a tighter embrace. He pressed his hips into hers, and slid both of hands down her back to grab and knead the muscles of her ass.

His cock stiffened. Morgan felt the growing erection against her lower abdomen. Morgan smiled into the ongoing storm of passionate kisses. Morgan never tired of witnessing this delicious man's arousal, knowing she had caused it.

Balthazar's right hand gave Morgan's ass another full squeeze. Then reached around to the front of her hips and cupped her mound of delicate flesh. Morgan spread her legs for Balthazar, and he reached down to slide her cunt lips apart, relishing in their warm wetness. Balthazar snaked one, then two fingers into her and made a circular motion, preparing her for him. Morgan sighed with pleasure.

A sexy smile formed on Balthazar's fantastic features. He plunged his fingers inside Morgan, pulled them out, tickled her clit, and penetrated again. Balthazar repeated this action until Morgan couldn't help vocalizing her bliss. He pulled them out, spreading her juices across her left nipple. Balthazar's mouth followed his fingers. He sucked on her breast, while tenderly stroking his hands up and down Morgan's body, forcing her to calm down to his steady pace. Balthazar loved controlling Morgan's pleasure, playing the instrument of her body like a virtuoso. He was just getting warmed up.

Balthazar stood up. Morgan gave him another barrage of kisses. She could taste herself on his lips. Any time a lip-lock lingered, his dick quivered with approval. It stood at attention in its full glory. Balthazar tightened his embrace with Morgan and waltzed her towards the dresser. Too intent on each other, they miscalculated a bit and crashed into it.

"Umpf!" they grunted in unison, laughing at their synchronized responses. Balthazar groped for the top right dresser drawer. He yanked it open, revealing a treasure trove of condoms and tubes of lube, a variety pack of good times. Balthazar found a Trojan Magnum Warming Sensation Condom, his favorite. Being a safe sex pro, he continued to unleash loving kisses on Morgan while tearing open the condom wrapper behind her back.

The two had made love on countless occasions. Morgan knew just when to move her hips away to give Balthazar enough room to pull the condom onto his pulsating penis.

They resumed their mauling of each other. Balthazar pushed Morgan against the wall. Holding his sheathed cock, Balthazar slid it up and down the outside of Morgan's pussy, using Morgan's wet excitement as lube, instead of one of the various tubes in the drawer. Morgan tilted her hips up a bit. Balthazar plunged his dick into her. They both moaned in response to the penetration. Morgan got leverage from wall against her back, and wrapped her legs around his waist.

Morgan's weight pushed Balthazar's cock even further into her. Balthazar pinned Morgan harder against the wall as his legs and hips flexed to rhythmically fuck her. Morgan's body matched his movements. When their pace began to pick up, the wall no longer served their purposes. Balthazar decided to give up their athletic position, and brought their sweaty bodies to the bed.

They rested for a while in the good ol' missionary position. Morgan and Balthazar turned the love-making into a study in detail. Their eyes locked, tuning in, hyper-aware of every breath, gasp, and movement. The slightest nuance of pleasure given or received was doubly experienced by the joy of observing the effect each was having on the other.

Morgan got a wolfish grin on her face, betraying a devilish intention. It gave him only a second's warning. She thrust with her hips, twisted to the left, anchored with her right leg that she'd entangled around his left leg, and flipped them over. Morgan took a turn to have some fun on top. Balthazar offered no resistance, as it gave his legs a bit of respite from their recent showing of sultry strength.

Morgan straddled Balthazar, sitting up to give him his favorite view of her riding his proud and plentiful cock. Balthazar put his hands on her thighs and then her hips, dictating how fast he wanted her to go. Morgan yielded to his direction and they slowed the pace of their hips to a simmering rhythm. Neither of them were in any hurry. Every moment was bliss and it'd be a shame to end it too soon. Balthazar loved watching Morgan's breasts jiggle and sway as her body bounced upon his own. She braced her hands on his chest and angled herself to give him room to fuck her while still getting a great view of seeing his dick thrusting in and out of her.

Soon the idea of taking it slow was forgotten. Balthazar knew

Morgan's body so well. He knew just how to entice her, get her going, drive her wild, and make her come harder, longer, and more times than she thought possible. Morgan's moans grew in volume while the headboard thumped against the wall.

"I love being inside of you... so hot... Ugnh... Morgan... Yes... Oh Fuck... Yes... Beeu... ti... ful.." Balthazar growled.

Morgan replied with another deep moan. She bent to kiss him, and Balthazar rolled her back over in the process. Balthazar brought her legs over his shoulders and fucked Morgan even harder. Their bodies slapped together. They grunted and sweated with pleasure. Balthazar, on a position mission, took Morgan's right leg and brought it to the other side of his head so they were side-saddle. They kept fucking away as Balthazar slowly turned her around. Soon Morgan's face was buried in the pillow, her ass in the air. Balthazar fucked Morgan from behind, his massive cock sending lightning bolts of electricity throughout her cunt, setting fire to every last nerve ending of both of their bodies.

Morgan did a push up, and Balthazar wasted no time in cupping her left breast with one hand and finding Morgan's clit with the other. Balthazar knew he had it when her body jerked against his. Balthazar gave her clit feathery touches and strokes, all the while continuing to ram her with his cock.

Balthazar slowed his pace, fighting the urge to pound her until he came. Balthazar retreated momentarily from Morgan's lovely body so he could turn her over onto her back.

Balthazar kissed Morgan deeply, settling his weight on her, and pushing his cock back inside of her. He rotated his hips in a circular motion, while pulling almost all the way out of Morgan. Then Balthazar slid his cock as deep inside Morgan as he could go, rolling his hips up at the end of each stroke, aiming for her G spot. Balthazar felt pleasure ripple through Morgan.

Balthazar was focused on Morgan, receptive to her every nuance. He felt Morgan's orgasm building and he rode the ecstatic waves with her, accelerating the gyrating pace of their writhing bodies.

Morgan gave out a long moan when she came. The walls of Morgan's vagina clenched on Balthazar's triumphant cock, causing an irresistible pulse of pleasure to break through his last resistance to coming.

After their bodies had finished their euphoric spasms, Morgan and Balthazar gave each other lazy congratulatory kisses and caresses. Morgan reached down to pull the sheet and comforter over them, while Balthazar took off and disposed of the used condom. They twined themselves into each other and fell asleep.

* * *

Twenty minutes later Balthazar awoke to Morgan's lips closing around his hardening cock. Morgan licked a bit of pre-cum off of the tip before taking Balthazar deep into her mouth. Morgan's tongue found the sensitive spot underneath the pulsing head of his dick. Balthazar moaned and his body jerked about from the delightful waves of bliss which were setting his senses reeling. He sighed, groaning with pleasure as Morgan sucked him off with zeal.

Morgan went into the bathroom to shower afterwards. Balthazar joined her while she finished slathering her hair with conditioner, right on time to rub Morgan down with the soap. Morgan did not turn around when Balthazar came in, shutting the frosty glass shower door behind him. Morgan felt Balthazar's body behind her and leaned back. Balthazar reached in front of her and took the rose petal bar of soap in his left hand. Balthazar's right hand brushed Morgan hair aside. While he gave her breasts a lot of attention with the soap, Balthazar trailed a path of kisses down her neck, licking and nibbling Morgan's flesh.

Balthazar assisted in rinsing the conditioner out of Morgan hair. Then he dropped to his knees and swung Morgan's left leg over his shoulder, intent on pleasuring her. Morgan could feel the bolts on the shower bar give a little as she gripped it hard for support.

When Morgan's right leg got wobbly from exertion and pleasure, Balthazar gave her one last long lick and then stood up. They kissed while stepping out of the shower. Balthazar threw a big towel around Morgan and rubbed her down with it. Then Balthazar picked up all five feet eleven inches of Morgan, throwing her over his shoulder. Morgan squealed in delight at his show of strength. Balthazar ducked a bit when going through the door frame, since they had already learned the hard way that there was limited clearance.

If asked or teased about it later, Balthazar would say he was only practicing for his job when he did this to Morgan. However, they both knew he loved to overwhelm her, and it always made Morgan giggle.

Balthazar carried Morgan until they reached the super soft fuzzy rug in the bedroom. Lying down, his skin still dripping wet, Balthazar slid Morgan's body on top of him. Ignoring his prominent hard on, Balthazar spread Morgan's legs apart and positioned himself to continue going down her. Balthazar's mouth administered to her clit, his fingers diving into her, until she unleashed a shuddering climax.

Morgan recovered a few moments later. She retrieved another latex sheath from the drawer. Morgan unfurled it onto Balthazar's cock, and pounced on him.

Finally exhausted, they passed out for a nap.

* * *

Morgan clapped her hands in front of Balthazar's stoic face. Every time she saw him in UnderLife, Morgan got excited, and then frustrated. There was never any reaction from Balthazar in UnderLife. Morgan wanted to connect with him so badly in this realm, but it seemed impossible. After many failed attempts, Morgan feigned disinterest, consoling herself that she would be seeing Balthazar in Waking Life. Morgan acted like it didn't matter.

Off in the distance, Morgan heard music. Was that Victoria Shine singing? Morgan scampered off in search for her favorite muse.

* * *

"Morgan."

"Hmm?" Morgan giggled in her sleep.

"Sweetie?" Balthazar brushed her lips with his.

Morgan kissed him back. Her eyes fluttered open.

"Hey," Morgan ran hands through Balthazar's hair, cupping his jaw.

"Time to get ready for your party."

"Oh yeah, it's my birthday."

"Before everything gets crazy I want to give you the first half of your present."

"Okay!"

Balthazar handed Morgan an envelope.

Inside were four tickets to the upcoming Victoria Shine concert. Victoria was touring to promote Harmony's Harem, the album which had been inspired by Victoria's character Harmony Moore from Love In Motion.

"Holy shit, front row seats? These must have cost a fortune! My God, you've certainly outdone yourself. Thank you!" exclaimed Morgan.

"You're welcome. We saved a ticket broker, Barry, a few weeks ago. It was a pretty dramatic call. Barry is ferocious about honor and debts. He said if I ever needed anything, and here we are. I got four, because I figured, the more the merrier. So if I wasn't an excited enough fan, you could invite friends to help you gush."

"What a thoughtful gift! Thank you, thank you, thank you!" Morgan said, showering Balthazar with affection. Balthazar reciprocated then retreated to clean up for the party.

Later, Balthazar approached Morgan while she was slapping on some make-up.

"I know it's your birthday, but while my parents are here, could you lay off the weed, or take it into our bathroom?" he asked.

"What am I, an idiot? I wasn't planning on puffing in front of your parents. I know how against it they are. Give me some credit."

"Okay, I was just worried."

Morgan turned and put a hand on his chest, "Well stop."

The doorbell rang.

Balthazar went to get it while Morgan finished putting blush on her face. Morgan heard Balthazar greet someone, let them in, and guide them back to where Morgan was.

"Morgan, may I present your Tarot card reader for the evening. This is Dorcha..."

"...LeTour?" Morgan finished.

Dorcha tilted her head to one side, "Yeah, do I know you?"

"Morgan Martel. Our Dads..."

"...Oh my God! No wonder you look so familiar! What's it been, a decade?" Dorcha said.

"Fifteen years," Morgan said.

"Wow, well, seems like the universe wants us around each other again," Dorcha said.

"I was just thinking that! This is awesome." Morgan bear-hugged Dorcha.

"Mysterious ways," Balthazar said. "I'll leave you two to catch up."

Morgan kissed Balthazar before leaving. "The best birthday presents ever."

"Thanks, honey." Balthazar went into the kitchen to continue preparing for the party.

Dorcha said, "What was the other present?"

"Do you like Victoria Shine?"

"Of course, she's great. I've been a fan of hers since I was a kid."

"Want to sit in the front row at her concert in December with us?" Morgan said.

"You're kidding? What a tremendous offer!"

"Please, I can't think of a better way to celebrate this surprise reunion."

"Well then, fuck yeah, I'll go."

"I'm delighted the cosmos decided it was time for us to reconnect," Morgan said.

"Absolutely!" Dorcha said.

"You know, we used to play together all the time."

"Didn't we have a pizzeria in the sandbox?"

"Yes! We'd sift the sand to shred the mozzarella cheese."

"So weird, I haven't thought about that in years. How is your Dad?"

"He's good. How are your parents?"

"Fine, happily married to other people," Dorcha said.

"Oh, I didn't even know they had split up. I'm sorry."

"It happened when I was seven. I barely remember it. Well then, are you ready for your birthday reading?"

"Yes! I've never gotten a Tarot reading before. I'm kind of nervous," Morgan said.

"Don't worry, there's nothing to be afraid of. Now, what would you like to focus on?"

"Balthazar said you can do relationship readings?"

"Yes. It's my specialty."

"Okay, I want one of those and then a quick one on me, since people are going to be arriving soon. That is, as long as I can get more extensive readings from you on another day?"

"Can do." Dorcha shuffled her cards, smiling at Morgan. Morgan stared back at her, awestruck and overjoyed to be sitting across from her first friend ever. Dorcha was the only other person Morgan knew that her mother had held as a baby.

Using the Druid Craft, Faeries' Oracle, and Lover's Path Tarot Dorcha had Morgan cut the decks. Then Dorcha laid out her favorite relationship spread.

Position 1 represents **how Morgan sees Balthazar**:
  Druid: #11 – Justice @
  Faeries: #30 – The Laume
  Lovers: #0 – Innocence @
Position 2 represents **how Balthazar sees Morgan**:
  Druid: 6 of Wands @
  Faeries: #1 - Unity
  Lovers: Prince of Arrows @
Position 3 represents **Morgan's focal point in the relationship**:
  Druid: Prince of Pentacles @
  Faeries: #28 – Penelope Dreamweaver @
  Lovers: Queen of Staves @
Position 4 represents **Balthazar's focal point in the relationship**:
  Druid: 3 of Swords @
  Faeries: #27 – Nelys the Alchemyst @
  Lovers: Queen of Arrows
Position 5 represents **where the relationship is now**:
  Druid: 8 of Cups
  Faeries: #50 – Arval Parrot
  Lovers: 7 of Pentacles
Position 6 represents **where Morgan wants the relationship to go**:
  Druid: King of Pentacles
  Faeries: #10 – The Singer of Healing

Lovers: Prince of Cups
Position 7 represents **where Balthazar wants to relationship to go**:
Druid: #5 – The High Priest @
Faeries: #52 – The Rarr
Lovers: Ace of Arrows
Position 8 represents **something to consider in the relationship**:
Druid: #14 – The Fferyllt @
Faeries: #19 – The Sage @
Lovers: Queen of Cups
Position 9 represents **the overall lesson each of you are learning in the relationship right now**:
Druid: #4 – The Lord
Faeries: #16 – The Bright Mother @
Lovers: Queen of Pentacles

"You want this union to last, for it to be a healing relationship, with Balthazar cast as the man of your dreams. Unfortunately, you don't trust him enough yet to be honest with him. Your lack of trust isn't completely unfounded, because he's being critical of you right now. Balthazar senses he doesn't know the whole story. He questions what you're doing with yourself career-wise. He's focusing on the dualities and differences, rather than seeing your strengths and the common ground you share."

Dorcha continued, "The good news is that, like you, he very much wants things to evolve between you. Balthazar needs to get out of his own way, to allow the energy to flow unimpeded. His clenched frame of mind compels Balthazar to aggressively question and monitor your progress, which doesn't help anything. Right now you are both being patient with each other about the communication avoidance. The advice for you is to realize you're undermining your own authority here. You're blocking your own imagination, or you're allowing Balthazar's limited perception of you to influence your attitude. Maybe you're caught up in a fixation with the physical: sex, money, material things. Something to consider is the underlying emotional quarrel going on here. One or both of you is withholding information from the other, or twisting it, which adds a manipulative element to the relationship. Until specific loving action is taken by one of you to begin unwinding this knot, the block on true romantic union will remain. This clog will sabotage an otherwise healthy intimacy." Dorcha ended her Tarot tirade, searching Morgan's face for a reaction.

Morgan, absorbed in processing the reading said, "Please continue with the second reading. I'll tell you everything when you're done."

Dorcha cleared the first spread and went through her usual process of shuffling the three decks. Then Dorcha handed the cards to Morgan so she could cut them.

"Okay, this spread is simple, only three placements. The first position represents your overall situation right now, what is affecting every aspect of your life. The second column will be the advice the Tarot wants you to follow. The third is your near future. This will also give us a clue of how you're going to need to use the advice."

Morgan nodded, eager to find out what the reading would say. Dorcha laid out the cards. She studied them a bit before speaking.

Position 1 represents **Morgan's situation**:
> Druid: #5 – The High Priest
> Faeries: #40 – Honesty @
> Lovers: 8 of Arrows @

Position 2 represents **advice for Morgan**:
> Druid: #18 – The Moon @
> Faeries: #44 – Lys of the Shadows @
> Lovers: 8 of Staves @

Position 3 represents **Morgan's near future**:
> Druid: 3 of Swords
> Faeries: #0 – The Guide
> Lovers: 8 of Pentacles

"You're not being honest about something in your spiritual belief system. It feels like you're in a nightmare, at the bottom of a cycle. Things are probably not as bad as they seem. Your falsehoods are causing you to project negativity on to others. Something dark is going on for you. You're being passive instead of talking about it. In your near future there is the spirit guide card, which I consider the slipstream of cosmic energy. It's a powerful card. Along with it is a sorrow card." Dorcha held up a grey image of three swords on a stone shaped like a heart. "The third card here represents talent, or work, or compensation. Maybe some special skill that you have?" Dorcha showed Morgan the third card which depicted a man laboring over a project well underway. "I'm not sure exactly what this means. Possibly it's about cultivating your talent, which is going to get you through a sad time. Or maybe it means that the work you have to do for the cosmos is going to be painful."

Morgan stared, first down at the cards, and then up at Dorcha.

"Does any of this resonate with you Morgan?" Dorcha asked.

Morgan was about to say that she didn't feel like she was in a nightmare when the shift occurred.

* * *

Morgan and Dorcha were dressed in rough wool hand-made peasant garb. The Tarot cards in between them were now one deck and it was an old school deck, something resembling an ancient Rider-Waite deck. There was also an uncorked bottle and two cups, half full of some pungent liquid, on the table. The room was lit by many candles.

They gaped at each other.

Before Morgan could explain how her talent had gotten them there, the door burst open.

In rushed several people, holding torches, cudgels, and swords. Outside stood at least half a dozen other people, ready for a fight.

"She's a witch!" yelled a bearded villager.

"They both are!" his companion said.

"Burn them!" snarled a greasy woman.

"Before they cast another wicked spell!" said the bearded man.

"Oh, c'mon, you gotta be fucking kidding me!" Dorcha said.

Morgan knocked over the bottle, hoping it was a high-proof alcohol. Then she set the tablecloth on fire with a nearby candle, and turned the whole table over, partially blocking the front door.

"Run!" Morgan screamed to Dorcha who stared back, incredulous. "GO NOW!" Morgan shoved Dorcha.

They dashed out of the back door.

Morgan and Dorcha found themselves in an ancient city. There were hundreds of buildings around them made of mudbrick.

Morgan and Dorcha ran right into three startled men who had been given the task of blocking their escape.

"What, you were waiting for us around the corner? That is so unfair," Morgan said. Morgan and Dorcha backed up into open ground with their hands in a defensive posture.

"Hey guys, c'mon, we can talk this through. We're not witches," Dorcha said.

The men continued to advance, immune to any parlay, persuasion, or charm. Morgan and Dorcha turned around and ran for their lives.

Dorcha, the swifter runner, led the way. They wove through the dusty city streets. The whole place seemed well kept but deserted, like everyone was congregating in some other part of town.

Panting from exertion, Morgan Dorcha entered a residential area. Again there was not another soul around. Everyone who lives here is out to get us, or hiding, or gone, Morgan thought. On both sides of the street there were at least two dozen houses marked with ascending Roman numerals. Morgan went for the door nearest to them. It was locked. Morgan threw her shoulder into the barrier, and was repelled. Dorcha saw a '0' above the door.

The angry mob was approaching. Morgan and Dorcha heard boots thumping on the cobblestone, curses, threats, and the clang of armor and weaponry. The mob was close, almost on top of them. Morgan and Dorcha had time to try one other door.

"Run," Morgan said.

"No, follow me," Dorcha said.

Dorcha sprinted for the door marked IX, with Morgan right on her heels. IX, Dorcha thought. In the Major Arcana in the Tarot, IX stands for The Hermit. Maybe we'll be safe in there. Praying she was right, Dorcha barreled into the door. It was unlocked. They rushed in and closed the door, right before the blood thirsty gang turned the corner behind them.

Morgan and Dorcha kept quiet and waited. After several tense minutes the noise outside faded. Morgan and Dorcha started to relax and inspect their surroundings. Both of them almost jumped out their skins. In the room were two women with long dark curly hair, olive skin, and dark eyes staring back at them. At first Morgan and Dorcha thought they had stumbled into the women's home, until they realized they were looking at a giant mirror dominating the entire wall behind them.

Morgan and Dorcha looked back at each other. Outside of the mirror, they looked like their normal selves dressed in medieval peasant garb. However, in the mirror they were Mediterranean maidens with features similar to each other, though mirror Morgan was still much taller than mirror Dorcha. Both women approached the mirror. Dorcha murmured, "It's like we're sisters." Dorcha waved her hand to see if the reflection mimicked the motion. It did. Then the scene shifted.

* * *

Morgan and Dorcha were back in the apartment like nothing had ever happened.

Dorcha shook her head, "What the fuck?"

"Remember that talent of mine you talked about before our trip to Renaissance Fair Hell?"

The screen door rattled on its frame as someone banged on it.

Morgan and Dorcha's heads both turned quickly toward the door. They were still paranoid from their recent UnderLife mob attack. Seeing each other being so jumpy tickled the hell out of Morgan and Dorcha. They dissolved into laughter.

"Well hello, ladies. What's so funny?" said a striking man entering the living room.

Morgan responded, "It'd take forever to explain, Bishop." She hugged him. "This is Dorcha. She is our Tarot card reader for the evening, and a dear old friend of mine from New Orleans."

Dorcha shook hands with Bishop, and excused herself to go to the bathroom.

In the bathroom, Dorcha felt bile begin to rise in her throat. She barely had time to lock the door and lift the toilet lid before throwing up.

It took Dorcha several minutes to recover from the UnderLife experience. Dorcha took a swig of the mouthwash on the counter. She hoped, given the circumstances, that her hosts wouldn't mind.

Dorcha re-emerged to find a line of people who wanted to get their cards read. Morgan winked at Dorcha, handed her some water, and said, "Are you okay?"

"Yeah, I think so."

"Hey, keep our adventure on the down-low. I'll explain everything later."

"No problem. I don't know how I'd begin to tell anyone anyway."

"Are you still up for giving some readings? I totally understand if you would rather just relax and hang out," suggested Morgan.

"Don't worry. I can do Tarot in my sleep. Hey, at least now I know why you have a hard time communicating what's going on with you."

"Tell me about it," Morgan said. She patted Dorcha on the shoulder. Then Morgan went to the front door to greet some guests.

Dorcha gave excellent readings for the next few hours, and was the hit of the party. Morgan proceeded to get merrily drunk. She was delighted to have another UnderLife companion. It was the first time since her experience with August that Morgan had brought someone into UnderLife with her.

* * *

Morgan and Balthazar were curled up in bed together, exhausted after a stupendous birthday bash.

"Thank you so much for being open-minded and hiring a Tarot card reader for my birthday. I know that kind of stuff makes you feel uncomfortable. It fucking blows my mind she turned out to be Dorcha LeTour! Can you believe it? What are the odds? Last time I saw Dorcha, she was a kid with an ice cream cone, getting more of it on the front of her shirt than in her mouth. Now Dorcha's all grown up and we're back in each other's lives. It's so cool."

"Dorcha tried to refuse payment. She told me that seeing you and the Victoria Shine ticket were more than enough. I insisted. Told Dorcha she worked hard all night and deserved it. I like Dorcha. A very sincere and insightful woman," Balthazar said as they dozed off.

That night Morgan dreamt she was Victoria Shine's new lover.

Morgan kept asking permission to kiss and touch Victoria. Morgan was awed when Victoria simply smiled and said "Yes." They started to make out. The scene shifted and Morgan asked Victoria again, still in disbelief that she was allowed to express affection towards Victoria. Victoria's energy felt so open and inviting.

Morgan snapped back into consciousness, drenched in a full body sweat. Morgan could taste Victoria's luscious lips against her own. The dream was so convincing that when Morgan realized she was being spooned by a hunky man, her stomach dropped with a surge of panic. Morgan thought she was cheating on Victoria with this strange man in bed with her.

My God, I've betrayed Victoria! Morgan thought. Wait, we're not...

Balthazar stirred, rolling over.

Oh, right, my boyfriend for the last few years, Morgan thought. Victoria Shine is my favorite rock star. She has no idea who I am, and she's not my new girlfriend, Morgan reminded herself.

Morgan felt guilty. She went to the bathroom to splash some water on her face and to judge herself for a bit in the mirror.

* * *

The next day Morgan took Dorcha out to lunch.

Dorcha sat enthralled while Morgan told everything. Morgan told Dorcha about the bulk of her experiences and the mechanics of how UnderLife worked. She discussed August, Louise, and her on-going chakra balancing. Morgan figured that her and Dorcha's UnderLife connection was all the vetting required to trust her.

"You're so open-minded about all of this," Morgan said after her exhausting narrative.

"Nothing like running for my life in some other dimension to alter my perspective about the nature of reality," Dorcha said. "What's Balthazar's take on all this?"

"I love Balthazar, but there are some places he doesn't want to go. All Balthazar wants is to share and enjoy an active life of intense work and pleasurable relaxation. That's what drew me to Balthazar in the first place: his physical vibrancy and versatility. Between the skydiving, hiking, basketball, and a bunch of other sports including an almost daily sexual Olympics, we have a lot of fun together."

"How did you two get together? He said it was in college but didn't elaborate."

Morgan explained the whole story.

After listening Dorcha responded, "He admires you a lot, your determination, and great attitude towards life. I know this from the cards, and from observing the two of you together. He's a charismatic guy with a lot of friends. That's something that's not easy to let go of. If you lose Balthazar, it will put a heavy strain on all of those friendships you've made together.

"True. That's something I haven't thought about." Morgan said.

"So it's safe to assume that the big secret looming in both of your readings is that you haven't told him about UnderLife?" Dorcha said.

"He'll think I'm crazy."

"Morgan, you're condemning him for not being capable of understanding something you're hiding from him. It's not fair to either of you. If you think Balthazar might break up with you when you tell him about UnderLife, that's the risk you have to take if you want to be closer to him. Balthazar thinks your narcolepsy is endearing. Your helplessness at those moments is when he feels you need him the most. Balthazar takes your detachment and secrecy to mean that he isn't essential to your life. You two won't know if there is a future in this relationship until you tell him the truth. Otherwise, the intimacy you've shared is going to continue to unravel. Give him a chance."

Morgan sighed, "You're right. I know I need to. Part of me always thought when the time was right we'd share an UnderLife adventure together."

"That's a cop out," Dorcha said.

"I don't want to hurt him. I wish I could unclench. Tell him everything. Give him the opportunity to adapt. I think I resent Balthazar a little for never coming into UnderLife with me. Well, I've seen him in UnderLife several times, but he's never aware of it. Usually he's in a trance, like a zombie. He doesn't recognize me, and afterward he never remembers anything that happened. I believe that I'm sent into UnderLife to investigate and facilitate healing when I can, both for myself and for other people. It's hard to call someone my partner if they're unable to support me in my life's work," Morgan said.

"Morgan, how can Balthazar be supportive about something he isn't even aware of?" Dorcha said.

"Why do you gotta to be like that?"

Morgan and Dorcha laughed.

* * *

August's cell phone vibrated. "Yes?"

"Hi August!" Morgan said.

Morgan's jubilant greeting was met with silence.

"Hello?" Morgan paused, uncertain if August was even there. "August?"

"Sweetie, how are you? How was your birthday?"

"Amazing! Balthazar got me front row tickets to the Victoria Shine concert! I'm so excited! I wish you could have come to the party."

"Me too," August said. "I have a present for you."

"Thank you, that's so sweet." Morgan took a breath, "August, I passed out again at my temp job and got fired. Balthazar is going to be pissed. He hates it when I'm not working. I don't know what to do. I've exhausted all of my dumb job options in town and I need some advice. I'm running out of money, and I've grown comfortable with a certain lifestyle that I don't want to sacrifice."

"I might be able to help you out. There's a counseling job coming up which would be perfect for you, if you're interested."

"Hell yeah! Who would I be working with?"

"I'll get into that later. How are things with Balthazar?" August said.

"I want to tell him about the UnderLife."

"What changed your mind?"

"Balthazar knows something is up and it's making him anxious. He's worried I might be cheating on him. Balthazar even got a Tarot card reading, he was so worked up. Funny thing is Balthazar liked it so much that he hired the reader to work my party. You'll never believe who the Tarot reader was."

"Who?"

"Dorcha LeTour," Morgan said.

"Wait, Remy and Marin's daughter? That Dorcha LeTour?"

"The one and only. I'm amazed we found each other again, but it's true, and I have Balthazar to thank. Isn't it a crazy coincidence that Balthazar hired my long-lost childhood friend? What are the odds?" Morgan said.

"Astronomical, but I stopped believing in coincidences a long time ago," August said.

"What's that supposed to mean? Why do you make it sound sinister?"

"I'll explain later. I think it's wonderful you two reconnected. You're destined to be friends. Unfortunately, I'm in the middle of something right now and have to go."

"Wait, there's more!" Morgan said.

"What is it?"

"Dorcha came into UnderLife with me. We…"

"She did?" August said. "Bring her in with you for your next balancing session."

"What are you doing?" Morgan said.

"Take care, we'll speak soon."

August hung up. Morgan snarled in frustration.

CHAPTER NINE
ASSASSIN

United States Army Ranger Captain Taylor Tess had been awake for fifty-seven hours and it was taking its toll. Captain Tess was on one of the remote Sabalana Islands in Indonesia. The island was home to Malik Aban, a local gangster who had built up a reputation for cruelty and secrecy, and for his obsession with wealth. The CIA had given Captain Tess the task of killing Aban in a black op.

There were too many sticky political issues involved for the mission to become public knowledge. The United States government wanted something important from the Aban gang's chief rival, the Jemaah Islamiyah, a well-known terrorist organization. To get it would require eliminating their chief competition.

Captain Tess didn't know the details of why they sent a top notch American commando to do the dirty work, but he wasn't trained to care about the whys of his job. Duty demanded him to follow orders. Captain Tess's ability to focus on the mission determined whether he would succeed, or even survive.

Malid Aban was forty-seven years old, and he had been involved in every criminal activity imaginable. Aban peddled in the human flesh trade which offered every kind of deviant sex possible, including pedophilia, bestiality, and all-out slavery. Nothing was too taboo for Aban as long as enough profit could be gained. Every sin was on the menu: drugs, piracy, weapons dealing, bootlegging, organ harvesting, maiming, torture and murder.

Captain Tess had no qualms about killing Aban. On the contrary, Captain Tess felt that Aban's karma had brought him there. Captain Tess saw the mission as a cosmic mandate to balance the scales of justice by eliminating this terrible excuse for a human being.

Captain Tess had been hiding for thirty-six hours within a tall bed of reeds on the back edge of Aban's compound, submerged in three feet of water. Despite being entrenched next to a nest of cutthroats, Taylor managed to catch some sleep while at his post.

Captain Tess slipped into a vivid dream. He was locked in a loving embrace with the lovely and supple Bao Hé, a Chinese intelligence agent he'd encountered over the years. It was wonderful, everything Captain Tess imagined it would be. He never felt such peace in another person's arms. Captain Tess worried about holding Bao for too long, so he slackened his grip to let her disengage, but Bao only hugged Captain Tess tighter, which he adored. Only then Taylor realized they were hovering at least a foot off of the ground.

The miniature communications device in Captain Tess's ear beeped him back to consciousness. The audio code transmitted to him was connected to a motion sensor alarm Captain Tess had installed at the perimeter gates to the compound.

Captain Tess blocked fatigue from his mind. His predatory senses went on high alert. The target was arriving. Often Aban would dock at another part of the island and drive in. This kept Aban's entrances and exits in a random pattern.

The United States government had funded and trained the Special Forces counterterrorism branch of the Indonesian National Police, Delta Eighty-Eight. There were several agents working in this division who were acting as the eyes and ears of the CIA in this part of the world. Delta Eighty-Eight was given the task of providing a diversion for Captain Tess by engaging Aban's forces off-shore, a few miles away from the compound.

Captain Tess re-positioned himself towards the back of the estate. He watched the house come to life as servants and guards scrambled to attention, ready to fulfill their master's every desire.

Captain Tess cast an I Ching reading with three tarnished Taiwanese dollar coins while watching his prey settle in. He flipped the three coins six times and calculated the I Ching results in his head. Hexagram Twenty-Three going into Hexagram Eight: Splitting Apart into Union. Captain Tess had studied the I Ching for the last five years. He had memorized entire passages from books containing commentators on the I Ching hexagrams. This was a favorable reading, marking an excellent time to challenge a criminal organization by removing its leader. Captain Tess needed to keep a level head, execute the plan, and follow his exit strategy.

After dinner Aban retired to his quarters. He sat on his private balcony and made a couple of phone calls while drinking a night cap.

Captain Tess turned on the night vision scope attached to his Mk12 Mod 1 Special Purpose Rifle. He flipped up the front sight, and zeroed in on his target.

Captain Tess hit the time delay trigger on his escape route explosion package. "5…" Captain Tess looked through the scope. "4…" He flicked the safety off of the gun. "3…" Captain Tess marked Aban in the crosshairs. He inhaled… "2…" And exhaled while squeezing the trigger, BOOM! The bullet hit Malik Aban in his right temple, and blew out the back of his skull. Then the explosives started to go off around the compound. Malik Aban was dead before his body slumped off his chair and hit the balcony floor.

Pandemonium ensued. Gut wrenching booms continued to echo throughout the compound. Machine gun fire rattled. Aban's security detail believed that they were being attacked by a sizeable force. Guards shot at the decoy guns Taylor had set up on the other side of the compound.

Once Aban's body was discovered, the chaos intensified as Aban's cutthroat lieutenants started to turn on each other. In the confusion, Captain Tess slipped away. He made it to his extraction point, and was transported to a CIA safe house.

After his debriefing, Captain Tess was commanded to return to the United States for his next mission. When he got into the military plane, there was a laptop waiting for him in his seat.

After the plane took off, Captain Tess opened up the computer. He put his right ring finger on the small scanner. Next he was prompted for a password, which he punched in. Captain Tess's next assignment came on the screen. It included a photograph of Morgan Martel.

* * *

Morgan brought Dorcha to her next meeting at the Skyscraper Space. August and Louise were waiting for them. In the northeast corner, next to the telescope, they had installed a square varnished redwood table with four matching chairs.

After warm introductions, Louise guided everyone to the northwest living room area.

Morgan and Dorcha recounted their unexpected adventure during Morgan's birthday. August took notes.

"That UnderLife episode displayed that you two are an effective team. The images of each other in the mirror, and the medieval setting were no accident. I believe you were sisters in a distant past life on the other side of the world," Louise said.

August spoke up, "Dorcha, I'm impressed you had the presence of mind to pick up on the Roman numeral hiding place. How was the UnderLife experience for you?"

"Fucking scary," Dorcha said.

Everyone laughed at Dorcha's reply.

August asked, "When did you start reading Tarot? What drew you to it?"

"My mom had a Cosmic Tribe Tarot set at our place in Berkeley. I started playing with Tarot in junior high school. I found that they provided honest counsel, and that it was fun to learn the meaning of the cards and to be able to find an answer to any question. It gave my teenage angst perspective. I've got a question for you as well. How do I know we can trust you?" Dorcha said.

"I assume you brought your trusted advisors, Dorcha. Ask them if we are honorable," Louise said.

"You want me to ask the Tarot if you guys are cool?"

"Indeed," August said. "We set up a table for your readings when we heard you were joining us."

They relocated to the redwood table. Dorcha opened up her black leather backpack. She pulled out her journal, a pen, her Druid Craft, Faeries' Oracle, and Lover's Path Tarot.

Here was Dorcha's reading:

Position 1 represents **what kind of business Louise and August are in**:
> Druid: 5 of Wands
> Faeries: #45 – Taitin the Slyph
> Lovers: 3 of Pentacles @

Position 2 represents **how do they fund their day-to-day operations? Where is the $ coming from**:
> Druid: 2 of Pentacles @
> Faeires: #35 – The Faun
> Lovers: #11 - Justice

Position 3 represents **their intentions towards Morgan**:
> Druid: 8 of Wands @
> Faeries: #7 - The Singer of Intuition @
> Lovers: 10 of Staves

Position 4 represents **their intentions with me**:
> Druid: 6 of Cups
> Faeries: #43 – Geeeeeooo the Slooow @
> Lovers: Ace of Pentacles

Position 5 represents **something they haven't told us about the overall picture**:
> Druid: 5 of Swords @
> Faeries: #63 – Indi @
> Lovers: 8 of Cups

Position 6 represents **their purpose for working with Morgan**:
> Druid: Queen of Swords

Faeries: #2 – Ekstasis
Lovers: 7 of Arrows
Position 7 represents **advice for Dorcha regarding August and Louise**:
Druid: Princess of Swords @
Faeries: #5 – She of the Cruach
Lovers: 2 of Arrows @

Dorcha considered the cards while the other three women looked on.

Finally Dorcha spoke, "Everything checks out. Your intentions are honorable. Morgan, under their tutelage you will learn how to defend yourself, and how to keep your joy and your mind free from threats. The intention is to help you sharpen your intuition. You're being trained to be more capable at handling whatever arises in UnderLife. Overall, things seem to be in a planning or research stage. There's a transition happening here. I'm still not sure where the money is coming from. Its source has something to do with taking responsibility, using natural magic, and administering justice."

"What about you?" Louise said. "Where do you fit in with us?"

"You can help me to become less detached, and more receptive to pleasures of the material realm."

"Is this a path you would be interested in following?" Louise said.

"It's something I'd like to consider," Dorcha said.

"By all means, take all the time you need. Now, if you'll excuse us, we need privacy at this stage of Morgan's balancing. August will give you a ride home. Thank you for meeting with us. I hope we can speak further in the future."

"Yes, I'd enjoy that," Dorcha said.

While Dorcha gathered her cards together, August retrieved a rectangular package hiding behind one of the steamer trunks.

"Happy Birthday, Morgan. We hope this is something you'll find useful," August said.

Morgan tore into the present. It was a leather bound collection of astrological reports that Louise had written for Morgan.

"How thrilling, a hundred pages about me, my favorite subject," Morgan said, leafing through the detailed tome. "Thank you, this is so cool."

"What an awesome gift, Morgan," Dorcha said.

Hugs were exchanged all around. August and Dorcha left.

Louise got right down to business. "I am satisfied that we have cleared the Crown chakra. Now we're going to be focusing on the Brow chakra. It's called Ajna in Sanskrit. It is the chakra of the mind, dreams, and psychic channels. Its corresponding stone is green moss agate. It's an excellent crystal for healing and cleansing, and it will aid in your recovery when UnderLife adventures go awry. Remember to be gentle with yourself while going through the balancing process. Be careful, there is a considerable amount of energy moving around you. It'd be easy to daydream and hurt yourself accidentally."

"Will do," Morgan said.

During the meditation, Morgan received another vision. She saw a long oval shaped room. In the center was a circular couch sunk into the floor. The surrounding walls were covered with doors. There were at least twenty of them. No door was the same. They were doors made of various materials, with different styles of design. A few didn't seem to have any locks or handles. Morgan opened one of the doors, which was made of rough, unfinished wood, and had a brass handle. She stepped through without hesitation. She found herself standing on a rooftop in San Francisco, with the sun blazing overhead, and a cool ocean wind caressing her skin.

* * *

That night in bed, Morgan was startled from her slumber by an awful nightmare.

It was the end of the school year. Morgan had enrolled in a science class that she had attended the first day and then forgot about.

Now Morgan was expected to take the final. Morgan had done zero studying. Her own negligence was causing Morgan massive anxiety.

The dream shifted and Morgan felt someone or something lurking near her. Whatever it was harbored malicious intent towards her, but Morgan's vision was too blurry to see it.

Morgan got ready in a hurry to leave wherever she was, but she didn't leave. Worry gnawed on Morgan's consciousness. She had forgotten something important. Morgan felt stuck in a maddening loop of prep and prelude, without getting to the next step.

CHAPTER TEN
ASTRONEWS

Dorcha awoke to an avian orchestra located in the venerable elm trees nestled next to her apartment building. The feathery musicians cleared their pipes with a few twerps and twitters before launching into a full chirping song. The heavy black curtains in Dorcha's bedroom were framed by sunlight.

Dorcha's cat Primo laid curled up at her legs. Primo rolled over, exposing his soft belly, achieving new levels of furry cuteness. Dorcha scratched him behind the ears. Primo nuzzled her hand. A sigh turned into a yawn. Dorcha got out of bed and put slippers on and a house coat to stave off morning chill.

After using the bathroom, Dorcha went back to her bedroom and did twenty minutes of yoga. It got her blood flowing and woke her body up. Dorcha promised herself to hike tomorrow.

Dorcha cruised into the kitchen and made a couple pieces of toast. After buttering them, Dorcha put strawberry jam on one and cinnamon on the other. She brewed a cup of Earl Grey tea and added milk and Splenda. Dorcha felt a dark glee upon hearing the hiss the artificial sweetener made when it hit the liquid's surface. It better not come out that this stuff is harmful, Dorcha mused, or else I'm done for.

While she was in the kitchen, Dorcha checked her cell phone resting on its charger. Dorcha noticed a text from Morgan which read, "Open your front door."

Dorcha opened the front door. There was a small box leaning against the door. On the box there was a note written by Morgan and signed by Morgan and Balthazar saying, "Something we thought you might enjoy. It reminds me of our birthplace."

Dorcha took the box back into the kitchen. She opened it while munching on the first course of her breakfast. Morgan and Balthazar had given her an Italian-made Gothic Vampire Tarot deck. Dorcha was thrilled. What a perfect gift, she thought.

Dorcha finished her toast with big bites, and then settled down at her desk. Dorcha's perch overlooked the street from her second story apartment. She cracked the window a bit, loving the crisp, fresh air and cool morning light. The only activity on the street was a paperboy in a station wagon going about his daily route.

Dorcha put on her iPod, so as not to disturb any neighbors still asleep. Then Dorcha got started with what she termed the Morning Staff Meeting.

Years ago, Dorcha's mother had had this desk built for her when it became clear Tarot cards were not a passing fancy, but that Dorcha had a real gift. Marin designed the modifications to the desk specifically for Dorcha's purposes.

On the left side of the desk, underneath the wooden surface, there were ten small drawers, in two columns of five drawers each. Each drawer was five inches wide by seven inches deep by two inches vertical. This offered Dorcha a discreet and convenient place to store her cards. The drawers were lined with black satin, to protect the cards from outside energetic influences. The desk made of polished dark cherry mahogany wood, which gave it a witchy, mysterious feeling.

Dorcha took the plastic off of the Vampire deck. The cards were glossy and clean, ready to be broken in by Dorcha's well-practiced hands. Dorcha spread out the cards, with their sultry, bloody images. Then, on an impulse, she stacked the cards back up, deciding to let their individual introductions happen during reading sessions.

The cards came with a small book which had been translated into five languages. It gave brief, vampire-themed descriptions of each card. Rider-Waite format: 22 Major Arcana cards, representing life lesson archetypes, and 56 Minor Arcana cards. The Minor Arcana cards, like a decks of regular playing cards, were split into four suits representing the four elements: Swords (spades) representing air, Wands (clubs) representing fire, Pentacles (diamonds) representing earth, and Cups (hearts) representing water. Each suit of the Minor Arcana had ten cards, numbered one through ten, plus four more court cards; King, Queen, Knight (or Prince), and Knave (or Princess).

It excited Dorcha to have a new addition to her Tarot team. Dorcha pulled out her three other decks. She shuffled the first deck, Druid Craft, and laid out the first spread of the day. Dorcha repeated the routine with each deck, layering them on each other. Dorcha recorded the results in her journal.

Position 1 represents **Dorcha's current situation**:
        Druid: Princess of Cups
        Faeries: #60 – The Pook
        Lovers: #15 – Temptation @
        Vampires: #19 – The Truth
Position 2 represents **advice for Dorcha**:
        Druid: Ace of Swords
        Faeries: #3 – The Guardian at the Gate @
        Lovers: #7 – Desire
        Vampires: Knave of Swords
Position 3 represents **Dorcha's near future**:
        Druid: 2 of Wands
        Faeries: #20 – The Dark Lady
        Lovers: 6 of Pentacles @
        Vampires: Knight of Swords

Dorcha knew that the reading was talking about her attraction to Balthazar. Of course Balthazar was unavailable, but this fact hadn't deterred the attraction. Maybe it had even enflamed it. Dorcha knew she wasn't going to do anything about it, nothing underhanded anyway. Morgan was lucky to have found him. Despite the plaintive mewlings of Dorcha's own sabotaging Ego, she felt happy for Morgan.

To satisfy her curiosity, Dorcha did a relationship spread on Bishop, the attractive guy Dorcha had met at Morgan's birthday party. Bishop had never had a reading before the other night. At first he had been reluctant, but his attitude changed when Dorcha started telling him about things in his life that there was no way she could have known about. Bishop was one of Balthazar's college buddies. During their brief time together, Dorcha had felt a spark of interest from him.

Position 1 represents **how Dorcha sees Bishop**:
        Druid: #17 – The Star
        Faeries: #28 – Penelope Dreamweaver
        Lovers: Prince of Cups @
        Vampires: 5 of Swords
Position 2 represents **how Bishop sees Dorcha**:
        Druid: #13 - Death
        Faeries: #8 – The Singer of Courage
        Lovers: Princess of Staves
        Vampires: 5 of Wands
Position 3 represents **Dorcha's focal point in the relationship**:
        Druid: 10 of Swords @
        Faeries: #44 – Lys of the Shadows

Lovers: 8 of Arrows @
Vampires: King of Wands

Position 4 represents **Bishop's focal point in the relationship**:
Druid: 8 of Pentacles
Faeries: #54 – Epona's Wild Daughter
Lovers: #21 – Triumph
Vampires: King of Pentacles

Position 5 represents **where the relationship is now**:
Druid: #18 - The Moon
Faeries: #10 – The Singer of Healing
Lovers: #13 – Transformation
Vampires: King of Chalices

Position 6 represents **where Dorcha wants the relationship to go**:
Druid: Ace of Wands @
Faeries: #56 – Gloominous Doom @
Lovers: 2 of Pentacles
Vampires: Queen of Chalices

Position 7 represents **where Bishop wants to relationship to go**:
Druid: Prince of Pentacles @
Faeries: #29 – Ta'Om the Poet @
Lovers: Prince of Arrows @
Vampires: 8 of Wands

Position 8 represents **something to consider in the relationship**:
Druid: #14 - Fferyllt
Faeries: #17 - Himself
Lovers: #0 – Innocence
Vampires: #3 - Passion

Position 9 represents **the overall lesson each of you are learning in the relationship right now**:
Druid: 6 of Pentacles @
Faeries: #60 – The Pook
Lovers: 8 of Pentacles
Vampires: Knight of Swords

What a surprising result, Dorcha thought. Well, maybe not as much as she would want to believe. The situation held decent romantic potential, but Dorcha knew she definitely had her own head up her ass. She would need a shift in her attitude for there to be any shot of this getting off the ground. Dorcha remembered giving Bishop her card. If he was interested and courageous enough, he'd call her. Dorcha needed to keep an open mind about the situation. It took humility to be receptive.

Next Dorcha decided to do a reading on August and Louise. Their benevolent natures and nurturing ambitions seemed too good to be true.

A Seven Questions Spread using Druid Craft, Faeries Oracle, Lover's Path, and Vampires Tarot.

Position 1 represents **Louise**:
>Druid: 2 of Wands @
>Faeries: #22 - The Master Maker @
>Lovers: #12 – Sacrifice
>Vampires: 10 of Swords

Position 2 represents **August**:
>Druid: #16 – The Tower @
>Faeries: #9 – The Song of Initiation
>Lovers: #3 – Fertility
>Vampires: #9 - Daytime

Position 3 represents **what Louise and August want from Morgan**:
>Druid: #19 – The Sun
>Faeries: #65 – The Fee Lion
>Lovers: 5 of Cups @
>Vampires: #10 - Fate

Position 4 represents **what Louise and August want from me**:
>Druid: Prince of Swords @
>Faeries: #14 – The Maiden @
>Lovers: 7 of Arrows
>Vampires: 8 of Wands

Position 5 represents **Louise and August's primary goal**:
>Druid: Princess of Swords @
>Faeries: #32 – Iris of the Rainbows
>Lovers: 2 of Arrows @
>Vampires: 6 of Swords

Position 6 represents **how Louise and August see my ability**:
>Druid: 10 of Pentacles
>Faeries: #39 – Losgunna
>Lovers: 4 of Staves
>Vampires: 8 of Pentacles

Position 7 represents **my best action with Louise and August**:
>Druid: Ace of Swords @
>Faeries: #51 – The Topsie-Turvets
>Lovers: 10 of Staves
>Vampires: 7 of Pentacles

It fascinated Dorcha how the Tarot always offered her a unique perspective. August and Louise were hard to read in person, but the cards told a different story. August struggled with the demands of her work and of her isolation. Louise took the long view, dealing with momentary sacrifices for the greater good. Dorcha couldn't get a bead on their overall goal, except that it was positive and it was some kind of ushering through the unknown.

Dorcha knew that Louise and August respected her Tarot abilities. She found it compelling that Louise and August wanted her to challenge them, to use her gift to determine if they were trustworthy. Their fearlessness to be examined inspired confidence in Dorcha. Dorcha wanted to interact with them further, and was glad that Morgan had introduced them to her.

Dorcha did a few more Tarot spreads and listened to a few more songs. Then she realized that in all her excitement about her new deck, she had forgotten that the latest AstroNews show was probably on-line already. Dorcha put her Mac laptop on the desk, still leaving room for her cards, so she could continue fondling the decks while watching the show. Sometimes Dorcha paused AstroNews for a minute to focus on a finished spread, writing it down in her Tarot Journal.

* * *

"Hello everyone, I'm Kyle Vihzor. Welcome to AstroNews."

The AstroNews animated opening sequence began. It started with a gigantic map of the solar system with the planets spinning at high speed in their orbits around the sun. The planets would periodically freeze and lines would connect them, revealing giant triangles and squares created by the planetary positions.

A close-up of Earth filled the screen, which zoomed towards Hollywood. A cartoon version of Kyle appeared with a crown on his head. Then he morphed into a lion still wearing the crown, and bellowed out a robust roar.

The screen widened, and the full moon sped from the horizon into the sky overhead. A beam of moonlight enveloped the lion, transforming him into a human-sized set of old-fashioned golden scales of balance.

The scales shrunk to the size of a fist and floated in mid-air. The animated Kyle reappeared, and the shrunken scales were absorbed into his chest.

Kyle approached a giant wardrobe with the astrological symbols carved into it. Kyle touched the Aries symbol which resembled ram's horns. The closet burst open and a furry costume on a hanger flew out.

The costume enveloped Kyle, and he changed into a ram. His hooves pawed the ground and he charged into the camera. There was the sound of breaking glass, and then the 'AstroNews' title dominated the frame.

The camera cut to real-life Kyle. "In case this is your first time tuning in, I am a Leo, Moon in Libra, Aries rising. Leo is the sign of love, entertainment, and royalty."

"Yes, he's our little prince," said a voice off-screen. The camera switched to a master shot, which revealed Darian Vihzor, star of Love In Motion, sitting in the guest chair opposite from her brother.

"Little? Look at these guns!" Kyle took off his suit jacket, revealing his sleeveless dress shirt. Kyle was not exaggerating. His arms were muscular, defined by countless hours at the gym.

"See, Jill, I told you I could get him to show off his guns!" Darian yelled.

Jill Vihzor, Kyle's youngest sister and the show's sound operator, walked into frame, with her boom mike in one hand and five dollars in the other. She handed the five to Darian and said, "That didn't even take five minutes." Then Jill walked back off-screen to her mark.

A voice came over the God mike. The voice belonged to Vespa Vihzor, Kyle's oldest sister and the show's producer. Vespa did her best to sound stern, "Put them away, Kyle."

Kyle mock huffed, "The lights are hot. I need this shirt so I don't sweat everywhere. What can I say? I'm a virile man."

Kyle Vihzor cleared his throat and began the top story.

"The astrological sign of the day is Scorpio. Scorpio's main mascot is the scorpion, of course, but they have two other mascots as well: the eagle and the phoenix. Scorpio rules sex, death, inheritances, the occult, and taxes. Being a fixed water sign, there is a set pattern to Scorpio expression. Scorpios are often mistaken for Earth signs because of this. However, don't be fooled, they are intensely emotional creatures. Scorpio drives and desires can be overwhelming if Scorpios are not taught to express themselves through positive channels. Many self-destructive habits may develop. Handle with respect and caution. They have an uncanny instinct for revenge.

Kyle continued, "You can tell there is an imbalance with a Scorpio if they are unnecessarily mysterious about trivial things, such as their age, middle name, or astrological sign. As with their watery peers Cancer and Pisces, there is, of course, a danger of being separated from their emotional lives. Sometimes, in order to cope, they try to cut off their intense feelings, or at least to dull them with escapism. This can be very difficult if the water sign person grew up in an environment where it was not permitted to communicate their feelings.

"Scorpios release energy in a geyser-like fashion, because of their tendency to let things fester until they explode forth. The blast can be perilous if you are close to the focal point. The fissure of frothy feelings seethes with searing steam. Like their animal counterparts, Scorpios possess a poisonous stinger capable of striking at any moment, especially in the name of vengeance.

"Please be careful interacting with their powerful energy, because it can melt your face off. On the other hand, if properly administered, this same poison facilitates transformation. This molting can revolutionize an individual who survives the dangerous blast."

* * *

Enchanted by the young astrologer, Dorcha practically drooled on her keyboard. Kyle had won Dorcha's affections with his lengthy blogs on the practicality of astrology. Dorcha never missed an episode of The Vihzors' monthly show. I was easy to tell that Kyle welcomed the love that had been lavished upon him his whole life. Kyle's genuine self-confidence bordered on arrogance, and he acted like a mischievous scamp.

Dorcha's lustful reverie for Kyle halted when she noticed the time. Only twenty minutes before work! The rest of the AstroNews episode would have to wait.

Why do I always act like taking a shower is going to turn back time? Dorcha mused.

The shift at the café was a monotonous eight-hour blur of mixing coffee drinks and making sandwiches. Dorcha prayed for a more compelling source of income.

After work Dorcha went grocery shopping, came home, fed Primo, got some water, busted out the cards, sparked a bowl, and went on-line to finish watching AstroNews.

An e-mail was waiting from Morgan asking if Dorcha had watched the AstroNews episode yet, and to call after.

* * *

"Want to go to a rock concert and sail into an ecstatic spiritual experience? Go see Victoria Shine! We're giving away two tickets to a lucky top scorer on our on-line Victoria Shine trivia quiz. Go to kylevihzor.com for details.

Kyle continued, "Speaking of Scorpios, we're going to have later in the show, two very special guests: My very own movie star sister Darian Vihzor and rock star actress Victoria Shine from the hit television show Love In Motion."

Vespa switched cameras. Kyle adjusted his position to give the viewer a visual break for the next segment.

"When speaking with people who know little to nothing about astrology, after we cover a few basics about their Sun signs, the next thing I'm usually asked is, what other signs am I compatible with? Based on Sun signs alone, it is difficult to make anything more than sweeping generalizations. Today we're going to explore one of the major elements in natal birth chart compatibility; the Sun/Moon conjunction.

"Your Sun sign is the dominant force in your personality. If you were a computer, it'd be your operating system. If you were a shoe it could be the difference between a sneaker and a stiletto heel, for personality typing purposes. The twelve signs have separate key traits which are the fundamental building blocks of the personality. Whether the trait becomes positive or negative depends on the choices and circumstances of the person in question.

"Taurus, Scorpio's opposite, is the other side of the energy coin. Taurus rules material possessions and money. At its best, this energy helps fuel the drive for a young Taurus to take care of themselves financially. They learn to provide, gently, for themselves and their loved ones, as fertile soil supports an abundant farm. At its worst there can be a disgusting materialism and an anxiety ridden and childish attachment to the trappings of wealth."

Next to Kyle in the corner of the screen and animated bull appeared hugging a big pile of money.

"Your moon sign rules your emotional life. The moon changes signs approximately every two and a half days. That's why they say, "changeable as the moon." There is also a past life connection with your moon sign. It's the lesson you're coming from. This lingering energy influences how you experience your feelings.

"In astrology it's easy to do a reading on a relationship through the use of composite charts. When you overlay two natal birth charts, you can see a third entity, which is the relationship itself. Some combinations are much more stable than others.

"Another interesting astrological phenomenon to take a look at is the Sun/Moon conjunction. This happens in a relationship when one partner's sun sign matches the other's moon sign. When a Sun/Moon conjunction occurs in a composite chart, it means that how one person's personality operates matches how the other person's emotions work. This karmic resonance gives a sense of comfort to each party, the feeling of being seen and understood for who they really are. In his research on synchronicity, Carl Jung found that the incidences of Sun/Moon conjunctions in marriage was so high that it was statistically significant. This showed that there was no way it could have happened by chance.

"All the more reason to explore the entire chart of someone who catches your interest. Don't just find out their Sun sign.

"And now to introduce my dear darling sister for one of my favorite segments, Secrets from a Scorpio, with Darian Vihzor:"

The camera cut to Darian dressed in a revealing red silk blouse and tight black skirt. Darian shot an alluring gaze into the lens and began, "Thank you Kyle. Today I want to shed some insight on the feminine mystique in regards to conflict management.

"Never forget that women have the ability to incubate their anger. A small ember of spite can be nurtured into a vitriolic tirade, set to be unleashed at will with volcanic proportions.

"Let's say, hypothetically, I'm dating a man who lacks a certain amount of tact and decorum. We'll call him Biff. Due to a gaping flaw in Biff's character, he doesn't think monogamy is an assumed arrangement between us after six months of steady dating. This so-called exclusive notion that Biff talks about never mentions the other women he's seeing.

"You can imagine my surprise, in this random example I'm throwing out here, when we're out to dinner one evening and are approached by an attractive lady who was shocked to see Biff out on a date.

"After Biff stammered a weak introduction, promising to call her later, the intruding female retreated. Through it all, I smiled calmly, and he thought that meant everything was alright. Yet what was really going through my mind was, Oh we're going to be fighting about THIS later.

"What made my lips curl into a savage grin was the sick fantasy of cutting his balls off and stuffing them into his mouth. Let him suck on them for once."

The camera cut back to a wide-eyed Kyle, who gulped and said, "Thank you Darian, very disturbing."

* * *

Dorcha hit the pause button on her computer. Her protesting stomach was insisting on eating. Primo followed her into the kitchen and rubbed against Dorcha's leg until she gave him kitty treats.

Thoughts of Darian Vihzor roved around Dorcha's mind while she made a burrito for dinner. Dorcha loved how Darian appeared regularly on her younger brother's astrology show.

Darian Vihzor was an effortlessly beautiful woman who was seemingly unaware of her power. Close proximity to Darian soothed and exhilarated. Darian Vihzor was a woman you wanted to have on your team, any team. Dorcha had seen every movie and TV show that Darian had been in since they both were kids. After all these years Darian felt like an old friend, despite the fact that Darian had no idea who Dorcha was.

Dorcha observed that as Darian grew older and more aware of her gifts, she was developing the unique talent of a master charmer. This wonderful effect also occurred through the camera lens, making everyone involved with Dorcha's romantic comedies a fortune.

Dorcha took a music break while her burrito was baking in the oven.

Dorcha did her favorite relationship spread on Morgan, for purely platonic purposes. Between their core past life witch UnderLife experience, and Dorcha's unbidden attraction towards her handsome boyfriend, Dorcha thought it wise to gain some perspective and wisdom in regards to her old friend.

The Relationship Spread using Druid Craft, Faeries Oracle, Lover's Path, and Vampires Tarot.

Position 1 represents **how Dorcha sees Morgan**:
    Druid: Princess of Cups @
    Faeries: #58 – Ffaff the Ffooter
    Lovers: 9 of Swords
    Vampires: Queen of Pentacles

Position 2 represents **how Morgan sees Dorcha**:
    Druid: Queen of Pentacles
    Faeries: #3 – The Guardian at the Gate
    Lovers: #6 - Love
    Vampires: 9 of Pentacles

Position 3 represents **Dorcha's focal point in the relationship:**
    Druid: #8 - Strength
    Faeries: #36 – Spirit Dancer
    Lovers: 6 of Arrows
    Vampires: #16 – The Grave

Position 4 represents **Morgan's focal point in the relationship:**
    Druid: 8 of Pentacles @
    Faeries: #14 – The Maiden @
    Lovers: 10 of Arrows
    Vampires: 4 of Swords

Position 5 represents **where the relationship is now:**
    Druid: Prince of Wands
    Faeries: #6 – The Singer of Connection @
    Lovers: Ace of Cups @
    Vampires: 10 of Swords

Position 6 represents **where Dorcha wants the relationship to go:**
    Druid: 3 of Wands @
    Faeries: #11 – The Singer of Transfiguration
    Lovers: 10 of Staves @
    Vampires: 9 of Cups

Position 7 represents **where Morgan wants to relationship to go:**
    Druid: #18 – The Moon @
    Faeries: #10 – The Singer of Healing @
    Lovers: King of Cups @

Vampires: #19 – The Truth
Position 8 represents **something to consider in the relationship**:
    Druid: 10 of Cups @
    Faeries: #64 – Gawtcha @
    Lovers: #3 - Fertility
    Vampires: 4 of Pentacles
Position 9 represents **the overall lesson each of you are learning in the relationship right now**:
    Druid: #6 – The Lovers
    Faeries: #16 – The Bright Mother
    Lovers: Princess of Cups @
    Vampires: 5 of Pentacles

It looked as though their rare talents and their need to be understood were going to bring them much closer together.

According to the cards, Morgan harbored an attraction to Dorcha, which startled the Tarot reader. Dorcha hadn't picked up on that at all. Morgan always just seemed friendly and enthusiastic towards her.

There was a certain fluidity and flexibility in Morgan's sexuality which Dorcha did not share. Dorcha had a hard enough time letting down her guard around men. It caused Dorcha great anxiety even to think about being physically intimate with a woman. Luckily, it looked as though Morgan's interest came from her excitement about Dorcha, and not from a wish to start up a romance with her. Dorcha was pretty sure that over time the character of Morgan's feelings would change, and that they would develop an enduring and nourishing friendship.

A Seven Questions Spread using Druid Craft, Faeries Oracle, Lover's Path, and Vampires Tarot.

Position 1 represents **the karmic reason Morgan and I were reunited**:
    Druid: Queen of Pentacles @
    Faeries: #39 – Losgunna @
    Lovers: Ace of Arrows @
    Vampires: 4 of Wands
Position 2 represents **an explanation for our sister witch persecution in UnderLife**:
    Druid: 7 of Pentacles @
    Faeries: #22 – The Master Maker
    Lovers: 6 of Cups
    Vampires: 6 of Pentalces
Position 3 represents **how I can help Morgan with her UnderLife ability**:

Druid: #14 – The Fferyllt @
Faeries: #36 – Spirit Dancer @
Lovers: 2 of Cups
Vampires: Queen of Pentacles

Position 4 represents **how Morgan will help me with my Tarot ability**:
Druid: King of Swords
Faeries: #14 – The Maiden
Lovers: Ace of Cups
Vampires: #2 - Temptation

Position 5 represents **our current mission and life lesson**:
Druid: #15 – Cernunnos @
Faeries: #7 – The Singer of Intuition
Lovers: 10 of Staves
Vampires: Knight of Pentacles

Position 6 represents **how do I to turn reading Tarot into a full time job?**
Druid: #16 - The Tower @
Faeries: #5 – She of the Cruach
Lovers: King of Cups
Vampires: #11 - Power

Position 7 represents **the near future with Morgan and me**:
Druid: #8 – Strength @
Faeries: #53 - Death @
Lovers: #6 – Love @
Vampires: #0 - Innocence

It was clear to Dorcha that she and Morgan had reunited for a cosmic reason. It was to keep each other in check about the important things in life, so they didn't stagnate or depart from their paths.

The current mission was about cultivating their intuition. By enhancing their psychic sensitivity, they would avoid Ego-generated destructive behavior. The reason they had successfully navigated their UnderLife adventure was because they were humble enough to work together.

Their friendship would provide a tremendous boost to their talents. Dorcha would keep Morgan from getting too self-absorbed and unbalanced by her passionate nature.

In Dorcha's Tarot pursuits, Morgan was a joyous collaborator with a discerning intellect. She offered Dorcha the perfect companion to discuss, dissect, and experience a deeper understanding of the archetypal energies which flow through life. Perhaps, Dorcha thought, future UnderLife adventures would help with this as well.

Dorcha's near future with Morgan looked a bit stressful. The cards knew Dorcha wouldn't admit to her attraction to Balthazar any time soon. Dorcha felt a little ashamed about this, especially after what had gone down between her and Morgan's parents. Until the lust went away, or Dorcha admitted to her attraction, it would be a snag in her relationship with Morgan.

The cards told Dorcha that it might take some time before reading Tarot would become a full-time career for her, but to stay patient and receptive, because it would happen eventually. Right now, focusing on the decks full time would be too overwhelming. Dorcha knew that, as a Capricorn, patience was her ally.

While recording the Tarot spread in her journal, Dorcha caught a whiff of her burrito baking. Time to eat. Dorcha heard escaped cheese sizzling on the metal cookie sheet.

* * *

Kyle: "Next up, our Predictive Astrology segment. I hope the powers that be in Hollywood hear me when I say that Aries women make fantastic leads for action television shows. Let's look at some examples: Jennifer Garner in Alias, Claire Danes in Homeland, Maisie Williams in Game of Thrones, Katee Sackhoff and Tricia Helfer in Battlestar Galactica, Lucy Lawless in Xena: Warrior Princess, Spartacus: Blood and Sand and Porn, and Spartacus: Gods of the Arena and Porn. Lawless was also heavily featured in Battlestar Galactica. Then there is Sarah Michelle Gellar in Buffy the Vampire Slayer and Sarah Jessica Parker in Sex in the City. Who are we kidding? Sex and the City saw a ton of action.

"And now, Granola Fashion Tips by my triple air sign, athlete Gemini sister, Jill Vihzor."

Anyone's first impression of Jill was that she spent most of her time outside. Jill's tank top revealed bronze skin, and her nose was red and peeling from sunburn.

Jill's dark skin made her sparkling blue eyes and white teeth pop. "Flip-flops are the sweats of footwear. Their presence says, Look, I didn't even try. I want to walk around a bit and can't be bothered with putting attention into this area of my appearance. Sure, some people manage to spend an obscene amount of money purchasing bedazzled thongs made from exotic materials. Let's face the facts, people. You're basically wearing slippers in public, no matter how you dress them up. That said, you'll generally find me cruising around in a pair no more expensive than lunch at Taco Bell. I will remain in these until they fall off my feet or as weather permits. Then I'll bust out my clogs. Boots are worn only if things get too meteorologically intense, or if it's time to hike or snowboard."

Jill swung a foot up onto the desk, revealing a well-worn turquoise flip-flop.

The young athlete continued, "Speaking of hiking, that brings me to the subject of our Creative Process segment. As with Life, hiking is not all about amazing views. The path traveled is as important as the final result. The bird's-eye perspective must be earned, which entails a ton of grueling, consistent effort. Stray too far from the path and you may fall flat on your face.

"Pay Attention, Pace Your Self, Keep Going.

"This is the same advice for having multiple orgasms."

The camera cut back to a smiling Kyle. "Thank you Jill, insightful as always."

Kyle addressed the camera, "Before we greet our esteemed guests, Victoria Shine and Darian Vihzor, I'd like to give a breakdown of their astrology. We know that both of these beautiful women are Scorpios, that's a given. Both are popular artists. However, Darian's Sun sign is in the Eleventh/Aquarian house. The Eleventh house rules ideals, friends, and allies. This makes the general population feel like Darian is warm and accessible. Darian's Moon in Capricorn denotes an emotional attachment to advancing her career, which makes my sister a bit of a workaholic. That's why during every hiatus of the Love In Motion, Darian stuffs in as many films as her schedule allows. This has given Darian an extensive international fan base that can't get enough of her.

"The eleventh house in Sun placement and Sagittarius Rising also illuminates Darian's passionate activism. She's involved in too many charities to keep track of. Sagittarius, Darian's rising sign and her energetic costume, so to speak, is the mutable fire archer. Darian's joyful attitude and love of travel has her traipsing around the world at a moment's notice.

"Now, Victoria Shine has a Sun and Moon conjunction in fourth house Scorpio. This is the house of Cancer. Victoria is intensely private. Her emotional needs come first. For the chosen few near and dear to Victoria's heart, she offers fierce loyalty. Victoria sequesters herself away for periods of time to rejuvenate her energy.

"Make no mistake, when Victoria wants attention, the whole world forgets what its doing and watches. Victoria is a woman with sexual and artistic gravitas. It takes a sophisticated dramatic palate to appreciate Victoria. She's not for the faint at heart.

"Victoria's Leo Rising gives her a refined creative sensibility in any medium. She was born with the innate knowledge that sex is power. Victoria's Leo Rising heightens her sexual appeal, aptitude, and appetite.

"Victoria's Sun/Moon conjunction in her own chart means that she entered this world under a New Moon.

"As you can see, Darian Vihzor and Victoria Shine are powerful women. Each contributes in a unique way to the growth of humanity by honing and sharing their crafts."

"Without further ado, ladies and gentlemen, we've got two of the stars from the hit show Love In Motion. Vespa, please cue our canned studio audience to welcome our esteemed guests."

There was the sound of loud clapping and cheering being piped into the studio. Vespa inserted a video of the four Vihzor siblings in bleachers, gesticulating wildly and acting as rabid fans.

The camera cut back to Victoria and Darian stepping onto the stage and settling into the guest seats. They waved and blew kisses to the imaginary audience.

Known to be a fan of campy humor, Kyle's broad grin was plastered across his face. "Welcome, let's get to it. Victoria, is it true you won't be returning for next season?"

"Most likely. I've been focusing on music full time again."

Darian cut in, "Oh, she's just playing coy, folks. I know how much fun you've had shooting Love In Motion. You won't be able to stay away for long."

"Well, I'm not promising anything," Victoria said.

"You rarely do, buddy," Darian said.

The women grinned at each other.

"I've put a new band together. We've got a show at The Wiltern next month," Victoria said.

"Remember folks, take the Victoria Shine trivia quiz. You could win two front row seats to the show. Go to kylevihzor.com for details."

"Victoria, it would be an honor if you agreed to guest host the Secrets from a Scorpio segment next month?"

"It ceases to be a secret if I tell you about it," Victoria said.

Darian chuckled, "Good answer."

"Ladies, I'd love to hear your thoughts on acting. Maybe you can offer our viewers some insight. You're both so young to have such a wealth of experience," Kyle said.

"That's funny coming from a fledgling like you," Victoria said. "Acting is the only profession where you can start working as an infant. Hell, as a fetus, with a bit of in-utero camera work."

"People train for years to get into and maintain a conscious innocence of the moment," Darian said with an air of superiority.

Never one to miss an opportunity to play with her friend, Victoria shot Darian a dismissive, "Others have a natural talent and instinct for acting."

"Even a raw talent must practice to harness their full potential," Darian said, looking pointedly at Victoria.

"Great actors have the ability to be vulnerable in any setting or circumstance. Their strength is generated by shedding all defenses to the experience of the moment," Victoria parried.

"Most actors are strong in some areas of performance and weak in others."

"True. It would take a tremendous amount of work for me to play a weak sniveling victim," Victoria said.

"Although you've certainly got the town whore character down pat," Darian said.

Victoria snickered, "Isn't that the pot calling the kettle black?"

"You've sure been great competition on the show," Darian said.

"What, for biggest slut?"

Both women laughed.

Kyle joined them for a few beats, and then asked, "Victoria, speaking of your active social life and open bi-sexuality, which do you prefer, men or women?"

Victoria narrowed her eyes at Kyle, considering for a moment whether or not to attack him for his brazen inquiry. Her delight about the subject kept the peace.

"As far as I'm concerned, the possession of a functional cock has nothing to do with a person's ability to give and receive pleasure."

"What qualities do you look for in a sexual partner?"

"Passion, creativity, sensitivity, and endurance," Victoria said.

"Wonderful. Thank you for joining us on the show. Victoria, it's always a pleasure to see you exploring your acute sense of style. You're living art.

"However, Darian, my dear and darling sister, please put some more clothes on, you sad hussy. It's never too late to start acting like a lady. Your new mantra is modesty. You don't want the boys to think you're a two-bit hooker, do you?"

The devilish grin on Kyle's face turned to surprise as his sister tackled him off of his stool. The frame cut to a master shot while they crashed to the ground.

"Is she mad enough to sacrifice the Yves St. Laurent outfit? Two to one, Darian wins," Victoria said up into the boom mike, looking at Jill.

Jill said, "You're kidding, he's a trained fighter."

"C'mon, my forty dollars to your twenty she kicks his ass," Victoria said.

"I'll take the bet," Jill said.

"Deal," they shook hands and pulled out some cash.

Kyle moved into frame with his sister in a standing arm-in-guillotine headlock.

"Thank you for watching AstroNews. This is Kyle Vihzor, signing off." Darian bit him and they resumed fighting.

Victoria was about to hand Jill money in the background, but when the struggle continued, Victoria took it back, cheering for her friend.

The end credits rolled over the mayhem.

* * *

Dorcha looked at the clock. It was well after midnight. Dorcha called Morgan anyway, figuring she might be up. Instead Dorcha got Morgan's voicemail.

Once the beep sounded Dorcha said, "Hey, it's me. Sorry to be calling so late. I thought you might still be up. Thank you so much for the vampire deck! I love them! Perfect gift, my friend. What a great AstroNews episode. I can't wait for Victoria's concert. Alright, call me when you get up tomorrow, around the crack of noon. Let's get lunch, we have much to discuss. Okay. Wow, this is a long message. I gotta go," Dorcha giggled into the receiver while hanging up.

Dorcha realized how stoned she was while she was talking. Good thing Dorcha knew it would amuse Morgan.

Dorcha turned on the television. An old Darian Vihzor movie was playing called The Test. The Test had been made during Darian's transition from child actor to grown-up movie star. Dorcha decided that the coincidence was par for the course with the way her life had been lately. Dorcha poured herself a glass of Pinot Noir, settled into the couch, and sparked the bong.

Dorcha laid out one more Tarot spread before retiring for the evening.

A Seven Questions spread using Druid Craft, Faeries Oracle, Lover's Path, and Vampire's Tarot.

Position 1 represents **who my romantic love reciprocated partner is**:
        Druid: 6 of Wands @
        Faeries: #27 – Nelys the Alchemyst
        Lovers: #2 – Wisdom @
        Vampires: #19 – The Truth
Position 2 represents **our karmic connection**:
        Druid: 8 of Pentacles @
        Faeries: #51 – The Topsie-Turvets @
        Lovers: 3 of Arrows @
        Vampires: 10 of Cups
Position 3 represents **what attracts me to him**:
        Druid: 8 of Cups @
        Faeries: #33 – Faeries of the Future @
        Lovers: 2 of Arrows @
        Vampires: King of Pentacles
Position 4 represents **what he will find attractive about me**:

Druid: 6 of Pentacles @
Faeries: #2 – Ekstasis @
Lovers: 5 of Staves @
Vampires: #5 – The Ancient
Position 5 represents **how he handles me**:
Druid: #20 – Rebirth
Faeries: #10 – The Singer of Healing @
Lovers: 6 of Cups
Vampires: #4 – The Liege
Position 6 represents **how I can recognize him?**
Druid: 6 of Swords
Faeries: #59 – The Bodacious Bodach
Lovers: 2 of Pentacles
Vampires: 9 of Wands
Position 7 represents **our near future**:
Druid: 9 of Pentacles @
Faeries: #32 – Iris of the Rainbows
Lovers: #10 – Fortune @
Vampires: Knight of Wands

Yikes, thought Dorcha while scanning the cards. It's going to get worse before it gets better in the romance department.

CHAPTER ELEVEN
THE CONCERT

Not since the childhood days of Christmas morning had Morgan woken up so excited. Finally, today was the day of the concert. Morgan had seen Victoria perform with Virtuoso twice, but both times had been in seats which required binoculars. Tonight was front row.

Morgan sat up to look at the clock on Balthazar's end table. 6:58 AM? Morgan groaned. She'd only been asleep four hours. Morgan lay back, forcing herself to relax and rest for longer.

* * *

The sun was setting as Balthazar and Morgan pulled into the parking structure at the Wiltern Theater. They had planned to meet up with Draven and Dorcha in front of the venue.

Morgan jumped out of Balthazar's Jeep Grand Cherokee. "C'mon, Balthazar. Hurry up."

"It's an hour before the doors even open, Morgan. Relax," Balthazar said, putting Morgan's iPod in the glove box and locking it.

"Do you have the tickets?" Morgan said.

"Uh-" he patted his pockets, "I thought you had them."

"What?! I specifically handed them to you for safekeeping. Fuck! How could y-

"Calm down, calm down," Balthazar said, producing the tickets from his jacket pocket. "I have them. I was only kidding," Balthazar laughed.

Morgan punched Balthazar in the shoulder, "Not funny, mister."

They found Draven and Dorcha in line, waiting for the theater to open. Security was earning their pay by keeping the crowd from overwhelming the sidewalk.

Morgan, Balthazar, Dorcha and Draven all got a kick out of observing the eclectic folks gathering for the show. Victoria Shine attracted all kinds, from prim to punk. Time passed quickly as they amused each other and got friendly with the people waiting in line around them.

A cluster of paparazzi coagulated near them at the front of the theater. They were shouting enticements, pandering for the attention of none other than Darian Vihzor, who had arrived with her family.

"Oh my God, it's them," Dorcha said.

"Who?" Balthazar said.

Draven replied, "Over there, see them, the older couple with the three women and the adorable young man?"

"They're hard to miss. Hey, isn't that…"

Draven cut Balthazar off mid-sentence, "Yep, Darian Vihzor, she's got a new movie coming out. I did a freelance article on the parents, Trevor and Tilly, for Technology Review. They're inventors."

"Oh yeah?" Morgan said.

"They made an insane amount of money a few years back for designing a microchip which revolutionized the computer industry. It quadrupled the fastest CPU clock rates at the time."

"Cool, I'm impressed. Technological wizards who've managed to raise four gorgeous kids. They all look so happy," Dorcha said.

Draven continued, "They're doing something right. Their children have all distinguished themselves in their chosen fields. See the brunette with the glasses? That's Vespa, she's a scientist. Works with her parents, and also moonlights as a midwife. We all know Darian. She's been performing since childhood. Darian's fucking hilarious, and underrated as an actress. She's so good at playing the disarming romantic lead that people think it's the only thing she can do. The petite one with the dirty blond hair is Jill Vihzor, an Olympic Bronze Medalist for ice skating. She fell doing a triple Lutz. Now Jill can be found all over the world surfing, snowboarding, and skydiving. Jill is one hell of an adrenaline junkie."

"Yeah with phenomenal balance," Morgan said.

"I've got the last one," Dorcha said. "The youngest is Kyle, astrologer and creator of my favorite monthly web show, AstroNews. One of Kyle's dreams is to compete in the UFC. Kyle trains in mixed martial arts at least four hours every day. I've been crushing on him for a while."

"Wow, I bet family game nights are competitive affairs at the Vihzor household," Morgan said.

"Try compound. They have a gorgeous property in the Hollywood hills, and vacation homes in France and Bali," Draven said.

"Well, someone's done their research," Balthazar said.

"Thank you. It was an easy article to write. They are a fascinating bunch."

The theater doors opened and everyone made their way inside. Morgan and Balthazar went to get refreshments while Draven and Dorcha went to the bathroom. Morgan positioned herself behind Kyle, Darian, and Jill, who were also waiting in the refreshment line. Pretty much everyone in the lobby recognized Darian, and quite possibly Jill and Kyle as well. Yet, in the wonderful style of Hollywood's studied indifference, they left the Vihzors alone to enjoy the show.

Morgan eavesdropped on the Vihzor's conversation.

Kyle was holding court with his two older sisters, "Even as a child you could tell how intense, private, and dramatic she is. It makes complete sense that Victoria would be a Scorpio."

"Here we go with the astrology again," Jill said.

"Don't act like it's not real, Jill," Kyle said.

Darian put an arm around her brother. "Have you been watching old footage again? Can't we let embarrassingly bad hair days die?"

"I wanted to see if I could tell what Victoria's sign was even when she was a kid," Kyle said.

"And?" Jill said.

"Oh, it's so obvious, just the core look in her eyes gives it away. However, Scorpio is also her Moon sign, which underlines, italicizes, and bold faces the Scorpio energy. Then there is her Leo Rising, which given enough attention, Victoria's sense of exhibitionism will often overwhelm her natural drives towards complete privacy," Kyle said.

"Your cosmic scrutiny sounds like a crush to me," Darian said.

"I defy anyone to stand in the path of her charm and not succumb. Attraction to Victoria only denotes good taste, which I have in abundance."

For the moment, Darian was satisfied. They ordered snacks and drinks for the entire Vihzor tribe, and then left to rejoin their party.

The six members of the Vihzor family were sitting two seats left of Draven, Dorcha, Morgan, and Balthazar. Sitting between Kyle and Draven were the AstroNews winners, Sally and Bob. Kyle was an attentive host to his guests.

"He keeps looking over here," Draven whispered.

"Well, you are staring at him," Morgan said.

"Dude, maybe he's cruising you," Balthazar said, which made the women giggle.

Dorcha had never been this nervous in her life. She was bouncing between the awesome concert about to start, her crush on her friend's boyfriend, Draven's charm, and her earnest worship of Kyle and Darian Vihzor. Dorcha was star struck.

Morgan squeezed Dorcha's hand and winked at her. "Hell of an exciting night."

"Yes," Dorcha said.

Morgan released Dorcha's hand. Morgan turned to Balthazar, and began to massage the back of his neck. Balthazar closed his eyes, allowing Morgan's gentle massage for a few moments. Then he responded with kisses.

Dorcha averted her eyes, and discovered Draven observing.

"They're disgusting," Draven joked to Dorcha in a low voice.

Dorcha laughed, "Bless their hearts. Balthazar sure went all-out with these seats."

"Yeah, good luck on him getting Morgan's attention once Victoria steps on stage. Enough about them. I am loving the front row. All concerts should be seen from here."

Draven turned around, basking in the buzzing sold-out audience. He recognized a dozen celebrities scattered throughout the crowd.

Draven decided to chat up Sally and Bob. The couple was beside themselves with joy, thankful for Sally's extensive knowledge of celebrity trivia. Kyle joined in the conversation. Soon Draven was introducing Kyle to everyone. Frozen, Dorcha managed to smile and nod. Morgan waved hello and said, "We love your show, Kyle!"

"Thank you! It's so much fun to do," Kyle said.

The lights dimmed. The crowd roared, drooling with heated anticipation. It'd been over three years since Victoria had stepped on stage as a musician.

From Morgan's ideal vantage point, she saw a person darting out onto the stage, heading for the drum kit.

Moments later a sultry beat rose, spurring the audience to near frenzy.

Another musician appeared at the edge of the stage, and bass notes twined elegantly into the percussion.

The lights rose enough to expose the two female band members setting the sonic stage for their leader.

The back of the stage, dominated by a scrim, was lit to reveal the outline of any object behind it. Another woman skulked on stage, appearing to the audience only as a silhouette. She raised a microphone her lips.

From the shadows Victoria sang the beginning notes of "Earthly Delight", a break out hit from "Harmony's Harem."

The fans roared their approval.

At the end of the bridge, Victoria held a powerful note. The lights dimmed on the scrim and lit up the front center stage where Victoria emerged from a trap door in the floor.

Surprised, the crowd got quiet then went wild as the music shifted. The song exploded into a breakneck pace. Everyone was on their feet.

Morgan forgot to breathe. Victoria's attire looked like a cross between

Mad Max Beyond Thunderdome, Fifth Element, and Elizabeth. It was a triumph of leather, lace, velvet, modified corset, perfectly styled hair and dramatic make-up, and it showed enough skin to tease without revealing the goods. Victoria dazzled Morgan beyond description.

* * *

Towards the middle of the show Victoria sang "Strip the Sun". During the drum-and-bass instrumental jam, Victoria scanned the crowd, enjoying them as much as they were her. Victoria zeroed in on Balthazar, sensing he was the only one in the audience who didn't want to fuck her. Victoria's Ego demanded she change his mind.

Morgan witnessed Victoria noticing Balthazar. Morgan watched in horror as Victoria sauntered over to him, sweat dripping off of her nubile, perfectly toned body. When Victoria planted a kiss on Balthazar, Morgan's jaw nearly fell off her face from shock.

Victoria made out with Balthazar for a bit. Then she looked over at Morgan and winked at her, with a sick grin on her face.

Balthazar, awestruck by Victoria, didn't notice the exchange between the women, or notice Morgan at all for that matter.

Morgan was livid. How could this be happening? Morgan turned to Dorcha and Draven, desperate for support from her best friends, only to discover they had disappeared. Startled, Morgan realized she was in an UnderLife episode. The scene zoom shifted.

Now Morgan was sitting with Victoria on a wooden raft sitting on the sand during evening twilight on the beach. Balthazar was standing nearby with his shirt off, and his hair grown down to his shoulders. Balthazar looked like a shaggy-haired, drug-dealing, band-stalking hippie in great shape.

Victoria and Balthazar were aware of Morgan's presence, but ignored her, staring at each other instead. Victoria murmured approval and attraction to Balthazar. Morgan saw the raw lust in his eyes, but he hadn't made a move on Victoria, yet.

Morgan felt devastated, ashamed, and mortified. She was in love with the woman who was hitting on her boyfriend. Morgan got up, heartsick, and while walking away said, "Go ahead and make out."

Morgan did not see their reactions. Morgan only looked back once she was very far away from them, and then ducked out of sight behind a building. Victoria and Balthazar were still sitting there, staring at each other.

Then it melted into another scene which held a pervasive apocalyptic disaster feeling. Morgan was with her father, Eddie, and Victoria, in her Dad's 1964 cerulean Plymouth Valiant, a car he never possessed in Waking Life. They stopped for some unknown reason. Victoria got out of their car and into an SUV packed with people, driven by Balthazar.

* * *

Suddenly Morgan came back to Waking Life at the moment right before "Strip the Sun" began, which Victoria already sung in the UnderLife.

When Victoria got to the same instrumental section of the song, Morgan looked at her. Victoria was looking right in their direction, just like she had been in UnderLife, but Morgan could see that Victoria couldn't see them because of the lights.

Of course, this was the song where Balthazar finally cut loose and started loving the show. Morgan watched Balthazar smiling and bouncing along on the balls of his feet to the infectious rhythm.

Morgan felt like her brain had melted. The rest of the concert went by in a dazed blur.

* * *

After the show was over they followed the herd of people into the lobby, Balthazar moved away from the group to throw their empty drinks away.

Morgan's face was ashen, like she'd seen a ghost. Her friends were expecting Morgan to be a hyper chatterbox after the brilliant display of musical prowess they'd just witnessed. Draven looked at Dorcha. Dorcha's face echoed Draven's concern. Draven leaned in towards Morgan, "Honey, what's wrong?"

"I'll tell you later," Morgan said.

Balthazar joined them, "So, do we want to go out for a night cap?"

Morgan shook her head no.

"Dorcha and I have early mornings," Draven lied. "We should probably go. It was an unbelievable show, Morgan. Call me when you get up so we can discuss this in excruciating detail."

"I will. Good night guys."

There were hugs all around.

The car ride home was spent in an odd silence. Balthazar wanted to tell Morgan how much he enjoyed the show. When Balthazar had gotten the tickets, they both had assumed he'd only be going to be a good boyfriend. Neither of them expected him to like it. But Balthazar had loved the show. He was dying to tell her. But Morgan was silent. Confused, Balthazar didn't say anything either.

By the time Balthazar parked the car, Morgan still hadn't said anything. Balthazar opened the front door to their apartment and decided to put out some feelers.

"What an fantastic concert! I loved how Victoria tricked us in the beginning by using a body double in the back and then appearing at the front of the stage," Balthazar paused momentarily. When Morgan didn't jump in he continued, "I was amazed. I never really got why you were so into her, but now I do. How about those outfits Victoria barely wore? Actually the whole band was hot, even the cute butch drummer. They fucking rocked it!" Balthazar watched Morgan for a reaction. This concert had marked the best musical comeback Hollywood had seen in years, and they had been in the front row. Balthazar expected Morgan to be bursting with jubilation.

Instead all Balthazar got was a subdued, "Yeah, it was an awesome show. Thank you so much for the tickets. It was exactly what I wanted for my birthday." Morgan leaned in and pecked him on the lips. She moved to cross the threshold of their apartment. Balthazar halted her progress by slipping an arm around her waist, and pressing his body up behind her.

"Hi," Balthazar said, his right hand brushing the hair off Morgan's shoulder, exposing her neck, where he put a row of feathery kisses on her soft skin. Balthazar cupped her breasts with his hands. Gradually the kisses became more insistent.

When Morgan felt Balthazar's teeth nibble on her neck, the familiar delicious heat of impending sexual delight rose throughout her body. Morgan knew it had to be now or never. If she hesitated a second longer her vagina would take over and jump Balthazar.

Morgan sighed, removing Balthazar's hand, which had traveled to her belly for a stroke. Then she took the hand fondling her breast and kissed the back of it, before releasing him. Morgan walked into the apartment.

"Wait," Balthazar said.

"What?" Morgan said impatiently.

"Hey, what the hell is going on with you? You've been so quiet since the show."

Morgan turned to face him, tears welling up in her eyes.

"I have to tell you something," Morgan said, voice choking up.

"What?"

"I…" said Morgan, faltering.

"Just say it. What is it?" Balthazar asked.

"I'm sorry. I don't think it's going to work out with us."

Balthazar stared at Morgan. Balthazar's eyelids fluttered open and closed a few times, like an unconscious tick, and he laughed nervously. "You're kidding, right?"

"No, I'm not kidding," Morgan said.

Balthazar stopped laughing. He looked like a young boy who had just been told the Easter Bunny, Tooth Fairy, and Santa Claus was complete bullshit, crossed with the news that the dog he's had his whole life, Sparky, got into a batch of chocolates Balthazar left out from his Halloween candy stash, and died during the night, violently.

It began to sink in for Morgan the finality of what she was doing to the man whom she'd spent almost every waking minute with for the past few years. Morgan took Balthazar's hands in hers. He was too numb from shock to do anything.

"You've been so wonderful to me Balthazar. The perfect boyfriend..."

"-But then why are you doing this?"

"Because I have to. Your generous birthday gift taught me a big lesson tonight."

"What lesson?"

"I'm not all here for you," Morgan said.

"Is this because you're in love with Victoria Shine? I get it. It's okay."

"No, it's not. I mean, yes, I am in love with her. I've loved her since elementary school. I rushed home every day to see Victoria and Darian's show. Your and my first conversation was about Victoria."

"You're obsessed."

"Whatever."

"You don't think you're going to actually know her or be with her, do you? There were thousands people at the show tonight who want to fuck her as much as you do," said Balthazar, incredulous.

Morgan sighed again.

"Don't do that."

"What?"

"That fucking you're-judging-me sigh, like I'm too dumb to get what's going on with you."

"No, that's not it, really."

"Well then, what the hell is it Morgan?"

"I'm not exactly narcoleptic like you think I am."

Balthazar burst into laughter, "Oh yes you are. I've seen it."

"The narcolepsy is a side effect. It comes from traveling into the collective unconscious, which I call UnderLife," Morgan said.

"What do you mean? You're having some kind of experience when you pass out cold?"

"No, it's a result of dying in UnderLife. I die there, I fall unconscious here. A successful trip happens almost in the blink of an eye in Waking Life. That's when I get disoriented for a few seconds, and play it off as a close call with the narcolepsy."

"You can get killed there?" Balthazar asked, playing along.

"Yes, if I get killed in the UnderLife, I pass out in Waking Life. Some kind of physical hard reset, I guess."

"So this UnderLife thing is why you suddenly fall asleep or get all dreamy-eyed and forgetful? Not the heavily documented and shared rare sleep disorder called narcolepsy?"

"Technically the failed UnderLife experiences result in a narcoleptic sleep episode. However, I usually know exactly why it occurred, and sometimes there's no avoiding an UnderLife fatality."

"How does it happen?" Balthazar asked.

"Any way you can think of. Remember when I passed out on my dinner at Señor Frogs, the night before we went sky diving for the first time?"

"How could I forget? It would have been really embarrassing if it hadn't been so funny. You were in mid-sentence then your eyes fluttered closed. You fucking face planted right into your burrito-enchilada combination plate."

"I wish I could have seen the look on your face," Morgan said.

"I was afraid you were going to be suffocated by Mexican food. I would forever have to tell people I lost my girlfriend from a refried bean related injury."

They both laughed hard, momentarily forgetting the grim nature of their conversation.

Morgan continued, "Well, the UnderLife adventure in question involved me getting shoved out of an airplane without a parachute. I plummeted with terminal velocity to the Earth. There was a great view of a mammoth forest, rolling fields of grass, and a crystal clear blue lake on the way down though. The thing is, it made skydiving in Waking Life with a parachute strapped to my back, and an instructor attached at four points behind me in tandem, a cake walk."

"I'm confused. What exactly is this UnderLife? Is it like Tron or the holodeck in Star Trek?

"It's like a self-programmed holographic experience. The environment of each UnderLife experience depends on the people involved, and what set of symbols they live their life by. I know you've heard the term, 'as above, so below', well, it couldn't be more true."

Morgan and Balthazar sat down on the couch for a long talk. Morgan proceeded to explain about all of her pivotal UnderLife experiences, and what lessons and events they represented throughout her life. Morgan started with her mother's frame invaders, then the tsunami with August, being drawn and quartered, the whip battle with his ex-girlfriend, and the witch persecution with Dorcha. It was such a huge relief to finally let Balthazar in on all of it.

Afterwards, they sat in silence for a few minutes. Then Balthazar shook his head, making a derisive snorting sound. "What an astounding imagination you have!"

"You sound like my father when I was child. I am not making this up.

You believe me, don't you?"

"You have to admit, it sounds pretty crazy. It's certainly a lot more exciting to think of it this way, rather than thinking that you're having hypnagogic hallucinations because of the narcolepsy. Are you being serious?"

"Fuck you. This is the truth. Why would I make something like this up?"

"I don't know. Why haven't I ever heard of this kind of special ability before?"

Morgan shrugged, "As far as I know, I'm the only one who can do this. Sometimes another person gets brought in with me, and they remember the experience as vividly as I do. I don't have a clue how it happens or what to do to control it."

"We've been together for years, why didn't you tell me about this before?"

"I didn't want you to think I was crazy."

"Well, I already know you're crazy. It's one of the things I love about you."

"Balthazar, I'm serious."

"Okay then, why have you not brought me in? Don't you trust me?"

"I've wanted so badly to tell you, but…"

"What?"

"You don't see me in the UnderLife. No matter what I try, I can't keep your attention and you never remember it."

"Well, maybe it will be different now since my conscious mind knows about it. Try it. Go!"

He looked at her, waiting. His body tensed with anticipation.

"It doesn't work like that. I can't regulate when I go in and out of it. As I said, sometimes someone else will go there with me and will remember the experience. You've been involved a few times, but I concluded it was my psyche's projection of you. You never remember your dreams. Once you mentioned something to me which was actually a tiny fragment of what we went through in the UnderLife."

"When was this?" Balthazar asked.

"Very early on, the third night we spent together."

"The zombie dream?"

"Yep," Morgan said.

"What a sick nightmare! The smell! They kept coming, and no matter how many we killed, there were more of them. You mean to tell me, you were there, like, for real?"

"Yes. The memory is as true for me as everything that we're experiencing right now. I fucking hate zombies. They're so depressing and almost impossible to kill without heavy artillery. No one should have to experience getting their brains eaten while still alive." The revulsion on Morgan's face showed that she knew exactly how it felt. "Now you know why I don't find those kinds of movies entertaining at all."

"This proves there's at least a small connection between us in UnderLife. Why didn't you tell me this before so I could try to help you?"

"You've never seemed receptive to it. Whenever I talk about a crazy story I've read, you always say how glad you are it was something you didn't have to deal with. Seriously, sweetie, it's not like I'm trying to exclude you from anything. These adventures aren't tropical vacations. I love you. Why would I want to drag you into my odd and often traumatic UnderLife? You don't know how long I've wished to be able to share this with you, but I've been afraid of how you'd react."

Balthazar nodded. "It's a lot to digest. I was just starting to get used to the idea that Tarot cards aren't total bullshit. This UnderLife place, and you're the only one we know of who can go there, is some fucking weird and heavy shit, Morgan."

"Tell me about it. I'm still often surprised when it happens. This gift could have been a curse if I hadn't been raised to embrace it and work with it."

"What do you mean you were raised to embrace it? Does your Dad know about this?"

"Yes, he does. UnderLife is not his favorite subject, but for the most part he's been very cool about it. For Dad it's the place where his paintings come from. All Dad wants is for me to take him to see my Mom again. He can't quite understand it isn't something I can operate like that. We don't talk about it much. However, there is my Aunt August."

"I love her. She's hilarious."

"Yeah, not my aunt, and she isn't exactly a FBI agent."

"Isn't exactly?"

"How about not at all. She's more like my handler."

"What are you talking about, your handler?"

"She guides me in my work," Morgan said.

"What work? All those fights we've had about money, and you've had a job this whole time? Why the hell didn't you tell me?"

"It's complicated. Secretive."

"What are you, a spy?" Balthazar asked snidely.

"No, far from it, but what we're working to accomplish isn't ready for the general public yet. It's not the right time. The streams are still feeding the river of change."

"What do you mean river of change? And who are we?"

"I can't really get into it." The truth was that Morgan wasn't quite sure what Louise and August's overall mission was, but revealing this to Balthazar didn't seem like a good idea.

"Okay, so why are you trying to break up with me? You told me your big secret. I haven't run for the hills or called the men in the white coats."

"It's because of what happened tonight at the concert."

"What? I thought we had a great time."

"During the show I slipped into UnderLife." Morgan told him of the experience.

"You're telling me we have to break up because I cheated on you with your fantasy girlfriend in UnderLife?"

"You don't understand. I hated you during the experience. I was outraged and jealous you were getting romantic attention from her. I wasn't focused on you in a positive way at all. You were an obstacle to who I really want, Victoria."

"Oh, how sweet, thanks. You wouldn't have even been in the front row if it wasn't for me."

"Thanks Captain Obvious, way to be gracious."

"Oh yeah, because abandoning me out of nowhere is such a civil thing to do." Balthazar took a deep breath, barely containing his temper. He did his best to reason with Morgan. "It was just a nightmare, an UnderLife torment, like the zombies. Unless you still hate me, which would be ridiculous because I didn't do anything wrong, Morgan! Now you are sounding nuts. What, you suddenly don't love me?"

"I do, but I don't think I'm in love with you anymore. Never mind the events from the concert experience. What became clear to me was who I wanted, and it wasn't you. I can't pretend I didn't feel the difference. It'd be deceptive and deceitful to continue a romantic relationship with you. It's not fair to either of us."

"I don't believe this! You've kept this fucking secret from me for years, and when you finally tell me about it, it's only to break my heart? What? Fuck, Morgan!"

"I'm sorry. I should have told you about UnderLife before," Morgan said.

"Forget it. This is officially insane. I can't deal with this right now. I need to get away from you and sort it all out." Balthazar stormed away yelling, "Way to show gratitude for all your birthday gifts! I liked you better when you just had an odd sleeping disorder!"

"Where are you going?" Morgan asked.

"What do you care? You're the asshole breaking up with me!" Balthazar screamed, slamming the apartment building security door on his way out.

CHAPTER TWELVE
HISTORY LESSONS

Exhilarated from the concert, Dorcha and Draven went back to Dorcha's place to smoke bowls and chat for a while. After he left, Dorcha was settling in to watch a DVD of her favorite Darian Vihzor romantic comedy, Affection, when Morgan called.

"Hello?"

"Dorcha?" Morgan asked, her voice choked up.

"Sweetie, what's wrong?"

"I... I broke up with Balthazar," Morgan began sobbing in earnest.

"You did? Oh no, what can I do? How can I help? Do you want me to come over?"

"Can I spend the night at your place? I don't want to be here when he gets back."

"Of course you can. Are you okay to drive?" asked Dorcha.

"Yes, thank you," sniffed Morgan, "I'll see you in a little bit."

Morgan showed up twenty minutes later with a couple bottles of wine. Dorcha had a fresh bowl of marijuana waiting for her.

They hugged for a long time.

Dorcha pulled back and made eye contact. "Morgan, what happened?"

Morgan regurgitated the whole story, including the UnderLife slip at the concert with Balthazar and Victoria, and the subsequent marathon break up talk. Copious amounts of weed and red wine were consumed during the conversation. Dorcha's beloved iPod shuffled along with them, providing their soundtrack.

"Did I just totally fuck up? We were happy together, right? Why didn't I tell him about the UnderLife sooner? I feel like such a jerk," Morgan said, worn out from the night.

"Do you want me to do Tarot on the relationship?" Dorcha asked.
"Please. I need some perspective right now."

The Relationship Spread on Morgan and Balthazar using the Druid Craft, Faeries Oracle, Lover's Path and Vampires Tarot.

Position 1 represents **how Morgan sees Balthazar**:
        Druid: Prince of Swords
        Faeries: #60 – The Pook @
        Lovers: 9 of Wands @
        Vampires: #15 – The Inner Demon
Position 2 represents **how Balthazar sees Morgan**:
        Druid: Princess of Cups @
        Faeries: #13 - Solus
        Lovers: 10 of Cups
        Vampires: Ace of Pentacles
Position 3 represents **Morgan's focal point in the relationship**:
        Druid: 7 of Cups
        Faeries: #15 – The Journeyman
        Lovers: #0 - Innocence
        Vampires: 7 of Swords
Position 4 represents **Balthazar's focal point in the relationship**:
        Druid: 10 of Cups
        Faeries: #38 – Laiste, Moon's Daughter
        Lovers: #1 - Magic
        Vampires: 8 of Wands
Position 5 represents **where the relationship is now**:
        Druid: 10 of Pentacles @
        Faeries: #57 – Luathas the Wild @
        Lovers: Ace of Wands
        Vampires: #18 – The Memory
Position 6 represents **where Morgan wants the relationship to go**:
        Druid: #14 – The Fferyllt @
        Faeries: #59 – The Bodacious Bodach @
        Lovers: #20 - Judgment
        Vampires: 10 of Pentacles
Position 7 represents **where Balthazar wants to relationship to go**:
        Druid: 4 of Swords @
        Faeries: #39 – Losgunna @
        Lovers: 2 of Pentacles @
        Vampires: 3 of Wands
Position 8 represents **something to consider in the relationship**:
        Druid: 9 of Wands

Faeries: #35 – The Faun @
Lovers: Princess of Cups
Vampires: #10 - Fate

Position 9 represents **the overall lesson each of you are learning in the relationship right now**:

Druid: 5 of Cups @
Faeries: #46 – The Friends @
Lovers: 9 of Pentacles
Vampires: Queen of Pentacles

Dorcha launched right into the meat of the reading, "For you, whether you realized it or not, telling him about the UnderLife was the harbinger of death in the relationship as it stood. Part of breaking up with him was about control. Hurt Balthazar before he has the chance to reject you. There was also the that fear he would be okay with it. Suddenly the blaring reality would come to light. You've never fully taken him into the UnderLife. I think bringing me into UnderLife for our witch persecution also confirmed a long held fear you've had. There's a lack of spiritual compatibility between you, otherwise he would be a lucid and cognizant participant in UnderLife."

"Jeez, Dorcha, don't pull any punches. You know I can't control the entrances and exits in the UnderLife."

"Maybe not consciously, but you know there's something to the fact Balthazar hasn't been able to engage with you in your inner universe. I'm sorry if I'm being harsh."

"No, it's okay, I much prefer honesty, and you're right. It's just tough to hear it," admitted Morgan.

"It says here in the cards, plain as day, you want the perspective of life without him for a while. See what it's like to be single. He needs time to digest everything," Dorcha said.

"Do you think the split is permanent?" Morgan asked before realizing how ridiculous she sounded, since Morgan was the one who wanted to walk away.

"It depends on what each of you discover while you're apart. There's still a lot love between you," Dorcha said.

"Okay," Morgan yawned. "I'm exhausted. Thank you for the reading. I might harass you tomorrow for another one."

"Anytime," Dorcha stood. "Here, I'll get you a pillow and some blankets. Do you need a toothbrush?"

"No, I brought my toiletries. Thanks for letting me crash on your couch."

"Stay as long as you want."

* * *

Dorcha didn't have to work the next day, so she and Morgan went to i Cugini in Santa Monica for brunch. After stuffing themselves, they took a stroll on the beach. The overcast day featured a stiff, chill breeze. Morgan felt it matched her mood perfectly.

"Every day I have to subjugate my Ego," Morgan complained. "While I slumber it seems to regenerate with frightening speed. My Superior and Inferior Self wake up at the same time."

"It's the same for everyone, Morgan. My Ego tried to shiv me in the shower this morning," Dorcha said.

"When I was with Balthazar, my Ego would lob over something like, 'Too bad he doesn't know the real you. If he can't see you in the UnderLife, where is he in your heart?' Waking up on your couch today, the first thing I hear from my Ego is, 'Oh look, now you're alone.' So it begins again."

Dorcha laughed, "There's no satisfying it, only subduing it. One of the reasons I love Tarot so much is that it helps me pierce the illusionary veil of my Ego, even if only for a moment."

"I love that you know how to read them. It's a helpful skill," Morgan said.

They stopped on a sandy knoll to watch a few brave surfers in wet suits taking advantage of the wave swell created by impending stormy weather.

"There's something I didn't tell you last night. I'm sure it contributed to why I took the UnderLife slip at the concert so personally. Louise and I have been working on my Vishuddha, or throat chakra," Morgan said.

"Which would go along with telling Balthazar about the UnderLife," Dorcha said.

"Louise said we were having a hard time getting the energy moving. She made some adjustments which I'm not allowed to talk about until after we're done. What I can say is during on our third meditation at Vishudda, I had a vision."

"What happened?"

"It was several years in the future. We owned a gorgeous house on a cliff next to the ocean. I could hear the waves crashing. It was dusk. The warm air carried a slight breeze. I stood on the wooden deck after dinner. The setting sun reflected off of the infinity pool."

"Wait, who is we?" Dorcha asked.

"Victoria Shine," Morgan said. "Yeah, I know, of course it would be the woman of my dreams. As the sun slipped further below the horizon, I could see her silhouette through the huge windows dominating the west side of the house. Victoria strolled around the kitchen and dining room, laughing with a friend on the phone. I stayed outside to give Victoria privacy and to enjoy the night air. When Victoria came outside, we were bathed in moonlight. Victoria approached with an irresistible expression on her face. We kissed for a while. It was ecstasy. Then Victoria got more aggressive with me. Victoria sunk to her knees, and then the vision ended." Morgan said.

"Wow, I can see how that would generate some self-conflict. Do you believe it was a prophetic message, or a fantasy?"

"I don't know. I hope it was precognition. I haven't been able to get the images or feelings out of my mind. Victoria and I were happy together. It haunts me."

The two friends went to see a movie theater to get lost in someone else's drama for a bit. When it finished, Morgan checked her phone. Balthazar had called.

* * *

The next day Morgan met up with Balthazar to talk. Balthazar expected Morgan to be apologetic and willing to beg for his forgiveness. When that didn't happen, things got ugly.

Dorcha got back from work in the evening to find Morgan on her doorstep, surrounded by luggage, her eyes red from crying.

"He thinks I've had some kind of psychotic episode. He says breaking up with him and this sudden talk about UnderLife are symptoms of a larger illness. Balthazar said he would stand by me while I sought psychiatric help."

"What did you say?"

"I told him to fuck off. To believe whatever he wanted, I was moving out."

"Subtle," Dorcha said.

"Draven said I could stay with him, but he lives downtown. If you don't mind, can I surf on your couch while I look for a place? I won't be here longer than a week."

Dorcha treasured her privacy, but she decided she could endure sharing her space with Morgan for a while. "Of course you can."

Morgan smiled, "Thank you." Morgan held up a half ounce bag of weed, tossing it to Dorcha. "I think this will help with the burden."

"You're welcome to stay as long as you want. Really," Dorcha said to the plastic bag. Dorcha opened it, stuck her nose inside, and inhaled the skunk bouquet.

Dorcha whipped up a simple pasta dinner. Morgan stayed in the kitchen to converse while Dorcha was cooking. They consumed a bottle of Syrah Morgan had bought. Morgan cracked open a second bottle. The women settled in on the couch for bong hits.

Morgan took a long drag, coughing a bit after exhaling. "You know, periodically I'll dream my mother is alive."

"You do?" Dorcha said, flicking on the blue lighter.

"Yeah, and usually it's so good to see her. When I was younger it would make me depressed. I'd wake up and be reminded it was only a dream. Mom was long dead, and there was nothing that I could do about it. As the years passed, I've learned how to enjoy Mom's appearances. This last month though, I've been having the same recurring dream a few times a week. In it, Mom is trying to tell me something urgent. She has her left hand cupped to the side of her mouth. Mom's lips are moving, but I can't hear anything. She looks worried, almost frantic. It's disturbing. You know, I've always wondered why Mom really killed herself," Morgan said.

"Oh honey, it was the tumor, Morgan. The doctors said it pushed on Gwendolyn's behavioral center. That's why she did it," Dorcha said.

"I'm talking spiritually. Why did Mom get the tumor in the first place? And what happened to our families all of those years ago in Berkeley which caused us to break up?"

"You mean you don't know?" Dorcha asked.

"Well, it's why I'm asking. One night I had an excruciating UnderLife episode where I was blinded with a hot poker and literally torn apart by being tied to four horses told to go in separate directions, and then my still living torso got thrown onto my own blazing funeral pyre."

"Yeesh," Dorcha said, exhaling a puff of ganja smoke.

"The next morning Daddy packed us up to move to Los Angeles. He refused to say why and forbade me to speak of any LeTour. I was too afraid of alienating Dad to argue. Now, what happened?" Morgan asked.

"They had sex," Dorcha said.

"What? Who?"

"My Mom and your Dad."

"No way! They did?" Morgan said.

"Yes. Mom never told me how it happened, but I think she had a thing for him for a long time. My father noticed right away you guys had left. Dad asked a lot of questions. He was shocked that Eddie gave no warning, explanation, or even a good-bye. Mom must have anticipated this, because I got shipped off to a friend's house for a sleep over. I didn't put this together until much later, but that night my parents got into a gigantic fight. Once the truth of the adultery came out, Dad packed up his stuff and moved to Seattle. Dad wanted to take me with him. Marin refused. Over her dead body, she said. If Remy was a more violent man I think he might have taken her up on the offer. She got in the way of a friendship which would make the closest of brothers feel envious. It made him hate her for many years. Mom said I could fly up to Seattle on some weekends, and stay with Dad for the entire summer."

"Holy shit, that's so core," Morgan said.

"It makes me kinda glad I was too young to remember much from those years."

"Damn, so how did you end up in Hollywood?"

"Wait, there's more. It gets worse," Dorcha said.

"Oh no." Morgan didn't know if she wanted to hear it.

"My mother covered it pretty well for a while, but after our families split her eyesight deteriorated rapidly. By the time I got back from Seattle after the first summer I spent with my Dad, it was too severe for Mom to deny. Shortly afterwards she was pronounced legally blind due to a rare case of aggressive bilateral Coats' disease."

"What the fuck? Oh my God, poor Marin. What did it do to her eyes, if you don't mind my asking?"

"It's a condition where there is abnormal development in the blood vessels behind the eye. The retinal capillaries eventually break open, leaking the serum portion of the blood into the back of eye. The leakage makes the retina swell, causing it to detach. It can be treated if it's caught early. Mom wasn't so lucky. By the time she made it to the doctors it was already too late."

"Dorcha, I am so sorry," Morgan said.

"Thanks. The weird thing is, Mom's attitude through the whole thing surprised me. She was devoid of self-pity. Mom manages pretty well these days. Well, she's still blind, but continues to practice law with some assistance. Mom lives in this cool apartment complex in the Bay Area. Pretty much everyone there is blind. They're a supportive community. It is fun to visit because everything is tactile. That's where Mom met Keith. Keith's blind-since-birth older sister lives there. Mom and Keith got married a few years ago."

"Have you ever asked Tarot about our family history?"

"No. My Tarot curiosity usually takes me into future possibilities. It also helps me to accept the present."

"Will you go with me to the Skyscraper Space tomorrow to do some investigation?"

"Yes. I'm curious about August and Louise. I've never met anyone like them before," Dorcha said.

"I know," Morgan said. "How they can seem so open while being so mysterious is beyond me."

* * *

On Sunday, Morgan and Dorcha arrived at the Skyscraper Space two hours before sunset.

It only took a "how are you?" from August for Morgan to well up in tears. Morgan gave a detailed narrative of the Balthazar break-up and the Tarot aftermath.

By the end of Morgan's story, the four women were settled on the couches drinking ice tea which Dorcha had retrieved from the kitchen.

"Remaining in a stagnant relationship is like sleeping in cold, defiled bathwater," Louise said. "I agree with Dorcha's reading. You want space from Balthazar right now, or you wouldn't have broken up with him."

"I'll help you look for a place tomorrow," August said.

"Thanks. I really appreciate everyone's help. Dorcha has been a trooper letting me stay with her."

Morgan went on to tell August and Louise about the Martel/LeTour family scandal years ago. Morgan finished by recounting the recurring dream of her mother trying to whisper something to her. Morgan demonstrated by cupping her hand to her face, and leaned over to say something in Dorcha's ear.

A neuron sparked in August's memory, triggering the image of Eddie's Secrets of Women painting, which August had seen many years before in New Orleans.

"Does your father have the original Secrets of Women painting?" August asked.

"I think so. I haven't seen the piece in years. Why?"

"It would be useful to your family investigation," Louise cut in, picking up on August's thoughts.

"I'll ask him about it," Morgan said.

"Go see him in person. Bring Dorcha along," Louise said.

"Me?" Dorcha sputtered. "I…"

"Don't worry, everything will be fine," August said.

Morgan and Dorcha made eye contact. Morgan nodded, "Come with me?"

"Okay," Dorcha said.

* * *

Morgan and Dorcha went to visit Eddie Martel the next day at his downtown studio.

"Dad?" Morgan asked after keying into the loft.

"Yeah, be right out sweetie." Eddie's muffled voice came from the storage room in the back of the space.

Eddie entered wearing a paint spattered t-shirt, light blue hospital scrubs, and pink bunny slippers. Eddie's hair and well groomed beard were streaked with grey.

"Morgan, c'mere doll," Eddie said, hugging his daughter.

Over Morgan's shoulder Eddie saw her companion. Releasing Morgan, he asked, "Who is your frie…" then Eddie froze.

"Hi," Dorcha said.

"Dorcha?" Eddie asked.

"Yes."

Tears brimmed in Eddie's eyes. Eddie opened his arms to embrace Dorcha. She reciprocated.

"Group hug!" Morgan said, enfolding them both in a squeeze.

They spent the afternoon and most of the evening swapping stories. Eddie was overjoyed to see Dorcha. He wanted to hear every detail of Dorcha's life. Neither Morgan nor Dorcha, brought up anything too controversial, such as infidelity, sister-witch persecution, chakra balancing, or anything UnderLife related.

It upset Eddie when he heard Morgan had broken up with Balthazar.

"How sad, I really like the kid. Honey, I thought you two had a future together. What happened?"

"At one point I did too. When we began dating it was a dream come true. Unfortunately, I've had a growing feeling for some time now that something crucial has been missing in the relationship. I don't know. My head is such a jumbled mess."

"I know Balthazar loves you, sweetheart. Just make sure you're not doing anything you are going to regret."

Morgan almost laughed when her father said that, but considering what she'd learned about Eddie and Marin, she didn't want to explain why his remark was so apropos. "Thanks, Dad, I'll take it into consideration."

Eddie turned to Dorcha, "What about you gorgeous? Got your eye on anyone?"

"No one at present," Dorcha lied. Dorcha was doing her best to starve and imprison any desire for Balthazar, with varying degrees of success. The closer Dorcha felt to Morgan, the more a strict sense of honor reminded Dorcha that her fantasizes of Balthazar needed to remain imaginary.

Morgan smiled. "What about Mr. Astrology?"

"Who?" Eddie asked.

"Kyle Vihzor," Dorcha said. "Kyle writes and stars in an astrology show on the Internet. Kyle doesn't count. We've never even had a real conversation."

"A minor detail. It sure hasn't stopped my many years of obsession about Victoria Shine."

"You mean loving focus," Dorcha said.

"Yes, loving focus," Morgan winked.

Eddie gazed at them, happy to see them together again.

Morgan continued, "That reminds me, Dad. Do you still have the painting with both of our Moms? I want to share it with Dorcha. Keep it at her place for a while, then at my yet-to-be found new apartment."

Eddie face paled. At first Eddie didn't react, like he hadn't heard Morgan's request. Eddie got a far off look in his eye.

"Yes," he said quietly. "It's here." Eddie hesitated, weighing whether or not he could let the piece go after having held onto it for so long, even though he had never displayed it. Eddie only took out The Secrets of Women when he was sunk into a quagmire of depression and in the mood to wallow.

Eddie nodded his head. Dorcha noticed Eddie and Morgan shared a physical tic of answering with their bodies before uttering any actual words.

"Yes. I'll get it for you," Eddie rose and headed towards the back of the studio, "You ladies should have it. Both of your mothers are radiant."

* * *

The next evening, after Dorcha worked a lunch shift at the café, they went back to the Skyscraper Space with the painting.

"How is your father doing?" Louise asked.

"Good, the same. Elated to see Dorcha," Morgan said.

"That was intense. I'm glad we went," Dorcha said.

"Why did we need to get this painting, anyway?" Morgan asked.

Louise walked towards the couches. "Follow me please. Sit down. Want to puff?" Louise asked.

"What?" The offer had caught Morgan off guard. They approached the northwest living room area of the Skyscraper Space. On the coffee table sat a brand-new foot long glass bong, with fresh water in the main chamber. Next to it was a small glass jar filled with premium grade ganja flowers.

"You're encouraging us?" Dorcha asked while inspecting the piece.

"It's a wonderful entheogen. It blurs the lines a bit. You two will need all the help you can get."

"Well, if you insist." Morgan giggled as she took a nug from the glass jar, and packed the bowl.

Louise continued to talk while Morgan and Dorcha puffed. "Our Inner Worlds or Under Lives, how they are comprised, and what goes on in them, is a reflection of the creative energy we manifest with each breath taken in Waking Life.

"Humans have a much longer and more dramatic history then our current, meager records would lead us to believe. The knowledge gained from our past has not been lost. There exists in every soul a buried memory of all its incarnations. Spiritual records exist, complete with the minutia of every thought, action, and event.

"There's a place where the spiritual records are kept and encoded. The

Hindus call it the Akashic Records. The word comes from the Sanskrit word that means "space" or "sky". The Akashic Records are located on a non-physical plane of existence. This is where I want you to go to access the true history of your families," Louise said.

"How are we supposed to do that?" Morgan asked.

"The exact path has yet to reveal itself. What I do know is that The Secrets of Women will act as a meditative base camp for your explorations."

"Dorcha, have you ever meditated before?" August asked.

"Yes, I've been doing yoga for years. My first instructor began and ended every class with meditation."

"Good, it'll make things easier."

"I want to consult the Tarot on this," Dorcha said.

"Excellent idea," August said. "I'll prepare the meditation area and hang the painting."

Louise turned to Morgan. "You're with me. I'm going to help you warm up. We'll do a series of breathing and stretching techniques to get your physical instrument ready for conducting energy."

Dorcha went to the table. She unpacked her cards and journal.

Seven Questions Spread using the Druid Craft, Faeries' Oracle, Lover's Path and Vampires Tarot.

Position 1 represents **how we enter the Akashic Records**:
> Druid: 6 of Swords
> Faeries: #10 – The Singer of Healing @
> Lovers: 6 of Wands
> Vampires: #14 - Blood

Position 2 represents **what I need to focus on**:
> Druid: 10 of Pentacles @
> Faeries: #14 – The Maiden @
> Lovers: #9 – Contemplation
> Vampires: 3 of Swords

Position 3 represents **what Morgan needs to focus on:**
> Druid: 5 of Cups @
> Faeries: #11 – The Singer of Transfiguration
> Lovers: 2 of Cups @
> Vampires: 7 of Wands

Position 4 represents **how to consciously enter UnderLife**:
> Druid: #3 – The Lady
> Faeries: #0 – The Guide @
> Lovers: 4 of Arrows @
> Vampires: King of Wands

Position 5 represents **something we should be aware of**:

Druid: #6 – The Lovers @
Faeries: #64 – Gawtcha @
Lovers: 6 of Arrows
Vampires: Knight of Wands
Position 6 represents **the essence of our exploration**:
Druid: #7 – The Chariot
Faeries: #51 – The Topsie Turvets
Lovers: 3 of Pentacles @
Vampires: 5 of Swords
Position 7 represents **our near future**:
Druid: 9 of Cups
Faeries: #65 – The Fee Lion @
Lovers: King of Pentacles
Vampires: Knight of Cups

"This is going to be difficult for me to deal with emotionally," Dorcha said after staring at the cards in front of her for some time.

"Do you still want to do this? We don't have to." Morgan asked.

Dorcha thought about it while continuing to read the cards. She decided she would regret it if she bailed. "Yes, let's give it a shot. I'm too curious not to. Besides, it might not even work," Dorcha reasoned.

Morgan smiled at Dorcha, loving her sense of adventure. "What else did you find out?"

"This mission is about healing. It's also about being careful what we wish for. If we're successful, it will create a revolutionary shift in our perspectives. The Tarot's advice is to let it flow. The path to the Akashic Records is receptive to our desire for knowledge. Our near future in this endeavor is promising, if we're willing to take the plunge."

"Sounds good to me. Let's get started." Morgan was excited to experiment with using conscious intention to enter UnderLife. "We're ready when you are," Morgan announced to her mentors.

August hung The Secrets of Women with a series of cables anchored to the ceiling. She lit many candles and sticks of sandalwood incense all around the meditation area.

Louise gestured for Morgan and Dorcha to sit front of the suspended painting, side-by-side in the lotus position.

"Observe the paintings of your mothers. Take them in, study every detail, burn their images into your minds. Set your intentions to reveal the truth of your parents' history and the spiritual reasons behind Gwendolyn's brain tumors and Marin's blindness. Close your eyes. Take several long, deep breaths, and settle into your meditations."

Louise was going to guide Morgan and Dorcha to the room of many doors, which she thought would be a good jumping off point. Before she could begin, though, Morgan and Dorcha shad already slipped into UnderLife.

* * *

Morgan and Dorcha found themselves in a cave. The cave was illuminated by a flaming torch secured in a bracket riveted into the rock wall. In front of them was a pool of water.

Underneath the surface they could see a pinkish glow. Morgan went closer to investigate.

Dorcha hissed, "Careful, something scary could be in there."

Morgan moved to the edge of the pond. The clarity of the water gave her confidence. It appeared to be devoid of any plant or animal life.

"I see some bubbles. I think there's an underground spring. The pink glow seems to be coming from something at the bottom of the cave. Maybe it's emanating from the rocks themselves."

Morgan put her hand in the water.

"Don't!" Dorcha gasped.

"It's warm. Those bubbles must be from a hot spring."

"I don't like this. I feel like we're in a horror movie and the monster is going to jump out at any moment."

"I'm going in," Morgan zipped open her hooded sweatshirt and dropped it on the ground.

"What?"

"It's the only way to proceed, unless you can give us an alternative path. No one said accessing the library of human history would be as easy as walking through a door.

"Maybe there's a secret passage on the rock wall. Why would there be a torch here? Someone must have brought it in here."

"Not necessarily. It's UnderLife. Our psyches could have provided the light source," Morgan said.

Dorcha knocked on the surrounding rock walls. She looked for nodules, as if she could turn a nodule that would unlatch a door. Dorcha took the torch out of its bracket and yanked on the metal, but nothing happened.

"Why not a nice, dry door?" Dorcha asked.

"I think we're out of luck on that count. Besides, you're the one who said the future was promising if we were willing to take the plunge." Morgan waded into the pool.

"I didn't mean literally." Dorcha's whole body tensed. She knew something awful was going to happen. When Morgan dove under the surface, Dorcha thought her heart would stop. Dorcha held her breath with Morgan.

On closer inspection, Morgan saw that the pink light was being emitted by crystals which were framing an underwater tunnel. Morgan went up for air.

"You're not going to like this," Morgan said once she caught her breath.

"Oh no," Dorcha said.

Morgan treaded water. "The pink light is coming from crystals surrounding the mouth of a tunnel."

"You're right, I hate this." Dorcha sighed, pulling off her favorite sweater, revealing a black tank top. Dorcha abandoned the sweater, consoling herself that she would see it again in Waking Life.

"How do we know there even is another side to get to?"

"Faith. Otherwise, you'll find out what it's like to drown." Morgan said.

"Fuck you, don't say that. I'm new to this, and it's scaring the hell out of me."

"Don't worry, we'll be fine. Do you want me to swim ahead and see if I can find a way through?"

"Hell no, you're not leaving me here. We go together."

"'Atta girl. I figure we should thank our lucky stars the water isn't freezing. Okay now, deep breaths. Refresh all the air in those lungs."

They dove. Morgan, the stronger swimmer, led the way. For Dorcha, fear and adrenaline helped her keep the pace up.

The walls of the tunnel were encrusted with the same glowing crystals. They breast stroked their way through it, but they were worried about how long their air would last.

The burning in their lungs became painful. Panicking was becoming an inevitable outcome. Morgan saw an opening in the tunnel ceiling. She knew there could be no hesitation. If Morgan was in bad shape for air, Dorcha must have been having an even harder time.

Morgan used the cave floor to kick off, and shot up into the opening, which led her into a pink crystalline tube. Dorcha followed.

The women exploded from the water, heaving air into their lungs. It took a couple of minutes of coughing and sputtering before they could get their bearings.

They were in a much larger cavern than the first one. The ceiling was so high up that they could barely see it. Morgan thought it looked like a natural cathedral. The walls surrounding them were ablaze with torches placed at regular intervals. Morgan swam to the shore. They noticed a sizeable door with a short whitish figure near it.

Morgan and Dorcha approached the door. The figure was a garden gnome carved out of white alabaster, about four feet tall, with a cherubic smile. The gnome's right arm was extended like it was about to shake someone's hand.

The statue was standing next to a large, ancient wooden door held together by bands of steel. Dorcha deduced the door must have been locked from outside, since there was no discernable way to open it.

"Hello?" Dorcha yelled, knocking on the door.

No reply.

They searched the area near the door but they found nothing of consequence. Morgan and Dorcha went back to the gnome. Morgan touched the statue's head then patted down the body like a bouncer doing a search, mainly for Dorcha's amusement.

Dorcha smiled. "Whoever made the gnome is a master. My Dad would get a kick out of seeing this detailed handiwork."

Morgan shook the gnome's hand, at a loss of what else to do.

Dorcha laughed. "Did you think he was going to shake back?"

Morgan swatted at her companion. Dorcha backed out of the way giggling.

"I don't know. You got any bright ideas about how to get out of here?"

Dorcha said, "You have to see how funny you looked." Dorcha approached the gnome statue. "Well hello, kind sir." She bowed with a grin then shook the proffered hand.

The small hand gripped back, "Hello," a deep voice replied.

"Ah!" Dorcha yelped.

Both of the women jumped back in surprise. The gnome came to life. Color bled into its skin and clothing. The pointed hat turned red, the trousers black, the robe purple, and the beard fluffed out, still white. His skin went flesh tone. The eyes were an iridescent twinkling blue.

The gnome smiled at their reaction. "Librarian, nice to meet you."

"Hi, I'm Morgan."

"Dorcha," Dorcha stammered.

"I know."

"So we're in the Akashic Records?" Morgan asked.

"I'd say this is more of a personalized annex, but for all intents and purposes, yes. I'm your Librarian. I'm here to help guide you to find what you seek."

"Really?" Dorcha asked.

"Go ahead. Ask anything. From the profound to the mundane, all information is available here."

"Is there a God? Show me God," Dorcha asked.

Nothing happened.

Librarian laughed, "They always ask that."

"Why didn't anything happen? You said this could give us everything," Dorcha said.

"Some things are self-explanatory. That knowledge is all around you. It's not my fault if you can't recognize it. I'm a librarian, not an optometrist."

"Okay, how about what's the spiritual reason I've always had dark circles under my eyes?" Morgan asked.

Librarian pulled a blue diamond the size of a human fist from his pocket. Librarian threw the diamond in a high arc towards the pool of water. When the diamond reached the center of the pool, it halted in mid-air five feet above the water.

The torches flared and amber beams of light shot towards the diamond. The underwater crystalline tube they had entered from pulsed red. A column of energy rose up from the water, creating a base for the hovering blue diamond.

The diamond spun clockwise. It started slowly at first, then picked up speed until it started to blur. Refracted light was thrown around the chamber for a few moments. Then the diamond sharpened in focus and expanded above the water to movie screen size.

The screen showed a high resolution projection of Morgan in the present. Then it showed a present and past-life montage of head wounds caused by many fists, hilts of swords, a Billy club, the butt of an oar, elbows, not looking and running into a pole, getting kicked in the head while sleeping, a heel in the face during a fight and a front kick feint into a roundhouse kick which nailed Morgan in the left temple. There was a momentary shot of a galley ship, and of Morgan hitting her melon on an overhanging bulkhead compartment.

"Oh," Morgan said.

"There's more. Do you need to see it?" Librarian asked.

"I think I get the point. Well if we can ask anything, then who am I going to marry?" Morgan asked.

Librarian smiled. "Just because Time is an illusion does not mean it isn't powerful in its deluded conviction. Your brains are bound to it. You both manifested here at the exact age you are in Waking Life. Even in UnderLife you cannot let go of Time's lures and rules. It is the measure of your mortal life, in which you are actively engaged. Therefore, if there is any question the Akashic Library does not respond to, know it is of your own doing. Your spiritual self is not allowing that particular truth to illuminate itself yet. You are not ready for it. Accept what you can learn and move on with your path. It will take you where you need to go," Librarian said.

"What is the spiritual reason my Mom developed brain tumors?" Morgan asked.

The librarian cocked his head to one side, like he was listening to something far off that Morgan and Dorcha could not hear.

"The entity which was your mother, Gwendolyn Martel, sold her soul in a recent Earth incarnation."

"What?" Morgan reeled.

"Gwendolyn Martel, formerly known as Luciel: Born September 27, 1790 in New Orleans. Luciel's father began raping her at twelve years old. Luciel's mother knew about the attacks, but did nothing to stop him.

"Luciel ran away from home at fifteen years old. She dreamt of being a professional singer, and endured many years of living hand to mouth. Luciel held the belief money and fame would make her happy.

"Enter Sadie: The Devil's Secretary, the Pimp, seducer of souls, destroyer of lives.

"New Orleans, 1810. Luciel sold her soul to Sadie. She made the blood pact without understanding the terrible price she was paying for the ephemeral pleasures of the material realm.

"Sadie delivered on her promises. Luciel became a background singer for someone very famous. She had more money than she knew what to do with.

"After Luciel took the path of darkness, Sadie gathered more souls by having Luciel fuck around and get pregnant. Any lives conceived by Luciel were tethered to Sadie.

"Over the next eight years, Luciel's heart slowly died and her tortured spirit retreated. Money and fame came to mean nothing to Luciel. Luciel became just a body, an evil duplication machine.

"Luciel tried many times to kill herself. Sadie always saved her.

"Luciel poisoned her breast milk to kill her babies, hoping this would free them from hell. It didn't.

"The ninth child, No-Name Baby, the entity currently manifested as Morgan Martel, saved Luciel's light. With No-Name's arrival, Luciel knew her cursed life had to end.

"Luciel crossed paths with a gifted young woman who would one day become the Voodoo High Priestess of New Orleans, Marie Laveau. Marie possessed tremendous spiritual strength."

Librarian turned his attention to the floating energy screen.

* * *

A delicately framed woman with dark skin and an expensive dress went through a curtain of beads. This was Luciel. Luciel entered a place which looked like a museum filled with religious icons.

Another woman was sitting with her back to Luciel in front of an elaborate altar, filled with idols of Catholic saints and Voodoo paraphernalia. The other woman did not stir when Luciel entered. This was Marie Laveau.

"Baboh say you pay great money for help. Tell me your name," Marie said.

When Luciel did not answer right away, Marie stood and turned in one fluid motion. Marie's eyes widened. "There is great evil around you," she said.

Luciel burst into tears. "My name is Luciel. Please help me."

Marie looked at Luciel. An image popped into Marie's head. Marie saw an old vulture picking apart hapless lion cubs who were too young to defend themselves from its razor sharp talons and beak. "Child, what did you do?"

Marie saw another vision, a demon feasting on Luciel's heart and those of her children, born and unborn.

"This will take big work, my time not easily had," Marie said.

Luciel's sobbing increased. "Please make it stop. I'll do anything." Luciel reached into her bosom and pulled out a wad of cash from a secret pocket sewn into her dress. "I can get more."

Marie agreed to help Luciel break the curse. Over the next several months the Voodoo priestess did everything in her power to lift the veil of darkness. Nothing worked. Marie suspected Luciel would not be permitted to heal in this lifetime. The only way to end Luciel's torment would be to release her soul from her body.

Desperate and broken, Luciel was ready to get out any way she could, even if it meant her death.

"I'll give you everything. I have thousands of dollars," Luciel said. "Please end this misery."

After much convincing, and several more failed spiritual experiments, Marie relented.

Marie Laveau borrowed two horses and a wagon. She took Luciel and the Nameless Baby a day's ride into the bayou.

As evening fell they found a wild pecan grove. Marie parked the wagon near an elder tree.

Marie prayed once again for another path for Luciel, but when no inspiration was forthcoming. Resigned, Marie said, "Any last words?"

Luciel said, "Promise me you will help virtuous people whenever you can. Use the power God gave you for good. He gave it to you for a purpose. If you don't your soul will rot like Satan Sadie's."

Luciel picked up a rope which had been fitted with a hangman's noose, and threw it over a thick branch. Luciel pressed the end of the rope into Marie's hands. She got up on the unhitched wagon and slipped the noose around her neck. If Luciel jumped, the rope would only pull tight if Marie braced herself and tied off her end.

"Child, there's got to be another way," Marie said.

"No. We both know there's not. Do it. Give us freedom. Please."

Marie Laveau cried out when she saw Luciel flex her body, leaping off of the wooden wagon towards her death. The heavy rope went taut, slipping a bit in Marie's gloved hands.

Luciel's neck did not break immediately. Luciel clutched at the noose tightening around her neck.

"I'm sorry," Marie said, jerking the rope as hard as she could. The knot around Luciel's throat constricted further. Luciel's oxygen-starved body finally gave up her wounded soul, releasing it to the angels waiting to take her home.

The Nameless Baby wailed, sensing her mother's departure.

Marie slowly unfurled the infant from the satin blanket Marie had given to Luciel as a gift. Marie proceeded to ball up the blanket and place it over the child's weeping face.

Marie Laveau smothered the cursed and dammed child, praying to Jesus that what she was doing was for mercy. It was the only way.

Now they were free.

Marie disposed of the bodies in the swamp. On the long ride home, Marie remembered the promise of charity she had given to Luciel. Marie had a fleeting thought to dismiss the pledge, as it would be mighty inconvenient and costly, but she realized the fate of her own soul hung in the balance.

Marie Laveau kept her promise, content with the knowledge that she had no obligation to have any mercy for the wicked at heart.

* * *

The diamond's spinning slowed. The screen faded.

"Luciel died in 1818," Librarian said.

"That was rough," Dorcha said.

"That's the answer?" Morgan asked. "How does it explain what happened in this lifetime?"

"Selling her soul in the previous life made her vulnerable to attack in this one. She had a curse on her. The negative energy surrounding her was fed by the darkness of her unresolved karma. It manifested as fatal brain tumors."

"Who cast the curse?" Dorcha asked.

Librarian waved a hand. The floating diamond sped up.

* * *

New Orleans – Springtime

Marin and Gwendolyn were nineteen. They had been best friends since junior high school. One day, Marin and Gwendolyn were having a picnic in Jackson Square. They saw a handsome man furiously sketching the Saint Louis Cathedral. After a while, Eddie Martel noticed the beautiful women observing him, and went over to introduce himself. Charming conversation ensued, and both women instantly felt a powerful connection to Eddie.

Gwendolyn told Marin immediately about her overwhelming attraction for Eddie. Marin was attracted to him as well, but she kept her real feelings quiet. Marin believed that once Eddie got to know the two of them, she would obviously be the more dynamic catch.

When Eddie asked if the ladies would meet him and his friend Remy for coffee at Café du Monde, the women accepted. All four of them were pleased to discover how fun and effortless it was to spend time together.

Gwendolyn was a big hearted, generous, sensitive soul. In those days Marin did not appreciate or reciprocate Gwendolyn's trust and adoration. Even though Marin thought of Gwenny as a sister, Marin secretly regarded Gwendolyn's tenderness as frailty.

So sad, Marin thought, Gwenny's going to be devastated when Eddie and I get together. It's for the best, though. The heart knows what it needs.

Gwendolyn and Marin had known Eddie for only six days when he called to ask them to sit for the painting that was to become The Secrets of Women. Marin stared at Eddie with intense focus for hours while he painted. Gwendolyn was shy, often remarking that her gauzy dress was too revealing.

Marin saw Gwendolyn's interruptions, anxious primping, and batting of the eyelashes as sickening petitions for attention. Eddie was enchanted by Gwendolyn.

Later, Marin convinced herself that Eddie would have loved her and not Gwendolyn if only Gwendolyn hadn't distracted and enslaved him that day with her helplessness and great legs.

They met Remy LeTour for drinks after the sitting. Remy hadn't been able to stop thinking of Marin since their first encounter. Marin responded to Remy's amorous attention in the hope that it would make Eddie jealous, but it was a feeble attempt. Eddie was too enraptured by Gwendolyn to notice or care. Marin wanted to run out of the bar, but her pride kept her from leaving. She was too much of a coward to be honest about what she was feeling. Marin began a relationship with Remy to stay close to Eddie. The men loved double dating. As far as they were concerned, it was the perfect opportunity to be surrounded by their favorite people in the world. A part of Marin enjoyed Remy's sexual devotion and reverence for her body. Marin's outward behavior was kind, but it was compensating for the guilt she was feeling about her wicked fantasies of betrayal.

Remy enjoyed the torment of Marin's enigmatic behavior and

inconsistent affection. Even after they got married, Remy felt Marin's emotional resistance. It was a total turn on for the Remy. Remy chased Marin relentlessly.

Marin's hesitancy gave Remy all the time and space he needed to be sure of his love for her. Slowly she began to relent. Marin knew Remy would be a good father. His sculptures were popular, so Marin never worried about Remy's ability to provide financial support.

A year passed. One day Gwendolyn confessed to Marin that she might be pregnant. Eighteen hours later, Eddie proposed to Gwendolyn. Marin was miserable, but she buried her desire. She made denial the law of the land. It's what ultimately drove Marin to law school. She craved distraction, a challenge, and the capability to be financially autonomous. It was a good fit for Marin.

The day after Morgan was born, Remy proposed to Marin. Marin accepted.

Years rolled by. Deep inside Marin's heart, the fire for Eddie grew. Marin and Eddie acted as friends, sharing an intimacy which Marin cherished. Marin often fantasized about how perfect everything would be if only she and Gwendolyn could switch husbands.

When Marin got pregnant with Dorcha, her silent obsession for Eddie began to recede. Remy was attentive and excited to become a father, and Marin thought she had finally fallen in love with him.

Unfortunately, by the time Dorcha was three years old, Marin's lust for Eddie flared again.

At Marin's favorite hair and nail salon, she had heard whispers of gossip about a man who granted wishes for a price. The stories were always told by someone several persons removed from the folks involved, such as, my old roommate's cousin dated someone who knew a man that visited this witch doctor. His son was in a coma. The doctors said it would be a miracle if the boy woke up without brain damage. The father begged the witch doctor to help him. He promised the witch doctor the deed to his expensive house if he revived his son.

A week later, the boy came out of the coma good as new. The father handed over the deed to his house, and promptly moved out. In all the stories, everyone always ended up giving the witch doctor what they had promised.

Marin started a quiet search for a witch doctor. After months of plying her more shady acquaintances with drinks, Marin was directed to the home of Khenan Catarino. Khenan lived on the North Shore of Lake Pontchartrain. It was said he accepted new visitors the first and third Monday of every month.

One Monday Marin went to Khenan's house. Marin noticed how affluent Khenan's neighborhood was, and she started to believe the story about raising the boy from the coma.

Marin rang the doorbell.

An aged man with dark skin and dreadlocks answered the door.

"Hello, Xavier sent me," Marin said.

"Welcome," Khenan said, motioning for Marin to enter his place. "Sit."

Marin entered.

"What wish do you want granted, my child?" Khenan rumbled in his Caribbean-accented baritone-voice.

Marin took a deep breath. "I want Edison Martel to make love to me and for him to want to explore a romantic relationship with me." Marin said it all in a rush, amazed to speak those forbidden words out loud.

"Give me your hands," Khenan said. He studied Marin's palms for several minutes, nodding and grumbling under his breath. Finally, he released Marin's hands. Khenan's eyes bored into hers. "I can grant your wish. It is $10,000 in cash, up front, for my services and for the materials required. Many moons will pass before your dream reaches fruition. You will know the spell has taken root when a permanent, undeniable change in the structure of this relationship occurs. However, $10,000 is not the true price. The true price is that you shall see the world in a radically different way. Do you still wish to proceed? Once the pact is made, there is no turning back."

Marin didn't like price or the mystic's quick answer. Her wiser instincts told her to leave the house and not look back.

Instead, Marin bartered, "I'll give you six thousand."

"This is not a negotiation. Ten thousand and I promise you will bed this man."

"How do I know this is going to work? What assurances can you give me?"

Khenan Catarino spoke with rapid condescension, "Do you think I would be allowed to live here all these years if I did not have great power? I've been helping people get their hearts' desires since you were a glimmer in your mother's eye. If you don't need my help, no one is keeping you here."

Khenan had unwavering confidence in his mystical abilities. His refusal to pander for Marin's business was persuasive to her. What Khenan said was making sense. Of course she would see the world in a radically different way! She would fulfill a desire that had burned deep within for so long, and it would alter her view and experience of life permanently.

The hard part was how to cough up ten grand.

Marin took out a thirteen thousand dollar loan against her house. Marin wanted the extra three grand for a new wardrobe and spending money. Later, Marin lied to Remy and said that the mortgage was her parents' remaining debt on the house.

Marin paid Khenan Catarino. Khenan told her to get a lock of Eddie's hair. Marin had to intertwine it with a lock of her own. Then Marin should cut her hand, soak the hair in her blood, and let it dry under the light of a full moon. Next Marin would wrap the bound clump of hair in red silk and sleep with it under her pillow until the new moon. Then she was to return to Khenan's house at eleven the following night to finish the spell.

Marin gathered and prepared the ingredients. By the full moon she was ready.

The plan seemed fated to work. During the two weeks Marin slept with the silk swathed hair under her pillow, Remy was in Austin for an art show.

Marin went to Khenan Catarino's house the night after the new moon. A small voice inside her cautioned her to walk away. Cut her losses. Another one argued Marin was setting things right. Why would she possess such enduring feelings if they were never meant to be together? Marin's Ego won.

Thick incense smoke wafted from the house when Marin opened the door. Marin found Khenan feeding a blazing fire with more logs.

"You did what I asked?"

"Yes," Marin said.

"Give the charm to me."

Marin obeyed. Khenan motioned for Marin to lie down face-up on the bear skin rug in front of the fire. Khenan started chanting in a language Marin did not understand. He anointed her forehead, hands, and feet with a pungent essential oil. Khenan unfurled the bundle Marin had prepared and he draped the silk piece over Marin's heart. Khenan's voice rose in pitch and he did a skipping dance, counter-clockwise, around Marin's prostrate form. The faster Khenan moved, the louder he got. At his crescendo, Khenan used a metal rod to plunge the blood-stained hair deep into the fire.

Across town, at the same moment, Gwendolyn got a full blown, light and sound sensitive, nausea inducing, tunnel-vision migraine.

Early the next morning, Gwendolyn could swear she heard knocking. Gwendolyn answered the front door. No one was there.

Over the next several months Gwendolyn often heard phantom knocking. One day she thought someone was on the roof, and made Eddie take a look. Later at dinner Gwendolyn had a bit of a meltdown. She was convinced something was in the walls. No one else heard it. Six year old Morgan felt a terrifying disturbance she could not articulate.

The whole thing scared and embarrassed Gwendolyn. After a few false alarms Gwendolyn stopped telling anyone when she heard knocking and tried to ignore the sounds.

* * *

Morgan – Age Seven
Martel Home – 12:45 AM

Morgan woke up in her bed with a start. Her little arm was clutching Teddy Bear around its neck in a vice grip. Some commotion was coming from her parent's bedroom. Morgan could hear rapid low muttering and rustling noises.

At seven years old Morgan had an adult awareness, and it felt as though she had awakened into a lake of anxiety. Curiosity overcame Morgan's fear. Morgan slid her legs out from underneath the covers to go investigate. The no-skid bottoms of Morgan's powder blue fuzzy long john footie pajamas made soft slapping sounds on the hardwood floors. Morgan was quietly panicking in a boogeyman-is-in-the-closet kind of way. She opened her parent's bedroom door and peered inside.

Morgan saw her mother moving about the room. Gwendolyn was agitated. She picked up a mirror and looked upon her face in horror. "This is not my face. Who am I? I'm a Vietnamese student. I have a twenty page paper due tomorrow which I have to finish after I get off of work tonight. No! Wait! That's not who I am. I'm an old lady and my show, my favorite show, Golden Girls, is about to start… got to get my medicine, my reflux is acting up. No, not right. I'm Candi. A fifty dollar hooker and it is cold outside. AGH! Stop talking! Oh the voices. If I could just get some quiet, I could figure myself out."

Gwendolyn continued to grumble and stare at herself in the mirror. Over and over she exclaimed her feelings, and then suddenly denied them. Gwendolyn paced around the room barefoot. The soles of her feet were black from accumulated dirt.

"Shut up! Don't contradict me. I'm fine. I've got it all together. MORGAN!" Gwendolyn wheeled on her frightened daughter, "Stop yelling at me, sweetie. I can't hear you in this crowd."

Morgan looked around the room. She and her mother were its only occupants.

Her mother raged, "Don't tell me you can't see them? Are you blind? They won't stop talking. Chitter chatter all day and night." Gwendolyn held the mirror up to Morgan. "See them, honey? There are hordes of them and their dirty words, their doubts, their fears edging into my good sense. Shut UP! What do I have to do?" Gwendolyn slammed the mirror on her bedpost, shattering pieces everywhere.

"I know! I'll cut them out. That's it! Oh why didn't I think of this before? If I can just show them how serious I am maybe they will give me some peace." Gwendolyn grabbed a large shard of the mirror and waved it around the room as if she were surrounded by foes. "See? I'm not afraid to do it."

"Mommy?" squeaked Morgan's voice.

"Be silent, baby, mommy is trying to get these strangers with their lecherous, needy, endless thoughts out of the house." Gwendolyn jabbed the shard at an unseen foe on her right. "I know what you all want and you're sick! You hear me? You are all sick panting dogs. There is a child present, for God's sake. I have half a mind to bleach out all of your thoughts. Clean them up. Cut them out. Where are my pills? Which one of you stole my pills?"

Petrified, Morgan stood there with her back against the wall, Teddy Bear clutched to her chest. Morgan's pajamas were soaked through with sweat.

"Morgan! Don't look at me like that, like I'm crazy. I'm the sane one! It's the world that's insane, all of the killing and suffering, swindling, sucking… And for what? We all end up worm food in the end. Yap yap yap, that's all you do. That's all anyone does. Talking in circles about how they are going to do this or do that. What does it matter? Nobody changes. Nobody grows. No one is really happy. Honey, listen to me and remember this, anyone who tells you they are happy is full of shit. How could they possibly be serene without being mentally retarded? You'd have to be nuts to think you're actually enjoying all of this restriction and dirt. People wearing torture devices around their necks and calling it faith… and if I get one more telemarketer call here I swear I'm going to rip my hair out. How dare they interrupt me while I'm trying to have a nice thought? I don't care about your long distance plan. Stop calling me! Take me off the list. Scratch my name out. I know. I know what to do, how to end this conversation once and for all."

Gwendolyn sliced the shard of glass across her throat. Morgan was paralyzed, horrified. Time slowed. For a second nothing happened. Then Gwendolyn convulsed and made a gurgling sound, and blood began to pour from her neck, soaking her robe.

Gwendolyn's eyes cleared into momentary lucidity. Gwendolyn looked down at her blood flowing down her chest, then up at her daughter, and she realized the sickening finality of her actions. Gwendolyn opened her mouth to speak, to apologize. It was too late.

Morgan pulled herself away from the wall. She sprinted towards her mother's collapsing body, throwing her little arms around Gwenny's waist as they crumpled to the ground.

"Mommy No, Mommy No, mommy please please nonononono…"

* * *

Akashic Records Cave - The Present

Morgan's scream echoed the scream of her seven-year old self on the energy screen. Tears were streaming down Morgan and Dorcha's faces. They collapsed into each other's arms.

"I had no idea," Dorcha sobbed.

"I know," Morgan gasped. She was doing her best not to hyperventilate.

Dorcha felt her infatuation with Balthazar evaporate like rain on lava. There was no way in hell she would be making the same mistake her mother made. Dorcha was confident that she could come up with all new ways to shoot herself in the foot.

Librarian's voice cut into their thoughts. "My condolences. It is important for you to see the energy-field version of those last moments of Gwendolyn's life."

The women looked up and saw an overhead still of Gwendolyn brandishing the mirror shard and Morgan on the other side of the room. Librarian snapped his fingers. An overlay of an energy pattern appeared on the screen. It looked like fine white spider webbing that Gwendolyn was projecting to hold Morgan at bay.

"Gwendolyn Martel possessed dormant telepathic and telekinetic abilities. These abilities became activated by the pressure on her brain from the tumors, and they were heightened by her emotional state. The tumors ripped apart Gwendolyn's natural psychic shielding, leaving her vulnerable to the thoughts of everyone in the neighborhood. Gwendolyn was bombarded with a flood of information. It overloaded her delicate psyche. It also engaged a latent telekinetic talent to keep her daughter at a safe distance."

For years Morgan had never forgiven herself for not doing anything to stop her mother's death. Finally Morgan knew the truth. Gwendolyn committed suicide to protect Morgan from the chaos erupting from her burgeoning madness.

"Do you want to see the last segment?" Librarian asked.

"No," Dorcha said, "But show it to us anyway."

* * *

Berkeley, California

The Martel and LeTour families lived together in Berkeley for a few years after Gwendolyn died in New Orleans. Marin was in love with Eddie as ever, and she was forced to stand by while Eddie dated many other women. Marin became jealous and aggressive with Eddie. Their banter, flirting, and intimacy grew.

Remy was too busy working to notice. All of Remy's work for the business was paying off in notoriety, and he was loving the attention.

One night they all were smashed after a wildly successful art opening. After locking up, Remy went home to pass out. Eddie and Marin stayed and continued drinking. Finishing a half bottle of Jameson seemed like the right thing to do.

Eddie was in a vulnerable place. The first series of girlfriend-turned-Gwendolyn portraits were the main feature of the show. Seeing all of the portraits together, Eddie's soon-to-be-ex-girlfriend Mona had gotten it right away, left shortly after, and never talked to Eddie again.

"Eddie! You'll never believe how much I got for True New Year!" Marin said, gesturing towards Eddie's painting of springtime in a redwood forest.

Marin showed him a receipt.

"You're kidding. Shouldn't there be a decimal point?"

"No sir," Marin said.

They embraced. Eddie kissed Marin on the cheek. The touch of Eddie's soft lips on her skin was too much for Marin to bear. She kissed Eddie on the lips. The first kiss was so gentle. They moved in for further contact.

Then the cold truth of whose wife Eddie was about to make out with ripped through his consciousness. He stepped back from Marin.

"No. This is wrong. I'm not allowed to do this. You're Remy's girl. Remy has loved you since he first set eyes on you," said Eddie.

"Which is how I feel about you," Marin said.

"I... I'm flattered... But..."

"Remy and I haven't been happy for a long time."

"Really? You two have always seemed fine to me. Remy only has wonderful things to say about you."

"He's blind to who I really am. You've always understood the real me. I knew it the first time I saw Secrets of Women."

"You and Gwendolyn were radiant. I remember thinking that whatever guys you ended up loving would be the luckiest guys in the world. I had no idea you both would become family to me. I miss Gwenny so much."

"I do too. It's only out of respect for her that I didn't tell you how I felt about you."

"Why now?"

"You're dating again and... it... my... heart cries out for you... I've loved you for so long..."

Marin leaned in and kissed Eddie. Then she pulled back. Marin searched Eddie's face desperately for the slightest hint of approval or desire.

Eddie saw how hurt Marin got when he didn't respond. He was edging towards the abyss of blackout drunk. Eddie decided to fulfill Marin's wish to have sex with him.

During a crazy moment of post-coital bliss, Eddie fantasized about being in a relationship with Marin.

Sobriety hit at the break of dawn. Eddie realized what a huge mistake he had made. That morning, out of shame, Eddie packed Morgan and himself up, and they drove to Los Angeles.

When Remy found out that Eddie was gone, he and Marin had a spectacular fight. Marin finally came clean. Dorcha was sleeping over at a friend's house and missed the fireworks.

"You're a great father, provider, and friend, but I've been in love with Eddie since the day we met. Don't look at me like this is all such a huge shock. A part of you has known the whole time. I think you excused it away because it was something we had in common. I don't know if you desire him carnally, and frankly I don't care."

"What? You bitch. How dare you put this on me? Like I somehow allowed this or gave you permission to betray me. We're divorcing," Remy said.

"Fine. I've long since outgrown you anyway," Marin said.

"You're fucking kidding me. The growth in your character over the years has seen about as much effort as a watered down block of clay. How could you be so selfish? If what you say is true, that you've been harboring this great passionate love for Eddie, did you ever stop to think of what you'd destroy along the way? If you cared about me at all you should've never married me, let alone bore my child!"

"Having Dorcha is the best thing I've ever done."

"I agree. It's beyond over for us, but let's not make this any harder on Dorcha. And fuck you by the way for taking Morgan out of all our lives. Great job. You've single handedly annihilated an entire family, marriage, decades of friendship, and a dear, loving sibling relationship as well. Congratulations, asshole."

Marin had never seen Remy this hurt or angry. Marin was hit with the reality of the devastation she had created.

"I'm sorry, I'm so sorry, you're right. Please Remy stop. What can I do? Tell me what can I do to fix this?"

"Live with what you've done. I don't want to ever see you again! I'm moving to Seattle. Dorcha will stay with you for the last couple months of school. Then she'll come up to be with me for the summer."

"Then what? You're not going to try to have full custody, are you?"

"I'm not sure yet, although you certainly don't deserve her. What a pathetic example of nurturing and loyalty you are. I loathe leaving my angel with the disgusting, adulterous pariah her mother turned out to be. However, I need time to fix up a new home for her. Plus, Dorcha's really going to need her playmates in kindergarten right now since you took away her closest friend."

When Dorcha got dropped off at home the next day, she found her father packing. That night Remy drove around aimlessly for hours, and then he slept uncomfortably in his car. In the morning he left for Seattle to start over.

Dorcha cried herself into a head cold.

Marin's vision deteriorated steadily after her night with Eddie. She did her best to hide it from her daughter, but by the time Dorcha came back from her first summer in Seattle, Marin was days away from being completely blind.

CHAPTER THIRTEEN
CHINESE HOLMIES

Morgan and Dorcha's eyes snapped open. They were back in the Skyscraper Space. August and Louise were sitting on either side of them in meditation.

"Oh…" started Morgan.

"My God," finished Dorcha.

August and Louise waited for the women to explain.

Morgan jumped up and paced around the room. Dorcha continued to sit, head in her hands, taking deep steady breaths.

The older women were patient, despite the slow torture of suspense.

A quarter of an hour passed before Morgan told August and Louise everything. Morgan knew that talking would help her to process the skeletons they had just ousted from the familial closet. Every so often Dorcha would speak up, adding details to Morgan's narrative.

"We need to know if what we saw was real, or if we somehow made it up," Morgan said.

"Why would you think it didn't happen?" Louise asked.

"The UnderLife can be a tricky place to interpret. Don't get me wrong, I know what we saw is true. Confirmation in Waking Life would help with closure."

"We could ask my Mom," Dorcha said.

"Do you think she'll tell us the truth?" Morgan asked.

"If what we watched is really what went down, Mom might be relieved to confess her secrets."

"I feel like I should be angry with her or hate her for what happened. But it's weird, I don't. Maybe I haven't absorbed all of this yet. Up until now my only perspective of Marin was memories of her love and kindness after Mom died."

Dorcha shook her head. "This is so confusing. I never understood cosmically why she went blind. I thought it was one of those fucked up 'That's Life' moments, where something tragic happens and the only thing to do is deal with it, because nothing is going to change it. And now, we find out she traded her eye sight, her best friend, and her marriage for one night of drunken sex with a man she had been fixating on secretly for nearly a decade."

"Yeah, it's kind of hard to be pissed at her knowing what a terrible price she paid for a desperate mistake born from unexpressed love."

Morgan thought about it while taking a bong hit.

Dorcha shrugged. "We could call?"

"True, although for something as delicate as this it would be better if we ask her in person," Morgan said.

"You're right, and it's been too long since I've seen her. Mom will be so excited we found each other after all this time."

"I hope so. Well, it looks like we're going on a road trip."

"Excellent idea, ladies," Louise said. August also nodded her assent.

* * *

A rare heavy rain had been drenching Los Angeles since early morning. Captain Taylor Tess appreciated the cover as he watched Morgan and Dorcha scurrying from Dorcha's apartment. They were carrying luggage and provisions to Morgan's dirt-shrouded white Ford Escort. Taylor sat in a black Chevrolet Tahoe LTZ 4x4 a couple of blocks away and studied the two women through binoculars.

Morgan and Dorcha got into the car. On the driver's side, Morgan cracked open a Diet Coke and took appreciative gulps of it before turning the engine over. Dorcha fiddled with her iPod while Morgan weaseled the car out of a tight parallel parking spot.

Captain Tess let Morgan and Dorcha get a considerable amount of distance ahead before starting his SUV. Captain Tess checked the laptop screen sitting in the passenger seat. The night before, Captain Tess had placed a tracking device on the metal framework of Morgan's car. A red dot moving across the screen of Captain Tess's laptop marked Morgan and Dorcha's progress. They were headed for Highway 101.

Taylor followed them up north to Berkeley. For most of the six hour trip he stayed out of eyesight. Every once in a while Captain Tess caught up with them and got a visual. He thought the women were clueless about being tracked, but, as an expert hunter, Taylor rarely underestimated a target.

* * *

The entrance to Marin's townhouse complex sported a staircase and wheelchair ramp. There was a directory in English and Braille. Morgan brushed her hand across the Braille version while Dorcha fished her keys out of her purse.

"I didn't tell Mom anything about you yet. I was going to say something on the phone when I told her I was coming up for a visit, except I froze. I don't know why," Dorcha said.

"I understand. I'm still overwhelmed by what we saw," Morgan said.

The interior of the complex was painted stark white and was O.C.D. clean. Dorcha took four blue plastic shoe covers from a box on the inside of the gate. She handed two of them to Morgan, and told her to put them over her shoes.

It took Morgan a few minutes to understand the need for such a high level of cleanliness and the tactile aesthetics of the complex. A blind person doesn't care what color the wall is painted, but the clean surfaces and the many Braille maps were important to the residents. Morgan enjoyed touching the velvety walls as Dorcha led her through the complex.

Dorcha knocked on the front door of her mother's townhouse before keying in. As she stepped inside, Dorcha took off her shoes and motioned for Morgan to follow suit. Morgan relished the feel of Marin's soft, plush carpet.

The women heard silverware being put down. Moments later Marin appeared. Morgan's heart sank when she noticed that Marin's eyes failed to track any movement. Marin's hair had gone grey since the last time Morgan had seen her.

"Dorcha! Baby doll!" Marin opened up her arms and moved side to side in anticipation of holding her daughter.

"Hi Mom," Dorcha said in a sweet voice about half an octave higher than she normally spoke. Dorcha smiled and moved forward to embrace her mother. Marin gasped.

"Morgan?"

"Holy shit, how did you know I was here?" Morgan asked.

Marin laughed, tears slipping from her sightless eyes.

Dorcha bear-hugged her mother, taking the breath out of both of them.

Marin stuck out an arm in Morgan's general direction, still holding her daughter tightly with the other.

"Well, get over here, girl. Let me touch you."

Any resistance, anger, or detachment Morgan had been feeling towards Marin melted away. Morgan went in for the group hug.

Marin stroked Morgan's hair.

"I wish I could see what beautiful young women you have turned out to be."

"Oh Mom," Dorcha squeezed Marin.

"Seriously, Momma M, how did you know I was here?"

"I've missed being called that. Well, honey, you've always had a unique smell which I had forgotten about until right now. Going blind and quitting smoking has done wonders to my schnoz."

A kind-looking man in his fifties appeared in the doorway to the kitchen.

"Hi, Keith." Dorcha disengaged from her mother and gave him a big hug. "This is Morgan, my first friend in this lifetime."

"Hello," Morgan said, clasping Keith's hand.

"Pleasure to meet you," Keith said smiling.

Marin moved towards the dining room, her hand grazing the wall to guide the way. "We just sat down to dinner. Have you ladies eaten? There's plenty. We made chicken enchiladas."

"Nice!" Dorcha said.

* * *

Dinner was a delicious combination of Mexican food and Marin grilling Morgan about her life. Morgan recounted the intervening years without mentioning UnderLife. She used Balthazar as a convenient shield subject.

After dinner, Keith retired to his study to give the women some alone time.

They congregated in the living room, which had been furnished with yummy-to-the-touch velour couches. Morgan and Dorcha sat on either side of Marin.

Marin leaned forward, over the coffee table, and inhaled the refreshing aroma of her peppermint tea. She blew on the hot liquid. "How did you two reconnect?"

"Before we delve into that," Morgan said. "I need to tell you about UnderLife."

At first, Marin didn't want to talk about the past. She admitted to wanting Eddie for many years, and to the one-night affair that had scattered the families, but Marin wouldn't go into further detail on the subject. Eventually Marin admitted to seeing a psychic and giving him money to cast a love spell on Eddie. "He said I would see the world in a whole different way. One year later, to the day, Gwenny died from a freak brain tumor. That night with Eddie was three years after Gwenny's death. By the following year I was blind. The voodoo man was right. Eddie did explore a romance with me, but for only one night. I don't know how Khenan caused such a sick and twisted result. It only amounted to a nightmare, a belated spark of an affair with Eddie, then more loss and sorrow."

When Marin uttered Khenan's name, Morgan and Dorcha looked at each other. Now they had undeniable confirmation.

Marin continued, "I understand if you hate me, Morgan. I was a foolish, selfish, naïve, and jealous woman. Your mother did not deserve any of my passive-aggressive spite or malice. Gwenny was a blessed soul, who loved us all with innocent, unconditional devotion. I owe her and you a tremendous debt."

"Hating you isn't going to bring Mom back. Granted, this is a lot to process. I know you didn't realize what terrible forces you were setting into motion."

Tears trickled down Marin's face. She reached for Morgan. "Thank you, thank you so much. I shall always feel shame for what I did, because I was too much of a coward to be honest about how I felt."

They embraced. Dorcha joined the hug.

"Lovely ladies," Marin said, holding their hands and squeezing. "I'm exhausted. I'm going to turn in. Have a good night, girls. Please help yourself to anything in the house. I'm so glad you're here."

The three women snuggled with each other for a bit. Dorcha hummed her happiness and Morgan murmured, "Thanks, Momma M," and kissed Marin's cheek.

Marin retreated into the hallway, and went to the bathroom connected to her bedroom. She had barely closed the door and flipped the fan switch on when she began to cry. Marin sobbed with relief and with a dash of self-pity for her reckless choices in the past.

A huge weight had lifted from Marin's heart. She had always felt gnawing guilt that her dark pact would somehow curse the girls. It was a blessed miracle that they had grown up healthy and whole.

Keith knocked on the door to the bathroom, "Honey, you okay in there?"

* * *

On the roof of the building next door, Captain Tess was hiding amongst the solar panels. He was holding up a super-sensitive shotgun microphone, ignoring the protesting ache in his arm from holding this position for the last several hours.

Taylor watched Marin and Keith getting ready for bed while Morgan and Dorcha continued to stay up and talk.

* * *

"They're totally going to smell it," Morgan said, looking over her shoulder at the empty hallway.

"No worries," (puff) (puff) "Here." Dorcha handed Morgan the pipe.

"Marin doesn't care if you smoke?"

"Nope, mom has general anxiety about my vision and thinks it could help prevent something. I think she's relieved I'd rather smoke pot than drink. Mom said those early years in New Orleans and Berkeley were drenched in alcohol."

Morgan glanced over again at the deserted hallway, shrugged her shoulders, and took the bowl from Dorcha for a toke.

They puffed for a while in contented silence. Both were amazed by the unbelievable things that had been happening since their reunion. Their gazes met. Each knew exactly what the other was thinking. They giggled.

Dorcha took another hit. She exhaled a hefty puff of smoke and said, "Do you think I should tell R-Dad about this?"

"And confirm that the ex-wife never really loved him all those years? I think it would make Remy go through the nightmare again, and for what purpose?"

Dorcha considered this. "You're right, it doesn't change anything. It's not like this is a subject Dad ever brought up because he wants to have a sensitive chat and a good cry."

"Yeah, your Dad's pretty old-school stoic about certain things. The only time I remember seeing him cry was after G-Mom died."

"He loved her, loved the whole family with his whole heart. Dad thought everyone was as happy as him."

* * *

Captain Tess waited for an hour on the roof after everyone went to bed before returning to his vehicle.

To the casual observer, Captain Tess's Chevy Tahoe seemed like it had been packed by a well-organized camper. There was enough gear, thermal blankets, and organic food rations to sustain four people for two weeks during a snow storm. The rear seats in the SUV had been pulled out to create storage space for extra equipment.

The casual observer couldn't see that there were various secret compartments concealed throughout the car's benign-looking interior. These compartments contained a sniper rifle, two handguns, plenty of ammunition, five pounds of C-4, three grenades, Dragon Skin body armor, four rolls of duct tape, plastic sheeting, a shovel, an axe, half a dozen knives ranging in size from throwing to hunting, a four person tent, rappelling equipment, and fifty feet of rope.

Captain Tess entered the back of the truck. He closed a black security curtain to block any view through the windshield. Then he pulled down privacy shades on all of the windows.

Next Captain Tess plugged the voice recorder in his pocket into his laptop and uploaded the conversations he had recorded.

While Captain Tess waited for the computer to download the information and clean it up through a filter program, Captain Tess decided it was time for an I Ching reading. Captain Tess picked up a thin briefcase which held several IDs, passports, cash, a velvet bag containing a dozen precious stones, and a small journal with a pen bound to it by a rubber band. He retrieved the journal, and flipped the pages to one half-filled with short and long horizontal lines.

This time Captain Tess used three quarters to cast the hexagram and got Thirty-Four into Thirty-Five: Power of the Great going into Progress, with four changing lines. He stood in an excellent position. Captain Tess opened a digital version of Carol Anthony's Guide to the I Ching on his laptop and studied her interpretations for the hexagrams and changing lines. He ate a protein bar while reading. The book counseled him to be careful about getting cocky and overplaying his hand, or else it would put his entire mission in jeopardy.

In Captain Tess's journal, next to the current hexagrams, he wrote, "Accepted, rejected, misunderstood, understood, all are ultimately irrelevant. Attend to the task put in front of me on my path."

Captain Tess unpacked a sleeping bag and stretched out in the back of the truck. He set the alarm on his watch to wake him in five hours. Captain Tess fell asleep with the recording of Marin, Dorcha, and Morgan playing softly in his left ear.

* * *

By the time Morgan woke up, showered, and dressed, it was almost lunchtime. Dorcha had gotten up a few hours earlier and had spent the morning curled up with her mother on the couch after breakfast. They talked in low voices, enjoying each other.

When the three women sat down to eat the turkey melts Dorcha had made for lunch, Morgan asked, "Where's Keith?"

Marin turned towards the general direction of Morgan's voice. "Keith left earlier to run errands. He'll be back tonight for dinner."

"Ah," Morgan said.

They ate in amiable silence for a few minutes before Marin said, "Did Dorcha tell you about when she blindfolded herself for two weeks? She wanted to be able to empathize with the difficult acclimation of living in darkness."

"No, she didn't," Morgan said. "What a cool thing to do."

"Yeah, two of the most challenging weeks of my life," Dorcha said.

"You got very grumpy," Marin said.

"No kidding. It was hard. I'd get depressed and bitchy. Then I'd feel enormous guilt for my bad attitude. I missed the Tarot so much I started seeing the cards in my head…" Dorcha's trailed off as an idea struck her. "I just remembered, I woke up thinking maybe there's a way we can use UnderLife to help Mom's eyes heal."

Morgan nodded, "It's certainly worth a try…"

"No," interrupted Marin in a stern voice, "Girls, you don't understand. I needed to lose my sight to see what was important in life. It's a blessing, believe me. If we can't bring Gwenny back to life, it wouldn't be fair for me to regain the use of my eyes. You have each grown into women I feel honored to know. Please use your gifts to keep yourselves in balance and to assist people who deserve the effort."

"Mom…"

"It was generous of you to offer. I am sure your paths are headed towards greater work than me."

They spent the rest of the day shopping with Marin. Dorcha was the only person Marin trusted to dress her in the simple, elegant style she favored. Morgan could tell this was a favorite activity between mother and daughter, and it delighted Morgan to tag along.

Morgan and Dorcha returned to Los Angeles the next afternoon.

* * *

A week later, Captain Tess was holed up on top of the building next to the parking lot of Morgan's gym. Through the scope of his sniper rifle, Captain Tess did a scan of the area while watching Morgan walking towards her car.

Morgan, her hair still wet from swimming, congratulated herself on a strong workout. The sun was setting. The smog hanging over Los Angeles filtered the light into rich pinks and purples. Morgan's eyes tracked a flock of birds as they flew over a nearby apartment building.

Morgan saw something on the roof in her peripheral vision and the scene shifted.

* * *

Suddenly Morgan was standing on top of the building, five feet behind the man crouched at the edge. Morgan was trembling from the adrenaline that raw fear had dumped into her body. It took Morgan a second to realize that not only was she standing where she had just been looking, but the man watching her was holding a rifle aimed at her in Waking Life.

Captain Tess's eyes widened with shock when his quarry disappeared from his sight. He felt a presence behind him and instinct took over. Captain Tess spun up from the ground with a sweeping low kick. This caught Morgan behind the knees and buckled her legs. Taylor pinned Morgan to the ground with a knife at her throat before she could react. It would take a miniscule amount of pressure for the razor edge of the blade to break the skin.

Morgan had no idea who the man was, but she was at his complete mercy. Morgan was aware that if he killed her here, she would pass out in Waking Life and be vulnerable to further attacks. Morgan would have berated herself for committing such a blatant error, but the cold steel against her jugular postponed any self-reproach.

Although, if he had intended to hurt her, wouldn't he have done it already? Morgan wondered.

His smell was musty and foreign. Not in the Italian-villa, let's-go-check-it-out kind of way, but more like an I've-stopped-breathing-deeply-through-my-nose-it's-so-overwhelming smell. But it wasn't an unwashed smell. No, it seemed clean. His pungent musk was distinctly not for her, no question. Morgan wondered briefly if her nose reigned over her physical attractions.

"Can I help you? What do you want?" Morgan sputtered, doing her best not to sound scared.

The man released her. Morgan scrambled to her feet and backed away from him, rubbing her neck.

"You are training with me tomorrow from three pm to seven pm," he ordered.

"What kind of training? Who are you?"

"Captain Taylor Tess, your man-at-arms. I'm assigned to assist you in developing martial, strength, and mental facilities."

"Really?"

"Yes. We are to meet in Century City at the Skyscraper Space. August and Louise sent me."

"They did? Why didn't they tell me you were coming?"

"It was determined this would be a good opportunity for a low risk test."

"Is that why you had a rifle aimed at me?"

"Not at you, around you, for protection," Captain Tess said.

"Well, you sure scared the hell out of me."

"Not my intention. I don't know how you picked up on my surveillance, or how you got behind me so fast. This must be UnderLife."

"Yes it is. How long have you known August and Louise?"

"Not long. Louise instructed me to tell you what I said before so you would know they vouched for me."

"Why couldn't they give me a heads-up themselves? We live in such a fancy age with newfangled gadgets like phones and computers. Even snail mail or a homing pigeon would have sufficed."

"I believe they want to keep things as clandestine as possible. Most forms of communication can be intercepted or overheard. You are too valuable and vulnerable an asset to let the rest of the world know who you are quite yet."

The UnderLife episode ended.

Morgan vaulted back to her Waking Self and staggered a few steps to regain her balance from the swift shift. She looked at the spot where Captain Tess had been standing on the roof. Morgan thought she saw a shadowy form disappearing into the building.

Three to seven tomorrow, Morgan reminded herself.

* * *

The next day Morgan arrived at the Skyscraper Space for training. Entering through the security door, the first thing she saw was Captain Tess sitting in meditation at the center of the hardwood floor. He was wearing a white karate uniform with midnight blue trim. Captain Tess's belt was also midnight blue, with a red stripe running horizontally along its length in the middle. He opened his eyes and rose when Morgan came in. Captain Tess stood at attention and bowed. Morgan mimicked him, not knowing what else to do.

Captain Tess's head tilted, indicating for Morgan to look at something behind her. A brand new white karate uniform was hanging on a hook near the door, waiting for Morgan to put it on. When she returned from changing in the bathroom, Captain Tess showed Morgan how to wrap and tie the white belt around her waist.

"The uniform you are wearing is called a do bohk," Captain Tess said. "My primary mandate is to protect you. The most effective way to do this is to train you to be able to defend yourself. I'm going to instruct you in Korean Karate, Gracie Brazilian Ju-Jitsu, and I Ching."

"Oh wow, I've always wanted to get into martial arts. What's Ee-Cheeng?" Morgan asked.

"I Ching is the easy way. It is one of China's oldest canonical texts. It has been around for over 2500 years. I Ching is a divination system based around Ego submission. Our lower selves, also known as our Egos, are constantly attempting to force us off our paths. The I Ching is a lantern illuminating these fallacies. It informs us how to subjugate our inner saboteurs." Captain Tess saw Morgan nod blankly. "Showing you is better than telling you."

Captain Tess handed Morgan three quarters.

"Cast them six times and tell me what you get," Captain Tess said.

Morgan complied, "Two heads and a tail, a tail and two heads, three heads, two tails and head, three tails, is that it?"

"Once more," Captain Tess said.

"Three tails," Morgan said.

Captain Tess scribbled for a few seconds and showed her his pad of paper.

All Morgan saw were two stacks of six broken and unbroken horizontal lines next to each other.

"I have no idea what any of this means," Morgan said.

Captain Tess smiled. It was a sweet facial expression on a man who was normally stony faced. "You will with practice. These six-line diagrams are called hexagrams. As you can see, the lines in the hexagram are either solid or broken. There are sixty-four possible combinations, and therefore sixty-four different hexagrams. I like to call the hexagrams my Chinese Holmies. Your first reading is excellent. Hexagram Eleven going into Hexagram Sixty-One, Peace into Inner Truth. This is applicable to every area in your life. You are definitely in the right place."

Captain Tess handed Morgan fresh copies of Carol Anthony's, "A Guide to the I Ching", and Stephen Karcher's "Total I Ching". He showed her where to look up the different hexagrams, and showed her how the throws of the coins determined her current reading.

The books counseled Morgan to go with the flow, to give her lessons full focus and effort. Morgan knew in her heart it was critical to learn everything she could from Captain Tess. It was a function of Ego to believe that Waking Life peacefulness would last forever. Morgan had already encountered several violent UnderLife episodes, and she needed to be more capable at defending herself. Morgan considered herself extremely lucky that so far she had only been found by allies. Morgan knew that her talent would sooner or later attract unwanted attention.

Captain Tess put Morgan on a rigorous training schedule. The routine consisted of four hour training sessions, four days in a row (or four-by-fours as Morgan referred to them), then one day off. It was grueling. Morgan did more kicking, punching, grappling, submitting, defending, jumping rope, sprinting, lunging, sit-ups and push-ups than she thought anybody should endure.

Captain Tess and Morgan complemented each other very well. His expert instruction and her sponge-like receptivity to learning combat skills had them burning through the material. Captain Tess was hyperaware of Morgan's physical limitations, and he knew how to push Morgan's boundaries without injuring her.

Before each work out, Captain Tess had Morgan throw the coins for her I Ching reading of the day. Captain Tess gave Morgan some time to read from the books of source material which Captain Tess he had given her. They discussed what hexagram or hexagrams Morgan got, their meaning in the larger picture of her life, and how Morgan could use the I Ching to maximize the effectiveness of their time together. Then they meditated, stretched, and trained, trained, trained.

CHAPTER FOURTEEN
THE ASTROLOGER

August, Louise, and Dorcha surprised Morgan when they arrived together to pick Morgan up for her meditation session. After three months, it was finally time to begin work on her heart chakra, or Anahata. This was the energy center governing sophisticated emotions, love, compassion, well-being, and equilibrium.

After living with Dorcha for two weeks, Morgan had found herself a new apartment, and a darling one at that. Morgan loved Los Angeles, and she insisted that her residence be in the heart of Hollywood. It overjoyed Morgan to be located in an old apartment building on Gardner Street, just south of Sunset Boulevard. She found out that Timothy Leary used to live in her apartment, #204. Morgan thought that Leary was a fitting former tenant, considering that her whole life frequently resembled one long acid trip.

Louise explained to Morgan that her attraction to Hollywood had partly to do with the fact it was a Leo town. Morgan had been surprised to learn that geographic locations also had astrological signs. Louise had listed several for Morgan. Cancer, the sensitive crab, represented New York. The twins, Gemini, were San Francisco, and London was Capricorn.

Morgan was fixated on the fact that New Orleans was a Scorpio town. She loved that her birthplace shared the same sign as Victoria Shine.

Morgan agreed with Louise's assessment of Los Angeles's energy. The illusionists of Tinseltown created and journeyed through alternate realities on a daily basis. Their work entertained and enthralled the majority of the world's population. It made Morgan feel right at home.

Dorcha had helped to expedite Morgan's search for and transfer into her new home. Dorcha had been gracious as ever, not to mention excited to be getting her own place back. She knew that her bond of friendship and sisterhood with Morgan had been consolidated by their adventures together, and by their exposure to a boneyard of family skeletons.

Morgan had assumed that once she got back from Berkeley with Dorcha, she would be advancing to the next chakra. Instead, Louise put Morgan in a holding pattern. During the entire spring season, their meetings consisted largely of relaxing meditations designed to assist Morgan's physical recovery from her workouts. Louise was a bit concerned about overloading her protégé. She felt that Morgan needed the time to train with her new bodyguard and instructor.

"Well this is new. Good afternoon ladies. Where are we headed?" Morgan asked while sliding next to Dorcha in the backseat of August's Saab.

Louise said, "We feel it's time you meet our partners."

"You have partners?" Dorcha asked.

"Yes, and they are excited to speak with both of you. They've been aware of Morgan for almost as long as we have."

"That makes me nervous. Who are they?" Morgan asked

"Yeah that's a little creepy," Dorcha said.

"Don't worry. You'll find out soon enough," Louise said.

"Of course," Morgan said.

"At least you don't have to wear the hoodie this time," August said.

"Hoodie?" Dorcha asked.

"I'll tell you later," Morgan said under her breath.

August took Laurel Canyon, climbing north into the Hollywood Hills. Once they reached the top they went west, winding along Mulholland Drive. Morgan and Dorcha were engrossed in conversation, and neither woman noticed the name of the street where they turned off of Mulholland. The road got steeper. They crested a ridge, and then descended rapidly as their path switched back and forth into a secluded valley. The landscape obscured the fact they were still in the middle of a bustling metropolis. It reminded Morgan of being at the Hollywood Bowl.

A tree-filled vale was obscuring a large gate blocking further progress along the road. August barely brought the Saab to a halt before the mechanized gates opened. As they drove by, Morgan saw a camera mounted on top of the gate tracking their entry.

They came upon a three-forked crossroads. August took the far left path. After another mile the tree canopy opened into clearing. Morgan saw a small cabin nestled snugly against a seventy foot canyon wall.

August parked the car, turned the engine off, and she and Louise got out. Morgan and Dorcha followed them, waiting for some explanation. They didn't get one. Louise took the lead, heading for the front door of the wooden structure. She took an old-fashioned iron key from her suit pocket and unlocked the door.

The interior of the house looked like a Norman Rockwell painting. Dorcha wondered if the place had been decorated in the 1940s. She half expected to see a man sitting in the leather chair in front of the fireplace, wearing a Harris Tweed suit, and puffing on a pipe.

Yet, the humble one room cabin was vacant. It was furnished with a simple table surrounded by four chairs, a broken-in chocolate-colored leather chair, a matching couch sitting in front of the fireplace, a closet containing a Murphy bed, an ancient wood-burning stove, an old fashioned rotary dial telephone attached to the wall, and a bookshelf stuffed full with old tomes. A fine layer of dust covered every available surface.

Louise sat down at the table in the chair facing the front door. August went over to the front of the couch and crouched down, slipping her hand underneath the furniture. Morgan and Dorcha anticipated something extraordinary. Their curiosity peaked when August pulled out a foot long, six inches wide, checkered wooden box. August brought it over to Louise, sat across from her, and opened it. The younger women were a bit disappointed when they realized it was only a walnut chess set. Without speaking, the older women set up and began playing. August was white and acted first. Knight to F3.

"What are you doing?" Dorcha asked.

"We're playing chess while waiting," Louise said, moving her knight to F6.

"What are we waiting for?" Morgan asked.

"For you two," August answered this time, placing a white pawn two spaces forward at C4.

Louise didn't hesitate to move a black pawn to G6.

"For us? What are we supposed to do?" Dorcha asked.

"That's part of the puzzle. Good luck," Louise said without looking up. She smiled when August brought her other knight into play at C3. Louise responded with a fianchetto, moving her bishop to G7.

Morgan and Dorcha searched the space, hoping it'd be easy to find whatever it was they were looking for in such a confined area. Thirty minutes of fiddling around yielded nothing. Everything seemed so normal. It was all outdated, sure, but it was almost eerily average.

Dorcha unzipped her backpack and brought out the Tarot decks, a notebook, and pen. She set her cards up on the unused half of the table where August and Louise were playing. Dorcha asked the Tarot for guidance:

Four Questions Spread using the Druid Craft, Faeries Oracle, Lover's Path, and Gothic Vampires decks.

Position 1 represents **what we are looking for?**

Druid: 5 of Swords @
Faeries: #64 – Gawtcha @
Lovers: Prince of Pentacles
Vampires: 4 of Pentacles
Position 2 represents **where is the location of what we're looking for?**
 Druid: Ace of Pentacles @
 Faeries: #31 – UnDressing of a Salad @
 Lovers: 7 of Staves @
 Vampires: #4 – The Liege
Position 3 represents **how do we find what we're looking for?**
 Druid: #18 – The Moon
 Faeries: #16 – The Bright Mother @
 Lovers: 5 of Cups @
 Vampires: 3 of Cups
Position 4 represents **our near future?**
 Druid: 8 of Wands
Faeries: #45 – Taitlin the Slyph
Lovers: 2 of Arrows @
Vampires: 4 of Swords

While Dorcha got advice from Tarot, Morgan pulled out some pennies from her pocket to ask the I Ching for assistance. How do we solve this puzzle? Morgan thought while tossing the three coins six times. Morgan borrowed Dorcha's pen and notebook and scratched the results.

Morgan looked up the hexagram. Number Thirty-Three: Retreat, no changing lines. Morgan read the corresponding passage in Carol Anthony's book. It made no sense to her. How would not concentrating on the puzzle solve it?

"What did the cards tell you?" Morgan asked.

"I'm not too sure. We're looking for something physically stuck, and move it. A manual switch, perhaps?" Dorcha proposed.

"Hmm, what else?"

"I don't know, it's too muddled to discern specifically what the Tarot is saying. We'll figure this out together, but it's not going to be easy. What did I Ching tell you?"

"To retreat."

"What's that supposed to mean?"

"I have no idea," Morgan said.

They searched the cabin for another twenty minutes. Dorcha got annoyed, and, feeling like she was chasing her own tail, went outside to get some fresh air and another perspective. Dorcha walked around the building, noting how the structure stood right up against the rock wall. She explored the clearing and tree line.

Morgan poked her head outside. "I don't think whatever we're looking for is out there, Dorcha."

Dorcha paused, staring at the building for a few more moments before re-entering the cabin. "It seems unusual to have a house flush against the ravine wall. Wouldn't it be vulnerable to falling rocks?" Dorcha wondered out loud. She did another lap of the cabin's interior, at a loss for what to do.

The chess game continued. The players concentrated on the board, ignoring the younger women. Dorcha watched the competition, curious about which woman was the stronger player, and frustrated by the analytical pop quiz they'd been given. August took Louise's queen. Louise seemed undaunted.

Morgan couldn't get Dorcha's comment about the impractical placement of the cabin out of her head. Morgan stared at the wall adjoining the cliff face. It was dominated by a Murphy bed, hiding inside a cabinet, built into the wall. For the fourth time, she opened its doors and pulled the bed down. Behind the mattress was a wooden wall. Morgan knocked on the mattress and the frame and patted the area down, but again found nothing. She lifted the bed back up and closed the doors.

On the adjoining wall, opposite from the fireplace, there was a large bookshelf. Morgan scanned the shelves again, which contained an array of impressive titles. A bit of everything was here: Rumi's poetry, Einstein's ground-breaking theories, David Sedaris's razor-sharp wit, Jane Austen's insight, Proust's fluid prose, and Shakespeare's timeless plays were only a few of the masterpieces.

Morgan started pulling books from the shelves randomly, hoping for some luck. It felt silly. She continued. A book entitled "The Holographic Universe" by Michael Talbot caught her attention from its place on the bottom shelf. Morgan picked it up. When she did, a low click reverberated inside the base of the bookcase.

The floor vibrated slightly, and they could hear the muffled rumblings of stone scraping against stone.

Morgan's eyes darted over to August and Louise. The only reaction Morgan witnessed was a slight curl in the corners of Louise's mouth. Louise moved a chess piece and softly said, "Check."

August gasped, eyeing the board more intensely, agitated by the attack.

Dorcha rejoined her partner, clapping Morgan on the back in congratulation. "What did you do?"

"I just pulled out this book, and something happened. I'm not sure what. Hopefully it flipped the switch the cards were talking about. I think the rumbling came from the Murphy bed cabinet."

The two women approached the closet. Morgan hesitated before opening the doors. When Morgan finally did, they both groaned, frustrated to be staring at the vertical Murphy bed once again. Dorcha looked to Morgan for inspiration. Morgan shrugged her shoulders and slumped against the retracted bed. Morgan yelped, struggling to maintain balance when the entire bed moved into the wall from Morgan's weight.

"That's it!" Dorcha exclaimed, reaching forward to steady Morgan. Bracing themselves, they shoved the recessed bed harder. It moved a few more feet, until it had cleared its outer frame. Then it stopped. They heard another click, more stone on stone movement, and the entire bed slid to the left, disappearing into a concealed side compartment.

Straight ahead was a passage carved directly from the rock.

"Classic hidden tunnel," Morgan said, thrilled.

"Retreat, withdrawal," Dorcha said. She referred to her journal and jotted down notes. "What does someone do when they want to retreat? Say, go into the woods and hole up in a cabin, read, rest?"

"These symbols always make way more sense in hindsight," Morgan grumbled.

"True, although I never tire of figuring it out beforehand if I can," Dorcha said and grinned. She peered into the tunnel with Morgan.

"Well done," Louise trilled in her British accent, then added, "Checkmate," in a low voice to August.

The younger woman muttered curses, cleared the board, put the pieces away, and slid the folded chessboard back under the couch.

Louise stood, extracted a small flashlight from her pocket, and entered the tunnel.

"So is this the part where we get to hear about your plans for world domination?" Dorcha asked as Louise passed. All the cloak and dagger stuff was worrying Dorcha a little. She preferred to be apprised of a situation before engaging.

"Sort of…" Louise trailed off. There was a long pause as the younger women waited for Louise to elaborate. Instead, Louise kept walking down the corridor. August followed, with Morgan on her heels. Dorcha trailed behind. The further they went into the mysterious structure, the more awkward Dorcha's mood got. Doubt ridden questions bubbled up, such as: Where are they taking us? And who are these people really? Who do they work for? What did they want with them?

Dorcha's skin crawled with fear as the secret door automatically ground shut behind them. Dorcha squelched her paranoia, knowing it was just her Ego getting riled with the anticipation. If Louise or August had any malicious intentions towards me or Morgan, Dorcha thought, they pretty much had them at their mercy anyway. She quickened her pace to catch up with the group.

Their path descended deeper into the earth as the tunnel twisted and turned. Morgan noted how the air in the tunnel tasted and felt fresh.

Somewhere there had to be a mechanism which was circulating fresh air, but Morgan couldn't see any vents or natural air shafts.

After ten minutes of walking, they reached a metal door. Louise reached out with her left hand to grip a rock bulging from the rough tunnel wall. Louise popped open a camouflaged cover, revealing a keypad, and punched in a series of nine numbers. The barrier slid open.

They stepped into an elevator, whose design reminded Morgan of the mysterious place where August had taken her by helicopter.

"Stasis," Louise said. The elevator came to life, ascending at least half a dozen floors before stopping.

When the doors slid open, Morgan and Dorcha blinked several times, agape at what stood before them.

The room was painted black, with either side roughly cut from rock. Three doors were spaced evenly apart on the crescent shaped far wall. There were people standing ten feet away.

One was a medium sized woman wearing glasses, with her brunette hair streaked with grey swept up into a bun. Next to her stood a lanky, stern faced man about 6'2" tall, and roughly the same age as his companion.

Louise strode into the room. "Morgan Martel, Dorcha LeTour, may I present Doctors Tilly and Trevor Vihzor."

At August's prompting, the young women stepped forward.

Morgan and Dorcha glanced at each other while entering the room.

Tilly shook hands with Morgan and then Dorcha. Trevor followed suit.

"They're you're partners?" Morgan sputtered out, once she found her voice.

"Yes," Louise said with a smile.

"Life just got weirder," Dorcha mumbled.

"No kidding," Morgan said more loudly. "Alright, please tell us what's going on. What are y'all about? What do you want with us?" Morgan asked, nervous energy blunting her communication skills.

"World peace," Trevor answered without hesitation.

"That's it?" Dorcha blurted out.

Trevor snorted in prideful derision, "What do you mean that's it? This is the ultimate in complicated and difficult on-going missions."

"Oh I don't doubt it. Please forgive my underwhelmed response. I was expecting for this to get nightmarish, in a horror movie kind of way. I even wore my bouncy, shapely, support bra and good running shoes," Dorcha said.

"Well, it's nice to know you've come prepared, as we have a ton of work to do. World peace isn't going to happen by itself."

"No conspiracy?" Dorcha almost sounded disappointed.

"Don't worry. There will be plenty of running for your life in

UnderLife."

Tilly chimed in, "Yes, we want Morgan to build a team of people who will be joining you at your job in UnderLife."

"Which is?" Morgan asked.

The question seemed to exasperate Trevor, like he thought Morgan should already know this. "Assisting people to recognize, strengthen, and repair their spiritual support structures. Aiding others in achieving and maintaining their happiness. Making progress in collectively manifesting heaven on Earth."

"Assisting who?" Dorcha asked.

Tilly answered, "Whomever we are guided to. Ideally those who are capable of, or are already in positions of power. Maximize the effectiveness of our endeavors by galvanizing people who will help others."

"A team?" Morgan asked. "Who is going to be on my team?"

"That's for you to determine," Tilly said. "I'm sure if you look within, the answers are there."

Dorcha addressed Louise and the Vihzors. "Will you guys pay me enough to quit my dumb job at the café?"

"How does starting at $50,000 a year sound?" Louise asked.

"Sounds like you've got a new employee," beamed Dorcha, high-fiving and hugging Morgan.

"How about Captain Tess? If we're going to be on safari in other people's psyches, we'll need his tactical knowledge and skill set. Everyone has some sort of psychic Ego defense system which is tricky and dangerous to navigate. Even consciously cooperative subjects have vicious Ego defense systems. I never got past Balthazar's UnderLife zombie army. It's part of the reason why I broke up with him."

"Done." Trevor said. "Captain Tess has already agreed to protect you and your companions in any setting, Waking or UnderLife. He'll be joining us later."

Who else? Draven? No, Morgan didn't think he'd be into it. Morgan still wasn't sure if Draven believed her stories about UnderLife. Sure, Draven loved hearing about the adventures, and the graphic novel project they had started together was going well. Morgan felt like a part of Draven speculated like Balthazar did. If this ability was real, why had Morgan not taken him in?

Sometimes it even seemed like Draven was accusing her of being lazy when she would tell him that it was hard to control entering and exiting UnderLife, and to control who she brought with her.

As much as Morgan wanted Draven to understand and experience UnderLife with her, Morgan didn't blame Draven's skepticism. It was natural.

Once again Morgan was reminded why it felt so good to have Dorcha in her life. Dorcha loved gazing under the fabric of reality with the endless maps she built with her cards. Dorcha's spiritual cartography skills were shockingly accurate. Morgan considered her counsel indispensable. The more they worked together, the more Morgan learned about the archetypal energy flowing through Life. It was exciting for Morgan to learn how to apply these lessons both in Waking Life, and in the endless realms of puzzles in UnderLife.

"Morgan?" Dr. Trevor Vihzor inquired.

"Yes?" Morgan replied with a dazed expression on her face.

"Did you have an UnderLife episode just now?"

Morgan startled Trevor by laughing. "No, unfortunately the blank stare was my thinking face."

This struck Tilly, Dorcha, and August as funny. Morgan got the giggles. Even Trevor and Louise couldn't help cracking smiles.

"Seriously," Morgan continued, "the team suggestion got me going. Dorcha and Taylor definitely, as I'm sure you know I've been working well with them already."

"I'm glad you recognize how valuable they are," Tilly said.

"Yes, they will be dynamic contributors," Trevor said. "Who else?"

"I don't know. How many do I need?"

"That's up to you. Four is a solid number..." Trevor said.

"I don't think it's flexible enough," Tilly said.

"Yes, it does seem too structured for this kind of work. Excellent observation, my love."

Morgan wanted so badly to blurt out Victoria Shine's name. She chided herself for the foolish impulse. What a fucking angst-ridden, nutty pipe dream to entertain the idea of her idol being an actual acquaintance, let alone her traveling companion in UnderLife. Morgan looked to August for support and got a warm smile in response.

"August?"

"Oh no, I'm not getting attacked by any more tsunamis. I might have gone for it if I was fifteen years younger."

"In which case, I'd be older than you. C'mon, it'll be fun."

"I know what your sick idea of fun is. No, darling, I don't believe this adventure is calling me."

"Now," Louise said in a commanding voice, "if you'll excuse August and me. We have a meeting we need to get to. Ladies, you're in excellent hands. The Vihzors will see you safely home. Morgan, we'll do your next mediation tomorrow at the Skyscraper Space. Good work today, both of you."

Louise and August left through the far right door, on the opposite wall from the elevator entrance.

Trevor motioned to Morgan, "Allow me to take you to see Captain

Tess and your new training partner."

"Who is that going to be?"

"Kyle," Dorcha blurted out. Her stomach lurched. Excitement and terror stunned Dorcha into silence. With all the commotion she had forgotten whose parents the Vihzors were until that very moment.

"Correct," Trevor said.

"Ladies, please don't tell him everything right away," Tilly said.

Trevor explained, "We want to see how he handles UnderLife with no briefing."

"How do you know I'll pull him into an UnderLife adventure? Do you really want to scare the hell out of him?" Morgan asked.

"No, we don't," Tilly said, tossing a stern expression towards her husband.

"It's a hunch," Trevor said. "Kyle can handle it. He's a prime candidate for an adventure. Whether Kyle realizes it or not, we've helped to prepare him for this his entire life. With all this Ultimate Fighter nonsense, the kid is looking for trouble."

"Kyle is just curious," Tilly said.

"It's definitely going to be a shock," Morgan warned. "I have no control over where we'll end up, or what will happen."

"He'll manage. I have faith in Kyle," Trevor said.

"Don't be too hard or expect too much from him, honey. You know Kyle only wants to make you proud."

"I am proud of him."

"Say it more."

"I say it all the time."

"Kyle is a Leo, so he wouldn't mind if you said it even more." Tilly winked. Her husband and son shared the same sun sign.

Trevor smiled.

Tilly turned to Dorcha, "Do you mind if I have a few words alone with you?"

Dorcha hesitated, "Uh… Sure."

"Follow me."

Tilly Vihzor guided Dorcha through the door farthest to the left. They entered a tiny metal room, which Dorcha realized was an additional elevator. There was a second inner door to the elevator which was made of the same dull metal. The walls swiveled closed.

"Study," Tilly said, and the elevator descended. The metal doors opened seconds later. Once Tilly and Dorcha had entered the next room, the elevator door shut behind them. Dorcha did a double take. The elevator door was disguised as a full-sized portrait of Trevor in his early twenties. Dorcha thought the resemblance between Trevor and Kyle was uncanny.

They were in a beautiful two story library, with shelf upon shelf of books lining every wall.

Tilly glided through the remarkable room, leading them to a homey den. A cool breeze was blowing through an open window. The room was furnished with an armoire, desk, fur rug, end table, and two overstuffed chairs in front of a fireplace.

Tilly motioned for Dorcha to have a seat. Dorcha complied.

Tilly turned a gas valve to ignite the logs in the fireplace.

"Do you want something to drink?" Tilly asked. "Some water? A glass of red wine?"

"No, thank you," Dorcha said. Should she be surprised that Tilly offered her her favorite alcoholic beverage? Just how much did these people know about her anyway? Dorcha did her best to look non-chalant.

Dr. Vihzor pulled a small, shiny, flat metal case from her coat pocket. Opening the case, Tilly produced a perfectly rolled joint, and placed it on the end table.

"We were wondering if we could borrow your Tarot journals to analyze their content."

"How do you know I keep a journal?" Dorcha asked.

"Oh, please. There's a sealed plastic crate of them, with Primo's fur on the lid, in the left back corner of your closet."

Dorcha blanched. Another illusion of privacy had been ripped away like an ornery Band-Aid. If they knew the precise location of her old journals, they certainly had seen the contents of her naughty chest. It scenario reminded Dorcha of her naked-in-public nightmares from grade school.

Tilly reached into her coat for a lighter, sparked the joint, and handed it to Dorcha.

"Do you want Shiraz or Amarone?"

Dorcha considered her choice while taking a long drag. Exhaling, Dorcha said, "Amarone, please." Clearly these people had Dorcha by the short-hairs. They knew Dorcha would have a hard time keeping herself from partaking in great weed and an amazing glass of wine. Dorcha adored how she was being handled, but she wondered about other shoes dropping.

Inside the armoire there was a small wine refrigerator. Tilly retrieved a bottle of 2001 Monte Faustino Amarone della Valpolicella Classico, and while using the corkscrew she responded to Dorcha's unspoken anxieties, "If seeming too good to be true is a fault, it's one we possess. I know what we're asking seems strange. This isn't about revealing your secrets or embarrassing you. There aren't many Tarot card readers who keep such meticulous records of their readings as you do. My husband and I wrote a computer program designed to analyze the raw data of your Tarot journals. We're looking for a higher pattern. It's a pattern so large in scope, that maybe you've felt its machinations, but weren't able to articulate them completely. We're also interested in understanding your process as a reader. We want to see if there's a way to build a useful computer program based on a combination of your interpretive style, the original intentions of each deck's author, and the archetypal current underneath each symbol."

"Sold," Dorcha said. "I've always been curious if a larger perspective could be gleaned from my daily divinations. As for the program, if it can give credible and consistent guidance, then I'm all for it."

"We will keep this project confidential," Tilly said. "I will need your help in examining the journals. The more I know, the better."

Dorcha nodded, "After all our recent family revelations, it'll be a relief to have a sounding board for unearthing and examining the minutia of my emotional life."

* * *

Back in the Stasis Room

Trevor watched his wife leave with Dorcha. In the decades they'd known each other, Trevor had never tired of watching Tilly move. She seemed to glide rather than walk. Tilly's footfalls whispered even on the most resonating terrain.

Once the door had closed behind Tilly and Dorcha, Trevor focused his attention on Morgan.

"Right this way," Trevor said, leading Morgan back into the first elevator.

"Corridor," Trevor said to the elevator, and they descended a few floors. Their destination was indeed a corridor.

While they walked through winding hallways, Trevor said, "Neither my wife, no I, relish the idea of our son getting into brawls with dangerous, highly-trained men. However, Kyle will not be dissuaded. We told Kyle that he has our blessing if he allows us to put together the coaching staff for his first fight. If Kyle insists on treading this path, I want to make sure he's well prepared."

"Understandable. Although I'm not sure how effective of a workout partner I'm going to be. Kyle is way stronger, faster, and more experienced than I am in combat."

"I'm not concerned about that. We have people to challenge Kyle's physical prowess and technical proficiency. Speaking of which, how is Captain Tess as an instructor?"

Morgan sighed in admiration, "Brutal and wonderful. The Captain kicks my ass. He knows exactly how much I can take, and pushes the line."

"Excellent. The man is doing his job. Believe me, Morgan, as rough as it is to train with such a diligent expert, you'll be grateful if you ever have to use your new skill set."

They arrived at double doors which opened into a small gymnasium. The gym had a comprehensive array of machines, weights, and mat space. Ten-foot mirrors, complete with a ballet barre, lined one wall. The reflection made the place seem larger than it was. Darkened flat-screen televisions were mounted on every wall.

"Please wait here," Trevor said. "I'm going to find Kyle. Taylor will join you shortly."

"Okay, I'll be here."

* * *

Trevor found his son lounging in the hot tub, drinking iced tea and flipping channels with a waterproof clicker.

Kyle turned off the television and said, "The new guy you've got me sparring with is frakking tough. Where did you find him?"

"Captain Taylor Tess is an Army Ranger."

"Cool. So he's, like, killed people?"

"Yes. Treat him with the utmost respect, son. Don't be bragging to your buddies about him. I know how much you love mixed martial arts, but always remember that Captain Tess is capable of killing you within seconds, in any circumstance. Conflicts for Captain Tess involve murder."

"Yes sir," Kyle said. Kyle knew his father was being serious. He appreciated the opportunity to work with an elite professional warrior.

"Under his tutelage, you will have all the tools you need to win your first fight."

Kyle smiled. "Thanks, Dad."

"We also have a new training partner for you."

"Who?"

Trevor opened a folder, and handed Kyle a piece of paper.

Kyle got out of the hot tub, and toweled off a bit before taking the paper. Kyle recognized it as a natal birth chart wheel, and scanned his favorite astrological indicators. First the top three: Sun Eighth House Libra, Moon Sixth House Leo, Pisces Rising. The North Node was Fifth House Cancer. Five planets in Libra told Kyle this person was a natural partner and mediator.

"Interesting character. Who is this guy?"

"Her name is Morgan Martel."

"You want me to do MMA training with a woman? I don't want to hit a chick."

In response Trevor gave Kyle another paper with a composite chart of Kyle and Morgan's relationship.

After analyzing the composite chart for a moment, Kyle said, "Oh. I guess we do need to work together."

* * *

Morgan paced around the circuit training/weight room, checking out the state-of-the-art equipment. The various machines had every major muscle group covered. Morgan decided to stretch out and get some reps in. Over the last few months, Taylor had inspired Morgan to become aware of how to channel her Ego driven emotions such as fear, desire, anticipation, anxiety and anger, into more positive and productive outlets.

Morgan had broken a sweat by the time Captain Tess entered the room. He was drenched from head to toe. Taylor's t-shirt clung to his ripped torso.

"Captain Tess, did you go swimming with your clothes on?"

"I rolled with Kyle," Taylor explained while retrieving a dry shirt from his gym bag. "The kid's got a lot of heart. It'll be interesting to see how Kyle reacts to UnderLife." Captain Tess sat a short distance from Morgan. He had never been this relaxed and informal with Morgan before.

"I'm surprised by how comfortable you are with UnderLife."

"The I Ching speaks of UnderLife. Carol Anthony describes it in her book under Hexagram Forty-Eight: The Well." Captain Tess grabbed A Guide to the I Ching from his bag. He showed Morgan a passage on page 218.

Morgan scanned the first page of Anthony's notes on Hexagram Forty-Eight. Four paragraphs down it said, "The well also symbolizes our self-development and education in the fundamental truths of life. The I Ching guides us through the hidden world that parallels and mirrors our external life, a world which may be seen in meditation, and sometimes in dreams. Receiving the hexagram means that we should develop our self through making a keener effort to understand the fundamentals of human behavior. Above all we must not remain locked in the conventional view of the way things work."

"Wow, the Chinese Holmies really do know their stuff."

"Yes, the I Ching is a reliable guide through the trials and tribulations of navigating the unknown."

Morgan said, "We're gonna need all the help we can get. Are you sure protecting and training me is something you want to do?"

"Yes, it is my duty."

Morgan smiled, "Well, if you ever change your mind, like say after you get attacked by whatever your worst nightmare is, I won't be offended, I promise."

"What were your hexagrams for today?" Captain Tess asked.

"This morning I got fifty-nine into twelve."

"Dispersion into Standstill. I see. Are you warmed up?" Taylor asked.

"Yes Sir."

"Then let's have you do five sets of triple fifteen/thirties while we wait for the Vihzors."

"Yes Sir," Morgan said, inwardly groaning. Captain Tess meant five sets of fifteen push-ups, lunges, and leg lifts followed by thirty sit-ups. Morgan had a love/hate relationship with the routine.

Captain Tess sensed Morgan's hesitation. He said, "We'll do it together."

* * *

By the time Kyle and Trevor arrived, Morgan was panting for oxygen.

"Kyle," Trevor announced, "meet Morgan Martel, your new training partner."

Kyle did a double take when he saw Morgan. "You look familiar. How do I know you?"

"Victoria Shine conce..." Morgan's voice faded like someone had sucked the air out of her lungs. Her eyes glazed over.

* * *

At first Morgan thought the roaring in her ears was coming from nearby rushing water. Flashing bright lights were everywhere. It took a few moments for Morgan's senses to acclimate. Morgan squeezed her eyes open and shut a few times. Looking upward she saw a stunning view of star-filled space. There were too many stars visible to be in Earth's atmosphere. Morgan saw that a translucent dome was keeping them from the vacuum of space.

Morgan's gaze leveled on Kyle, who was standing about fifteen feet in front of her. Kyle was way more thunderstruck by the experience than Morgan.

They were standing in an arena which Morgan recognized as a version of the Ultimate Fighting Championship's Octagon. The roaring sound was coming from the massive crowd surrounding them.

Morgan gulped. Not only was the crowd not human, but they were the most varied and scary bunch of monsters she'd ever seen. It was as if Clive Barker, Jim Henson, Stephen King, and George Lucas had fused their imaginations together to create thousands of terrible beings. Leave it to Kyle to have an intergalactic alien nightmare for an UnderLife.

On one side of the arena, there was a giant scoreboard lit up in a language Morgan had never seen before. Morgan guessed it showed odds and results for betting. Most of the creatures were holding glowing chips.

It reminded Morgan of rabid crowds clutching tickets aloft at the horse races.

In any other circumstance Morgan would have paused to marvel how UnderLife had taken them to a spaceship arena. However, Morgan knew they were in a dire situation. The talon and fanged crowd pressed against the chain link fence of the Octagon.

Morgan stepped closer to Kyle and bowed. Kyle returned the courtesy.

Morgan exploded into action. She executed a left front kick aimed at Kyle's right knee cap, which he blocked with his right forearm. Morgan followed up with a right jab, striking Kyle on the upper lip and nose.

"Ow! Stop hitting me!" Kyle yelled.

Morgan danced back. She relaxed, dropping arms to her sides, signifying that she would stop attacking. Kyle followed suit. Morgan executed a swift-step jumping right side kick into Kyle's stomach.

Kyle slammed into the chain link fence of the cage. Claws from a member of the crowd swiped at Kyle's exposed flank, slicing open several gashes on his skin. Kyle cried out, and pushed himself off of the fence, stepping directly into Morgan's left hook. Morgan then sent a wicked right ridge hand to Kyle's neck.

Out of desperation, Kyle grabbed for Morgan, trying to overpower her with his superior height and weight. Morgan pulled Kyle into a Muay Thai clutch and kneed him right in the family jewels.

Cradling his crotch, Kyle dropped to his knees, wheezing, "No below the belt."

"Young man, this is not the UFC," Morgan said.

The bloodthirsty audience bellowed their approval and roared for more blood.

Morgan circled around her befuddled opponent, and executed a powerful front kick to Kyle's spine, forcing Kyle to his hands and knees. Morgan stretched her right hand to the sky, palm open. She closed her fist and rotated her hand one hundred and eighty degrees, and then plunged her right elbow into the back of Kyle's exposed neck. Morgan felt Kyle's bones break.

Kyle rolled to the ground in agony. The last thing Kyle saw was Morgan's foot speeding towards his head right before she kicked him in the temple.

Lights out!

* * *

Kyle regained consciousness twenty minutes later. His eyes snapped open, wide with fear. Kyle recoiled from Morgan, who was the first person to notice that he was awake. He sprang to his feet, hunched into a defensive crouch.

"What the hell? That was so fucked up! Where did we go? Why did you attack me?" Kyle yelled.

"I had to," Morgan said. "We were plunged into a vicious blood sport. Rules of the cage. One of us defeats the other for the demons' amusement, or they kill us both. And don't think they'd be quick about it. I'd rather take you out than get mutilated slowly by evil creatures. No one said UnderLife was a safe place to travel."

Morgan gave Trevor an I-told-you-so look.

"UnderLife, what the hell is that, some kind of virtual reality?" Kyle asked.

Morgan explained. It was easy to sell the concept to someone who had encountered it first-hand.

"How do you know they would have come after us if we didn't fight?" Kyle asked.

"Instinct and experience. I've seen such a horde of quasi-civilized nefarious monsters before. That crowd wanted blood, one way or another. I avoid exacerbating already horrendous situations. Believe me those monsters would have pulled out our fingernails slowly to see which one of us screamed the loudest. I won't even get into the permanent scarring from repeated rapes. If kicking your ass was a quick exit, I'd take it again. Every UnderLife episode carries a lesson, purpose, and possible punishment." Morgan said.

"What if their plan was to feast on the winner?" Kyle asked.

"That would have been unfortunate," Morgan said, shrugging.

Kyle turned to Trevor, "Dad, you knew all about this UnderLife, didn't you?"

"Yes, we've had our eye on Morgan since she was a child," Trevor said.

"Why didn't you tell me about this years ago?"

"The secrecy was for everyone's safety. It was too dangerous for Morgan and potentially for many others as well. What if Morgan had been raised to use her ability as a weapon?"

"You mean she hasn't been? Could have fooled me." Kyle muttered.

"Ms. Martel needs to know how to defend herself," Captain Tess said. "Morgan executed the best course of action given your circumstances. Good day of training. We all learned something new, and no one got hurt."

"Son," Trevor said, putting a hand on Kyle's shoulder. Kyle wanted to shrug his Dad off and walk away. Kyle's jaw clenched. Trevor continued, "Remember that where we come from, a lapse in discipline is the difference between life and death. Of course I've wanted to tell you. We needed to be patient, to give room for certain truths to surface in proper time. I didn't work this hard and long to let vain enthusiasm ruin it."

From the tone in his father's voice, Kyle knew it was time to shift his attitude, and not act like he'd been victimized by fate. Kyle began to understand how a professional fighter could be grateful for a defeat, as it could become transformed into a significant lesson and a blessing. No one had ever knocked Kyle out before, and Morgan, a woman, had done it in a matter of minutes.

"So is UnderLife like the Matrix? Can I do flips and dodge bullets?" Kyle asked.

"Not unless you can do those things already. Sometimes in UnderLife you'll have special abilities, but it depends on the specific UnderLife experience. UnderLife has malleable physics, but things generally adhere to Waking Life rules. In the Matrix they were able to download entire skill sets and disciplines into their brains. We don't have the technology for that. I wish we did," Morgan said.

Kyle looked at Trevor.

"No son, we don't have that tech… yet."

Morgan saw Kyle's mental wheels cranking. The UnderLife encounter had rocked him. It's one thing, Morgan thought, to have faith, to believe in following a path of love. It's another wondrous thing altogether to get a taste of the eternal Source, the confirmation of a higher power from a miraculous event.

Kyle's first trip into UnderLife had been harsh. Would he have had it any other way? Kyle had difficulty accepting things which came easily to him. Slowly, Kyle's youthful chiseled features broadened into a dazzling smile. "This is going to be fun! What other secrets you got tucked away, Dad?"

* * *

After Kyle's debriefing had finished, Captain Tess escorted Morgan through a series of halls, stairways, and elevators. Captain Tess moved through the maze of twisted hallways so swiftly that Morgan figured he must have memorized the blueprints for the building. Morgan had no clue where they were. She didn't know which way they were facing, or if they were above or below ground. One thing she did notice was that the architecture and design wasn't uniform throughout the building. It seemed like different sections of the Vihzors' compound had been built at different times, over the course of many years.

Soon they were in a winding maintenance hallway, with visible pipes, minimal industrial décor, and a stale, damp, brackish smell. They turned a corner and passed a long row of dozens of large, floor-to-ceiling steel lockers. At locker number forty, Captain Tess stopped and dialed the combination lock so quickly Morgan couldn't see the numbers.

The locker was empty. "Get in," Taylor ordered, lightly nudging Morgan.

"Wh-" Morgan's momentum already had her halfway in the locker before she realized what Taylor was doing.

"Stop!" Morgan shouted as Captain Tess sealed the door behind her. Morgan banged on the door. The locker room was lit with red light, kind of like a darkroom.

"Calm down," Taylor commanded in a hard tone Morgan had never heard him use before. Morgan stopped thrashing about. "Wait at the dirt road," Taylor continued. "I'll bring the car around."

"What?" Morgan asked.

The entire chamber shuddered once then started to ascend.

In a couple of minutes the tiny room ground to a halt. When the doors slid open, gentle moonlight spilled in. Morgan stepped out of the locker onto spongy moss covered earth. She felt relieved to be in the fresh air again.

Morgan found herself in a forest clearing, in a circle of mulberry trees.

She heard the locker moving behind her. Morgan turned around in time to see it sink back into the ground. All that was left was an innocuous green patch which blended in perfectly with the surrounding underbrush.

Morgan shook her head in bewilderment. Who needed to have this many secret entrances and exits? Interesting how they showed me these things, Morgan thought, but they didn't explain how or why they maintained such a high level of security. Certainly the place had cost a fortune to create. No telling what else they had going on in here.

Morgan was grateful for the light of an almost full waxing moon. She checked out her surroundings. It took only a few minutes of searching to find the dirt road Taylor had mentioned just beyond a cluster of trees.

Obediently, Morgan waited for Taylor.

Ten minutes went by. Morgan heard a noise coming from the trees. She heard rustling, then a branch snapping, and someone saying, "Ow, shit, that hurt."

"Dorcha?"

"Morgan? Where are you?"

"Just beyond the trees. Follow my voice."

"Morgan!" Dorcha said with a big grin, bounding up to Morgan for a hug. "Those people are so core," Dorcha stage-whispered after their embrace. "I think I've hit my quota of secret elevators to last me quite a while."

Morgan chuckled, glad to see Dorcha in such a good mood. "What happened with Tilly?"

"Amarone."

"What's that?"

Dorcha gasped, mockingly appalled, "I'm going to pretend you didn't say that."

That's when Morgan smelled the wine on her friend's breath.

"Are you drunk?"

"Shh," Dorcha put her finger up to Morgan's lips, "Don't speak."

Morgan laughed at Dorcha's reference to Dianne Wiest's masterful performance in "Bullets over Broadway", their favorite Woody Allen film.

There was a flash of headlights and the sound of a truck engine. In moments Captain Tess's SUV came bumping along the road towards them.

"Yeah," Dorcha admitted as their ride approached, "maybe I'm a bit liquored up. It was so tasty."

CHAPTER FIFTEEN
REVOLUTIONARY TRANSITION

Morgan and Balthazar had always had a strong sexual connection. For years they had had constant contact, living together and making love at every opportunity. Morgan's abrupt break up with Balthazar had started a game of Lust Chicken. Morgan's departure had eradicated the boredom and complacency they'd been feeling. After the relationship had lain fallow for a season, the buzzed late-night phone calls and texts began.

The certainty of sizzling sexual synchronicity wore on Morgan's resolve, and similarly on Balthazar's wounded heart and pride. They avoided all personal and metaphysical differences in conversation, which helped to diffuse any break-up rancor. This eroded their collective will to stay away from each other.

Morgan realized there were countless free brothels for women. These brothels were called "bars". Bars provided Morgan with a few nights of haphazard passion, but no long-term liaisons came from these nights. Both Morgan and Balthazar tried to unleash their boiling sexuality on other partners. Unfortunately, Morgan could not help but compare the cool, casual feelings she had for her new partners to the hot lust she had experienced with Balthazar. Balthazar had the same problem. Their respective nights of alcohol-fueled rebound sex with other people were fun, but neither Morgan nor Balthazar could feel consumed by them.

Morgan's random partners also seemed to show an appalling lack of sexual education. Their enthusiasm for her flesh was pleasurable, but it only made her appreciation soar for Balthazar's talented technique. Even Balthazar's predictability was charming to Morgan now. She missed it like a long lost comfort.

Morgan wondered how many people were aware that women could

have two different kinds of orgasms: clitoral and vaginal. A skilled lover managed to get both lit up, blending the two pleasures into an Earth shattering, crying-out, headboard-smashing, leg-twitching, blinding, what's-my-name cum fest.

Morgan longed for the ecstatic oblivion that Balthazar could take her to. Balthazar made Morgan feel safe with his physical strength, his sultry voice, his stunning compliments, and his luscious lips which Morgan could kiss for hours without being sated.

Why did I break up with Balthazar in the first place? Morgan wondered. What am I doing? An ever-growing fear gnawed inside of Morgan. Maybe I made a huge mistake, she thought, the biggest mistake of my life.

The night after Morgan got back from meeting the Vihzors and from beating up Kyle, she couldn't settle down. She hoped a few bong hits would mellow her out, but instead it ratcheted up her energy as if she'd taken a few shots of espresso. Morgan decided to go for a drive to clear her mind and to do some late night grocery shopping.

Memory flashes of passion shared with Balthazar bubbled up in Morgan's consciousness like fresh soda. At the stroke of midnight, the beginning of the witching hour, her resolve snapped.

Balthazar was dozing on the couch while half-watching SportsCenter when his phone rang. Balthazar stared at the screen for a moment, considering. Finally he hit the answer button and put the speaker to his ear without saying anything.

"Hi," Morgan said.

"Hi."

"What are you doing?"

"What are you doing?"

"I don't know. I miss you," Morgan said.

"Are you break-up booty calling me?"

"Would you be offended if I am?"

"I'd be more offended if you didn't try at least once," Balthazar said.

"You've probably got some hot chick there that's been waiting to bag you for a long time, and now here's her chance."

"If that were the case, do you really think I'd answer the phone when my ex-girlfriend called me at midnight?"

"The slut in your bed would be upset if she knew we were speaking. She's probably asleep, worn out from the recent championship sex. She's also an early riser. Midnight is already well into bedtime for her."

Balthazar whispered, "What are you, some kind of psychic? How did you know? Did you plant a camera in my bedroom?"

"Yes, and now I've got dirt on you because she's married to a rich and vengeful man," Morgan said.

"Oh, she's married, is that it?"

"Yes, you can't handle any promises or commitments right now and just want a good ol' roll in the hay with a sexy babe. The immense sorrow of not having me around weakened your normally impeccable ethical behavior."

"I do miss you."

"Can I come over?"

"Why?"

"To get a good night's sleep, of course. I'm used to this big bear I like to cuddle with," Morgan said.

"You want to cuddle?"

"Or not, I'll just lie there, resting peacefully, naked. I'm sure nothing will happen."

"Liar," Balthazar chuckled.

"Yeah," Morgan said.

It only took a few moments for Balthazar to ponder his options. "Are you on your way?"

There was a knock on his front door.

* * *

Morgan left while Balthazar was slumbering. Despite being knackered, something in Morgan's brain wouldn't let her fall asleep in Balthazar's bed. Morgan justified her stealthy retreat by thinking that the night had been just a momentary lapse of passion. Sex doesn't mean I've announced an official plan of action to get back together, she thought.

One thing was for certain. Balthazar's sexual skills were epic. Morgan entertained herself on the drive home by recalling a montage of luscious moments. Balthazar's knowledge of Morgan's erogenous zones, combined with the comprehensive shorthand of gasps, moans, and groans they had developed over the course of their relationship, had made for a terrific night.

The first rays of dawn were peeking over the horizon by the time Morgan returned to her apartment. Morgan was glad to have a day off of training. Between the cabin, the Vihzors, the demon spaceship arena, and the volcanic sex with Balthazar, it'd been a thrilling and exhausting twenty-four hours.

* * *

By sunset Morgan was at the Skyscraper space, ready to take the next step in her chakra balancing.

Louise put on some music, a pleasant hodge-podge of rain, bells, birds, drums, and flute sounds. Morgan lay down on the white feather comforter in the usual position, on her back with the crystal wand positioned between her sternum and belly button. The smell of sandalwood incense wafted throughout the spacious room. Louise lit a fresh set of seven chakra candles.

"Now, take a deep breath," Louise instructed, "and slowly let it out." Morgan exhaled, and after repeating the process a few times, she shifted into her meditation.

"Listen to the music. Relax. Keep breathing. Just let things flow by."

Images of from the night before surfaced. The sex with Balthazar was aggressive, demanding, everything unspoken acted out in a tangle of lustful limbs and undulating bodies.

The ride home from the Vihzor's floated through Morgan's mind. It was the first time Morgan had seen Dorcha drunk without being inebriated right alongside her. All in all, Dorcha handled herself pretty well. Dorcha surprised Morgan with how flirtatiously she had asked Captain Tess if they could stop at Astro Burger.

Morgan realized Dorcha had not mentioned Kyle. Even when Morgan told the monster space arena story, Dorcha never took the opportunity to question Morgan for further details.

Dorcha probably wasn't happy about that Morgan and Kyle would be sweating all over each other during workouts. Morgan knew about Dorcha's infatuation with Kyle. She vowed to herself to keep things platonic with Kyle. As attractive as Kyle was, Morgan didn't think it'd be too difficult.

Morgan fixated on one fact: Darian Vihzor was Victoria Shine's best friend. Maybe, by the grace of the Great Goddess of the Galaxy, Morgan would be able to meet her cherished idol.

Next Morgan envisioned the graphic novel she was working on with Draven Powers. A yet-to-be-drawn full-frame page of an elegant hotel lobby floated into view.

When Morgan had told Draven about UnderLife a few months ago, Draven had misunderstood, thinking Morgan was pitching him a potential story idea. Draven had gotten enthusiastic over the prospect of them creating their own graphic novel based off of UnderLife. At first Morgan had tried to explain UnderLife was real, but Draven had just laughed and said, "Seriously, this would be a great project for us. I know a few really talented artists who could draw this."

Usually Morgan's meetings with Draven disintegrated into hanging out, and talking about everything under the sun instead of getting any work done. This was fine with Morgan, as she thoroughly enjoyed Draven's company.

"And take another breath," Louise's gentle voice floated in. "3…

2…1," Morgan's eyes opened. After a few moments, Louise asked, "How do you feel?"

Morgan told Louise everything she could remember. Recalling all the details of a meditation was tricky. Often tidbits would hide, and reveal themselves later, like day-old answers to trivia questions.

Louise said, "You're entering a new phase, one in which you're learning how to use your influence and power. Be careful. You're likely to feel very sensitive right now. Take it easy. Drink plenty of water. Your emotional state will be heightened. Everything seems to be sequencing nicely. I'll look into your wand tomorrow morning to get a deeper perspective of how things are going. Call me if you need anything. Otherwise, I'll see you next week."

* * *

The next afternoon Morgan took the Metro Rail downtown. She went to Draven's apartment. They had scheduled a meeting for their graphic novel project. Morgan assumed that this meant cocktails would be forthcoming, so she had opted not to drive.

From the moment Morgan walked through Draven's front door, she felt a tension in him and in the room which had never been present before.

"Hi. Come in," Draven gave Morgan a quick hug. "Let me wrap up what I was doing."

Morgan watched Draven return to his desk to type whatever notion he was expounding upon. Morgan hoped Draven wasn't actually expecting her to be productive that day.

Morgan wandered into the kitchen to get something to drink. She retrieved a glass and put it under the water cooler. While it filled, she admired an old blown-up black-and-white picture of Draven as a toddler. The photo was a bit blurry, with the framing askew. One side of Draven's laughing face was visible, the other in deep shadow, and somehow it all came together as an adorable shot.

Morgan settled down on Draven's couch, and flipped through an Annie Leibovitz photography book. Several minutes later Draven's printer came to life with a whirr.

Draven joined Morgan on the couch with a stack of papers in his hand. "It's a fluffy article for Details Magazine, due at the end of the week. I'm not finished yet. Can I read you what I have so far?"

"I'd love to hear it," Morgan said.

"The current title is "Family Matters"."

Draven read, "Choose wisely when courting amongst a family. Doing the slutty sibling shuffle is a daring and dramatic maneuver. It gives masters of seduction pause. Too much emotional paperwork involved.

"However, if you cannot resist their charms, here are a few tips:

"1. Be patient and kind. This is politics. They are already deciding amongst themselves who gets to have you. Sometimes the sibling who wins is not the match with the best chemistry. This is where many run into trouble. They consummate with the easy temptation, only to regret their hasty lust when they realize that the true passion lay with the other sibling.

"2. If you can, trust the real attraction and let the other down easy. Be honest and tactful. Lead with a compliment. If you don't mind your manners, there is a chance a disgruntled family member will galvanize the rest of the clan to boycott your ass.

"3. Remember that if it works out with your new sweetheart, you'll have to socialize with various family members for the rest of your life. Be careful."

"I trust this article sprang from experience?" Morgan asked, while putting the finishing touches on a joint.

"The truth must be investigated. It was for scientific purposes."

"Right, how did it go?"

"Messy."

"Learned these tips the hard way?"

"Always do," Draven said with a smile, sparking up the ganja flowers.

"Since you've been toiling away so hard, I think it's time for a break. We can hash out the project later." In theory Morgan had planned on being productive, but in practice Morgan wanted to play with her buddy.

Draven nodded, "I think we need to feed and lubricate the creative wheels with some dinner and cocktails."

"Excellent, our first executive decision… sushi?" Morgan asked. Whenever Morgan came over, they always went to Sacred Meal across the street. Morgan couldn't get enough of their baked salmon rolls, Crazy Milk Sake, and Sapporo.

They spent dinner in labyrinthine conversation. A banquet of subjects was discussed, from serious political issues, to heartfelt revelations, to catty gossip. Drunk and giggling, the two of them were like a free floorshow for the other patrons. They talked about Draven's many dating adventures, and Morgan told modified versions of what she was doing with her training and meditations. As far as Draven knew, Morgan was training in martial arts, was doing a program of energy work and chakra balancing to help her narcolepsy, and was being paid to be a part of a research study.

Whenever Draven's probing came close to prying open Morgan's levee of secrets, Morgan distracted him however she could. Draven's cleverness was making this increasingly difficult. He smelled secrets like a hardened detective. Draven always knew when there was more to a story, or which straight guys were curious about exploring their sexuality.

Morgan hated bullshitting him. She decided to focus on splitting the hairs of her relationship with Balthazar, telling Draven all about their night together.

Keeping all the details about UnderLife from Draven was causing Morgan a lot of stress. Telling Balthazar about UnderLife had been disastrous, and Morgan didn't want to lose Draven's friendship. Even if Draven believed her, which was unlikely considering how big of a skeptic Draven was, Morgan knew he would still grill her with a litany of questions. Morgan probably didn't have answers for most of Draven's questions.

Ultimately, Morgan knew that if she wanted to be a real friend to Draven, she had to tell him the truth. It wasn't Morgan's place to try to control Draven's reactions.

Revealing her UnderLife ability would also expose Morgan's spiritual ambitions. Morgan didn't want to sound like a pompous ass, giving Draven all of her white-knight, saving-the-day fantasies. Morgan wasn't even sure if her UnderLife explorations could really make a positive difference in anyone's life.

Over the months, Dorcha had also grown very close with Draven. Dorcha regularly berated Morgan for taking so long to tell Draven about the UnderLife. She told Morgan she was getting tired of holding back all of the experiences that she was unable to share with Draven. It wasn't fair to keep one best friend silent, Dorcha said, and the other in the dark.

Somewhere around the third bottle of sake and Morgan's second twenty-ounce beer, she decided that tonight was the night to tell Draven the whole story.

After dinner Morgan asked, "Are we stopping by the corner market for more beer? Do you still feel like playing?"

"Of course. You can pass out at my place tonight. I'll drive you home in the morning."

"Sounds good, I love your fuzzy couch."

They bought a twelve-pack of Stella Artois and a couple of fudge-centered Drumsticks.

Back at Draven's apartment, Morgan cracked open a couple of beers. "As usual, we were models of industrious productivity with the graphic novel."

"We're practicing passive brainstorming."

"I'll say. During meditation yesterday with Louise, an image stuck with me. It was a full-page panel of an opulent hotel lobby. I jotted down a terrible version of it. Unfortunately my father's drawing talent isn't genetic."

Morgan showed Draven a rudimentary sketch of a boutique hotel lobby with labels indicating an elevator, a descending staircase, and the front desk.

Draven considered the paper. "I don't know how it will fit in our detective story yet. Maybe a setting for our hero to meet an important informant?"

"Possibly. Well, I think that satisfies our literary quota for the evening."

Draven paused a moment before saying, "I called Dorcha a couple of nights ago and she drunkenly gushed about her new job."

Morgan's stomach dropped. Here we go, she thought.

Draven continued, "Fifty grand a year to read Tarot cards, on what? How ridiculous! I don't get it, what's the catch?"

"No catch. Dorcha has a valuable skill."

"You're both being naïve. Think about it. People aren't this generous for no reason."

"Their intentions are virtuous, I swear."

"I don't like it. Something's not right here. It's like they own you."

"What? No, they don't. August and Louise are my friends. When my mom died, August stepped in as my surrogate mother. I trust her."

"Why? What did August ever do to do deserve such blind faith?"

"It's not blind. August wouldn't hesitate to risk her life for my protection."

"Right," Draven muttered with no confidence.

"It's true," Morgan sighed. "This isn't the way I wanted to tell you. UnderLife, it's real. The graphic novel has just been an excuse to talk about it with you."

"What? Are you kidding?"

Morgan gave another exhaustive UnderLife explanation. Morgan wasn't sure if Draven believed anything she said, but he played along. Morgan had underestimated how thorough a cross-examination Draven would give. Mind melds were less intrusive.

"Something doesn't add up with these people," Draven said. "If they're so legit, why isn't there a paper trail? Why can't I find anything on August Cannon? Do you even know Louise's last name?"

"Who asked you to do a background check on them?"

"I'm worried about you. They could be a cult."

"They're not a cult, Draven. You don't know what you're talking about."

"Oh, I don't? Enlighten me, please." Sarcasm dripped off of Draven's tongue like a deadly acid.

Anger burned away Morgan's buzz. Had Draven been listening to me? Yes, he's humoring me, she thought.

Morgan's realization that Draven wasn't buying anything she was saying disappointed her tremendously. Morgan wanted to tell Draven about meeting the Vihzors, but Draven's lack of receptivity prevented Morgan from continuing.

"If you're so sure of their virtue," Draven continued, "why are you getting so defensive? It's because you don't really know who these people are."

The truth in his statement stung Morgan. Morgan didn't know the whole story with August and Louise, or with their partners the Vihzors. The arrival of Captain Tess was (or could be seen as) suspicious as well. Morgan surmised someone would have to be very well connected to transfer an Army Ranger from active duty to the training of an obscure civilian. If Captain Tess was an Army Ranger at all. He seemed to have that kind of training, Morgan thought, but how would she know? August had deceived Morgan about not being in the FBI for how many years? Draven's doubts were starting to infect Morgan, and it was pissing her off.

"We'll talk about this later. I'm going home." Morgan grabbed her jar of weed off of the coffee table and stuffed it into her bag.

"Oh, you're going to leave now? Don't want to face the truth about your parasitic mentors? Coward. Fine, go!"

Morgan shot Draven an icy glare, "If you weren't being such a jackass right now I would tell you more."

"Whatever, Morgan, weren't you leaving? I'm getting tired of your delusions."

Morgan slammed the door on her way out.

The Metro was no longer running, so Morgan began to stomp the five miles home in a huff. Frustration, anxiety, and sorrow were keeping tears at the precipice of her eyelids. Morgan didn't expect to get such friction from Draven. Normally he was much more understanding.

Morgan's dark mood got even worse when her iPod's battery died in the first mile back to her apartment. At least the five miles didn't seem like a big deal. With all of Morgan's punishing workouts, the walk just felt like a nice warm up.

As Morgan approached her building, she heard Victoria Shine's song Subtle Approach playing nearby. Morgan glanced at her iPod, double-checking that it was indeed off.

Morgan was still upset from her conversation with Draven. She punched in the security code for the front gate and entered. Two of her neighbors were coming home late from a party, and were talking to each other next to the bank of mailboxes. Morgan turned to Roger, an actor/bartender who lived in the unit underneath her.

"Do you hear that music?"

"What music?"

"Really, Victoria Shine isn't blasting right now from somewhere in here?" asked Morgan.

"Nope. Sorry." Roger said this to Morgan with a strange look. Morgan turned to Kiki for some support. Kiki shook her head, confirming that if there were any tune playing, it was coming from Morgan's imagination.

Morgan, embarrassed, gave a self-conscious smile. She laughed, shrugging her shoulders like this was a dumb joke and they shouldn't pay her any mind. Morgan retreated into her apartment.

"Subtle Approach" continued on a loop.

Morgan opened up a window, wondering if someone outside had their music cranked up, but the music still sounded like it was coming from inside the room. Opening the window didn't change the volume of the music at all.

Morgan went over to her speakers, feeling for vibration. Nothing, silent. They aren't even hooked up to my iPod anyway, Morgan thought as she picked up the loose wire.

A dark voice inside of Morgan suggested this might be a symptom of some kind of brain tumor growing inside of her. Morgan squashed this idea. She knew how her mother's bizarre condition had manifested.

Maybe someone put a curse on me? She thought. But who and why? Only a few people were even aware of UnderLife, and Morgan didn't know anyone who bore ill will towards her.

Morgan chalked it up to nerves from the fight she had had with Draven. She decided she needed a relaxing soak in her tub.

The music continued while Morgan was drawing a bath. In fact, it sounded like someone was incrementally turning up the volume. Morgan felt the bass line in her body while undressing and submerging herself in the hot bath water.

* * *

Subtle Approach shifted into a dance remix, and now it was blaring. Morgan found herself in a packed, dimly lit nightclub. People were everywhere. Scratch that. Men were everywhere. Any woman whose path Morgan crossed while winding through the crowd turned out on closer inspection to be a transvestite.

For a fleeting moment, nestled deep in the crowd, Morgan thought she saw Draven dancing with several men. As Morgan approached he moved further away.

"Draven!" Morgan shouted, to no avail. The thumping music drowned out Morgan's voice.

Draven disappeared into a hallway on the far side of the dance floor.

Following, Morgan went into the men's bathroom. Intermittent moans and groans were coming from the stalls. The place smelled like urinal cakes, sex, and alcohol. At first, Morgan was afraid she would have to search the area, but then Morgan saw another exit on the opposite wall.

The door opened into a tiled steam room. The haze of steam and male pheromones was so thick that Morgan felt her knees weaken with desire. Naked panting flesh danced just beyond Morgan's limited peripheral vision. Morgan fought the impulse to linger amongst the debauchery.

The scene shifted and Morgan was in a locker room. The music changed to Victoria's song *Concubine Discipline* from the second and last *Virtuoso* album. This amused Morgan. It was no surprise to find the room filled with naked men changing their clothes and posing. None of them noticed her. Morgan found it next to impossible tear her eyes away from them. An inordinate number of the men were blessed specimens of physique, bone structure, and endowment.

It took some effort, but Morgan kept moving, reminding herself that all of the man-beauty was a part of Draven's UnderLife defense system. The succulent sentries didn't seem alarmed by Morgan's presence, and aside from radiating indifferent sex appeal, they did nothing to obstruct her path.

The next set of heavy doors opened into a weight room. The trance version of *Return, My Love* from Harmony's Harem reverberated through the space. A multitude of muscle-bound men worked out in Speedos, blasting their pecs, doing squat thrusts, curling biceps, and a mélange of other exercises.

"Oh, Draven, of course it would be raining men in your UnderLife," Morgan said while taking an appreciative gander at the world-class body of a handsome gym bunny.

Morgan looked away in time to catch another glimpse of Draven at the far end of the expansive room, leaving by the front exit. Morgan followed Draven. She waded through the equipment and denizens as fast she could. Morgan burst out the front door of the weight room and stopped dead in her tracks.

Morgan was standing in the exact same hotel lobby she'd seen in her meditation. On closer inspection, Morgan discovered that the building was a renovated gothic castle. The large stone bricks, common in medieval construction, were married perfectly to the modern architecture that had been grafted upon them.

A string version of Victoria Shine's *Strip the Sun* was playing. The music echoed off the vaulted ceilings.

No one else was around. The place felt spooky.

Ding! Morgan's attention focused on an elevator which was flanked by two bronze lion statues. She moved closer.

A shiver went through Morgan's spine, and the hair on her arms rose as if it were electrically charged. When Morgan got within ten feet of the elevator, an eerie translucent little blond girl materialized, blocking the way.

"Ah!" Startled, Morgan jumped back.

The girl didn't respond, and continued to stare ahead blankly.

Morgan crept forward, intending to hit the elevator call button. The apparition sidestepped, barring her way.

The ghost's neck jerked suddenly. Her soulless eyes bored into Morgan. The girl ran a finger across her own throat while shaking her head no. Morgan shivered. The petite blond pointed to a nearby staircase.

Moran walked to the staircase. The granite steps wound down deep into the bowels of the building. She descended at least a hundred feet before reaching a huge bank vault at the bottom. The door to the vault was open. Morgan didn't know whether to feel happy or suspicious. If this was a trap, Morgan was about to cruise right into it.

Morgan entered the vault. She was astonished to find that it was filled to the brim with every imaginable piece of Victoria Shine memorabilia. There were souvenirs, promotional materials, and photographs from her entire career. From cereal boxes to film posters to blow-ups of tabloid scandals, Victoria's face was everywhere. An old-school film projector was playing Victoria's episode of True Hollywood Story on a pull-down screen.

Did I create this? Morgan thought. Am I seeing my own UnderLife? Cause if so, yikes. This is too much.

On the far wall of the vault, there was a huge blow-up of "Moment Before", a candid shot of Victoria taken just before she stepped on stage during her first world tour with Virtuoso. It was one of Morgan's favorite pictures. There was a marvelous array of emotions in Victoria's eyes. The picture showed Victoria's anticipation, excitement, fear, hope, and determination.

Morgan had first seen the picture many years before in a Vanity Fair spread. She had taken a scalpel from her father's studio, carefully cut it out of the magazine, and pinned it up on her bedroom wall.

Morgan was so entranced by the enormous photo that it took her a few minutes to realize Draven was standing at the foot of it. His attention was focused on moving around boxes of memorabilia.

"Draven?"

"Morgan! Where are we? Am I dreaming this? I think I just saw a ghost," Draven said in rush.

"Yeah, that little girl was pretty creepy."

"What little girl? No, I'm talking about my father."

"Your father? Isn't he…"

"Dead three years from a heart attack? Yes. I saw him leave the bar. I followed him to this vault, and he disappeared somewhere inside of here." Draven looked around and whistled. "So either this is UnderLife, or you rented a warehouse to store one hell of an extensive shrine to Victoria Shine."

Morgan laughed, "Yeah, no kidding. I'm the big fan, so I guess this is a slice of my unconscious."

"Looks like the whole pie to me." Draven paused. "I'm sorry about our fight earlier."

"Me too," Morgan said.

"I can see why you prefer to show rather than tell with UnderLife."

"Yeah, and the settings rarely repeat themselves. Each UnderLife domain seems to be specific to whatever spiritual lesson is currently on the docket. Did you hear me earlier? I've been following you for quite a while."

Draven shook his head. "No. I got absorbed with chasing my father. At least I think it was him. I only got a few clear looks at his face."

"Was your dad solid-looking or was he kind of see-through?"

"He looked as real as you do."

"Maybe there's a secret door around here. Those seem to be going around."

"That's why I was moving around boxes of this marketing crap. I was hoping to find a trap door or hiding place."

"Then let's keep looking," Morgan said.

Draven nodded and they split up.

Morgan started at the perimeter. Draven searched the floor. Neither of them found another way out of the vault.

Morgan was familiar with all of Victoria's published photographs, magazine articles, and authorized and unauthorized biographies. Scanning the room, Morgan recognized almost everything she saw. Morgan rifled through the treasure trove surrounding her. There were many photographs of Victoria and Bunny Jones, her mother and former manager.

Morgan picked up an antique ornate silver frame. Inside the frame, the picture was ripped in half with the left side missing. It depicted Victoria as a child with her arm around a toddler boy. She was kissing the top of the boy's head.

"I don't think I've seen this one before," Morgan said. The photo in Draven's kitchen leapt into her mind. "Draven, come here. Check this out."

Draven approached, but got distracted by something behind Morgan. Draven's eyes widened in alarm, "Mor…"

CLANG!

Something heavy hit Morgan on the back of the head.

* * *

Morgan awoke with a start. The frigid water of the bathtub made her gasp. Morgan's pruned phalanges seized the rim of the tub. She reoriented herself to Waking Life.

Morgan tried to get up, and yelped out in pain instead. She had no idea how long her lower back had been locked in its present position, and it was now in full spasm, turning any movement into torture.

Morgan grimaced while extracting herself from the tub. By the time she'd toweled off and put on her bath robe, lightning bolts of agony were making Morgan's breathing erratic and labored. Morgan hobbled to her bedroom, and sprawled out on the hardwood floor to try to relax her traumatized back muscles. Eventually Morgan was able to calm her aching back. She crawled into bed and passed out.

* * *

Early the next morning, Morgan woke up to the sound of her phone ringing in the living room. Morgan's back was still jacked up from the night before, so Morgan remained in bed and let the call go to voicemail. Morgan drifted back off to sleep.

A couple of hours later, Morgan dragged her aching carcass out of bed.

Checking her phone, Morgan saw that it was Draven who had called. Morgan punched in the code to retrieve the message.

"Hi, it's me. Okay, last night was awful. I want to make sure you got home okay. Something weird happened in my dream last night. Call me when you get this. Let's talk."

Morgan called him back. Draven picked up after a few rings. "Hi."

"It wasn't a dream. You were in UnderLife."

"I knew it! So that's what it's like. Wild," Draven said.

"Did you see what hit me on the head?"

"Yeah, you were bludgeoned by a frying pan, and then I was back in my bed. This sounds crazy, and I guess under the circumstances how would we know, but I think Bunny Jones was the kitchenware commando."

"Victoria Shine's mother? How odd. Well, the blow killed me in UnderLife, which means I passed out in Waking Life. Luckily I was propped up in the bathtub, otherwise I might have drowned. My back got totally tweaked out, though."

"Ow, sorry to hear that. Do you want me to come over?"

"Nah, I'll be okay. I just have to rest and I'll go see a chiropractor tomorrow."

"Let me at least give you a ride. I feel bad."

"Alright, thanks, Draven. I'm sorry we got into a fight."

"Me too, that sucked. What were you trying to show me before scary stage mom arrived?"

"I found a picture I'd never seen before. It was ripped it in half, with the left side missing. It showed Victoria cuddled up next to a small boy."

"So what's that got to do with anything?"

"The kid looked exactly like you."

"Really? Maybe I have a doppelganger out there."

"Or maybe it was you. You've said before you don't remember your childhood very well, or who your biological mother was."

"Yeah. Maybe I met Victoria at a meet-and-greet for the kids show she was on."

"I don't know. Victoria looked too young for that. The relationship seemed more intimate than a fan photo. I wonder what or who is on the ripped off side," Morgan said. "Do you know who took that baby picture of you hanging in your kitchen?"

"No. I found it in my Dad's stuff after he died. I guess I assumed he'd taken it since I don't know a thing about my real mother."

"Hmm," Morgan said.

"What? You think I'm somehow related to Victoria Shine, don't you." Draven said.

"I'm not sure. I know it sounds impossible," Morgan thought about it for a moment. "You do look alike, and you both have sexual drives bordering on addiction."

"You're one to talk." Draven paused. "Oh, this is silly."

"You're right. I want it to be true, though. I guess I don't have any real clarity. I'll ask Dorcha and Captain Tess to do readings."

"And Louise," Draven said.

"Yes. Everyone will be interested to know that this is the first time I've brought someone into UnderLife who wasn't standing in front of me that remembers the experience. Usually whenever a random person shows up in UnderLife they typically represent some kind of archetype for me. I call those interactions solo experiences, like how it is in dreams."

"Okay, this is a bit much," Draven said, interrupting Morgan's analysis. "You gotta ease me into Narnia here. I'm gonna go get a massage. I need it. When do you want me to pick you up tomorrow morning?"

"Ten-thirty. Thanks again, Draven. I'll see you tomorrow."

* * *

Later in the evening, Morgan left her front door open for ventilation with the screen door locked. The temperature had reached a record high that day, and it still hadn't cooled down after night had fallen. Morgan was lying on the couch with an ice pack, listening to music, when Balthazar arrived unannounced.

"Morgan?" Balthazar said.

Startled, Morgan attempted to sit up quickly. She grunted when her beleaguered muscles screamed with searing pain.

"Ugh- Ai- Hi." Morgan said.

Balthazar tried to open the screen door, only to find it locked. It took

Morgan some time, effort, and gasps of suffering before she was able to get herself up.

"Oh, honey, what happened?" Balthazar asked.

Morgan gingerly made her way to the door. "My back…" Morgan winced as her back seemed to respond to hearing its name with a series of spasms, "…is very angry with me."

"What did you do to it?"

Morgan got to the door and opened it for Balthazar. "I passed out in the bathtub, and fucked it up royally. What are you…?"

"I thought I'd stop by on my way home from work to see if you wanted to get it on. Clearly I should have called ahead first."

"Sorry, I'd love to ravage you, but as you can see I can barely move."

Balthazar kissed her softly. "Don't worry about it. Have you eaten dinner?"

"Not yet," Morgan returned to her position on the couch. "I was working up to dealing with food."

"Whatcha in the mood for?"

"You don't have to do this."

"What do you mean? I'm hungry too. What kind of gentleman or paramedic would I be if I didn't help a lady in distress?"

"Only if you insist. I wouldn't be offended if you want to take off."

"Please shut up and relax. You've got to start learning to let people help you."

"Alright, thank you, Balthazar." Morgan reached out and touched Balthazar's arm. "You really are a classy guy."

"Oh, you're gonna owe me big time. I expect many sexual favors for this unexpected blue-ball role playing game we've got going on here. Does it turn you on, having me as your nurse maid?"

"I don't know. Does it come with a little outfit?" Morgan's eyes twinkled. "I promise, once I'm able to, mind-boggling pleasure shall be yours."

"I look forward to it. Now, what do you want to order from Bossa Nova?"

* * *

It took a week before Morgan was able to return for light training at the Skyscraper Space. Morgan arrived to find Dorcha giving Captain Tess a Tarot reading. They waved hello to Morgan. Morgan retreated to the kitchen to make some tea.

Morgan took out some coins and cast her daily I Ching reading. Number Nineteen, with no changing lines. Approach. An auspicious hexagram. Good fortune was in Morgan's future as long as she adhered to the path of humble, self-correcting behavior.

Dorcha entered the kitchen as Morgan was finishing the entry on Hexagram 19 in Carol Anthony's book.

"Hi Morgan. How's your back?" Dorcha asked, embracing her friend.

"Better, still pretty sore. Captain Tess is going to take me through some stretches today to help speed up the rehabilitation. How are you?"

"Great! I've got two new Tarot decks I'm working with. Taylor gave me the Tao Oracle by Ma Deva Padma, which is based on the I Ching. The artwork of the deck makes it a cinch to learn the sixty-four hexagrams. Tilly Vihzor sent over The Gendron Tarot by Melanie Gendron. The vivid images of that deck are composed from a smorgasbord of symbols from many cultures. It's heavy on the Sacred Feminine. They're gorgeous. I love them."

"How many decks are you using now?"

"Five. I figured it was a good number. Five represents the Hierophant/Spirit card in the Major Arcana of the Tarot. We have five senses, which are our sources of input to navigate our bodies and our interactions on this plane of existence. I retired the Lover's Path deck. The current lineup now is the Druid Craft, Faeries' Oracle, Gendron, Tao, and Vampires."

"Awesome, I can't wait to get a reading."

"Anytime," Dorcha said.

"How did Captain Tess's reading go?"

"Good. Taylor is a fascinating man."

"Yeah he looks pretty interested in what you've got going on."

"What? No," Dorcha blushed.

"I think the Captain is into you. He gave you a deck which will teach you his divinatory language. How romantic," Morgan said.

Dorcha got a Diet Dr. Pepper from the fridge. The thought of the stoic soldier finding her attractive hadn't even occurred to Dorcha. She was too preoccupied with wondering whether or not Kyle would be joining them.

Louise arrived, just in time as far as Dorcha was considered. Louise gathered Captain Tess, Morgan, and Dorcha in the living room section of the Skyscraper Space.

"Morgan, please recount the details of your last adventure," Louise said.

Morgan told them the whole story, from when she first arrived at Draven's house to waking up in the icy bathtub.

"Morgan's ability is evolving," Louise said. "She got an image of a future UnderLife location in meditation and a musical warning of an impending episode, and she was able to bring in another person from five miles away. These are excellent signs of progress. This may indicate that the Vault episode has a particular significance. Captain Tess, Dorcha, we need your help deciphering the lesson of Draven's maiden voyage in UnderLife. Use your divination systems to translate the symbols of the experience. I've got August doing research on the Shine and Powers families. If August can dig up accurate birth information, we'll ask Kyle to create some astrology charts and get his perspective."

Morgan said, "The question I want answered is whether or not Draven was the little boy I saw in the picture with young Victoria. If so, what is his relationship to Victoria? Who or what is on the missing half of the picture? Why did Bunny Jones come after me with a frying pan? Why did Nikolai Powers, Draven's father, lead him to a vault filled with Victoria Shine memorabilia? Basically I'd love a full analysis from you all. There's something I'm missing here. It's on the edge of my brain and won't let me rest until I figure it out. Thank you for your help."

"Alright, everyone," Louise said. "We'll reconvene in an hour to discuss what we've learned."

Louise left to go meditate on the roof of the building. Taylor retrieved his I Ching books, journal, and coins.

"Morgan," Dorcha said. "Will you help me with this?"

"Of course," Morgan said.

"May I listen in on your reading?" Captain Tess said.

"Y-Yes," Dorcha said.

They moved to Dorcha's Tarot table. Dorcha shuffled the decks. Captain Tess cast a few I Ching readings and observed the two women.

"Shouldn't we include Draven in this process?" Dorcha asked.

"I called him last night and left a message about coming here today. I haven't heard back from him yet."

"Draven is probably dealing with the complete upheaval of his perspective on reality," Dorcha said.

"Trips to UnderLife have that effect. Even for me after all these years."

"Do you think the Vault was from your UnderLife or from Draven's?" Dorcha asked.

"I'm not sure. "Moment Before", the blown up photo on the wall, is one of my favorites, but all the clutter strewn about disturbed me. I've never been a big collector of Victoria Shine memorabilia. I'm more into the substance of Victoria's art, not the promotional packaging. I'd prefer Victoria to show up personally in UnderLife, not just her souvenirs."

"That's true. Alright, bear with me. I've got two new decks involved. I might have to look some things up."

"Dorcha, it's been a couple of hours, I can't believe you don't have those memorized yet," Morgan said.

"Oh, ha ha, very funny," Dorcha said. "Give me a week." she said under her breath.

Morgan and Taylor chuckled.

Dorcha and Morgan came up with two separate spreads to analyze the various elements of the episode.

Eight Questions Spread A using the Druid Craft, Faeries Oracle, Gendron, Tao, and Vampire Tarot.

Position 1 represents **is the little boy Draven?**
  Druid: #3 – The Lady @
  Faeries: #16 – The Bright Mother @
  Gendron: 6 of Swords @
  Tao: Hexagram 32 - Duration
  Vampires: Queen of Swords

Position 2 represents **Victoria's relationship to the boy**:
  Druid: #7 – The Chariot @
  Faeries: #26 – O! That Gnome @
  Gendron: 2 of Wands @
  Tao: Hexagram 44 – The Attraction of Opposites
  Vampires: 5 of Pentacles

Position 3 represents **who is in the missing half of the picture?**
  Druid: 2 of Swords
  Faeries: #33 – Faeries of the Future
  Gendron: #12 – The Hanged One
  Tao: Hexagram 29 – The Abysmal
  Vampires: 2 of Wands

Position 4 represents **what does Nikolai Powers represent?**
  Druid: Ace of Cups @
  Faeries: #61 – G. Hobyah @
  Gendron: 5 of Pentacles
  Tao: Hexagram 64 – Before Completion
  Vampires: Knave of Pentacles

Position 5 represents **what does Bunny Jones represent?**
  Druid: King of Pentacles
  Faeries: #55 – The Soul Shrinker
  Gendron: Queen of Swords @
  Tao: Hexagram 36 – Darkening of the Light
  Vampires: King of Swords

Position 6 represents **what does Victoria Shine represent?**
  Druid: #20 – Rebirth
  Faeries: #51 – The Topsie-Turvets @
  Gendron: Prince of Cups
  Tao: Hexagram 13 – Companionship

Vampires: Queen of Wands
Position 7 represents **the lesson of the UnderLife Vault adventure**:
Druid: 7 of Swords @
Faeries: #36 – Spirit Dancer
Gendron: #15 – The Deceiver
Tao: Hexagram 26 – The Taming Power of the Great
Vampires: King of Cups
Position 8 represents **advice for Morgan**:
Druid: 7 of Cups
Faeries: #41 – Ilbe the Retriever @
Gendron: #2 – The High Priestess
Tao: Hexagram 48 – The Well
Vampires: 9 of Swords

Eight Questions Spread B using the Druid Craft, Faeries Oracle, Gendron, Tao, and Vampire Tarot.

Position 1 represents **the hot indifferent men**:
Druid: 9 of Wands
Faeries: #6 – The Singer of Connection @
Gendron: 10 of Swords
Tao: Hexagram 45 – Gathering Together
Vampires: 10 of Swords
Position 2 represents **the hotel lobby**:
Druid: 3 of Wands
Faeries: #22 – The Master Maker
Gendron: 6 of Wands @
Tao: Hexagram 53 – Development
Vampires: 3 of Swords
Position 3 **why did Bunny Jones attack Morgan?**
Druid: 9 of Swords @
Faeries: #31 – UnDressing of a Salad @
Gendron: 9 of Pentacles
Tao: Hexagram 12 – Standstill
Vampires: #14 - Blood
Position 4 **why did Nikolai Powers lead Draven to the vault?**
Druid: #17 – The Star @
Faeries: #61 – G. Hobyah
Gendron: 3 of Swords @
Tao: Hexagram 58 – The Joyous
Vampires: Knave of Wands
Position 5 represents **lesson for Draven**:
Druid: 5 of Wands

Faeries: #5 – She of the Cruach @
Gendron: #16 – The Tower
Tao: Hexagram 27 – The Corners of the Mouth
Vampires: 8 of Swords
Position 6 represents **the message Morgan needs to know**:
Druid: #16 – The Tower
Faeries: #54 – Epona's Wild Daughter
Gendron: Ace of Cups
Tao: Hexagram 36 – Darkening of the Light
Vampires: #0 - Innocence
Position 7 represents **the ghost girl**:
Druid: King of Cups
Faeries: #10 – The Singer of Healing
Gendron: King of Wands
Tao: Hexagram 7 – Discipline
Vampires: King of Swords
Position 8 **where does the elevator lead**:
Druid: #0 – The Fool @
Faeries: #15 – The Journeyman
Gendron: #8 – Strength @
Tao: Hexagram 17 – Following
Vampires: #13 – The Embrace

Dorcha analyzed the spreads and wrote down notes on her findings. Fifteen minutes later Dorcha spoke. "It's hard to confirm whether or not Draven is indeed the boy in the picture. The cards seem muddled on the answer. There is scandal present in Victoria's relationship to the boy. Something got covered up, hidden deep away. Who says the picture you saw exists in Waking Life?"

"Good point. I don't have any solid proof. But my gut says there's more to this than masturbatory fantasies about a beloved famous artist."

The next words flowed out of Dorcha as if she was in a trance. "There is a lot of sadness surrounding Nikolai Powers. Bunny did something terrible, and somehow Nikolai is involved. Victoria is the connector in all of this."

"How so?"

Dorcha shrugged. "I don't know. Those words I just said made me feel like a conduit, like it flowed through me involuntarily." Dorcha scanned the cards, "There is definitely a mystery here for us to solve. Don't get impatient. Work on tasks available to you, rather than beating your head in frustration on obstacles. The ghost girl is a very positive, healing ally. She represented a test for you, which you passed by heeding her advice. You're not ready for where the elevator leads. Maybe you're not quite mature or strong enough for the life changing adventure it promises yet. Bunny Jones was definitely the security system in that realm. She was there to neutralize anyone who got close to the truth. I guess it's good that Bunny knocked you out just when you were about to tell Draven about the picture, because that means it's important."

Louise returned from her meditation. Captain Tess brought Louise up to speed.

"What do you think?" Dorcha asked Taylor. "What does the I Ching tell you?"

Before Taylor could give his analysis, August entered the Skyscraper Space with a smile on her face. "I found something!"

"Great!" Morgan exclaimed. "What is it?"

"Actually, it's what I didn't find that's so compelling. Someone went to great lengths to bury the past of both of these families. The hard copy and electronic birth records of Draven Powers and Victoria Shine are unavailable. There is no official documentation on Bunny Jones anywhere. It's like she doesn't exist. There's nothing on Nikolai Powers either. The information has either been wiped clean, or those are both aliases."

"Victoria and Draven are in the same family," Taylor said with certainty. No one argued.

They all gazed at each other for a full minute before Morgan broke the silence. "How do we prove it?"

CHAPTER SIXTEEN
BOUND

Meanwhile, twenty miles up the coast in Malibu

Victoria Shine sat in her music room with her elbows propped up on a Bösendorfer grand piano, and her head in her hands. A distant melody whispered and echoed in Victoria's mind. Victoria struggled to will it closer.

There were dozens of musical instruments lining the walls, held aloft by specially designed mountings. Victoria was in the habit of collecting unusual pieces which caught her eye. A bansuri flute from India rested next to a prima-sized Russian balalaika, which was a three stringed guitar-like instrument with a triangular body. Victoria's collection was eclectic and comprehensive.

Victoria's dyed blond hair was swept back in a loose pony-tail, exposing her brunette roots. She was wearing a simple knee-length purple cotton skirt with a matching form-fitting tank top, and no undergarments.

Victoria possessed a gift for mimicry, a useful trait in acting. However, this gift was proving to be a tremendous obstacle for her songwriting. Victoria was suffering from an infuriating case of writer's block. Everything Victoria wrote these days eventually melted into another musician's song.

Victoria wanted to bust into the bottle of Auchentoshan 1973 32 Year Old, an expensive lowland whiskey which had been given to her recently by an old friend. Luckily the impulse was fleeting. Victoria didn't really want to get drunk. She just knew it would get her to stop courting the elusive and fickle muses for that day.

At least put the allotted time in, Victoria reminded herself. Then I can relax.

A svelte naked man strode into the room. Victoria heard him

approaching, but pretended to be too wrapped up in her songwriting to notice.

Strong hands touched Victoria's shoulders, massaging her taut trapezius muscles.

"Mm, stop it," Victoria said. "I have to work."

"My plane leaves in five hours," Aidan said. "Who knows when we'll be in the same city again? You can work later."

Aidan leaned in to make out with Victoria. Victoria responded.

In between kisses Victoria said, "I was having a hard time getting into the flow."

"Let me give you some inspiration." Aidan's hand stroked Victoria's leg and squeezed her inner thigh.

Victoria's resolve disintegrated. She spread her legs wider.

Aidan smiled, kneeled, put his head under Victoria's skirt, and began to lick.

* * *

Back in Culver City at the Skyscraper Space

Kyle arrived for training to find August, Louise, Dorcha, Taylor, and Morgan in the living room area.

"Well hello everyone!" Kyle said. "What's going on?"

At the same moment, Morgan heard the muffled sound of her cell phone ringing in her bag. She knew it was Draven because she'd changed his personalized ring tone to The Weather Girls version of It's Raining Men.

"Hi Kyle," Morgan said as she passed her training partner. "They'll catch you up on what's going on."

Kyle nodded.

Morgan answered her phone, "Draven, hi, how are you?"

"Pretty good, so... are you there, at the Skyscraper Space?"

"Yes, please join us."

"Who's there?"

"Dorcha, Taylor, Louise, August, and Kyle just came in."

"Wow, the whole gang. Figure anything out yet?"

"There's definitely a connection. Come over, we'll tell you what we've got so far."

"Okay, I'll be there within the hour."

"You've got the address?"

"Yeah, you left it on the message."

"The security is pretty major. Call me when you're downstairs."

"Will do," Draven said. "See you soon."

"K, bye," Morgan said, and they both hung up.

Morgan rejoined the group. When they had finished getting Kyle caught up on the situation, Morgan asked him, "Will you help us get in contact with Victoria?"

Kyle grimaced. "I don't think it's a good idea without irrefutable proof. Victoria is not very forgiving to people who waste her time. To be honest, she kind of scares me. I'd rather fight a heavyweight blindfolded than incur Victoria's wrath."

"What if it's true?"

"I know. If you're right, and Draven is a long lost family member, Victoria will be eternally grateful for the reunion. You're wagering your only chance to get to know Victoria."

Morgan nodded, "It's a risk I'm willing to take."

Kyle sighed, "Victoria redefines private. I don't have her personal cell number."

"I'm sure Darian has it."

"Truuue," Kyle said. He scanned the faces of the crowd. Everyone looked as sincere as Morgan did. They all seemed to believe Victoria Shine and Draven Powers were somehow related. Well, stranger things happened every day, Kyle thought.

"Darian is on location, shooting in New Zealand," Kyle thought for a moment. "It's tomorrow morning there. Darian is probably already busy on set. I'll call later and feel her out. I can't promise anything, but now you've got me curious. I want to find out what the truth is."

"Good, because I think we should go back to the Akashic Records and ask Librarian," Morgan said.

"I can't believe you'd suggest that!" Dorcha said.

"What? It was pretty easy to access before. We shifted right into UnderLife once our intentions were set."   "Oh yeah, other than almost drowning, taking forever to figure out how to wake up the gnome, and still being haunted by vivid recall of what we found, the whole thing was a breeze."

"Gnome?" Kyle asked. "Where were you?"

Dorcha started to answer, "Well..."

Louise interrupted, "There might be another obstacle with that course of action. The soul histories you want to understand here are not your own. The truth of your own families was ripe and begging to come to light. This may not be true with regards to the truth about Victoria and Draven."

"Are you suggesting that we don't go to the Akashic records?" Morgan asked.

"No, I'm simply pointing out this mission could prove to be much more difficult than the last one. We need to wait until Draven gets here. If Draven agrees to participate, he will be a spiritual compass for this journey."

"Dorcha, will you..."

"Already on it, Morgan," Dorcha rose and went to go hole up at the

Tarot table.

Eight Questions Spread A using the Druid Craft, Faeries Oracle, Gendron, Tao, and Vampire Tarot decks.

Position 1 represents **how to enter the Akashic Records – Focal Point**:
  Druid: 3 of Cups @
  Faeries: #59 – The Bodacious Bodach @
  Gendron: #1 – The Magus
  Tao: #33 – Retreat
  Vampires: Knave of Cups
Position 2 represents **something we should be aware of**:
  Druid: #13 – Death
  Faeries: #10 – The Singer of Healing
  Gendron: 6 of Swords @
  Tao: #17 – Following
  Vampires: 4 of Cups
Position 3 represents **how to consciously enter UnderLife together**:
  Druid: Queen of Wands @
  Faeries: #30 – The Laume
  Gendron: King of Wands
  Tao: #10 – Treading
  Vampires: #10 - Fate
Position 4 represents **Captain Tess's Focal Point**:
  Druid: Ace of Cups @
  Faeries: #6 – The Singer of Connection @
  Gendron: Prince of Swords @
  Tao: #58 – The Joyous
  Vampires: 10 of Cups
Position 5 represents **Morgan's Focal Point**:
  Druid: 5 of Pentacles
  Faeries: #9 – The Singer of Initiation
  Gendron: 8 of Pentacles
  Tao: #47 – Exhaustion
  Vampires: 9 of Pentacles
Position 6 represents **Kyle's Focal Point**:
  Druid: 9 of Pentacles @
  Faeries: #54 – Epona's Wild Daughter
  Gendron: 5 of Wands
  Tao: #55 – Abundance
  Vampires: 8 of Swords
Position 7 represents **Dorcha's Focal Point**:
  Druid: #2 – The High Priestess

Faeries: #61 – G. Hobyah @
Gendron: 9 of Pentacles
Tao: #19 – Approach
Vampires: Queen of Pentacles
Position 8 represents **our near future**:
Druid: King of Wands
Faeries: #39 – Losgunna
Gendron: 7 of Wands @
Tao: #31 – Influence
Vampires: King of Cups

Seven Questions Spread B using the Druid Craft, Faeries Oracle, Gendron, Tao, and Vampire Tarot decks.

Position 1 represents **Draven's Focal Point**:
Druid: #11- Justice @
Faeries: #13 – Solus @
Gendron: Princess of Pentacles @
Tao: #54 – The Marrying Maiden
Vampires: #19 – The Truth
Position 2 represents **the UnderLife setting we're going to**:
Druid: 8 of Pentacles
Faeries: #10 – The Singer of Healing
Gendron: 3 of Cups
Tao: #64 – Before Completion
Vampires: #4 – The Liege
Position 3 represents **advice to solve the UnderLife puzzle for a safe exit**:
Druid: 4 of Cups @
Faeries: #34 – Sylvanius
Gendron: Queen of Swords @
Tao: #9 – The Taming Power of the Small
Vampires: 5 of Cups
Position 4 represents **how to find the evidence we seek in regards to Draven & Victoria's possible genetic connection**:
Druid: Prince of Wands
Faeries: #19 – The Sage @
Gendron: 3 of Swords
Tao: #40 – Deliverance
Vampires: Queen of Cups
Position 5 represents **the nature of Draven and Victoria's relationship**:
Druid: #2 – The High Priestess
Faeries: #6 – The Singer of Connection @

261

Gendron: #1 – The Magus @
Tao: #43 – Resoluteness
Vampires: #12 - Abstinence

Position 6 represents **the spiritual lesson of this journey**:

Druid: 10 of Wands
Faeries: #26 – O! That Gnome @
Gendron: 8 of Cups
Tao: #18 – Work on What Has Been Spoiled
Vampires: Ace of Wands

Position 7 represents **the challenge we will be presented with**:

Druid: Queen of Cups @
Faeries: #27 – Nelys the Alchemyst
Gendron: #16 – The Tower @
Tao: #55 – Abundance
Vampires: #3 - Passion

While Dorcha analyzed the two Tarot spreads she'd done, Captain Tess did an I Ching reading on the mission and got Hexagram 63 (After Completion/Already Crossing) going into Hexagram 58 (The Joyous/Open/Expression).

"This looks good," Captain Tess said.

Captain Tess checked his reference books on the three changing lines and nodded. "Yes, we're flowing with the streaming moment. There are the usual warnings to be careful, but we should keep going."

Morgan's phone rang. It was Draven. Morgan excused herself to go get him.

They returned a few minutes later.

Draven was on edge walking into Skyscraper Space. Why is there so much security here? Draven wondered. It makes me nervous. What was behind the closed door in the lobby, on the other side from the elevators?

Despite his trepidation, Draven tried to act unfazed. "Wow, you weren't kidding Morgan. There's a whole team forming here," he said.

Introductions were made. Everyone was cordial and welcoming. Dorcha gave Draven a big hug. They gathered around the living room space and brought Draven up to speed.

"I'm assuming all of you have been in UnderLife?" Draven asked.

"I haven't," Louise said.

"Then how do you know it's real?"

"Faith." Louise shifted her attention to Dorcha and Captain Tess. "What did you two come up with in your readings?"

Captain Tess answered first, "Everything checks out. We're flowing with the cosmic current."

Dorcha consulted her notes. "This is a necessary expedition, whether or not we find the information we're looking for. I agree with Taylor. A lot of healing cards came up in the spreads. Unfortunately, healing can be a painful process. I believe we're ready for the challenge."

Dorcha continued, "I also did individual divinations to advise each of us for this journey. Taylor, despite your best intentions, this could be an emotionally rough trip for you. Any hardship you endure is for a good reason. Morgan, an initiation is occurring. Let go. Overcome barriers, oppression, or exhaustion by industriously using what you've learned so far. Kyle, the difficulties you encounter might seem insurmountable. Don't give up. There is a way through. Draven, you're a concubine to the truth right now. You may be treated unfairly or be put into a stagnant position. Brace yourself. As for me, I need to heed my own intuition. If something feels wrong, it is. Good luck everyone," Dorcha finished with a smile. Morgan could tell that, despite Dorcha's protests, she was starting to enjoy excursions into unpredictable UnderLife.

Louise nodded to August and stood up. "We're going to go to the roof to meditate. Neither one of us want to get drawn into an UnderLife episode with you if we can help it."

"It might even happen up there," Morgan said.

"True," Louise said. "Then that shall be our path. Don't want to tempt fate, now do we?"

"Understandable."

"Actually," August interrupted. "I want to stay here and keep an eye on everyone. It doesn't feel right leaving them alone."

Louise's eyebrows were raised in an unfamiliar look of surprise. "Really? You do."

"Yes."

"You are well aware of the possible consequences?"

"I'm still capable," August said.

"It's not your attributes which cause concern," Louise said.

Suddenly everyone else wasn't too sure what they were talking about. No one intervened.

August continued, "Someone should be here to guide their meditation. I take full responsibility for my participation."

"As you wish," Louise said. Addressing the group before leaving, she said, "Safe travels. Be careful. Work together. Inherent in every problem is its solution. Cheers."

August arranged everyone in cross-legged poses around Morgan. August positioned Draven to the west of Morgan, Dorcha to the east, Kyle to the south, and Taylor to the north.

Getting the group to go into meditation took almost no effort. All present had previous meditation experience. However, after fifteen minutes of deep, steady breathing they still hadn't entered UnderLife.

Morgan considered stopping the attempt. What was taking so long? It was so much easier last time. Maybe they weren't ready for this mission after all.

Then a trio of deep bass notes thumped. Morgan felt it vibrate in her gut.

* * *

Morgan found herself at the dead end of a deep, narrow canyon. The walls rose at least one hundred feet on either side. Indirect sunlight lit the area with a muted yellow glow.

"Hello?" Morgan yelled out, "Anyone out there?"

Where is everyone? Morgan wondered.

Since there was only one way to go, Morgan started walking. Every so often Morgan called out to her companions, but she only heard the echo of her own voice in reply.

Soon the path hit a crossroads. There were three different passages Morgan could take. Morgan knew that the entire place could be a never ending maze, so she decided to wait for a while to consider her options. She hoped someone else would find her.

Morgan heard whistling. She called out, "Hello? Who's there?"

"Morgan? Is that you?"

"Kyle?"

Morgan heard a flurry of thudding footfalls. Kyle burst from around the corner on Morgan's left side.

"Morgan!"

"Kyle!"

They embraced, happy to see each other.

"Where are the others?" Kyle asked.

"I don't know. You didn't see or hear anyone else?"

"No, you're the first person. Found myself in a dead end canyon..."

"Me too," Morgan said.

Kyle continued, "I've been walking for an hour at least."

"Time is an unusual experience here," Morgan said.

"You'd think Mr. Military would be the first one at a rendezvous point if his terrain set up was the same as ours."

"Yes. Unfortunately, there's no way of knowing if the rest of this place is designed as we've seen it, or where everyone else appeared. Captain Tess not the one I'm concerned about. He's a master survivor and combatant. It's..."

"Dorcha and Draven, yeah. What are we going to do?"

"Split up? One person waits here while the other goes down one of the paths we haven't explored yet?" Morgan asked.

"I don't like that idea. It took too long to find you the first time. Let's stick together."

"Alright, which way do we go?"

Kyle looked around, "Do you have any idea which direction we're facing?"

"No, the valley walls are too high and I don't know if that's supposed to be a morning or afternoon sun. Why do you ask?"

"August was deliberate in placing us on the four cardinal points around you during the meditation. I thought that might affect our corresponding UnderLife locations."

"Well, look who's adjusting to alternate realities like a champ."

"Hey, I grew up on first-person point-of-view computer role playing games. These UnderLife realms seem to have a similar design structure."

"Okay, when we were in Waking Life, I was facing west, towards Draven. When I arrived in UnderLife, my back was towards the dead end of the ravine. I continued walking forward, so I was still heading west? You arrived on my left side, so that means you came from the south? Which is where Dorcha was sitting in Waking Life. So where is she?"

"Now I'm confused," Kyle said.

"Yeah, me too," Morgan said. "Well, we have a choice before us. Which way do you want to go, left or right?"

Kyle considered for a moment. "Right," he said.

They had not gone far through the twisting passage before they saw a body splayed out on the ground a hundred yards ahead of them. Quickly Morgan and Kyle ran to the body. They found Captain Tess laying face up in a pool of blood. His face was twisted in a horrific expression. His head was almost completely severed from his body.

"What the fuck?" Morgan asked.

"I don't believe it," echoed Kyle. "Who or what could have done this?"

"And where is it now?" Morgan asked.

They both glanced around, shocked that their expert instructor had been defeated.

"Remember that in Waking Life Captain Tess is healthy," Morgan said.

"I know. That's the only reason I'm not having a full meltdown right now."

They heard a vicious snarl.

"We're dead meat," Kyle said.

Whatever creature was stalking them howled. It had picked up their scent.

"Run!" Kyle yelled, sprinting away from the noise. Morgan followed.

Kyle and Morgan ran full tilt through the canyon maze. Whatever was following them seemed close. There were ominous, monstrous sounds at their heels. They continued running for about a quarter of a mile before Morgan had had enough.

"Wait," Morgan said while panting for air. Morgan halted and turned around.

Kyle looked over his shoulder and noticed her stop. "What are you doing? Run away!"

There were booming foot falls in pursuit. The bone-chilling roars and growls were intimidating. Morgan steeled her nerves.

"I hate running! I need a sports bra! Fuck this! I want to fight this fucker!" Morgan screamed.

"Are you crazy? Did you see what it did to Taylor? He's like a ninja, and it ripped his throat out! How could we possibly stand a chance?"

"Dorcha said that this episode was going to be tough for Captain Tess. Maybe he got attacked by a personal demon. Personal demons are the most dangerous to their owners. It explains why he looked so afraid. You go ahead, Kyle. I'm facing this villain."

"Right, like I'm going to leave my wing woman," Kyle said. He stood his ground.

A minute later, a soft white bunny rabbit hopped into view.

Morgan erupted with laughter. Kyle was dumbfounded.

"It figures Taylor would be a Monty Python fan."

"What? I don't get it," Kyle said.

Morgan pointed, "There's the boogey man."

"You're joking, right? A cute bunny is Taylor's worst nightmare?"

"Careful. Don't get too close. It's much more dangerous than it looks. Let me handle this."

Morgan took two steps forward. The bunny leapt to attack Morgan's neck, its deadly elongated razor sharp teeth bared for the strike. Morgan sidestepped to the right and snapped a well-timed outside-to-inside, close-fisted, right forearm block on the bunny's neck, knocking it to the ground. Before the blood-thirsty bunny could recover, Morgan punted the unholy thing into the earthen wall.

Like sadistic, unruly children, Kyle and Morgan ran over to the wounded abomination and eagerly stomped Taylor's nightmare to death.

* * *

Morgan and Kyle slid back into Waking Life in the blink of an eye. They found Captain Tess slumped forward, unconscious. They went to Captain Tess and gently repositioned his body so he was lying down comfortably on his back.

Dorcha, Draven, and August were still sitting in the lotus position. They opened their eyes when they heard Morgan and Kyle moving.

"Did you go into UnderLife?" Dorcha asked.

"Oh yeah," Morgan said. "Wait. You didn't?"

"No," Draven answered. "I've been sitting here with my eyes closed, breathing up a storm."

"What happened? Did you see Bunny Jones?" August asked.

"Or my Dad?" Draven asked.

"Oh, a bunny was involved," Kyle chuckled.

"But it wasn't Jones," Morgan said.

August went to the roof to get Louise. When they returned Morgan and Kyle explained what had happened.

Twenty minutes later Captain Tess woke up. There was a rare look of embarrassment set on his chiseled features.

"It's odd that the three of you were pulled in, but the rest of us were left out," Dorcha said.

"Yeah, I was all set for another spiritual safari," Draven said.

"It was wishful thinking to believe UnderLife would be so easy to control," Morgan said. "There are always unpredictable complications. As far as we knew, everyone else was lost somewhere in the canyon maze."

"Killer rabbits, Sir?" Kyle asked Captain Tess with a big smile.

"I've always been afraid of things which seem innocent but turn out to be deadly, and I don't figure it out until it's too late," Captain Tess said. "Usually this means things like land mines, ambushes, and martyrs with hidden bombs strapped to their chests. I guess it all started with growing up watching Monty Python. I never thought I would literally be attacked by a childhood nightmare."

"All of those healing cards were accurate," Dorcha said. "I just didn't realize it meant that Taylor would battle a manifestation of his fear. The Tarot advice in regards to Draven and me also makes more sense now. I only wish I could interpret the Tarot so clearly beforehand."

"You will," August said. "You're still learning to adapt your gift to the practical challenges of UnderLife."

"Should we try again?" Kyle said. "It's one hell of a ride."

"Not a good idea," Morgan said. "The collective unconscious isn't receptive right now to our inquiries about Draven. It wouldn't even allow him in."

August said, "Louise and I have a theory about how to create an image-space for group entry into UnderLife. It involves picturing and focusing on an oval-shaped room with many doors. We were going to try this theory for Morgan and Dorcha's trip to the Akashic Records, but they shifted into UnderLife before we had the chance."

Louise said, "This would give everyone a common image to anchor themselves. August, why didn't do that today? No wonder they lost focus and slid into a spiritual lesson for Captain Tess."

"I…" August said.

"Regardless," Morgan said. "I think we're going to have to do this mission the old-fashioned way," Morgan said. "Draven needs to meet Victoria in Waking Life. Victoria is six years older than Draven is. If they spent any time together as kids, maybe Victoria would recognize him."

All heads turned to Kyle.

"Alright, alright, I'll call my sister."

Kyle left a message for Darian. He promised to contact Morgan as soon as he spoke with Darian.

Everyone parted ways, except for Draven and Dorcha. They went back to Dorcha's apartment for an extensive Tarot extravaganza. Draven and Dorcha invited Morgan to join them, but she declined. Morgan made plans to have dinner with them the following night.

Morgan was still riled up from the adrenaline of the UnderLife adventure. She knew just who to take it out on.

* * *

Balthazar was fast-forwarding through commercials from a pre-recorded Laker game when Morgan got to his apartment. In anticipation of Morgan's arrival, Balthazar had left the door unlocked, and his clothes off.

Morgan was touched that Balthazar had taken such good care of her the other night. She eagerly made up for her previous invalid status.

In the afterglow of awesome sex, Balthazar started drifting off to sleep. Morgan resisted the post-orgasm drowsiness, and sat up to leave.

"You should stay," Balthazar said, reaching out his hand to stroke Morgan's back.

Morgan sighed. A part of her really wanted to. However, she didn't want to jerk Balthazar around with her indecisiveness. Well, not any more than she already was.

Morgan's body tingled with pleasure from the feathery strokes to her lower back. "C'mon," Balthazar said. "I know you don't want to drive home. You're exhausted. I made sure of it."

"Bastard," Morgan grumbled, turned, and allowed the contours of her form to meld with Balthazar's.

Morgan snuck out in the morning.

* * *

The next evening Dorcha took Morgan and Draven out to dinner to celebrate Dorcha's first pay check from the best job she'd ever had.

"You should see the reading list Louise handed me," Dorcha said. "The thing is enormous. Over a thousand titles, fiction and non-fiction, touching on almost every topic conceivable. I'm expected to give an oral book report once a week. Its fifth grade all over again."

"Except this time you're getting paid an exorbitant amount of money to learn," Draven said.

"True, I'm not complaining."

"I'm glad they're making you study mixed martial arts with me," Morgan said. She took a bite of her delicious medium-rare steak.

"Traveling with you, it's only a matter of time before I'll have to throw down with a rabid Care Bear, kill some tribbles, or wrestle a talking dragon. Plus it gives me a chance to wrap my legs around Kyle while practicing my ground game."

"Gotta love the ground game," Draven said.

"Speaking of Kyle," Morgan said. "What do you think now that you're getting to know him personally?"

Dorcha got dreamy look in her eye. "He's brilliant, and a real sweetheart. I..."

"Alright, before we get into boy talk, I've gotta say I'm kinda pissed it took the two of you so long to tell me about UnderLife. Poorly handled, ladies," Draven said.

Morgan reached for Draven's hand. "I'm sorry Draven. It's my fault. Dorcha wanted to tell you right away."

"C'mon, Draven," Dorcha said. "It wasn't about keeping something from you. You know you thought Morgan was bat-shit crazy when she first told you about UnderLife. She was afraid you'd pick a fight, and you did."

"And now here we are, wondering if I'm related to a famous rock star actress," Draven grinned. "Everything is so much simpler now."

They all laughed, brought their wine glasses together in salute, and drank.

"It's such a huge burden off of my shoulders to have everything out in the open," Morgan said.

"One thing keeps popping in my head," Draven said. "Tell me again, how did Balthazar get those front row Victoria Shine tickets?"

"Balthazar resuscitated a grateful ticket broker, Barry, who said if he ever needed a favor to please ask. Why?"

"I don't think it was a magical coincidence that we got those seats. Back at the Skyscraper Space, Kyle and I chatted for a bit. Kyle assumed his parents gave me the tickets because I wrote such a glowing interview about them. Victoria hand picks who gets front row seats. Apparently Darian has been known to take over that duty when she's going to attend a show. Rarely are those tickets sold. How did Barry get four of them?"

"Are you saying Louise hatched some elaborate plan? Staged a fake illness while Balthazar was on duty at a location where they'd be sure he would get the call? Barry is an alias for whom?"

"Another partner?" Draven said. "How long did it take Louise and August to introduce you to the Vihzors? Even after you mysteriously ran into the whole clan at the concert?"

"And what about how you met Taylor?" Dorcha asked. "It's not like surprise maneuvers are foreign to their cloak-and-dagger modus operandi."

"Why not simply give me the tickets themselves? Save all the hassle."

"Maybe to see what would happen. You've lusted after Victoria since before you even knew what sex was."

"True," Morgan said. She shrugged, "It seems far-fetched, but so does everything these days. When the opportunity arises, I'll ask August about it."

"Doesn't it bother you that you're being manipulated?" Draven asked.

"I don't see it like that. They have their reasons for being secretive. Trust me. These are not sinister people we're dealing with."

Dorcha broke the tension, "Okay, can we talk about what's really important here, our love lives?"

"Please," Morgan said.

"You're right," Draven said. "We're being far too serious. This is a celebration. Obviously we need another bottle of wine."

The three of them proceeded to enjoy a delectable meal with plenty of scrumptious banter. Afterwards they walked back to Morgan's apartment. Morgan checked her voicemail.

"Kyle called and left a message!" Morgan said.

Morgan put the message on speakerphone. "Hey Morgan, good news. Victoria is performing at the MTV Movie Awards in ten days. You and Draven can use the AstroNews press passes I got. The rest is up to the two of you. See ya at training!"

* * *

A few days later, Balthazar, clad in his usual t-shirt and jeans, stopped by Morgan's apartment unannounced again, only to find her not at home. Balthazar realized that he had little imagination about what Morgan did when they weren't together. Balthazar always pictured Morgan as taking bong hits on the couch while watching a favorite television show, or giggling on the phone with a friend, waiting to jump his bones when Balthazar walked through the front door.

This was peculiar. Two o'clock in the afternoon was generally tea, toast, and toke time for his sort-of-ex-girlfriend.

Balthazar left to go get some lunch, and on the way back he picked up a newspaper. Balthazar decided that if Morgan wasn't around by the time he finished reading it, he'd go home.

Balthazar was about to leave when he saw Morgan pull up in Kyle's dark purple BMW. Morgan hugged the handsome driver, and exited the vehicle. They each looked sweaty.

Balthazar was confused. Was this Morgan's new boyfriend? Was she dating them both?

Kyle saw Balthazar as he drove away. Kyle gave him a friendly smile.

"Who was that?" Balthazar asked.

"That's Kyle, my training partner," Morgan said.

"Training for what?"

"I've been practicing martial arts for a while now."

"Martial arts? You?"

"Yeah, Korean Karate and Gracie Brazilian Ju-Jitsu."

"Really? Huh," Balthazar grunted. He noticed that Morgan was indeed wearing a tank top and shorts. "Wait. Isn't that Kyle Vihzor? Now I remember where I've seen him before, the concert. How do you know him?"

"His parents are colleagues of Louise. They suggested we train together," Morgan said. "So what has you waiting on my doorstep?"

"This," Balthazar said, stepping in to kiss Morgan.

Morgan and Balthazar had barely gotten past the threshold of the apartment before half of their clothes were already off.

Balthazar closed the front door by pressing Morgan's underwear-clad form up against it. Rather than yielding her body to him as she normally did, Morgan distracted Balthazar with a deep kiss, hooked her foot behind his ankle, and tripped him. She controlled Balthazar's fall so as not to hurt him. Morgan landed on top of him in full mount.

At first Balthazar struggled to get out of the vulnerable position. Morgan wrapped her legs around Balthazar's hips and thighs and squeezed, stabilizing her base. She pinned Balthazar's arms using her full weight, neutralizing his superior strength. Balthazar stopped fighting when the kissing ensued. Morgan playfully nudged the sizeable bulge in his jeans with her clothed sex.

Balthazar could tell Morgan had spent extensive hours practicing martial arts. There was a fluidity and power in Morgan's hip movements which she didn't possess when they lived together.

A disheartening image flashed in Balthazar's mind of Morgan rolling around in the gym with Kyle and who knows how many other men, or women. He pushed the thought away, and flipped a compliant Morgan onto her back.

Soon their remaining clothes were stripped off, and they got busy tasting each other's sex, singularly and simultaneously. Balthazar stood up to retrieve a handful of condoms from Morgan's bedroom. Morgan followed him, draining the remaining contents of the water bottle she'd dropped near by.

The duo collapsed onto her bed and fucked.

Morgan had gotten used to Kyle, Taylor, and Dorcha's physical creativity during ju-jitsu. Balthazar's sexual predictability, normally comforting and quite sufficient to get Morgan off umpteen times, had lost some of its magical lure. Despite this unfortunate revelation, Balthazar's relentless determination and physical stamina soon had Morgan moaning and twitching with pleasure.

Morgan and Balthazar cleaned each other off in the shower. Then they sprawled out and nestled on Morgan's couch together, with their damp naked bodies lazily entwined.

"When are you going to come home?" Balthazar breathed into Morgan's ear in between lingering kisses to her neck.

When Morgan didn't answer right away, Balthazar lifted his head, his eyes searching hers.

"I am home," Morgan said, leaning up to kiss Balthazar's lips.

It was an ambiguous answer, but for the moment Balthazar took it to mean that she felt at home with him, and he cuddled closer.

Morgan woke up a couple hours later to her stomach growling. The living room was dimly illuminated by ambient street light spilling in from the window. When Morgan shifted to get up, Balthazar also stirred.

"Hey, do you want me to go out and grab some dinner for us?" Balthazar asked while looking around for his clothes.

"Sure. Thank you," Morgan said over her shoulder on the way to the bathroom.

Morgan heard Balthazar talking on his phone, ordering their favorite dishes from Sunset Thai. She heard his keys jingle, and the front door shut.

Twenty minutes later Balthazar returned with bags of food and a six pack of beer. Morgan flipped on the television and DVD player. Disc One of Season Two of Arrested Development was in the machine, and Morgan hit Play All. They ate while watching the show. Morgan was reminded of the hundreds of times they had gone through this evening ritual. She felt herself slipping back into the pattern. It felt somewhere between comforting and stifling. Morgan knew she couldn't continue into the cycle if she really wanted things between them to change.

Morgan reached for the remote and turned off the TV.

"Hey…" Balthazar said in a voice muffled by a mouthful of silver noodles.

"Let's move to the kitchen table and do this like a proper date."

Balthazar nodded, got up, and helped to move their dinner over to the kitchen. Morgan lit some candles and put on music.

At first it was an awkward move for both of them, but soon they were conversing easily. Morgan got Balthazar to talk about work. She asked about his friends, and about Gregory.

Soon Balthazar realized he was dominating the conversation. He began to inquire about what Morgan had been up to during the months they had been apart.

Morgan held off from talking about UnderLife as long as she could, but the subject inevitably flowed in that direction. Balthazar seemed like he wanted to know more about it, so Morgan told him. The more Morgan talked, the more fired up she became. She wanted to share everything with Balthazar. Morgan felt a wonderful sense of completion. Now Balthazar knew who she really was, and they were free to love each other fully.

Morgan delved into the story of how Draven found out about UnderLife. She told Balthazar about the fight they had had, Morgan storming home, hearing music out of nowhere, getting into the bath and slipping into UnderLife. Then she told him about the journey through Draven's layers of men, the hotel lobby, the shrine vault, and Morgan's frying pan exit.

At this point Morgan was so comfortable that it felt perfectly natural to end the tale by saying, "I think Draven and Victoria Shine are related, possibly even siblings."

Balthazar stood and went to the kitchen for some water.

"I swear it's the truth," Morgan said. She told him about the team's investigation and their findings. Morgan finished with, "We're going to try to meet Victoria this Sunday at the MTV Movie Awards to see if she remembers Draven."

Balthazar shook his head. "I talked to Father Finnegan about your alleged UnderLife ability. It disturbed him greatly. Father Finnegan thinks you've fallen under the spell of dark forces to believe such a bizarre story."

"What's your opinion?"

"You believe something is going to happen between you and Victoria Shine, don't you?" Balthazar asked.

"I... uh... I don't know," Morgan stuttered. "Hey, I'm as shocked as you are that this connection exists."

"I'm not shocked. You've been obsessed with Victoria Shine most of your life. Morgan, sweetie, this is all a delusion, a fantasy. Why other people play along with it, I'll never know. It's cruel of them and does you no good," Balthazar said.

"You think I'm making this entire thing up? That UnderLife isn't real?" Morgan asked.

"Look, I think you're a vivid dreaming narcoleptic with an incredible imagination. I'm not trying to offend you, but we have spent a ton of time together. I'd say I know you pretty damn well. Sometimes you can get carried away, especially when you get passionate about something."

"Fuck you. Stop talking to me like I'm some sad schizo that needs to get on some meds."

"Okay then. Why does everyone else seem to be having these experiences with you except me, your boyfriend for the last four years?"

"I don't know! I can't figure out how or why it works the way it does. I've always wanted to share this with you. I want to include you in all aspects of my life."

"Have you? Really? Why did it take you so long to tell me about it?"

"Honestly, I didn't think I'd have to say anything at all. Every day I thought, maybe we'll shift into UnderLife together. And when I'd see you in there, I'd always try to get your attention. I hoped you would remember being there. My worst fears came true anyway. You obviously don't believe what I'm saying. I always worried that when you found out, you would think I was crazy, and I'd lose you. It sure doesn't help that this is exactly what you've accused me of."

"You can be so frustrating!" Balthazar shouted.

When Morgan didn't retaliate, they sat there in silence, staring at each other.

"I don't want you out of my life," Morgan said.

"You know that we're all or nothing. I can't just be your friend. Please get some help. You're willing to fight harder for someone you've never met than you are for me. It's a fantasy. I don't see where I fit in. It's not fair to either of us if I stick around."

"Then go. Let's stop dragging this out."

Balthazar gazed at Morgan. They were both crying. Balthazar stood and left.

* * *

The MTV Movie Awards were held at Gibson Amphitheatre in Universal City.

Draven and Morgan waded through the elaborate parking and check-in procedures. The event coordinators were managing the celebrity-filled chaos with a legion of personnel and an arsenal of communications equipment. The venue was specifically designed to accommodate these kinds of special events.

Morgan and Draven received their identification badges. They went to the viper-pit B-list press trough, and waited for Victoria to appear.

The place was a complete zoo. There were constant bursts of deafening screams from the packed horde of fans on the bleachers. The havoc provided an excellent cover for Draven and Morgan. No one realized they weren't actually doing any reporting.

Dressed in his best suit, Draven fidgeted with his plastic badge. "Oh honey, this is crazy. Victoria is going to think I'm just some beguiled fag who wants either to be her or to latch onto her. Isn't there another way to

274

do this?"

"I'm open to suggestions," Morgan said. She shifted uncomfortably in the dark emerald gown August had bought for her. The dress showed off Morgan's ample bosom and well trained legs. Morgan always forgot the names of famous designers moments after hearing them. Fashion had never been her forte.

Yesterday had been a whirlwind of preparation. There were manicures, pedicures, massages, Tarot, I Ching, an hour of physical training, meditation, wardrobe fitting, and mane shearing.

Louise brought in a professional hair and make-up team to put the finishing touches on Morgan and Draven. Coiffed, scrubbed, and painted, they fit in seamlessly with the well-groomed crowd.

"Aren't you going to freak out when you meet her?" Draven asked.

"Over the years, the inner salivating fanatic mellows out. I'm so glad this is happening now, and not in my teenage stalker years. Although I say that now, but who knows what will happen?"

"Yeah, you're going to lose your mind," Draven said.

"Probably," Morgan laughed.

* * *

Victoria Shine completed sound check, had an early dinner with her band, and finished hair, make-up, and wardrobe. Then she retreated to her limo. Victoria asked Ryan, the chauffeur, to find a secluded spot nearby where she could rest until it was time to make her entrance.

Victoria fell asleep. She was tired from another songwriting fiasco the night before. Victoria dreamt about her first piano lessons as a kid. Victoria hated them. They were so boring, hours of drilling dumb scales and silly songs. Mother insisted, said it "made her more well-rounded," whatever that meant. Little did either of them know what an important part of Victoria's life music would become.

Mrs. Weatherford, her teacher, had stale coffee breath and wore a sharp flower-walloping perfume. Mrs. Weatherford was a perfectionist. Victoria always knew when she was about to be criticized, because Mrs. Weatherford would begin with a disapproving smack-click sound, which she made by sucking her tongue to the roof of her mouth, and then releasing it. Mrs. Weatherford's criticism was constant and intense.

If it wasn't for her number one fan Chompy, Victoria would have quit. Chompy loved hearing her play, no matter how awful it sounded. With Chompy, Heart and Soul made sense, and was a joy to play.

Victoria woke up to the alarm jingle on her iPhone. She felt haunted by a long held ache of grief.

Victoria rummaged through her gig bag. She pulled out a mirror, and inspected her hair and make-up for any sleep-induced smudging or frizzing.

Victoria pressed the button to lower the privacy screen between herself and the driver.

"Time to roll Ryan," Victoria said.

"Yes Ma'am," the driver responded. Ryan closed the graphic novel he'd been reading: The Sandman - Preludes and Nocturnes. Ryan turned the car key and the engine roared to life.

Victoria prepared herself for her performance and for the maelstrom of attention. She smiled, feeling the first stirrings of a familiar and thrilling energetic jolt which the stage provided. Victoria hummed to warm up her voice.

It took a few minutes for Victoria to realize that the tune coming from her lips was unfamiliar, and it was exactly what she'd been hunting for these past few weeks. The terrible timing of her fickle muse annoyed Victoria to no end. Of course the music would come to her when she couldn't sit down and work on it.

Victoria called her own number and left herself a musical voicemail, praying she could sort it out later.

All too quickly, the door to Victoria's limo was opened from the outside by a helpful page, and Victoria was lit up by a blinding number of flashes.

Victoria exited the vehicle with feline grace, and basked in the rush of adrenaline and the paradoxical modesty her celebrity stature inspired. Victoria strutted along the red carpet like a seasoned pro, smiling and waving at the crowd. She cruised right past Draven and Morgan.

It's her, Morgan thought. Victoria Shine is standing in front of me. What a thrilling beauty!

Morgan's brain struggled to reconcile having this talented woman who had spent so much time in her imagination right in front of her. It had been easy to disassociate Victoria from the real world. Even at the concert, all of it felt too fantastic to be real. The lights, the music, and the disturbing UnderLife shift had seen to that. Right now Victoria was right there, in the flesh.

"Victoria!" Draven bellowed. He was at a loss of what else to do, and determined not to miss the golden opportunity. Despite the paparazzi and numerous fans yelling her name, Victoria's attention focused on Draven. Victoria stopped cold in her tracks, staring.

Victoria's eyes narrowed at Draven. So familiar, she thought, he looks like… No, it's a wishful fantasy… What he would have looked like? But he's dead, Victoria sighed. Uncanny resemblance, though. Victoria felt deranged and crestfallen from the sliver of hope shivering through her. She turned away.

"Victoria!"

Victoria walked away thinking, He's simply a reporter who happens to be a grown up ringer for...

"IT'S ME! DRAVEN!" Draven yelled.

...her brother, Chompy, finished Victoria in her head. There were butterflies fluttering in her stomach.

Victoria spun on her heel, approaching Draven with silky swiftness.

"No. You're dead." Victoria reached up to stroke Draven's face. Draven let her, and then he took Victoria's hand in his hands and kissed her palm.

Victoria smelled Draven's scent. A memory flashed of when she was a young girl. Her toddler brother had a bad nightmare, and cried out in his sleep. Victoria let him crawl into bed with her, and she held him gently. Feeling safe, he fell back asleep. Victoria cradled her brother. The same sweet musky smell, uniquely his own, lulled her into slumber as well.

Victoria's eyes filled with tears. Her mouth fell slack. Victoria put her free hand up to her lips, overwhelmed.

The rest of the world, momentarily forgotten, came roaring back. Bulbs flashed. At least three camera crews were focused on them.

Victoria grabbed the lapels of Draven's coat and pulled him closer.

"Come with me," Victoria said.

Draven followed a couple of steps and then stopped.

"But, my friend..." Draven said.

Victoria glanced at a wide-eyed and stupefied Morgan.

"Bring her too. Let's go."

Victoria asked Draven in a low voice, "How did you figure out I was your sister?"

"That's a long story," Draven said, not having a clue where to begin. Draven could scarcely believe this was real.

"I'd love to hear it. Let's find a place where we can get comfortable and talk." Victoria guided them to her dressing room. She wondered for a split second where her band mates were. The self-named Drum and Bassie were notorious troublemakers and prodigiously talented musicians.

Victoria held Draven's hand, and sat him down on a black overstuffed leather couch. Victoria caught Draven's reflection next to her own reflection in the light bulb-framed make-up mirror. She was startled by how much they looked alike.

Morgan stood with her back against the wall near the door. Witnessing Victoria and Draven experience utter astonishment and joy was a sight for Morgan to behold. Morgan's body tingled with excitement. She had to remind herself to breathe.

Cam Wolfram, the high powered publicist, knocked once and then opened the dressing room door without waiting for a response. Cam was known for being effective and expensive. He was usually able to manipulate even the worst public relations nightmares into something beneficial for his clients. Victoria kept Wolfram on retainer.

"Victoria, you skipped the interview lines. If we hurry you can make them," Cam tapped his watch.

"Cam, this is my brother, Draven."

"Hi," his eyes flitted briefly to Draven and then back to Victoria. "Can we go now?"

"Stop being an asshole," Victoria said.

"Hey, that's what you're paying me for. Get moving. Talk to them after. I'm sure they will be happy to wait," Wolfram said.

Victoria sighed and turned to Draven. "Do you mind waiting?"

"Are you kidding?"

"I'll return as soon as I can," Victoria said.

"Go," Draven hugged Victoria. "We'll be here." Draven put his arm around Morgan's shoulders.

Morgan smiled weakly. She was so nervous that she was struck dumb and sweating profusely.

"You can watch Victoria on the monitor. She's singing the first song," the publicist said while ushering Victoria out of the room.

After the door closed, Morgan and Draven stared at each other in total shock.

"Can you?" he stammered.

"No..."

"She..."

"So beautiful," Morgan said.

"My sister," Draven said, loving the sound of those words.

"Wow."

"Victoria knew. She recognized me."

"Yes."

"Thank you."

"No, thank you Draven, that was..."

"Amazing," Draven said and hugged Morgan.

Morgan and Draven settled in, too afraid to leave the dressing room. They didn't want to get booted out of the backstage area by security, and Victoria had asked them to wait, so that was exactly what they were going to do.

"Should we snoop around?" Draven said, pointing to Victoria's gig bag.

"No way, she'll know."

"No she won't."

"Don't be stupid. Why take the chance of pissing Victoria off?"

"You're right," Draven said pacing around the room. He was too amped up to sit still.

Morgan flipped on the large flat screen television mounted on the wall, and watched the live coverage of the event. Draven joined her.

The time passed while Morgan and Draven kept up a running commentary of praises and jabs aimed at the presenters and performers. Morgan and Draven whispered their more vitriolic slurs, knowing they were only a few hundred feet away from the celebrities.

Victoria's performance electrified the audience. She was in rare form, pulling out all the stops. It was definitely a hard act to follow.

"This is better than the video of Earthly Delight," Draven said.

"I know, and I love that video..." Morgan trailed off.

"Me too," Draven said.

Minutes after Victoria left the stage she came back to the dressing room, and made a beeline for the make-up mirror. Victoria batted away the attentions of the staff make-up artist, preferring for the moment to do her own maintenance.

"Draven, please come with me. I have to work this circus a bit, or my handlers are going to give me hell," Victoria said. She continued to gaze at herself in the mirror long enough to mop the sweat off of her face and do a retouch.

"But... Morgan is the reason I found you," Draven said.

Patting blush on her face, Victoria turned and really looked at Morgan for the first time. "Now how did you pull something like that off, my dear?"

"It's a long story," Morgan said, having a hard time summing up the implausible truth.

"She's psychic," Draven said.

"A medium?" Victoria asked. "You're a fortune teller?"

"No, I can't see the future."

"Well, however you did it, thank you. You're a blessing. I want to speak with you further." Victoria moved in a little closer to Morgan. "Do you mind if I steal Draven from you? We have a lot to catch up on."

"Oh, of course not," Morgan said, "I totally understand."

In truth, Morgan was crestfallen, but she was determined to be gracious.

Victoria winked at Morgan, squeezing her hand briefly.

Then they were gone.

For a moment, Morgan entertained a "I'll never wash this hand again" moment then laughed at herself. She wasn't that crazy.

However, Morgan did smell her hand. Victoria's intoxicating scent lingered ever so slightly.

Morgan drove directly over to Dorcha's apartment to dish, analyze, and celebrate.

CHAPTER SEVENTEEN
EXCHANGE

Later That Evening, Hollywood, 2:14 AM

Morgan was getting ready to leave Dorcha's apartment when Draven texted. Morgan kicked off her shoes, packed another bowl, and waited.

Twenty minutes later, Draven burst through the front door of Dorcha's apartment, looking like the cat that'd caught the canary.

"Draven!" Morgan and Dorcha bounced to their feet. They cheered and hugged him.

"How was it?" "Tell us everything," overlapped the two jubilant women.

"Oh my God, she's... Wow. I..." Draven's eyes shimmered with tears, and a silly smile of happiness graced his features. "Definitely my sister." Draven perched on the couch, and scooped up the bong for a toke.

Morgan could barely sit still. Dorcha shuffled her Druid Craft Tarot deck to give her hands something to do. The silent, giddy energy ricocheting around the room could have powered the entire building for a week.

Dorcha and Morgan marveled at how their bizarre talents had been able to reveal the mother lode of discoveries. They felt volcanic enthusiasm for Victoria, Draven, the Vihzors, their talented mentors, and the further adventures beckoning on the horizon.

Unable to contain herself any longer, Morgan blurted out, "How was it? What did you do? Talk about?"

"Victoria had me by her side for the rest of the award show. Wolfram, Victoria's publicist, insisted she work the room at the post show party."

"Did she get mad at him?" Morgan asked.

"Victoria swore a bit then laughed. She's glad she's getting her money's worth from him."

"Did Victoria refer to you as her brother around other people?" Dorcha asked.

"Only when she introduced me to Wolfram," Draven said. "After telling someone else I was her good friend, Victoria whispered that she wasn't ready to get the third degree from the media quite yet. We always see the polished, guard up, professional side of Victoria Shine, but she's a person doing her best, like the rest of us."

"Yeah, a beautiful, smart, internationally famous, wildly successful, rich, sexy, talented woman, nothing to get too excited about," Morgan drawled.

Draven laughed, "With a great sense of humor."

"Lest we forget," Morgan said, still reeling.

"Unfortunately," Draven continued. "We didn't really get to talk privately. Victoria got swarmed at the party. Then she received an unexpected call from Kendrick Hawke, a corporate maven who co-produced Promotion, the indie pic Victoria acted in five years ago."

"Oh, we're quite familiar with Promotion," Dorcha said. Morgan had come over recently for a Victoria Shine and Darian Vihzor movie/television marathon.

"Victoria said she's wanted to jump Kendrick's bones ever since they worked together eons ago. Kendrick is single for the first time in years, and he flew into Burbank Airport tonight to take Victoria to the Cayman Islands."

"For how long?" Morgan asked.

"Two weeks."

"We have to wait two more weeks? No fair!" Morgan pouted.

"I could tell it was a point of pride for Victoria to have an affair with Kendrick. Definitely something a sister of mine would do. Victoria apologized for bailing so soon after our reunion. She wants to meet everyone when she gets back," Draven said.

Dorcha laid out several Tarot cards on the couch pillow next to her. "Lovers aside, I think Victoria wants the time to do some investigating on her own, and get a background check on Draven. I'm sure she's wondering how something like this could have been hidden from her for so long."

"Victoria showed me an old Los Angeles Times article which reported a lethal car accident involving Nikolai Powers and his toddler son, Draven. Victoria asked if our father was still alive, and for a moment her face held such innocent hope. I felt like a complete ogre for having to tell her the truth."

"She had a newspaper clipping of your alleged death? How is that possible?" asked Morgan.

"I don't know," Draven said.

"It could be a forgery," Dorcha said. "I wonder if it actually ran."

"Who would do such a thing? Why?" Draven asked.

"I bet Bunny Jones is in for an earful from her estranged daughter," Morgan speculated.

"No kidding," Dorcha said.

Draven shook his head in disbelief. "Do you really think my own mother would fake my death?"

"From the gossip I've heard about her over the years, yes," Morgan said.

* * *

The next afternoon Morgan and August went to the Hollywood-Wilshire YMCA to swim laps. The place wasn't busy, and they were alone warming up in the hot tub.

"In retrospect," August said, "an event being broadcast around the world was maybe not the best setting for delivering a truth bomb. Victoria prefers to be in control. You both took her totally by surprise. It was too big for Victoria to process in front of either of you."

"So Victoria sprints away to a tropical island with Kendrick for orgasms and time to mull things over?"

"Exactly. Would you expect anything less from someone with their birth chart dominated by Scorpio and Leo energy?"

"You're right," Morgan said, "predictability has never been an attribute of Victoria's."

"It's unfortunate all signs point to Bunny Jones as being the culprit for the fabricated fatalities. Mothers are meant to represent the Sacred Feminine. I hope Victoria has found a more virtuous role-model to carry that archetypal energy for her."

"I bet Darian Vihzor helps to fill the position. Those two are close," Morgan said.

August placed her lower back in front an underwater air jet and decided to change the subject. "Ever wonder why you don't ever go into UnderLife while in the water?"

"I don't know. Lucky, I guess. I like swimming here, because there's always a lifeguard, in case something happens."

"I think it's more than that. I believe you can learn to control your entrances and exits from UnderLife. Your primal survival instincts already help with this."

"Remember when I passed out here in the steam room? That's a dangerous place to fall unconscious," Morgan said.

"Privately, yes, but you know that it gets regular foot traffic. The risk is relatively low."

"I could hit my head on the tiles."

"I doubt it. You're too cautious to put yourself in a position where that might happen."

"How am I supposed to train to control it? Do you know how many times I've tried and failed to get in and out of UnderLife?"

"Don't worry about the past. I don't believe you were far enough along in your development to consider having control over shifts. Right now your task is to dismantle your doubts about this goal, and to keep treading your path modestly."

Morgan nodded, and closed her eyes, sinking further into the water.

A few minutes passed. August waded towards the steps of the hot tub. "Time to swim, Morgan. Do your best to follow my lead and keep pace."

"Alright," Morgan said. She was anticipating a brutal work-out. Morgan took long drafts off of her water bottle, and joined August in the lap pool.

* * *

During the next two weeks, Louise stepped up the frequency of Morgan's meditation meetings. They had a session almost every day. This stage of the chakra balancing was focused on Morgan's solar plexus, or manipura, which governs will power and the distribution of energy through the body. The manipura is located in the stomach region. Digestion is a physical manifestation of this chakra's process. Its flow is blocked by shameful thoughts and deeds. Citrine is the corresponding crystal for the solar plexus chakra, which helps to cleanse, protect, and energize.

Morgan was finding that waiting for Victoria to come back from the Cayman Islands was excruciating, but focusing on Louise's and Captain Tess's training sessions was helping a bit. Still, Morgan was driving herself nuts with a daily microscopic examination of every detail from her encounter with Victoria.

Draven told Morgan that Victoria called him every day to chat, and that she set a date to meet with everyone as soon as she got back Los Angeles.

* * *

One day the following week, Morgan arrived early at the Skyscraper Space to help August and Louise to prepare for the celebration of Victoria's return.

Morgan was nervous about describing UnderLife to Victoria. She spent many hours rehearsing explanations. Morgan's body hummed with anticipation.

The Skyscraper Space had been reorganized into a comfortable informal party atmosphere. There was abundant greenery strung with lengths of small white Christmas lights.

The west half of the room was now a pseudo-pub. Louise had been exercising her gourmet cooking skills all day. A cornucopia of exotic smells wafted in from the kitchen.

August had arranged a full bar, complete with a twelve bottle wine refrigerator filled with several outstanding vintages. She placed the bar against the middle of the floor-to-ceiling thick glass wall. In the northwest corner there was a circular dining table, draped in white linen, with eight silverware settings.

August had placed a substantial amount of foliage around the Tarot table, so there would be more privacy during readings.

Finally, in the southeastern part of the room, Louise had added two curved couches and a coffee table.

As always, they had a spectacular view of Metropolitan Los Angeles and the Century City corporate high rises.

Morgan mused at how Louise and August downplayed their leadership roles by acting as the modest prepares of provisions. It was clear that they wanted Morgan to stand out as the leader of the team.

Dorcha showed up shortly after Morgan with her Tarot cards and an extensive playlist ready on her iPod. Morgan and Dorcha had spoken at length about what background music they wanted for the event. They knew that most musicians were very aware of their sonic atmosphere, and this would certainly be the case for the guest of honor. Morgan knew that Victoria's taste in music varied greatly, so the women decided to put on all of their favorites. They included Tori Amos, Muse, Goldfrapp, Kylie Minogue, Arcade Fire, A-Ha, Sia, Garbage, PJ Harvey, Nine Inch Nails, Sinéad O'Connor, Depeche Mode, and Nina Simone.

Victoria Shine arrived twenty minutes late with Draven and Kyle on each arm. They were escorted by Captain Tess. Captain Tess slipped out of the front door to secure the perimeter.

Victoria was exquisite, thought Morgan. Morgan became dazzled all over again by Victoria's beauty and incredible magnetism.

Kyle bounded up to Morgan and Dorcha, greeting them each with big bear hugs.

After brief introductions, Kyle confessed, "My sister is still mad at me for my lack of tact and personal attention in how I handled the situation. Darian said I was being selfish. Victoria got ambushed rather than ushered into the truth. Everyone please accept my sincerest apologies."

"No worries, Kyle. It's in the past," Victoria said. She focused her attention on Morgan. "Quite an interesting set up you've got here. Mind if

I look around?"

"Please do," Morgan said.

August took drink orders and Louise returned to the kitchen.

Victoria wandered around the Skyscraper Space with Morgan, Dorcha, Kyle, and Draven in tow.

Morgan and Dorcha caught each other's eye and shared a can-you-believe-this-is-happening look.

Victoria gravitated towards the Tarot table where Dorcha's decks were fanned out.

"Are these yours?" Victoria asked Dorcha.

"Yes."

"Will you please give me a reading?"

"I'd love to," Dorcha gushed.

Victoria glanced around at her companions, "Would you excuse us?"

"Of course..." "Certainly..." Morgan and Kyle overlapped.

Draven winked, "You're in for a treat, sis. Dorcha knows her stuff."

Morgan and Kyle and Draven retreated to the pub side of the room for refreshments.

Victoria sat down. She scanned the multitude of cards before her, "Do I choose which deck I want us to use?"

"No, we're using all of them."

"Nice," Victoria said.

Darian continued, "If you like, you can design your own reading, or we can do a more standard reading. A general four placement reading could cover Love, Career, Advice, and Near Future."

Victoria thought about it for a few moments then asked, "How do I design my own reading?"

"You choose a series of questions, up to fifteen. Each card placement acts as an answer to each question. Any more than fifteen questions for one reading can get too confusing. In that case it's better to break up the questions into multiple readings. You can also do an in depth focus on one particular subject, or get an overview of many subjects. The process is all about creating spiritual maps to guide you."

"Will you keep this reading confidential?"

"Yes." Dorcha said, knowing it'd be difficult not to tell Morgan everything. Dorcha trusted that Morgan would respect Victoria's privacy, and not give Dorcha too hard of a time about not sharing the reading with her.

Victoria gave Dorcha an appraising eye. Then she said, "Okay, how about:

1) Who is the best match for me as a loving, sexy partner?

2) Songwriting

3) The acting gig on the table

4) Acting in general right now
5) Lesson I'm learning from Draven
6) What's going on with Kendrick?
7) General advice
8) Near future

"Wow, you sure fired those off with confidence. Have you had your Tarot read before?" Dorcha asked.

"Many times," Victoria winked.

Dorcha shuffled each deck before handing them to Victoria with instructions to cut the cards three times.

Yikes, Victoria is a connoisseur, Dorcha thought. I'd better rust my buddies. Even though Dorcha wasn't head over heels in love with Victoria like Morgan. She still respected the hell out of the artist, and wanted to make a good impression. Dorcha realized that Victoria never specified how Dorcha should perceive the specific inquiries. Did Victoria want advice? An overview? Or both? It dawned on Dorcha that Victoria was being vague on purpose. She was testing Dorcha. Dorcha grinned. This was fun.

Morgan watched Dorcha and Victoria from the other side of the room. Morgan was desperate to listen in on what they were saying, but intruding was not an option. Morgan's Ego whined, feeling awkward and jealous. Morgan sighed, turned away, and joined Draven and Kyle for a drink at the bar.

Everything is fine, amazing, Morgan reasoned to herself. This is going well. It's a dream come true that Victoria is here. Relax. Enjoy the moment. Eventually Victoria will speak with me privately.

Back at the Tarot table, Dorcha laid out the cards.

Eight Questions Spread using the Druid Craft, Faeries' Oracle, Gendron, Tao, and Vampire Tarot decks.

Position 1 represents **the best match for Victoria as a loving, sexy partner?**
>>> Druid: #13 – Death
>>> Faeries: #63 – Indi
>>> Gendron: Princess of Swords
>>> Tao: #57 – The Gentle
>>> Vampires: 8 of Cups

Position 2 represents **songwriting**:
>>> Druid: #3 – The Lady
>>> Faeries: #45 – Taitin the Slyph @
>>> Gendron: 8 of Swords
>>> Tao: #24 – The Turning Point

Vampires: Knave of Pentacles

Position 3 represents **the acting gig on the table**:
Druid: 6 of Pentacles
Faeries: #32 – Iris of the Rainbows @
Gendron: #12 – The Hanged One
Tao: #8 – Holding Together
Vampires: Ace of Swords

Position 4 represents **acting in general right now**:
Druid: #1 – The Magician @
Faeries: #17 – Himself @
Gendron: #21 – The Universe
Tao: #4 – Youthful Folly
Vampires: #2 - Temptation

Position 5 represents **the lesson Victoria's learning from Draven**:
Druid: 5 of Cups @
Faeries: #51 – The Topsie-Turvets
Gendron: 4 of Pentacles
Tao: #59 – Dispersion
Vampires: #6 – The Bond

Position 6 represents **what's going on with Kendrick?**
Druid: Prince of Wands @
Faeries: #34 – Sylvanius
Gendron: 7 of Wands
Tao: #17 – Following
Vampires: #20 - Dawn

Position 7 represents **general advice for Victoria**:
Druid: Ace of Wands @
Faeries: #54 – Epona's Wild Daughter @
Gendron: #10 – Wheel of Fortune
Tao: #22 – Grace
Vampires: Queen of Wands

Position 8 represents **Victoria's near future**:
Druid: #19 – The Sun
Faeries: #6 – The Singer of Connection
Gendron: 5 of Pentacles
Tao: #61 – Inner Truth
Vampires: Queen of Cups

Dorcha's first thought in scanning the cards was about Victoria's work on Love In Motion. Dorcha knew the Hollywood rumor mill was wondering if Victoria would return for a second season. The word on the cyber-street was that Victoria and one of the producers hated each other, and that it had been a constant source of friction. Dorcha decided to start the reading there. "The acting gig is only good for you if you're willing to be generous and sacrifice your pain, anger, conflict, and desire to fight. It's okay if you're not. The Faeries card here is called Iris of the Rainbows. It indicates hopes and promises for the future. However, since it's reversed, Iris is saying the storm isn't over yet."

Dorcha continued, "In regards to acting in general, you're learning something new here, spiritually. You're a bit burnt out on acting. This is the end of a cycle. The blocked energy can inspire manipulative and draining behavior. Your songwriting is connected to this creative clog. Right now there is a considerable amount of mental static and anguish surrounding your songwriting. The difficulties feel humiliating, but you need to realize it is all part of the process. Do not give up. There's an electrical storm going on in your mind. It won't last forever. The sun of inspiration will shine again."

Both women smiled at Dorcha's accidental reference to Victoria's surname.

Dorcha continued, "The best match for you romantically is someone who is consistent, gentle, clever, and brave. The Death card in this placement, along with this decision card, leads me to believe this could be someone who isn't of romantic interest to you right now. Possibly over time your priorities and wishes will change, and your desire for this person shall blossom. Or maybe there's another way of looking at it. Maybe just knowing this person will shift the way you look at love.

"The lesson you're learning from Draven is all about love, dispersing and dissolving negativity, and seeing things from different viewpoints. The sadness is passing, which will create space for new growth. This will benefit every area of your life.

"As for Kendrick, there is some kind of delay to a full expression of passion. This will take him some time to sort out. The other interpretation of the Prince of Wands reversed here is that he has a temper, or that he isn't being honest about where he's at emotionally. Maybe he's still healing and can't really handle this adventure until later. It's tricky though, because all the other cards here are favorable and indicate a positive outcome with him.

"You can apply the general advice to everything: This is a fallow time for you and it feels like a horrible nightmare. Don't worry. Wonderful things are on the horizon. Take care of your body with plenty of exercise, rest, and good food. Surrender to the moment and everything will improve before you know it.

"In the near future you're going to do something which won't be making you much money. In fact, you might lose out on an opportunity because your energy is focused elsewhere. However, eventually you will begin to feel a sense of connectedness, and a gut response of emotional awareness and sheer joy. This will show you that you're on the right path.

The money aspect of it won't even seem important at all."

Dorcha scanned the spread once more, making sure she had gotten everything. "Any questions? Something you want me to elaborate on?"

"No, you were comprehensive and accurate. Very interesting, you're quite talented. Thank you, Dorcha."

"Anytime, Victoria," Dorcha said.

By the time Victoria and Dorcha returned to the group, Captain Tess had returned. August handed the women their drinks. Victoria received a flute of 1995 Perrier Jouet "Fleur de Champagne Belle Epoque". Dorcha and Morgan each got a glass of 2001 Châteauneuf-du-Pape "Cadettes" Chateau La Nerthe.

August served the appetizers which included sweetbreads, Australian Wagyu carpaccio, a variety of oysters, and a Farmers Market green salad tossed with balsamic vinaigrette dressing.

Everyone, except for Louise the busy chef, sat down at the dining table to enjoy the haute cuisine.

After sucking down a Falsa Bay Oyster, Victoria focused her attention on Morgan, who was sitting on the opposite side of the table. "Draven and Kyle told me I've got you to thank for this fateful revelation." Victoria punctuated her words by grasping Draven's forearm.

"I helped, but something larger than us all facilitated everything."

"Who? God?" Victoria laughed. Morgan wasn't sure if Victoria was amused or if she was mocking her. Victoria continued, "So tell me about this UnderLife the fellas keep talking about."

Morgan said, "We all have our issues. Billions of people are acting out every personality nuance in the spectrum, from cute character idiosyncrasies to debilitating insanity. Problem solving is a cornerstone of human experience. UnderLife functions as a conduit to gain new perspectives on the battle occurring within each of us between our fully realized Soul consciousness and our blind Ego. The Ego is a devilish saboteur, which unleashes on all of us every day an army of evil mental tendencies and sensory obsessions. Ego always wants to take control of our personalities, usually under the guise of only trying to help. Despite its best intentions, the impulsive Ego chooses paths of self-destruction. The essential nature of Ego is like a clever, ravenous beast with zero wisdom."

Listening to Morgan talk, Victoria's eyes twinkled. Victoria's presence was so bewitching, Morgan thought, even as Victoria was simply listening, she pulled focus.

Morgan did her best not to lapse into a sexual fantasy and trail off while speaking. "UnderLife is a venue for healing, growing, and subduing our Egos ideally through non-violent conflict resolution, but most episodes aren't resolved that easily. Honestly, I'm shocked and overjoyed an

UnderLife episode led to Draven and you finding each other," Morgan said. "Although after what Dorcha and I discovered about our family's history, I should have known anything can happen."

During dinner everyone shared their own UnderLife experiences. Halfway through the meal, Louise joined the party, and humbly absorbed a barrage of compliments for her cooking.

Victoria Shine prided herself on having a stellar bullshit detector. Victoria could smell a scam or spot a grifter from a hundred paces. The weird thing was that none of the bells and whistles were going off in her head like they normally would during a con-artist hoax.

Whether Victoria did or didn't believe a word of what anyone said, she certainly found it entertaining. Victoria thought her hosts might be total nut jobs, but they sure knew how to put together a fantastic feast. Victoria kept tripping over the fact Draven, her brother, was alive. She still hadn't quite figured out how these people learned the truth.

Obviously this UnderLife thing was a great metaphor, Victoria thought, even though it couldn't possibly be real. To her credit, Morgan spoke with total conviction. What Victoria couldn't wrap her brain around was everyone else's sincerity about their visits to UnderLife Realms, as they referred to it.

While she was in the Cayman Islands, Victoria had called a few friends to get recommendations for a top-of-the-line private sleuth. She was led to someone so secretive, expensive, and effective, people just referred to him as The Detective.

The Detective's findings confirmed Draven was indeed Victoria's brother and he also confirmed that their mother was responsible for the cover-up. Victoria and Bunny already weren't on speaking terms. The discovery only confirmed for Victoria why she stayed away from the woman.

Louise elaborated on Morgan's earlier speech, "What we all need to understand is that our Egos bear a sacred responsibility to represent the shadow-side emotions for us, such as fear, anger, desire, greed, alienation, envy, pride, shame, and cowardice. These malignant emotions should be acting as benign signals for us, gently guiding our way. However, we all know that these emotions can be wild animals. They're essential to the psyche, but they require vigilant boundaries. Ego is relentless in its sword duty, and it can only be subjugated temporarily. Eventually it will regenerate and find a new tactic to wrestle away control from our higher selves. At their heart, all life lessons are about recognizing and self-correcting Ego-oriented behavior."

"How do these UnderLife episodes occur?" Victoria asked. "Are they drug-induced?"

"No," Morgan said. "None of us are sure how it happens. Usually they're anchored around whatever life lesson I'm working on, whether I'm aware of the lesson or not." Morgan launched into the retelling of the UnderLife episode from Draven's psyche. Draven interjected the details of his experience.

Victoria took in what everyone told her without criticism or complaint. She had the impulse to ask if they could help with her writer's block, but she was worried about exposing the problem. Victoria did not want any more fodder for the press about her creative difficulties, and she couldn't be sure that there weren't cameras or bugs recording everything at the dinner. It had been risky enough to have her cards read.

Victoria was careful not to consume too much of the expensive wine. The more open and friendly everyone else was behaving, the more suspicious Victoria got. Any minute they were going to hit her up for money, or worse, a public endorsement for some self-help program.

Louise knew it would be best if the first private encounter with Victoria would stay succinct. The clock was already approaching midnight. The group had unleashed a tremendous amount of information on Victoria, and it would take her time to digest it all. Louise said to the group, "I want to thank you all so much for joining us this evening," and then she and August began to clean up.

Victoria heartily embraced each person during the good-byes. When Victoria went to hug Louise, Louise quietly said to her, "If you're receptive, I'm sure we can help you with the composing conundrum you've been experiencing. No reason for anything to be in the way of such a brilliant talent."

Victoria's glare intensified into a laser beam, as if attempting to slice the thoughts right off the top of Louise's head. Had Dorcha told Louise about the reading? Victoria hadn't seen Dorcha and Louise interact closely the whole evening. Maybe a note had gotten passed through August, or there was a recording device hidden at the Tarot table. Victoria decided not to interrogate Louise at that time.

Morgan approached Victoria tentatively, "Do you need a ride home?"

"My driver is waiting downstairs. Thank you for the offer, though," Victoria replied, producing an iPhone from her clutch purse to signal Ryan via text that she was ready to leave.

* * *

The next afternoon Morgan met with Louise to work on her sacral chakra, Svadhisthan, the seat of sexuality, creativity, and emotional balance.

The deep orange carnelian stone associated with the sacral chakra would help to ground Morgan, increasing her energy, courage, and compassion.

Louise wanted to begin the work on this chakra right away, knowing that Morgan meeting Victoria had fulfilled a dream for Morgan, but it had also left her vulnerable. As Louise knew, it was often the greatest test to maintain balance when things were going so well. Morgan needed all the help she could get to stay centered.

* * *

A week later, Victoria returned the Skyscraper Space, armed with non-disclosure agreements. Victoria had contacted Morgan via Draven requesting a meeting, and she had asked that Morgan make sure that Louise and August were in attendance.

Victoria arrived on time. Morgan was waiting for her. Morgan said, "August and Louise are running a bit late. Can I get you something to drink? Water? Soda? Iced tea? Shot of tequila?"

"Iced tea, thanks," Victoria said.

They sat down on the circular couches.

"I don't know how August can stand having her mother as a boss," Victoria said. "Do they live together as well?"

"What do you mean, August's mother?"

"Louise, obviously," Victoria said, mimicking the older woman's British accent perfectly.

It dawned on Morgan that she didn't know anything specific about August's family. August hadn't brought it up, and Morgan had been so self-absorbed over the years with receiving August's nurturing and guidance, that she had never thought to ask.

"How did you know that?" Morgan asked.

"It was the first thing I noticed about them. These days I'm pretty sensitive to recognizing genetically-inspired physical resemblances. They have similar facial bone structure, a few key mannerisms in common, and despite the different accents, their vocal inflections overlap frequently. Weird they never told you. How long have you known them?"

"For most of my life," Morgan said quietly.

"What else are they keeping from you?" Victoria asked.

When Louise and August arrived, Morgan controlled her impulse to pounce on them with questions.

Cordial hellos were exchanged, and the legal papers promising confidentiality were signed.

Louise dove in, "Victoria, how is the song writing going?"

Victoria shot her a dirty look and said, "Well now, we're just gonna go right for the jugular, aren't we?" Victoria narrowed her piercing eyes.

"Look, we know it's all over the press. Since Cuneo died, molasses moves faster than my ability to crank out a new song."

"After writing Left, which is a spectacular tribute, the well went dry," Louise said. "Years passed, with you in full retreat. Then the role of Harmony Moore on Love In Motion fell into your lap. You hoped acting would get the creative juices flowing. You're an excellent actress, capable of a fine career. Unfortunately, it doesn't get you off quite as much as music does."

Victoria loved acting, but she always challenged the perspectives of the directors, writers, and producers she was working with. This behavior had a way of swelling budgets, and there were no guarantees the trouble would translate into lucrative box office returns.

Early in her adult acting career, Victoria had turned in stellar performances in several films in a row. Each one had achieved excellent critical attention and box office success. Unfortunately, she had gotten into a big blowout with a huge director and their producer on an astronomically expensive movie. Victoria had gotten neck deep into Industry politics, which she found revolting. It wasn't that Victoria was box office poison. Far from it. But Victoria was very finicky about which projects she chose to do, and there were many in the business who were afraid to work with her because of her reputation for being antagonistic.

Morgan was amazed at how well Victoria manipulated the press into ignoring her lack of musical output. That's why Victoria had hired a shark publicist to keep her in line for the MTV Movie Awards. The goal was to maximize Victoria's exposure, and at the same time give her space to rekindle the creative fires.

Victoria spoke, "Sometimes I feel like Kate Bush and I are in some kind of contest. It took her ten years to put out Aeriel: A Sky of Honey. Hell, after two years I was ready to stab myself in the eye with a lit cigarette if it meant I would write something good. I'm grateful Love In Motion came around. Playing Harmony Moore fueled an album's worth of material. Granted, it was like a campy musical theater soundtrack, which is something I never thought I'd collaborate on, but overall we had a lot fun."

"And since Harmony's Harem, your creativity has been blocked again?" Louise asked.

"What's your point, Louise? Have you got some magic spell that can cure my writer's block, for the low, low price of only $30,000?"

"If only the muses could be lured by money. No, I do not possess a magical creativity spell. What do you think is the reason for your difficulty?"

"Sounds like you're kindly counseling a dude because he can't keep his dick hard, the poor bastard."

"It is a form of impotence, and it can be just as traumatic as if you were suffering from penile erectile dysfunction."

"Awesome, I've always wanted to feel empathy with some schmuck who can't capitalize on a hot sex opportunity because his equipment isn't working."

"Your sarcasm is counter-productive."

"Alright, alright, you're so serious, Louise," Victoria said. "I think I have problems with my writing because of my perfectionism. I get paralyzed by the desire to bust out songs which will grab you in the head, grind you in the gut, and set your sex on fire. I am haunted by fragments of melodies and lyrics. Unfortunately, corralling them into some kind of song structure makes me want to get a lobotomy. It was a whole hell of a lot easier when Cuneo was around. He knew exactly how to translate my feelings into music. Sometimes all I had to do was read Cuneo some lyrics, and he would build a song right around them. Cuneo spoiled me. We pounded away on piece all night until we got it to where we wanted it to go. I used to think he didn't even need me at all. Cuneo said before I came around his songwriting was lame, hackneyed, bullshit."

Louise considered this for a moment, and then said, "There is a fountain of musical self-expression dancing inside of you. The only person getting in the way of the fountain flowing is you."

"Yeah, yeah, we're all our own worst enemies. Doesn't really help me reconcile the self-conflict. It pisses me off. I'm the asshole who's causing all of my problems? Great, I don't even get the luxury of blaming someone else."

"What if you could go through an ordeal to remove your creative block? Never again would you have to hunt for inspiration. It shall always be at your fingertips."

"I'd say you're conning me. An ordeal, huh? Sounds tedious and expensive. What makes you so sure this can be done?"

"Faith, and the cumulative wisdom gained from many years of experiences which can only be described as mystical. I possess an oracular gift. I've seen your capability to be a prolific songwriter. If you are willing to take a leap with our friend here, this vision will become a reality. As we've explained before, Morgan has an ability to travel through and manipulate the collective unconscious, or UnderLife, as she calls it. It's the reality most of us only experience in dreams and visions, but Morgan travels to and from these realms as easily as it is for the rest of us to enter or leave a room."

"I can't control it like that." Morgan blurted out. She felt the heat rise in her cheeks when the three other women looked at her. Morgan felt like a happily freaked out child on her first roller coaster ride.

Louise corrected Morgan, "Yes, ultimately you will. There exists a hidden part of you which does not want to control it. That part of your

Ego must be hunted down and exposed. This will help you overcome the very dangerous tendency you have of abruptly falling unconscious with little or no warning."

"Do you think I like this? I hate it! I've spent endless amounts of time in planes of existence which are just one puzzle after another. Or I come to in Waking Reality with a splitting headache because I've cracked my head on the floor, again. And then I inevitably say something about my trip which makes me appear even more insane."

Morgan flashed to when she was out to dinner with Balthazar a couple of years ago. During their meal she had been sucked into another UnderLife adventure. Of course Balthazar had no clue what was going on. He saw only that Morgan's eyes glazed over for a bit, then her head nodded forward like she was going to pass out, and then she frantically blurted out "Dragons!" so loud everyone in the restaurant turned to stare at her. Thank God Balthazar had had such a healthy sense of humor about the whole thing when he told Morgan what had happened.

Victoria broke in on Morgan's reminiscing. "What does this have to do with me? Why does it matter that Morgan can do this? According to Morgan, UnderLife doesn't sound like much fun."

August didn't miss a beat. "How do you think your brother found you?"

The question made Victoria stop in her tracks. Victoria still had no idea how Darian had discovered that he was her brother. "Exactly what do you want me to do?"

"I want you to travel in UnderLife with Morgan for a while. I am confident that during the journey, both of your control issues will be resolved. One of you can't control the accessibility of her gift, and the other is being controlled by her gift."

"Why is this so important to you, Louise? What do you get out of it?"

"I believe both of you were meant for a greater purpose which cannot be fulfilled unless you each stop your subtle self-sabotaging behavior. My personal spiritual beliefs call me to support the people I am drawn to, in any way that I can," Louise said.

August nodded in agreement.

"Are you saying you are secretly trying to Oprah the world into a better place, one oddball psychic nut job at a time?"

"Something like that." Louise smiled.

"Louise, I want to speak with you alone," Victoria said.

"By all means, follow me," Louise said, leading Victoria up to the roof.

The moment Victoria and Louise left the room, Morgan wheeled on August. "Louise is your mother?"

"What?" August asked.

"You heard me," Morgan said.

August sighed, "Yes."

"Victoria knew it from the start."

"Perceptive woman," August said.

"Tell me, when we first met when I was a kid, there was a mysterious man in a dark suit? The one waiting at the house when we got back from my swimming lesson, who made you leave early."

August was surprised Morgan remembered him.

"You mean Mitchell Cannon?" August said.

Morgan erupted with laughter.

"See? Now you know why I kept it from you," August said.

"Wait, wait. Are you telling me that after all this time your big secret is that you still live at home and work for your parents?"

August stuck her tongue out. "Well, sort of."

"Why don't you ever call them Mom and Dad?"

"Mitchell is adamant about this rule. He considers it a weakness to advertise our relationship. The Cannon family prefers to keep a low profile."

"What are you, spies?"

"Oh no, of course not. Well, at least not anymore. Let's say we like to travel a lot, gather information, and trade."

"Is that the watered-down version of what I just said?"

"If it was, I wouldn't be allowed to admit it."

"Gotcha. So, is my shaky fledgling too vulnerable to leave the nest and stake out her claim in the big scary world, hmmm?"

"You're enjoying this far too much. It's embarrassing and I wouldn't say I live with them. I have some of my stuff at their place for storage purposes only."

"Yeah, in a place called Your Bedroom," Morgan said.

August couldn't help laughing.

Then another idea popped into Morgan's head, "Mitchell Cannon pretended he was Barry the ticket broker!"

"Yes ma'am."

"You guys are sneaky."

"It's why we're still alive."

Morgan heard the muffled ding of the elevator, and moments later Louise and Victoria walked through the door.

"If I say yes, what will you do?" Victoria asked as they approached.

"Light candles and incense all around. Have you face each other, and state your intentions. Then put you back-to-back in meditative poses in the center of a circle, say a prayer, and bind you both with a symbolic string. Meditate for a spell, and we're finished."

"Then what?"

"Then the next time Morgan goes into UnderLife you shall go with her, and your adventure will have already begun," Louise said.

"For how long will we be bound to each other in this way?"

"Depends, either until you decide to break it, or until the work has been completed."

Morgan was equally excited and terrified to have Victoria as a companion in UnderLife. "What I'm more concerned about is if Victoria really understands what is going to happen. It's entirely unpredictable. Be prepared for a whole new relationship with traveling and chaos."

Victoria said, "Actually, I think you're all full of shit. If you really believe a simple string and candles are going to take me with you into some magical Under-whatever, you're more delusional than I thought. But hey, if you want to play this game, by all means, wow me."

The binding ritual was performed.

"Now what?" Victoria asked.

"Wait here for an hour," Louise said while unwrapping the string from Morgan and Victoria. "If nothing occurs during the allotted time, we part ways and carry on with our lives."

"Don't worry," August said. "Generally there's no mistaking an UnderLife entrance."

Louise and August rose and gathered their belongings.

"You're leaving?" Morgan asked.

"Yes," Louise said. "Have fun ladies. Give one of us a call after your UnderLife jaunt."

The Cannons exited.

Victoria set the alarm on her iPhone to ring in an hour. She checked her messages, and fired off a few texts.

Morgan pulled out three coins from her pocket to ask the I Ching for guidance. Morgan got Twenty-Two going into Twenty-Six. Grace going into The Taming Power of the Great. Morgan cast another reading on her optimal action and best attitude regarding Victoria, and she received Hexagram Sixty-Four: Before Completion. Morgan pulled out her copy of Carol Anthony's interpretations of the hexagrams and fought to focus on the readings, but was utterly distracted by Victoria.   Nothing could have prepared Morgan for the onslaught of raw physical lust she felt in Victoria's presence. Morgan's earlier shock was giving way to a primal craving. A ravenous desire to please Victoria surged through Morgan's every thought. Morgan was stunned by the realization that Victoria's beauty in person made her appearances on film or in print pale by comparison.

Victoria finished her electric correspondence and said, "If we have to wait around for an hour, let's go up to the roof."

Morgan was so focused on Victoria that she forgot to put the I Ching tome down. Morgan closed the book on her pen and scratch paper, and tucked it under her left arm.

They took the elevator to the top floor, and proceeded up a couple of flights of stairs to the door of the roof. A moderate breeze buffeted the women as they walked outside.

The design of the roof was an excellent example of Louise's philosophy; functionality, elegance, and durability. About a dozen three-foot-tall potted trees were placed around the open space. An all-weather table, umbrella, and a set of four chairs stood on the other side of the stairwell. In front of them there was a two hundred square foot meditation and training area made out of high-tech recycled plastic decking.

Their timing was perfect for catching a spectacular view. Victoria walked westward, enjoying the reflective ocean embracing the remaining rays of sunshine. Victoria stopped near the edge of the building. Morgan was several feet behind her.

A flock of seagulls flew by, framed in a gorgeous pink-and-purple lightly-clouded backdrop. It looked like something out of movie. In fact, chances were it was being immortalized by several filmmakers and photographers right at that moment.

"Another beautiful smog-enhanced Los Angeles sunset," Morgan said.

"Why do you want to do this?" Victoria asked. She leaned against the waist-high guard rail next to the ledge. "What do you get out of it?"

"Spending time with you alone is more than enough of a reward."

"On the stalker meter, where are you?"

"Completely devoted and totally benign. I'm not sure where that falls on the scale."

Victoria smiled, "Generally at an acceptable level." Victoria glanced at the book tucked under Morgan's arm, "What are you reading?"

"My I Ching hexagrams for today," Morgan said, showing the book to Victoria.

"What do those chicken scratches mean?"

"They're a warning about my Ego's dangerous influence, and about discerning true grace from false grace. Under Ego's tremendous pressure, I have to be careful about not being too stiff or too lax in my behavior. Focus on the chin and not the beard."

"What's this second bit of writing here?" Victoria asked. "BA w slash V? What does that mean?"

"Oh, well," Morgan blushed, "it's the I Ching's council on the best way to handle you, in energy terms."

Victoria frowned. "Handle me?"

"Best disposition or action. The cosmic perspective of our current connection," Morgan said in a rush, flustered by Victoria's tone. "Have you used the I Ching before?"

"Once at a party, years ago. Honestly, I don't remember much of the reading."

Morgan offered the coins to Victoria.

Victoria cast the three coins six times. Morgan calculated the results and announced, "You got Hexagram 5: Waiting going into Hexagram 2: The Receptive, Earth."

"What does that mean?"

"See for yourself," Morgan said, indicating the passages in Carol Anthony's book for Victoria to read.

Victoria examined the pages for several minutes and then said, "Interesting," without further comment.

"You know, I've felt drawn to you since I was a kid," Morgan said. "I love your work. If you ever need a compliment, I'm always ready to pontificate about your many wonderful attributes."

"I appreciate your good taste," Victoria said.

"My Ex would have a kitten if he knew who I was talking to right now," Morgan felt dumb as soon as she brought Balthazar up.

"Draven mentioned your old boyfriend. Why did you break up?"

"I didn't tell Balthazar about UnderLife until years after we got together. I assumed that eventually we'd meet there spontaneously. In retrospect I think I made a fatal mistake by not being honest once things got serious. I was afraid if he didn't have first-hand proof of UnderLife, there would be no way he'd accept the truth. Turns out I was right, unfortunately. I think Balthazar would have stayed with me if I recanted and continued the simple narcolepsy charade, or if I just never brought it up again. When I told him about how UnderLife guided me to the connection between you and Draven, we had a big fight, and that was the final straw."

"How many other people have you told about Draven and me?"

"Balthazar, and everyone who was here the other night. No one else, I swear."

"Disgruntled lovers have a knack for complication."

"Don't worry, Balthazar isn't a gossip. I'd be surprised if he told anyone. Besides, who would believe him? He doesn't even buy it."

Victoria shook her head. "I give it two weeks. News like this is an aggressive virus. It finds a way to spread."

"Shall we ask the I Ching for the best way to handle this?"

"Don't you think you might be getting in your own way with all of this stuff? Open your eyes and move on. You know I'm not going to give you what you want." Victoria said.

"I think you're misunderstanding. Tarot, I Ching, Astrology, these are metaphysical tools. I use them to investigate the motivations of my desire. Just because I have romantic fantasies about you doesn't mean I'm not your friend as well. I can't stop the desire from being there. I trust that my heart is guiding me on a true path, whether or not it actually leads to you. If I don't tend to the garden of delight I have for you and deny how I feel, it will turn on me. Cruelty is passion gone sour and insane. The last thing I want is to have any negative thoughts towards someone I love. I don't have guilt or shame for feeling this way about you even if I have no hope of ever being with you physically. I am already blessed and think it's a fucking miracle to be here speaking with someone whose musical genius and brilliant acting has had such a monumental impact upon my life."

"What musical genius? I've never written anything without help. I'm a natural mimic. It's easy for me take the seed of what someone else has already created and mold it into my own style, but I hate needing someone else to help me write songs. I want to create music on my own. It sickens me and it shows how desperate I am engaging in this bullshit UnderLife charade."

"It's real, Victoria. You'll see."

"You know what I see? I see a bright, sweet, gullible woman who is being taken for a ride. I don't know how this Louise character convinced you that you have this so-called ability. Maybe she gave you some drugs, or you're already psychotic, and Louise plays right into it. I still don't know how you tracked me down and found out about my brother. It was only out of gratitude that I listened to you in the first place. I'm flattered you love my music and you think I'm sexy, but don't you dare act like you really know me, because honey, you don't."

Morgan had a massive grin on her face.

"Why are you smiling, crazy?" Victoria asked.

Morgan could hear Massive Attack's song "Angel", and she knew it wasn't coming from the Skyscraper Space's state-of-the-art sound system. The volume rose. Coordinated with the music, Morgan and Victoria's environment began to melt. Vines grew from the shadows, creeping over every surface of the building.

Victoria was too intent on delivering her tirade, and she didn't notice what was happening until the shift had completed.

"Fuck me, how did you…" Victoria looked around in bewilderment as a breeze swept through her hair. They were in the middle of a sequoia forest. The sun was shining and birds were chirping.

Morgan bowed and opened her arms in a gesture of greeting.

"Welcome to UnderLife."

"I don't know what drugs you guys slipped me, but I want to buy a whole case."

"No drugs were involved, Victoria. It's the collective unconscious."

CHAPTER EIGHTEEN
CURRENT

"Where are we?" Victoria touched the bark of a tree to verify its existence.

"A forest," Morgan said.

"Thanks, Professor. I meant where on the planet?"

"It's UnderLife, as far as I can tell there's no geographical location. Think of it as another plane of existence. I'm sure you've heard of the phrase, as above, so below? Well our waking consciousness resides in the above..."

"...and somehow your particular talent consists of taking trips into the below?"

"Yes."

"Whose psyche are we in, mine or yours?" Victoria asked.

"I don't know, possibly neither, or both."

"What do you mean?"

"I call them Tweener Places. Like a spiritual airport or bus station. Common realms used for further traveling, not dwelling places, unless we're dealing with gypsies."

"Gypsies?"

"Well, I figure if someone's idea of home is to be traveling continually, then their UnderLife would somehow reflect it," Morgan said.

"Have you ever met anyone else who can do this?"

"No. That doesn't mean they don't exist, though."

"This is fucking trippy," Victoria said.

Victoria walked into the forest along a faint path. Their route through the forest led to more forest. They could tell they had entered a different part of the forest because of the change in terrain. There weren't any significant landmarks. The terrain was rather flat, with no good vantage point of the surrounding countryside. None of the trees were climbable. They were all either too young or they had no branches low enough to get a hold of.

"Did you hear music during the UnderLife transition?" Morgan asked.

"Not that I can recall. You did?"

"Yes, Massive Attack's "Angel". At the crescendo, it got pretty loud," Morgan said.

Victoria concentrated on her memories for a few moments then shrugged her shoulders. "If "Angel" was playing, I didn't hear it."

After a few more minutes of walking Victoria asked, "How do we get out of this?"

"It's a puzzle. We have to figure out why we're here. Solve the lesson of this place."

"What if we don't figure it out? Then what, we're trapped in here?"

"Well, yes." Morgan sighed. "There is another way out. It's not pretty."

"Tell me," Victoria said.

"Suicide. Dying in UnderLife is similar to what happens in a dream. Right before you croak, you come out of it."

"Great! Let's find a cliff and Thelma and Louise off of it." Victoria said.

"The problem is it will cause us to pass out in Waking Life. The shock of the experience is really jarring. Your physical body gets overwhelmed, and needs to shut down for a while. It's not fun. That's how I got diagnosed with narcolepsy," Morgan said.

"So every time you pass out, it means a traumatic and fatal UnderLife episode occurred?"

"Yes. Most of the time it's the result of some type of combat."

"Combat? With whom?"

"The unconscious self can generate any creature or person for you to fight with. It's infinitely resourceful. Things tend to depend on whatever personal mythology you nourish yourself with."

"Alright, so let's off ourselves, get the hell out of here, and faint in Waking Life. Big deal."

"It's more dangerous than you think, Victoria. There's no way to fall gracefully when you get knocked out. I've had far too many blows to the head, twisted ankles, and accidental trips down the stairs. In Waking Life we're not protected from real physical harm. Think about where you were when we transitioned. Leaning against the railing on the roof of a skyscraper, right? I should have moved us when I started to hear and feel the shift, but you were yelling and I... I forgot. What happens if one or both of us ends up over the railing? Do you want to take the chance?"

302

"Okay, okay, I get it. Let's keep going then. What if the lesson is to see how much boredom it takes before we kill ourselves, just to be released from this purgatory?"

Morgan laughed. "That's sick and I hope it's not true. C'mon. At least walking feels like we're going somewhere."

"Does all this cardio count in the Waking Life?"

"I wish. It'd be great to work out in no time, and always look fantastic without sacrificing any hours in the day."

They continued onward.

Victoria groped in vain for her lip gloss. "I guess my purse didn't get a ticket into UnderLife."

"Usually personal effects don't make the trip, unless they're going to be useful in the Realm."

They wandered around for what seemed like hours. "Some puzzle," Victoria said. "It's all forest. Is my unconscious telling me I should be a park ranger? Regretting the binding spell yet?"

"How could I? This is an honor. It's my pleasure. If I can help you in any way, I want to. Your work is a continual source of nourishment for all of your fans. I also believe what August and Louise said. Working with you will teach me how to gain more control over my UnderLife entrances and exits."

Victoria stayed quiet for a while and they kept moving.

"You'd think the landscape would have a little more variety in the vegetation," Victoria said.

"I'm delighted to be with you on this journey, even if it's tedious." Morgan cringed internally. It was difficult to resist gushing.

"That's sweet, and you're certainly interesting to be around. However, despite the spectacularly swift entrance, this Realm, as you call it, is a dull one-note song. Which reminds me," Victoria said, giving Morgan an appraising eye, "I think we need to talk about the manner of your attire."

"No fair! You have a personal stylist."

"Honey, I had to dress myself long before Ja'Mei came along."

"Yeah, I think the whole world remembers your big bracelet phase."

"We shall not speak about that further, missy. We're getting off the subject." Victoria gestured to Morgan's jeans, tank top, hoodie, and sneakers ensemble.

Morgan covered her body in mock shame. "I've gotten in the habit of dressing for comfort and functionality. You can see why. I never know what's going to happen next."

"Well, no need to look like a butch farm-hand, even if you can get sucked into this UnderLife place so easily."

Morgan laughed and feigned wounded shock.

Victoria continued, "Since this is UnderLife, where anything can happen, shouldn't we be able to change our appearances or clothing at will?"

"Yes, in theory, on this spiritual plane we are capable of doing whatever we can imagine. But my experience has been that our physical form on the material plane usually becomes the template for our manifestation in UnderLife. It acts as an anchor point for our psyche while we roam around here." Morgan said.

"Or maybe you haven't tried hard enough. Obviously hair, make-up, and costuming aren't exactly passions of yours," Victoria said.

"Indeed."

"Now if I'm plunged into a surprise lengthy gig, I'd want to have on some foxy attire. My feminine wiles might be needed to handle a situation."

"Who are you kidding? You could conduct effective negotiations in tinfoil if you needed to."

"In the Eighties, I probably did."

"Yes, in 1985. The Jiffy Pop commercial. They popped all of the kids out of a gigantic foil-covered popcorn pan."

"Aren't you the budding TV historian? Yeah, I remember, the frying pan was a giant trampoline. What a fun day getting paid to bounce around the office. Mother finally unclenched for a moment because it was a national spot."

"It must have been tough to be managed by her. You know I saw a piece of your mother's UnderLife?"

"Now that's enduring a difficult ordeal," Victoria said.

"The Vault with all your stuff was a study in obsession over your stardom. Talk about living vicariously. Every success you've had she's felt responsible for. Any failure was your own, and proved that you still needed her guidance. It's a convenient, self-indulgent way of thinking."

"Bunny is certainly a master of self-indulgence. For the most part I enjoyed her attention, at least until I hit puberty. Maybe it's because show-business is all I've ever known. My first memories are on set. I don't feel like I missed out on any other kind of upbringing. I was happy working as a kid. For a while I thought I had a gigantic family because I was surrounded by people who bent over backwards to be nice to me. All I had to do to satisfy them was follow their simple instructions and stay calm, except of course when they wanted me to freak out. Things got rough with Bunny when I was old enough to start questioning her authority."

"Do you mind satisfying my curiosity about something?" Morgan asked.

"Depends on what you want to know."

"How did you end up back in television?"

"Oh, it was all Darian's doing."

Victoria thought about how much she wanted to tell Morgan. Even though they were out in the open, the forest couldn't have felt more private. Victoria still couldn't get past the suspicion that somehow those crazy bitches had drugged her.

"Darian knew I was in a vulnerable place. It'd been over two years since Cuneo's death. I wasn't any closer to writing anything new. One night over dinner and many drinks, Darian convinced me to meet with her agent and producer about having me guest star as a rival on Love In Motion. Darian said they'd add me to the cast if everyone gelled. She made it sound like she and the producers had already discussed it, but they hadn't. She was already sure it was a brilliant idea, and if she could sell me on it, everyone else would be easy. However, Darian knew I wouldn't even entertain the possibility if I found out she was only speculating about the deal."

* * *

The meeting with Victoria, Victoria's agent Gary Kander, and Owen Loviatar the Producer was in a miserable state. Loviatar and Victoria were bickering. Their voices were rising in volume. Victoria was poised to storm out dramatically when Darian entered.

"Sorry, sorry, my sincerest apologies for the unforgivable tardiness. Now catch me up. Have we signed a year contract, and the shouts I heard in the hallway were out of jubilation?" Darian asked.

"Quite the contrary, Darian," Loviatar said. "Your friend here has much less enthusiasm for joining this award-winning show than you led me to believe."

* * *

Victoria mimicked a whiny cadence when impersonating Owen Loviatar.

Then Victoria switched back to her own voice for her response. "I bellowed in my full-theatrical, projecting-to-the-back-row-of-the-theater voice, 'I refuse to work for this man!'"

Morgan could see the years of training and experience Victoria had as a performer. Victoria was aware of every movement of her body. She knew what all of her facial expressions looked like, and she was alert to the nuances of her surroundings. It thrilled Morgan to be able to make such an intimate observation about someone who she had spent countless hours studying from afar.

"'What the hell did I do?' Loviatar asked. 'Who says I want to offer you a job?'" Victoria continued.

Morgan interjected, chuckling, "Uh-oh, you're a bad person to fight or have a power struggle with. What did you do?"

"The truth is I wanted to do the show. I knew it'd be good for me to be acting. Give the stagnant songwriting a bit of a break. However, I had a long-festering hatred for Owen Loviatar. He had screwed over a friend of mine many moons ago during his first marriage. It was a classic scenario. My friend was his mistress and Loviatar promised to leave his wife. He told my friend that his heart belonged to her, and if she remained patient everything would work out. None of it was true. Loviatar was motivated by greed. He would have never left his heiress wife. In fact, it was she who left him, after her detective gave her photos of Loviatar fucking my friend and three other hapless women."

Victoria continued, "By that time he had established himself in the entertainment industry as a man who got the project done, on time and on budget. How that bastard snagged his gorgeous second wife, I'll never know. Loviatar's a lying, unfaithful sack of shit, but unfortunately he's an excellent producer. He'd tear someone's kidneys out of their body with his bare hands if it meant getting a film of his in the can."

"So what happened next?" Morgan couldn't get enough of the backstage dirt.

"Darian did."

* * *

"Alright, time out. Gentlemen please give me a minute to speak with Victoria."

"Fine with me," Loviatar said, scooping up his Blackberry and stalking out.

As the men left the room, Darian said to Gary Kander, who was her agent as well, "Way to be a presence, Gary."

Kander was ready to say something in his defense, but he knew damn well that Darian had accomplished more diplomacy in fifteen seconds than he had the entire disastrous meeting. Defeated, Kander walked out.

"I don't know how you work for that slime bag Loviatar." Victoria said.

"I barely ever see him. We should have set up this meeting with Hank Bellamy, the other producer, but he's in Cannes promoting a film he directed during hiatus."

"This was a bad idea. I can't believe you snowballed me into thinking this was already set up. I don't know why I came here."

"Because you love acting and Love In Motion is a ton of fun to do?"

"Darian, I don't I have any real passion for acting anymore. It's all about music now."

"Oh, get off it, Victoria. You know this is a beautiful opportunity and you're a performer, in any medium or setting, plain and simple. You're acting all the time as this rock star persona you've developed. Maybe your passion for the craft is muffled, but I know it's still there."

"You don't know me. You don't know anything about me."

They stared each other down for a full minute. Darian's eyes narrowed with mischief and Victoria cracked with laughter.

"Damn it!" Victoria said.

"Darian Vihzor is the reigning champion of The Staring Contest! Aah!"

Darian waved and bowed to an imaginary standing ovation, accepted flowers, and even worked up some humbly overwhelmed misty-eyed gratitude. This was all part of a long running competition and inside joke they'd carried on for years.

"Oh you're good," Victoria said as the fake tears welled up in Darian's eyes.

"Thank you, a lifetime of practice." Darian snuggled up next to Victoria on the couch. "This is a no-brainer, Victoria. Join Love In Motion. We'll have a blast! This is one hell of a great paying gig."

"It's tempting, but you know how much I hate all of the politics and lack of privacy that come with it."

"Like the music industry isn't lubricated by bullshit? Sweetheart, you'll basically be playing yourself, maybe a bit tamer since this is network television, not Cinemax."

"Everything is more fun with hot sex thrown in."

"Except child care," Darian said.

They cackled with laughter.

Victoria sighed. Images fired through Victoria's mind of being on set again, memorizing lines and blocking, playing around with her fellow actors, a studio audience erupting with laughter, Victoria singing a new song inspired by the whole experience.

"I have a few terms of service," Victoria said.

"That sounds like a Yes to me! Oh Vick, this is awesome!" Darian bear-hugged her. Returning to business mode, Darian said, "I'm sure they can meet your demands. What are they?"

* * *

"That's the story of how I joined Love In Motion. How I got temporarily fired was much more entertaining for me."

"Do tell," Morgan said. "Wait, didn't Loviatar object to having you on the show?"

"Once Darian and I were a united front and she got Hank Bellamy on board, Loviatar couldn't say no. I was still considered a bankable movie star. He knew I would help the show to flourish. Loviatar may be a complete asshole, but he knows a gold mine when he sees it."

"And how did you almost get kicked off the show?"

"I fucked Loviatar's second wife Dominique," Victoria said.

* * *

Victoria mused about the first time she saw a framed wedding photo of Dominique Loviatar in Owen Loviatar's office. The beautiful model in the picture could be found in a copy of the Academy Players Directory, or on Ford Models' roster of devastating beauty. It'd be a pity if such a ravishing creature shackled herself to that vile man.

Two months later at a Love In Motion Emmy Party, Victoria Shine picked Mrs. Dominique Loviatar out of the crowd the moment she arrived.

Shine saw Loviatar getting caught up in man-time with visiting Italian advertising executives looking to pour at lot of money into the show. This left Dominique alone in the social shark pit. Victoria saw Dominique meander over to the open bar. She watched Dominique being chatted up by one of Loviatar's many predatory underlings.

Victoria couldn't resist approaching the woman. She was curious to see if Dominique had half a brain, and what possessed her to be with Loviatar. Maybe Dominique was a psychiatric nurse in disguise, there to administer Loviatar's anti-psychotic meds at regular intervals. Or she could be a long term working girl, top of the line, of course.

Victoria arrived in time at to hear Dominique order a club soda with lime.

"Are you driving?" Victoria purred with conversational familiarity.

"No, we have a driver," Dominique said smoothly. "I have an early morning."

"Do you like wine?"

"Yes, very much, but I don't think my patients will appreciate a hung-over therapist."

"Who said anything about getting wasted? I've got a succulent vintage here you've got to try. The nose on it reminds me of sex. You'll love it," Victoria said.

Victoria was thrilled to feel a controlled flare of attraction from the other woman. "If you insist," Dominique said.

They flirted effortlessly. For the life of Victoria, she couldn't understand how Owen Loviatar landed such a dynamic and attractive woman. Victoria said as much. Dominique laughed. She explained that despite his numerous faults, privately Owen revealed an unguarded, penitent side.

"Owen is decisive and goes after what he wants with a single-mindedness I respect," Dominique said.

"He's also an untrustworthy asshole. Pardon me for saying, but you could do a whole lot better."

Victoria stepped closer, caressing Dominique with psychic flutters of desire. Dominique's olive-skinned face flushed.

A couple of glasses of wine later, Dominique's tongue had loosened a great deal about her tumultuous marriage.

"I am Owen's confidant. He tells me everything. Yes, even about how he deserves the vitriol you feel for him. The man wants to evolve, be happy, and not act out so much."

"I get it. You're his salvation. It's understandable, since you're a natural healer," Victoria said.

"At first I thought I was really helping him. I thought I was a strong, positive influence. Now I feel more like an enabler, a salve or a Band-Aid. Once the sparkle wore off his pretty new thing, Owen's true character reasserted itself. His nightly penitent confessions are a sham. Owen vents his wickedness and gets off on my bountiful compassion. It's a game to him. He has no interest in improving his behavior. Owen is in love with the endless analysis of his own self-aggrandizing and driven character." Dominique's stopped short, her complexion blanching, "Oh God, I'm sorry. Here I am piling all my shit on to you about a man you already despise. With all my ranting, if I don't divorce Owen I'm essentially doing the same thing he is."

"Don't worry," Victoria said, touching Dominique's arm, "the last thing I want to do is judge you. I'm enjoying you thoroughly. You're dealing with the shock of realizing the man you fell in love with is an illusion. He wishes he had the strength to be a benevolent leader, rather than just a tyrant. Maybe you don't want out of the relationship and just need to shake it up a bit. Get his attention back." Victoria lips curled into a feral smile. "Do you do house calls? I have so many things I want to express to you."

Dominique wordlessly surrendered her phone to Victoria. Victoria punched in her number, and slipped the phone back into Dominique's clutch purse lying on the bar.

Darian arrived at the bar. She was well aware of the mischief Victoria was sliding herself into. Darian knew all about Victoria's vendetta for Loviatar, and seducing his wife would make for a satisfying revenge tactic.

"Excuse us for a moment, Dominique," Darian said. Darian put an arm around Victoria's waist, and guided her to where they could have some privacy.

"Are you really going to fuck the boss's wife?" Darian asked.

"I'm thinking about it," Victoria said, peering over Darian's shoulder to glance at Dominique.

Darian leaned in closer, demanding Victoria's focus. "How do you even know she's into women? Or you, for that matter?"

Victoria leveled her gaze on Darian, took a beat, and smirked. They both laughed.

"Thanks for the parenting, Mom. We're all adults here. No one is going to do anything they don't want to do." Victoria said, leaving to go back to the bar.

"Exactly my point drama queen," Darian hissed to the back of Victoria's head.

By the time Victoria returned to Dominique, Owen had joined his wife at the bar, and they were getting ready to leave. Victoria pretended to ignore them. Dominique covertly locked eyes with Victoria while exiting. Victoria winked at Dominique.

* * *

Victoria finished her story with, "It seems I hold an unconscious fondness for playing the role of temptation."

"In other words, you have a knack for fucking up other people's relationships?"

"Yes, exactly, and it's completely unintentional. Well, except in this case," Victoria said.

"Accidentally sexy?"

"M-hmm, I prefer to think of myself as a herald for change."

"A revolutionary," Morgan said.

Victoria smiled a big smile, "I like you," she said in an awkward rush, for comedic effect.

"How long did it take for Dominique to call you?" Morgan asked.

"Five days, and a few hours after Loviatar left for a film set in Prague. Dominique capitulating into hot forbidden sex is not something I'll soon forget. She's quite a sensual woman."

"Did they break up?"

"No. Actually, in the end I think Loviatar gained a great deal of respect for his wife, and begged Dominique to give him another chance."

"But Loviatar tried to fire you?"

"Initially yes, none of the brass appreciated my behavior, but they couldn't terminate my contract without it costing a lot of money. I'd brought a solid ratings bump to the show, and it made me a valuable asset. Loviatar let it go after throwing a few tantrums. I used the attention to get backing for a Harmony Moore mini-tour. All in all, it worked out for the best."

"So you were only together one night? How did things end with you?"

"Who said it was just one night?" Victoria asked. "And things didn't really end, they're more like, in suspension."

Victoria's eyes narrowed on the path they were walking. She picked up the pace. "Look, the landscape changed."

Victoria led them to a rocky landing offering an outlook of a fertile valley. It reminded both women of Yosemite in full spring bloom.

Victoria was energized by telling Morgan stories during their marathon walk, but now she felt depleted. No way in hell Morgan has more endurance than I do, thought Victoria.

"We found our exit," Victoria said, pointing to the cliff.

"Really? You want to jump off?"

"You said it was a way home, and I don't think I'm in any danger of going over the railing at the skyscraper."

"You don't you think we can solve this Realm any other way?"

"We haven't been very successful thus far," Victoria said.

"Well, of course not, we'd be in Waking Life already if we'd been successful."

"What do you suggest?"

"Given the monotonous terrain, I believe the reason for this UnderLife visit has been for us to have a lengthy conversation. We arrived at this gorgeous valley after you revealed personal details. Coincidence? The cliff is a test to see if we'll take the easy way out."

"You think if we talk long enough, at some point we'll trigger a shift back into Waking Life?" Victoria said, sitting down to rest on a nearby boulder.

"Yes, and I'm not just saying that because it's been so cool to hang out with you. Even if it did require a binding ritual and a hike through a forest in another dimension to make it happen. I don't think the key to this Realm is about meeting a quota of idle chatter. Your writer's block, what's obstructing the flow? Is it really such a mystery to you? What's your gut reaction? The first thought that comes to mind?"

Victoria sighed, exhausted. "Aren't you tired from all that walking?"

"No. You are? How can that be? You're in, like, Olympic shape."

Victoria yawned, moving from the boulder to sit on the ground with the rock at her back. "I don't know. Maybe I'm coming down from the drugs you gave me."

"Very funny," Morgan said. "This is strange, Victoria. Hey…"

Victoria's head lolled as she struggled to remain conscious. Morgan kneeled next to her.

"Victoria?" Morgan shook Victoria's shoulder.

"Yes…" Victoria replied softly.

"Stay awake. Please focus," Morgan said.

"…so tired…" Victoria submitted. "…You're right. I know why I'm blocked."

A rush of energy jolted through Victoria's body, bolting her upright. The landscape blurred around them.

* * *

"We're free!" Victoria hollered. She stepped away from the railing of the rooftop. Victoria hugged Morgan in jubilation. Morgan reciprocated gladly. The moment Morgan felt Victoria relax her grip, Morgan pulled away.

The sun dipped below the horizon.

"What the hell?" Victoria asked. "We must have been in there for hours! You're telling me no time passed?"

"Yeah, creepy, isn't it?" Morgan said.

"Total mind fuck!" Victoria shook her head in amazement, and headed towards the stairs. Morgan followed.

Back inside the Skyscraper Space, Morgan conference-called August and Louise, and put them on speaker phone.

"We had a lengthy UnderLife episode," Morgan said.

"Excellent. Well done," Louise said. "May we pick you both up for lunch tomorrow? We want to show you something. We've been working on it for many years. A car will be at your respective homes at eleven."

Louise did not wait for their reply before hanging up.

Victoria laughed. "I gotta give it to that woman. Louise sure has a sense of showmanship."

"Are you gonna go?"

"Well now I have to! The curiosity is unbearable."

* * *

There was a Town Car was outside Morgan's apartment at eleven sharp the next day. Morgan slid into the back of the vehicle. The driver then stopped to pick up Dorcha, and took them both to Burbank Airport. They arrived at the helicopter pad at the same time as Kyle and Draven. Captain Tess was busy doing preflight checks on the chopper when everyone arrived, and he informed them he'd be piloting the Pave Hawk "Pegasus".

Fitted for transport, the helicopter held ten fully-equipped seats. Kyle, Dorcha, Draven, and Morgan were giddy as children hanging around the impressive machine. "Captain Tess said Pegasus was designed for dangerous search and rescue missions," Kyle said.

"I hope we never need it for more than a glorified taxi service," Dorcha said.

Victoria got to the heliport half an hour later. Morgan had anticipated the delay, since she knew Victoria lived much further from Burbank Airport than she did.

Victoria sat in the unoccupied second pilot seat next to Taylor. She strapped herself in, put on the aviation helmet, and clicked on the microphone like a pro.

"Where are you taking us, Captain?" Victoria asked.

Captain Tess smiled. "Somewhere in the mountains. I've never been there before. Received coordinates and a list of who to take last night."

Victoria turned to glare at her fellow passengers. Morgan and Dorcha mirrored her look. Everyone had thought Captain Tess dwelled much deeper in the loop with the Cannons and the Vihzors.

Captain Tess made sure everyone was secured, contacted air traffic control for clearance, and got them into the air.

The trip was much more fun for Morgan the second time around, because of the wonderful company, and the fact that she was able to see where she was going. Captain Tess guided them at moderate altitude over the mountains.

An hour slipped by, and before long their speed slowed until they were hovering a couple thousand feet in the air over a patch of uninhabited wilderness.

Captain Tess double-checked the coordinates and frowned.

"Status report, Captain," Victoria said.

"We're there."

"I don't see anything," Victoria said, scanning the terrain below.

Captain Tess began to descend.

"What are you doing?" Victoria blurted out in alarm. Then she saw two camouflaged landing bay-doors sliding open in the mountain beneath them. "Never mind," Victoria said. These folks must have a mammoth operating budget for a set up like this, thought Victoria.

A large hydraulic platform rose up from the cavern beneath the ground. It was painted with a giant white letter "H", and it was lit up with running lights.

Taylor landed Pegasus and powered down the engines.

Kyle clapped in approval. "What can't this guy do?"

The platform sunk back into the mountain, and the giant doors closed once more.

It was dark inside the cavern. Rough-hewn rock walls drifted by as the helicopter descended deeper into the mountain. It reminded Dorcha of the Haunted Mansion portrait room at Disneyland. Dorcha felt claustrophobic. She fidgeted with her harness, unsure about unbuckling it.

When the platform came to rest, Taylor extricated himself from the pilot's seat and opened up the helicopter to let everyone out.

There were sleek tunnels dug into the walls on three sides of the platform. August Cannon and Tilly Vihzor were waiting at the perimeter of the hidden helipad.

"Tilly!" Victoria exclaimed upon exiting Pegasus. "You sneaky woman, I can't believe you'd hide something this fabulous from me, your fourth daughter."

"If it's any consolation, Trevor and I kept it from the whole brood."

"Hi Mom," Kyle said while hugging her. "Now I understand why Dad made me sign a non-disclosure agreement last night."

"Darian is going to be so jealous that Kyle and I saw this place first," Victoria said.

"Jill's gonna be pissed," Kyle said. "You know how competitive she is."

"Vespa will be fine." Victoria and Kyle said in unison, and laughed.

"This isn't even the best part," Tilly said. "Louise is almost done preparing our lunch. We want to show you something before we feast."

August grinned and walked with Tilly. Everyone followed to an elevator and got inside.

August ordered, "Elevator: Current."

The lift dropped them deeper into mountain. It opened into a non-descript hallway. Their guides took a right, and everyone followed along a winding path to an arched doorway. It reminded Morgan of a giant mouth.

The doors parted automatically, and the company passed through the archway.

They stepped into an octagon-shaped arena, one hundred yards in diameter, with fifty foot-high ceilings. Five tiers of polished redwood benches wrapped around the cavernous room.

The floor/staging area was made from giant slabs of onyx. In the center of the floor was a silver disc, wide enough for a person to be able to sit on it without touching the onyx. There were five identical silver discs spaced evenly around the center disc forming a circle. A ring of amethyst crystals bonded to the onyx floor surrounded each of the silver discs.

High overhead, there were thousands of quartz crystals of all shapes and sizes embedded in the stone roof. The crystals became larger towards the center of the ceiling.

Kyle let out a low whistle of appreciation

"Wow! This is awesome. Who designed this?" asked Draven, who had been unusually quiet during the entire trip.

"Amazing!" Dorcha said. "Who did you get to do the construction? It must have taken team of master craftsmen, metallurgists, and crystallographers to make this work."

"It's better if you don't know," August said.

"Are you kidding?" Victoria asked. "Why are you still being so secretive? The jig is up. We all know where the Bat Cave is."

"Ladies and Gentlemen," Tilly said, "We prefer to call this chamber Current."

CHAPTER NINETEEN
THE GARDEN

Draven asked the question floating through all of their minds, "What is Current for?"

August answered, "It's a harmonic psychic amplifier intended to boost Morgan's UnderLife ability."

"To what end?" Victoria asked.

"Assess, Acknowledge, Assist. Help people exhume and neutralize any self-conflict restraining them from fulfilling the full bloom of their purpose this life," August said.

Victoria snorted in disbelief, "Oh, that's all."

"Let's discuss this over lunch," Tilly said. "Follow me."

Leaving Current, the group traversed another series of passages and staircases to the living quarters.

Secure doors led into a courtyard with a seventy foot high ceiling, and three floors towering above them. Balustrades wrapped around the upper-floor hallways. The design of the space had an open-air quality, despite being buried deep in the earth.

A large dining table stood at the center of the floor, with formal place-settings and tapered candles aflame. Depeche Mode's Dream On was playing over an invisible sound system.

Louise and Trevor, in complete chef regalia, appeared to greet everyone before diving back into the nearby kitchen for finishing touches.

August played bartender. Trevor buzzed in and out of the kitchen holding platters of food. Against the wall near the kitchen, Trevor set up a self-serve banquet. It was filled with mouthwatering Middle Eastern cuisine. The menu consisted of hummus, tabouleh, falafel, swordfish shish kebab, ardy shouki (artichoke casserole), chicken and beef and lamb shawarma, grilled vegetables, pita, and saffron rice. The desserts were baklava and faloodeh (rose-water sorbet).

Everyone dug in. Their appetites were worked up from the exciting and bizarre field trip.

A tall, gray-bearded man wearing a dark suit and glasses arrived at the serving table and helped himself to some food. Captain Tess noted the bearded man's entrance, but he continued eating without saying anything. Everyone else at the table was too busy eating and chatting to notice the bearded man.

Kyle, who ate like a wood chipper, was already on his feet for seconds. "Who's this?" Kyle asked, pointing a thumb in the direction of the newcomer.

The man froze. All sound in the room stopped.

"Darling, please join us and introduce yourself," Louise said.

The man flashed a glare at Louise before approaching.

"I'm Mitchell Cannon," he said, sitting down at the previously-vacant head of the table.

Victoria, sitting at the opposite end, said, "Mitchell! Finally the man behind the curtain! Answer me this, what's the overall goal of this little group here? Please don't tell me you're starting a new religion."

"World peace," Mitchell said.

"How do you plan on achieving that?"

"Effective use of non-violent conflict resolution."

Victoria chuckled, "And then what?"

"Space travel. Let's pull ourselves together, and see who else is out there."

"You seem pretty sure intelligent extraterrestrial life exits," Draven said.

"It would be narrow sighted, arrogant, and ridiculous to believe otherwise," Mitchell snapped.

"Here we go," Trevor mumbled.

"Why haven't they contacted us yet?" Kyle asked, delighted by the subject.

"I don't know," Mitchell shrugged.

"Maybe we're tucked away in a hard to reach place in our wheel galaxy," Dorcha said before taking a big bite of her chicken shawarma pita sandwich.

Tilly jumped in, "My favorite pet hypothesis is we're in someone's backyard. Earth has been categorized as a developing planet dominated by a humanoid race hitting a defining moment of time in its spiritual growth. Before we're allowed to play with others we must learn to control our violent and self-destructive tendencies."

Kyle sat down to devour his second plate of food. "I think they're placing bets to see if we'll survive as a species or if we'll kill ourselves. I wonder what odds they've got on us at Galactic Vegas."

"Oh, Kyle," said Tilly in a mother's tone of sweet coddling.

"Alright, alright, obviously y'all are a bunch of space nerds," Victoria said. "But before we boldly go anywhere, let's talk about how you plan on accomplishing the first task of your agenda. What do Morgan's UnderLife and Current have to do with attaining World Peace?"

Mitchell stared blankly at the party.

"Tell them, dear. All of it," Louise said, smoothly dropping the British dialect for her natural standard-American cadence, "or I will."

Mitchell sighed. "For two decades of the Cold War, Louise and I were black-ops agents. Off the books, very active. We were the people sent in for the tough jobs. Over the years we witnessed, sometimes prevented, and sometimes caused many horrors in the name of patriotism. If we had been caught, our clandestine status would have given the United States government convincing deniability about any connection to us."

Mitchell took a drink of water and continued. "Trevor and Tilly Vihzor's birth names are Jurek and Halina Zarinsk. They were Mother Russia's most innovative young inventors. Each were prodigies in their own right, and once they teamed up, it made them capable of solving problems that whole teams of scientists had scratched their heads about for decades. The Zarinsks knew that their comrades were intent on using them to work on military applications, which they were adamantly opposed to. The Zarinsks had no interest in helping anyone kill anything, and they chose to disappear entirely. They hatched a plan to barter some positive, environmentally-harmonious technology to the United States in exchange for the freedom to live in peace."

Mitchell continued, "Our handler found out about the Zarinsks' plight, and decided to step in. Louise and I were given the task of setting up the Zarinsks' defection. It was the last mission our handler gave to us before he died. Louise and I got Jurek and Halina safely to the States. We created new identities for them, and went through the rigorous process of teaching the newly-anointed Vihzors how to blend into American culture."

"It was so dee-fee-cult to lose my native accent," Trevor said, slipping back into a thick Russian dialect. "Mitchell would get so frustrated with me."

"Stop elongating your vowels! You know how to split an atom, and you can't change your vocal pattern?" Tilly laughed while mimicking Mitchell.

"We were all surprised by the intense friendship that developed during the mission," Mitchell said. "After our handler died without preparing a successor, we were in a unique position to get out of the game while still being able to keep access, contacts, assets, and our lives. Let's face it, not many spies survive the game long enough to see old age, and we had August to think of. August was only four years old. How many more missions until we made a mistake or someone got lucky? The thought of leaving her alone in the world was terrifying."

It shocked August to hear her father speak this way. Never had she heard him be so candid about his feelings or his recollection of the past.

Mitchell continued, "The main reason why we were even still alive was Louise's oracular ability. After I went against her visions a few times and met with disaster, I learned to heed all of Louise's advice. Missions tend to go much smoother when you have psychic intel."

Louise smiled at Mitchell, touched his hand, and spoke. "I had recurring nightmares of the suffering our actions caused. We were instruments, puppets for a king-of-the-heap game in tribal politics. Our talents were doing more harm than good. The more experiences we went through, the less I could deny taking responsibility for my actions, orders or no. On the other hand, I entertained no delusions. If we tried to leave, agents would hunt us relentlessly around the world until we were dead. I didn't want a life on the run." Louise said.

Trevor spoke up, this time in full Leo majesty, and a perfect Californian upper class dialect, "Instead, the four of us decided to disappear from the political/espionage/warfare landscape together, and work on a non-violent revolution for all of humanity."

While listening to Louise and Trevor, Victoria's gaze fixated on Mitchell. Her eyes narrowed, penetrating. Then her lips curled into a smile. Victoria winked at Mitchell while scratching her chin.

Mitchell leaned back, impressed. Victoria knew he had faked the beard, despite his skillful craftsmanship. August had told him Victoria was exceptionally perceptive. Mitchell chided himself for underestimating his daughter's assessment.

"How did you manage to fall off of the grid?" Draven asked.

"Keep in mind it was 1973," Mitchell said. "Global surveillance and tracking have evolved exponentially since that time period. Being black ops, paper trails were practically non-existent, and we made sure to destroy any lingering documents. I'm glad our handler was too paranoid and proud to groom a successor in a timely fashion. His death created the perfect window for our escape."

"How does Morgan figure into this?" Victoria asked.

Inwardly Morgan beamed. Having Victoria Shine acting protective, even if only out of devil's advocate curiosity, felt like a giddy aphrodisiac.

Louise answered, "A vision haunted me after we went to ground with the Vihzors of a redheaded woman sitting in a crystalline cavern surrounded by beings of light. I knew we had to make sure this happened. It was the most important mission of our lives. At the time I didn't have a clue how it would manifest."

"I think you're on to something," Tilly said.

Louise laughed. "Yeah, well, there was a time not too long ago when all of you thought I'd finally cracked," she gave pointed looks to her husband and the Vihzors. Then Louise explained to the group, "It took seventeen years to find Morgan. When we did, there could be no mistake she was the one we were looking for. I used every possible divination method possible during my quest. Crystal balls, tea leaves, chicken bones, augury, you name it, I've probably given it a whirl. Many times I wanted to let it go, move on. The meditative beings of light image had burned itself on my psyche. Neglect made it ache like a fresh tattoo. So I continued onward. I'd become fond of using newspaper stichomancy as guidance. It's how we found this mountain. I saw a picture of it in an endangered species article, and knew I had to have it."

"Louise has a habit of getting what she wants," Mitchell said before taking the lead. "Meanwhile, the Vihzors continued exercising their talent for prolific creation, in children and technology. At first we couldn't risk much contact with each other. We didn't know if we'd been successful in removing ourselves for quite a while. Our brethren have a knack for being patient hunters."

"We must have done something right. No one has come after us," Trevor said.

"That you know of," Mitchell retorted.

"What?"

"There were a few loose ends to tie up here and there," Mitchell said.

Louise said, "Once we confirmed the redhead was real, yet still a child, and severely wounded from the violent loss of her mother, our focus shifted. Insulation and support for Morgan became vitally important. Let her grow up as normally as she could with UnderLife beckoning at any moment. Meanwhile, we worked on finding, designing, and creating a setting where Morgan could use her gift most effectively. Turns out we needed another fifteen more trips around the sun to make Current a reality."

"How can you be so sure Current will function the way you want it to?" Draven asked.

"Faith," Louise said.

"What if it doesn't work?"

Mitchell answered, "Then we've built an astronomically expensive ashram."

* * *

Once lunch was finished, the entire group returned to Current.

After being quiet throughout the meal, Morgan finally spoke. "It's beautiful. You've obviously invested a massive amount of time and money to create this. That's quite a risk, not to mention a ton of pressure to put on my elusive UnderLife ability."

"Don't worry, Morgan," Tilly said. "None of this was done lightly. You've been well prepared for the challenges which lay ahead."

"Unfortunately, we have hit a bit of a snag," Trevor said.

"Pray tell," Victoria said.

"Current is not finished yet."

"What's needed to complete it?" Draven asked.

Trevor said, "My readings indicate Current has power, yet its flow is muffled by a remaining design flaw we can't quite put our fingers on."

Draven balked, "Readings, from what?"

"We've rigged this entire chamber with advanced sensor modules. They help us to monitor Current, the people, atmosphere, hell, we've even got a seismograph here. There must be some kind of physical evidence of Morgan's UnderLife ability, especially the remote transport of another person's consciousness. We haven't had the opportunity to study her properly during transition."

"We're missing someone," Louise announced suddenly.

"How do you know?" Morgan asked.

"How do you know how to access the UnderLife?"

"Good point. How do we find them?" Morgan asked and realized the folly of her question. "Oh, right."

"Our unknown future ally knows how to complete Current?" Dorcha clarified. "You want us to go into UnderLife to find the final team member?"

"When did I join a team?" Victoria asked.

Dorcha blushed.

Kyle said, "The last time we tried to go in as a group, Captain Tess and I were the only ones who transitioned with Morgan, and we got dropped inside Captain Tess's homicidal bunny nightmare."

Mitchell said, "Current's primary purpose is to magnify her ability. Even unfinished, our hope is that Morgan will be capable of transporting all of you in at once. Perhaps together, if the UnderLife circumstances allow, you will find the remaining," he glanced at Victoria, "associate."

"As you may have guessed," Louise said, "we've brought you all here to ask if you'll accompany Morgan on her next mission."

"Of course!"

"Hell yeah, can't wait!"

"Yes, Sir!"

Dorcha, Kyle, and Captain Tess confirmed, their eager voices overlapping.

Draven looked to his sister for direction.

Victoria smiled, and said to Draven, "Well now, it'd be rude to say no. We've come all this way. Can't let them have all the fun."

"Excellent. It's settled, then," Louise said.

"Yes," Tilly surveyed the group, "We have muscle, youth, charm, a cartographer, a guide, and desire. What a fine group of adventurers."

"Do whatever you need to prepare," Louise said. "The meditative UnderLife entrance attempt shall begin in an hour."

Dorcha and Captain Tess went over to the redwood benches to conduct divinations for the impending UnderLife mission.

Kyle slipped away to explore the mountain compound.

Trevor turned to Tilly.

"I was thinking…"

"We need to…"

"Exactly…"

"Let's go…"

Trevor and Tilly exited Current.

"Where are they going?" Draven asked.

"The Think Tank, to fondle their instruments," Louise said.

Victoria and Mitchell hung back as everyone else went over to observe Dorcha and Captain Tess's readings.

"You'd make a good spook," Mitchell complimented Victoria.

"Rather play one on camera. I'd never want to live with such a high level of paranoia. Rabid fan bases are dangerous enough, and they like me."

Over by the benches, Dorcha huddled with Captain Tess before offering their collective insight and advice.

"First we cast general readings on the mission. Then we did individual analysis on everyone, which we'll give each of you privately."

Kyle returned to Current while Dorcha was speaking, and stood next to Mitchell Cannon.

"Could this place double as a fallout shelter?" Kyle asked Mitchell.

"It's a defensible position. We are generally safe here," Mitchell said.

"Should we wait for the Trevor and Tilly before you give us the metaphysical briefing?" Morgan asked.

"We're here," Trevor's voice echoed over hidden speakers, "Proceed, Dorcha."

"Creepy," Kyle muttered.

Dorcha smiled, "Very well. The Tarot has confirmed what we already know. Current is unfinished, and the solution is in UnderLife. For this mission we're searching for someone nurturing and strong, most likely a woman, or a man incredibly in tune with his feminine side. The best way to find this person will be to integrate the fires of head and heart, and not to be separated by their contradictions. I'm confused, though. There are cards which indicate a cosmic warning we need to heed. Somehow gathering together loving, dreamy energy of unity is a bad thing. I don't know how this applies to us, but I'm sure we'll find out. The adventure's key is to not be fooled by the surface of emotional turbulence."

"What's that supposed to mean?" Victoria asked.

Dorcha shrugged, "I wish I could be more specific. Hopefully the individual readings will provide further illumination. Captain Tess, what do you think?"

"The warning hexagrams I cast were Sixty-Four into Thirty-Eight, or Before Completion going into Misunderstanding. A misinterpretation of the UnderLife puzzle could very well be our undoing. In conjunction with Dorcha's Tarot analysis, I'd say there's a gilded trap waiting for us."

"Your favorite," Kyle said.

Captain Tess continued, "The I Ching focal point for the mission is Forty-Nine into Forty-Three: Revolution into Breakthrough. This is a pivotal endeavor for us."

"Indeed," Dorcha said. "Everyone else, please relax as best you can to prepare. Victoria, we'll start with you for the private readings."

One by one they each spoke with Dorcha and Captain Tess. When it was Morgan's turn, Dorcha didn't pull any punches.

"This is going to be a difficult journey for you, to say the least. You will be sorely tempted to try to intervene on your companions' behalf, and keep them out of harm's way. Generally your chivalrous impulse is fantastic. In this case you must focus solely on the mission. Find the person who has the missing piece to Current. Modest conduct, inner independence, listening to the gentle promptings of your intuition, and your vast UnderLife experience will all be required if we're going to accomplish our task. Do your best not to worry about the rest of us, we're a resilient bunch."

The hour galloped by, and soon they were gathered in the center of Current.

"Morgan, please take your place at the center platform," Louise said. "Victoria, Kyle, Dorcha, Captain Tess, and Draven please choose which silver disk you want to use, and settle in.

"Any suggestion about how I'm supposed to guide us to whom and what we seek?" Morgan asked.

"Keep an open mind," Louise said. "Anything is possible."

Morgan's eyes flitted over Victoria's curvaceous body. The impossible was standing mere feet away.

"You've got that right. Let's give this a whirl, see if and where it takes us."

"Here we go again," Dorcha whispered to Kyle as they approached their respective silver platforms.

Kyle sat down. "I feel like we're getting on a roller coaster."

"Or jumping out of a plane," Captain Tess said.

Draven's nerves frothed over. "Wait. What are we doing? Where are we going? I don't know if I want to do this."

"Calm down, Draven," Victoria commanded with more confidence than she felt. "Be charming."

Morgan couldn't help chuckling.

Louise brought out a wooded box three feet long, a foot tall and deep. Louise opened it, pulling out a big pale-yellowish-grey cylinder. "Morgan created this giant hand-made candle out of melted down wax plates from the chakra candles used during our many meditations. This journey is the final step of Morgan's chakra balancing. We are at the root, or Muladhara in Sanskrit. Located at the base of the spine, beneath the sacrum, this chakra is literally the seat of our power. Its stone is onyx, a powerful protection stone which absorbs and transforms negative energy. This is same material we used for the flooring of Current, to aid in everyone's grounding, and if needed, healing. Part of Morgan's training has been to open up, purify, and protect her energy centers. I wanted to make sure there was no past life karma holding Morgan back, and give her all of the support possible for UnderLife travels."

Louise placed the candle in front of Morgan and lit the wick. It flickered to life and burned strong. The three Cannons retreated to the threshold of the main door.

"Mitchell, Trevor, Tilly and I shall be monitoring from the Think Tank. I will guide you over the speakers into a meditative state. August will be on the other side of the main door watching the digital video feed just in case anything goes awry. Given the timelessness of successful UnderLife adventures, from our perspective this shouldn't take long at all."

Louise stood at the edge of the main door to Current and popped open a control panel hidden in the rock wall. "Here's a little something that our geniuses came up with for your visualization. Morgan, glance at what we've created, then keep your attention on the candle, even after shutting your eyes. It will light your path. Trevor, Tilly, initiate the hologram."

"Affirmative," Trevor replied.

The three Cannons left Current. The main doors sealed behind them. The lighting dimmed in the room until they were plunged into darkness.

The oval room of many doors flickered to life directly above Morgan's head. The whole group gasped. Morgan looked up to marvel at a perfect rendering of the UnderLife Ready Room she saw in her dream.

"Everyone ready?" Louise asked over Current's speaker system. Gentle meditative music filled the room. They heard gentle rain, birds chirping, the trickle of a stream, and periodic thunder. It sounded like they were in a rainforest.

"I want you all to breathe deeply," Louise continued in a soothing, hypnotic voice. "In... and out. Listen to the music. Close your eyes. Let everything go. All thoughts float by. Breathe. Picture the oval room with many doors. Concentrate. Breathe. Inhale... and exhale."

* * *

Victoria, Captain Tess, Dorcha, Kyle, and Draven's eyes snapped open. They discovered that they were sitting on comfortable couches instead of silver disks. Morgan was in the lotus position on top of a circular coffee table in the midst of her companions.

"Morgan! It worked!" Dorcha said.

"That's a relief," Morgan said, peering around to make sure everyone was accounted for. "After all that build up it would have been embarrassing if we remained in Waking Life."

"Now this is way more interesting than the endless forest we visited before," Victoria said, jumping up to explore their location.

It looked just like Morgan's vision and the Vihzor's subsequent hologram creation. The room was shaped like an elongated oval, with fifteen-foot-high ceilings, sunken circular couches in the middle, and numerous doors on the walls around them. From a bird's eye view, the place resembled a giant partially-closed eye.

No two portals were the same. An ancient oaken door stood next to modern metal doors with a barely visible seam in the center, alongside a rusted submarine hatch. Everyone spread out, searching for some sort of clue on how to proceed. No one dared touch anything.

"This place feels a bit claustrophobic to me," Victoria said.

"But there are so many exits," Draven said.

"Where do they all lead?" Kyle asked.

"And which one do we choose?" Dorcha asked.

A slight movement caught Captain Tess's eye. He turned. In front of Captain Tess there was a stone block set in an adobe frame. The motion had come from a small green sprout growing out of the doorjamb.

"Morgan," Captain Tess said, and the team gathered.

In the handful of seconds it took for them to reach the portal, more plant life sprung from around the door. Before their very eyes vines filled the frame, snaking around until the adobe itself was a mass of underbrush.

"I think we found our gateway," said an astonished Morgan. The UnderLife never failed to surprise her, despite a lifetime of adventures.

"How do we know this is the way to go?" Draven asked. "Didn't we get a warning about a pretty trap somewhere around here?"

"Let's see if we really have any options," Kyle said. He tried every other door in the room. None of them would budge.

Before anyone could stop her, Morgan stepped forward and pushed on the stone. It slid back easily. When the seal broke on the door, a musty earthy smell wafted over the group, and a cloud of gnats surrounded everyone.

Morgan couldn't help but have a spastic "Gross! Bugs!" response. She shuddered, hands frantically pawing at herself and the space around her to dissipate the minor swarm.

"Eww, unclean, unclean, this person better not have a close connection to Indiana Jones and the Temple of Doom. I definitely do not want to enter a dark room filled with creepy many-legged wildlife," Morgan said.

"Don't jinx us, pussy, just get in there," Victoria said.

"Shiny, always the gentle coach," Kyle said.

"Morgan, would you like me to enter first?" Captain Tess asked.

"No, I can do it. I'm not afraid," Morgan said, not sure if she was lying or not.

The vines continued to grow from the lintel of the door frame, and hung down like a beaded curtain.

Morgan shoved the stone barrier, and disappeared inside the foliage-obscured darkness.

Kyle followed without hesitation. Victoria sighed and marched in after them, then Draven, Dorcha, and finally Captain Tess brought up the rear guard.

* * *

Everyone was transported to an expansive clearing at night. The moon and countless stars twinkled overhead.

Cricket, cicada, and frog song were heard all around.

Their eyes adjusted to the swollen moon's glow.

Kyle noticed poured chalk lines on the raw earth. Kyle's head swiveled left, then right in confirmation.

"Hey guys, I think we're on an old football field," Kyle said, motioning towards the towering field goal posts fifty yards away from them on either side. Kyle pointed to a few sets of bleachers a hundred feet behind them.

"Why isn't there any grass?" Draven asked. Draven secretly loved professional football. Buff men in tights mauling one another, working together to get an imitation pigskin article into some else's back field. A fabulous affair, all the sweating, grunting, groping, and running around playing hard-to-get. Draven couldn't get enough of it. His only criticism about living in Los Angeles was that the city hadn't figured out how to support and keep a NFL team yet. Good thing San Francisco, Oakland,

and San Diego were only a short plane ride away.

The first rays of sunrise broke across the sky.

"What happened to the slow, dramatic, pre-dawn light? We just went from darkness to morning," Victoria said.

Blades of bright green grass spontaneously shot up from the earth around their feet. The field began to expand at an accelerated pace radiating away from them.

They stood still in shock, dumbfounded by seeing Mother Nature operating in fast forward.

"Don't forget about the pretty trap," Kyle said, echoing everyone else's anxieties.

"This is so beautiful," Dorcha said.

"And creepy..." Draven retreated to the bleachers as he spoke. "Is anyone else afraid of the insta-lawn?"

Everyone followed Draven to the bleachers.

Looking around, the light of the sun revealed foothills to the North, a stream flowing from the hills into the forest to the West, to the distant East a mountain range, and to the South there was flat farmland.

The vegetative surge soon covered any exposed earth with green.

"This place is as fertile as a Petri dish," Captain Tess said.

They sat on the bleachers for a while, expecting something sensational to happen. Yet after the initial glorious sunrise and Chia-Pet-on-mutant-hormones grass explosion, things seemed to settle into a normal day outside.

"Now what?" Kyle asked.

"I'm not sure," Morgan said. "I've never seen anything like this before. Obviously this is the gilded trap, but negotiating it is the only way we'll find who we're looking for. How do we go about this? What dangers really lurk here? How do we defend ourselves against them? Any suggestions?"

Victoria leaned over and stroked the blades of grass next to her to see what would happen. Nothing happened. Then she put her feet on the grass. Still no reaction.

"I think it's safe to step on the ground," Victoria said. Everyone watched her, but no one was foolish or daring enough to impede Victoria's curiosity.

Slowly Kyle, Taylor, and finally Draven also tested out the safety of stepping on the ground. Morgan and Dorcha stayed put. Morgan felt like she should be leading the charge to check out the surrounding landscape, but an indefinite sense of unease gave her pause.

Dorcha shared Morgan's trepidation. They sat together, trying to wrap theirs brains around how this environment was supposed to lead them to the mystery someone, and how to use it without springing the terrible trap.

After walking around a bit, Victoria sprawled out on the now lush field. It amused her to see Captain Tess was surveying the area methodically, and how Kyle was following the soldier around like a playful puppy.

Morgan decided to get up and join Victoria on the ground. Draven lay down with them. Dorcha stayed in the bleachers.

Victoria hummed to herself. A green stalk rose from the earth next to her. Draven and Morgan gasped. Victoria sang softly to the new born plant, "You are my sunshine, my only sunshine…"

The plant stalk grew heavy on the end as a bulb developed, and by the time Victoria stopped singing it unfolded into a brilliantly pink and purple vanilla orchid.

Thrilled, she continued, "You make me happy, when skies are gray. You'll never know dear, how much I love you. So please don't take my sunshine away."

A ring of identical flowers grew around the seated musician, blooming just as swiftly. Victoria laughed, gesturing her hands like she had planned the floral spectacle.

"Maybe we're supposed to transform this place," Victoria said, "Create our own gateway we're looking for with Nature."

Morgan knew she possessed zero defense against any cheerful proposition made by Victoria. If Victoria had said, "Let's burn it all" in a bubbly way, Morgan would have gone looking for sticks to rub together.

"C'mere Draven, I've got an idea," Victoria said while getting up to approach a towering goal post.

Positioning their bodies with the post between them, Victoria held out her hands for Draven to hold. He complied, completing the circle around the metal pole.

Victoria smiled at Draven, and inclined her head back, indicating for him to follow her lead. Victoria hummed "Ring around the Rosie", while skipping around the metal shaft like it was a maypole of Germanic paganism.

First one vine appeared from the ground. Then several others followed, defying gravity to crawl up the pole. Draven and Victoria continued to dance, coaxing the growth of the vines until the goal posts were completely covered.

Victoria and Draven dropped back, gasping with exertion and elation, to admire their handiwork.

Meanwhile, Dorcha had left her perch on the bleachers to get a closer look at the new tree. Everyone else had also gathered around, and began to clap in amazement.

This was only the beginning of the goal post's transformation. Once kick-started, the process continued. On their own volition, the vines hardened, shriveled, and turned brown. Soon it resembled retiform bark more than supple greenery. Branches sprouted forth from the lanky structure. By the time leaves were unfolding, the main trunk was so thick that a robust tree was standing before them instead of a large metal game marker.

During the tree metamorphosis, Captain Tess approached Dorcha. Captain Tess observed Dorcha watching Kyle watching Morgan watching Victoria.

Captain Tess casually picked a loose hair off of Dorcha's shoulder. She was oblivious to his presence. Thirty seconds later Dorcha turned abruptly, startled by how close Captain Tess was standing next to her. Captain Tess smiled and stepped back to give her more breathing room.

Dorcha blushed, realizing that Captain Tess was flirting with her.

"You guys have to try this!" Victoria said, practically glowing with joy.

"Yeah, I feel fantastic!" Draven said, beaming like a kid who just learned how to a bike without training wheels. "Victoria's right. This place wants us to play with it. Grow our own gateway to find what we seek."

"Show me," Kyle said, taking Victoria and Draven by the hands, and crossing over to the other goal post.

The three of them danced, singing childhood ditties, around the second goal post. It responded even more eagerly than the first. Soon Victoria, Draven, and Kyle were giggling at the foot of a mighty Sweet Chestnut.

Kyle jumped up and grabbed Dorcha. He did a dance pantomiming the earth taking over the bleachers like it did to the goal posts. Chunks of sod burst from the ground and splattered themselves against the metal framework.

Dorcha grinned. She realized that Kyle was copying elemental manipulation move from Avatar: The Last Airbender.

"C'mon, Capricorn, do some earthbending with me. It's your element, after all," Kyle ordered playfully. Dorcha wasn't about to refuse him.

Soon where the bleachers had once stood was a grassy knoll.

"Bravo!" Victoria applauded. She was immersed in creating a simple hedge maze of bushes bearing blue roses.

"Oh c'mon, Captain Tess, live a little," Victoria beckoned for him to help with her fanciful project. "It's Revolution into Breakthrough! Go with it, man."

Captain Tess mimicked Victoria's gathering hand movements over the soil. When the earth responded with immediate shoots, Taylor belly-laughed. It was exhilarating! Life lit up every molecule in his body.

It started raining, causing everything around them to grow even more. Morgan's fears dissolved with the rain. This place felt wonderful, energetic, and alive.

Captain Tess exploded into a sprint straight towards the mammoth tree trunk of the first goal post. He used it as leverage to do a spectacular back flip. Everyone cheered, clapping at his exhibition of agile strength.

Captain Tess felt like a super hero with volcanic energy coursing through his limbs.

Then Victoria saw herself reflected in the calm water of a nearby puddle, and all hell broke loose. She saw that she was getting visibly old and grey. Victoria's vanity flared. She wanted to fight the combustible creative process ignited by the garden, but it was too late. Victoria's skin started to itch like she had chicken pox, was covered in scabies, and was being attacked by a swarm of starving mosquitoes.

Victoria tried to resist scratching her arm, but it was impossible, "What the fuck is this? Why am I itching everywhere?"

She started scratching, initiating the maddening itch-scratch-itch cycle. Soon the chaotic irritation got so intense that Victoria was tempted to peel off her own skin if it would offer some relief.

Everyone gaped as Victoria aged before their very eyes.

"NO!" Victoria screamed. Horrified by the expressions on their faces, she looked down at her hands. Wrinkles were growing, liver spots were blooming, her hands and arms were shriveling, the flesh becoming loose on the brittle bone. The energy, so exhilarating moments ago, seemed to be eating away at her from the inside out. Victoria began to howl, sounding like a deeply-wounded animal. She dropped to her knees, curling into the fetal position, sobbing.

The group took two steps forward to help Victoria until they realized that they were ripening just as rapidly as she was. Draven, Kyle, and Captain Tess found themselves unable to halt their bodies' malignant aging.

Dorcha and Morgan were the last to be hit with the nasty backlash of energy from the deadly garden. Morgan reasoned that her and Dorcha's minimal engagement with the growth explosion had delayed the deadly onset.

"Whomever we're looking for, their unconscious natural defense system is in optimal condition," Captain Tess said before succumbing to the Garden's voracious energy.

The rush of growth made Morgan's skin crawl and burn. Now she knew what a molting snake felt like during its periodic shedding. That was the key! Whereas everyone else was fighting the accelerated growth until it consumed them, Morgan knew that wasn't how a proper revolution should commence. It was like winning an argument by attempting to kill the opposition, or wiping out a community of innocents in the name of freedom.

Morgan sat down in meditation and closed her eyes.

"Let the energy pass through. Stable. I am floating. No matter what happens my friends are safe. Detach. Focus on the mission. You are here to find a new friend. Breathe. Relax. Flow," Morgan chanted, doing her best to ignore the extreme discomfort.

It took considerable effort to let the seething environment breathe through her rather than envelop her, as it had done to her companions. She knew that if she gave in, her consciousness would be ejected from UnderLife realm, and they would be no closer to finding the last team member.

Nearby, Dorcha was stretched out on the knoll. She was having a similar experience as Morgan. Dorcha the Capricorn tapped directly into her astrological make-up to harmonize herself with the environment, "I am Earth. Life eternal, timeless, this garden and I are in harmony. My limbs are roots. I gain sustenance here. Symbiotic, there is no need for alarm or aggressive measures, peace."

Morgan kept working to force a detachment from the wild nature of the psyche fueling this UnderLife realm. After umpteen amounts of chanting, Morgan felt like the wild energy had died down to a controllable roar, and she peeked out from behind her eyelids.

"Dorcha?" Morgan asked, surprised, delighted, and concerned to see her friend lying on the ground intact, but possibly unconscious.

"Morgan?" Dorcha immediately perked up. "Where is everyone else?"

"They didn't make it. I think the garden, umm, ate them."

"Yikes. I don't know whether to be happy or sad I made it through that."

"Well, I'm happy you're here."

"What do we do now?" Dorcha asked, standing up.

The vegetation had reached such heights that they could not see beyond the former football field.

Morgan didn't know if they were in the unknown ally's Inner Kingdom. This could be a gateway place, or a testing ground on the way to wherever they needed to go to gather the information necessary to find Person X in Waking Life.

Morgan led Dorcha into the vast and virile vegetation. It didn't take long for them to find a familiar-looking hatch on the ground.

"Whoever this is, it looks like they are a fan of Lost," Morgan said.

"At least we know they've got good taste in television."

"So many gorgeous and sexy people on a mysterious island, what's not to love?" Morgan smiled at Dorcha, who shook her head at Morgan with bewilderment.

"Living the mystery is infinitely more terrifying. Do we really have to go down there?" Dorcha asked.

"Yes."

"How can you be so sure?" Dorcha argued.

"It's obvious this is the way to go. UnderLife tends to have clear gateways," Morgan said.

"Alright, you're the boss. Let's just hope this leads to a vast pile of rose petals and not something yucky."

They spun the wheel door handle, and opened the hatch. A "CHSsshh," sound slithered out as the air pressure from the two environments equalized. One whiff from the air inside the hatch made them both gag.

"No such luck, it's definitely a sewer system." Morgan said, "Oh this is going to be ugly."

"Like watching our team decomposing in front of our eyes wasn't horrific enough. Whoever this person is that we're looking for, they've sure got sickly creative psychic security layers."

Morgan covered her mouth with her shirt sleeve, and looked in the hole. All she could see was a dull metal ladder going into halitosis-infected darkness. Morgan stepped away from the entrance and stretched out her muscles while taking deep, steadying breaths. Dorcha followed suit, but she couldn't handle how calm Morgan was being about this.

"Why do we always have to wade into something scary or gross?" Dorcha asked.

"Life is messy."

"There has to be a neat-freak UnderLife out there somewhere." Dorcha peered down the passage. "I wonder if I can be grossed out to death. Why do people have to have such impeccable imaginations for unpleasant things?"

"Whatever you do, whatever happens to me, you have to keep moving, Dorcha. This is a gateway, a test, albeit an extremely revolting one," Morgan said.

"Why aren't there any pampering tests involving manicures, massages, and playing with kittens in fields of lavender?"

"Yeah, tell me about it. That would be a fantastic change of pace. Now, are you ready?"

"No, but let's go anyway."

After wading through disgusting water for an unknown length of time, they hit a crossroads in the tunnel.

"Sonofabitch!" Dorcha cursed.

Morgan investigated and found an arrow drawn in blood pointing downwards over the left archway.

"What if the arrow is a trap?" Dorcha asked in a voice muffled by her shirtsleeve makeshift air filter.

"Keep moving." Morgan said.

"Morgan… eww… so barfy…" Dorcha whined.

Morgan did not respond, and continued to push through the shitty brine. They penetrated deeper into the sewer. The spongy ground underneath their feet was squishy and slippery.

Dorcha struggled desperately to maintain control. She kept telling herself this was UnderLife, and therefore a subconscious illusion, a trick of the senses. She had to persevere. However, Dorcha couldn't stop her eyes from fixating on the raw sewage caked on the walls and on their legs.

Dorcha couldn't take it anymore. She stopped to regain her composure. The palpable stench made her unbearably nauseous. Dorcha was afraid if she succumbed to retching, she'd never be able to stop.

Morgan would have done something to help Dorcha, but she was having a difficult enough time herself staying conscious and going forward. Morgan knew if she halted, that'd be it for her.

Bile rose in Dorcha's throat, not throwing up became impossible.

* * *

Morgan had cut off all breathing through her nose the moment they stepped into the gigantic underground pipes. Her hand was clasped over her face and she took shallow, short breaths. Morgan wasn't sure if Dorcha was still behind her, but couldn't risk looking back. Morgan's sense of urgency was tempered by the extreme desire to avoid being fully submerged in the rotting liquid. In her haste to get out of there Morgan internally begged for no slips into the oil of aromatic torture.

After another hundred feet, the passage got narrower, until there was barely an inch of space between Morgan's shoulders and the walls.

At this point Morgan was almost sure that Dorcha was no longer following behind. Morgan prayed for accuracy about her earlier decision at the crossroads, because she didn't think she could trace her steps back.

Morgan slogged on. She felt a mixture of relief and worry as the passage came to a dead end. It only took a few more paces to close the distance. Then Morgan discovered the most beautiful rusty old ladder she had ever seen.

* * *

Morgan struggled to break through the gate above her head. Scraping metal-on-metal sounds rang out. Morgan heard a loud screech as the stuck barrier freed itself. Morgan opened the grate. She popped her head out and heaved herself into the room. Morgan looked around. She appeared to be in the basement of a large house.

Before she had even made it all the way through the hole and into the basement, vomit started to spew from Morgan's lips. She marveled at how horrific the journey had been. After so many years spent between worlds, Morgan's senses no longer made much distinction between UnderLife and Waking Life. Still, she tried to console herself that this was an illusion, a rotting, disgusting, incredibly convincing illusion.

It took Morgan some time to stop dry-heaving, long after the contents of her stomach had been ejected onto the floor. She wanted to discard her clothing, but decided it would be better to face whatever came next smelly rather than naked.

The room looked like a typical basement, filled with partially-organized clutter and unused furniture. Her attention focused on a cracked mirror hanging on the wall. It was etched with a big XI over the profile of a mustached man with a helmet. Morgan caught site of her haggard and filthy reflection, gasped, and looked away.

There were boxes, an old bike, a sports pennant hanging on the wall, a bench, a worn couch, a baseball bat, an unfolded lawn chair, a big wardrobe half covered with a rug, and dozens of other random items. She saw snow packed on the high-placed windows of the basement. Morgan heard and felt the furnace turn on.

The floorboards creaked above her. Someone was home.

A man came down the steps. He carried two ice-cold bottles of Samuel Adams Boston Lager. When he saw Morgan, he put the bottles down on a chest-sized freezer at the bottom of steps.

Did he know I was here? Is that second bottle for me? Morgan thought to herself. A beer sounded fantastic after the sewer rat experience Morgan had endured.

"Where did you come from?" the man asked.

"I… I'm not sure," Morgan said.

"Oh look, you're shivering." He couldn't help but notice the reeking sewer smell emanating from her. "…and are all dirty! You should get out of those wet clothes."

He went to a pile of boxes and started rummaging through them. "I know I have a box of old sweats around here somewhere."

"Thanks, that's very kind of you. I'm so glad to be out of the stinking mess down there."

Is this the person we're looking for? Morgan thought. He seems nurturing enough.

"Let me help you get those off."

Before Morgan could respond, he put his hand on the bottom of her shirt and started pulling it up.

"No thanks, I can do it myself." Morgan pushed his hands away.

He ogled Morgan's breasts. Her nipples were at attention underneath the wet top. His stare felt more disgusting than the clothes she was wearing. Morgan stopped disrobing, which made the man agitated.

"Here," he said, and reached for her clothes again.

"Hey!" Morgan shoved him back a few steps.

He held up his hands up in supplication, "Don't be frightened, I'm only trying to help."

The man's attack came out of nowhere. He sucker punched Morgan in the gut. It took the wind out of her, but Morgan recovered faster than he anticipated. She blocked the second punch which was headed for her face. Morgan countered with a shot to his liver. Regrettably, there was not enough force behind it to slow him down.

Morgan saw stars when his left hook landed. The force of it spun her whole body ninety degrees. He pounced on her from behind, his arms reaching around to put her neck into a deep choke hold. He flexed his right bicep for emphasis, squeezing the carotid artery in her neck. Morgan knew if she continued to resist he would render her unconscious, and she'd be utterly defenseless. Morgan changed tactics, forcing her body to go limp in his arms.

His deep, scratchy voice breathed into her ear in triumph. "What do we have here? A thief who has come to steal my valuables? You picked the wrong home to invade, missy." His rancid breath stank of cheap vodka and rotting meat. Suddenly the sewer seemed like a fond memory.

Confident he had her at his mercy, the man put his left hand on Morgan's hip and stroked her body upwards, cupping her breast for a moment, gauging her reaction.

Morgan stomped the heel of her right foot on the man's foot as hard as she could, then slammed the back of her head into his nose. He grunted in pain and loosened his grip. Without hesitation, Morgan bent over to get him off balance, clutched the arm around her neck with both of hers, and did a hip throw, flipping him onto the ground.

The man popped up to his feet, barely out of striking distance. He crouched into a boxing stance. She left round-kicked him hard into the meat of his right thigh. He ate the hit and charged her. At about six foot four inches and two hundred and forty pounds, he was much heavier and stronger than Morgan.

The tackle was timed perfectly, catching her off balance from the kick. The man executed a double leg take down, landing on top of her in the mount position. Before Morgan could defend herself and recover her guard, he slammed his right elbow into her head. The sharp bone cut Morgan under the left eye. Morgan's face throbbed and she could feel the swelling instantly. She cried out with surprise and pain. Despite Morgan's recent martial arts training, she was not at all used to really getting hit, and it threw her off her game. Unfortunately for Morgan, the man was no stranger to a bloody brawl.

"Now look at what you made me do," he scolded. "Here I am trying to help a stranger who has broken into my home and you attack me."

Morgan stared back at him in disbelief.

"Wh...?"

He interrupted her, "Please you need to get out of those drenched, disease-infested clothes. You'll catch your death with this cold snap we've been having." Concern was etched on his face.

Did I misread this? Morgan thought. Is this guy cool, did I just surprise him? Wait, the groping fucker punched me first!

Morgan's questions were answered quickly. He hovered over her for a bit too long. When Morgan did not move, he reached out to stroke her hair and cheek.

Morgan found the dark glint in his eye more putrid than ten more miles of the wretched sewer, but it gave her a daunting idea.

Morgan could feel the man flexing above her, ready for her to attack or try to escape. Morgan lifted her hips, pressing them up against the erection she knew he would have. Deranged fucks like this always got off on violent domination of the women they preyed upon. Morgan gyrated against him just long enough to convince him of her budding desire, like the fight had really been sadomasochistic foreplay.

He leaned in to kiss Morgan. She let him. His tongue thrust into her mouth, daring Morgan to resist. As much as she wanted to bite down, she committed herself to giving him a sensual lip lock. Morgan slid her legs up his body and loosely wrapped them around his waist. When the man leaned back and smiled, he saw Morgan's hands going to the waistline of his pants, he didn't stop it.

"The others were never so cooperative. I had to teach them discipline. But you understand the overwhelming strength of my love," he said.

Kneeling, he postured up. A feral expression formed on his lips as she unbuttoned and slowly unzipped his trousers. He leaned down and stroked her cheek again, so relieved to have found a woman who finally comprehended the innocence of his demon, and welcomed it.

Morgan opened her legs, inviting him to fuck her. He put his right hand on her chest and his left on the floor to reposition his body, so he could undress her.

Morgan held his right hand to her chest and shrimped her hips to the left, making her torso perpendicular to his body. She slid her right hand inside the crook of his left knee. The man's arousal turned to alarm when she bucked her hips, threw her right leg over his head, and clenched his neck with the back of her knee. Morgan repositioned both of her hands into a baseball grip on his right arm, effectively locking his exposed limb into an arm bar.

Morgan stretched out, hyper extending his arm, and put the collective force of all her muscles into forcing his elbow to bend the opposite way.

Using his superior strength, the enraged man struggled to keep his arm flexed. He lifted her entire body several feet off of the floor and slammed her back to the ground. Morgan held on for dear life, and even managed to cinch her body tighter onto his.

Morgan knew that if he got free he would beat the shit out of her before brutally raping her. Her legs gripped tighter and she flexed every muscle in her body.

Despite his considerable strength, Morgan held tight to her superior position. Morgan felt the bone in his arm snap and he thrashed with pain. She let go, kicking him off of her. Morgan did a backwards somersault to get some distance between them, and rolled to her feet. He was on his knees, bewildered at what she had done, but clearly not finished.

The man stood and growled, "You stupid bitch, do you think mere broken bone will stop what I am going to do to you?"

Morgan stood in a back stance with the majority of her weight on her right leg, her feet perpendicular to each other. She reached out with her left hand and grabbed him around the waist. With his right arm broken, he couldn't stop her. Morgan chambered her right open hand to her rib cage, palm facing up, fingers flexed and pointing towards the floor. Fluidly, explosively, she engaged her hip and lunged into a deep front stance. Morgan struck his exposed genitals with a right-handed palm strike, using all of her might and momentum. Then she gripped his testicles like a vice, and snapped her hip back. Reversing the motion of her hands, she now pushed off his body with her left arm while pulling with her right. This provided her with the extra leverage she needed to remove his precious jewels from their unholy temple.

Morgan ripped off his balls with a savage scream. She held them back behind and above her head in a gruesome catch-of-the-day pose.

Blood sprayed everywhere.

The man might have been able to handle a broken arm, at least while still in shock. But no man could withstand the violent manual severance of his testicles and even think about continuing to fight.

Morgan threw the flesh in her hand at him in abhorrence. He wailed in agony. Morgan was reminded of when the horses ripped her apart. Out of mercy for her own ears, she retrieved the baseball bat lying against the wall to finish the job. It took only one well-aimed and hard blow to the back of his head.

Screaming, THUNK, then silence. All Morgan heard now was her own labored breathing and the gurgling sound of blood and bodily fluids escaping from their vile and thankfully dead host.

Wood creaked, as something or someone moved.

"Hello? Who's there?" Morgan asked.

Morgan's heart was beating so fast she could hear it pulsing in her ears.

"Hello?" Morgan repeated.

A faint "Help me" floated to her.

Morgan scanned the dimly lit basement. In the corner amidst the ocean of clutter and old furniture there was an old wardrobe. It was half-covered by a heavy rug like it was some kind of birdcage. Morgan hadn't noticed before that it had a heavy chain and padlock on it.

"Are you in the wardrobe? Who are you?" Morgan asked.

"Please get me out of here." The voice was feminine, young, terrified, broken.

"Hold on!"

Morgan lifted the rug off, struggled with the lock for a second, and then got a bright idea. She went back to the mangled corpse of the attempted rapist to check his pockets. Morgan fished out a silver horseshoe-shaped key chain.

She unlocked the wardrobe, opened the doors, and the UnderLife episode ended.

Morgan never saw the teenage girl cowering inside.

CHAPTER TWENTY
INFLUENCE

Morgan found herself back at Current. All of her UnderLife companions were unconscious.

"Morgan," August said. She had entered Current the moment she saw the majority of the group slump, sprawl, or tumble their bodies to the floor. If everyone observing didn't know better, it could have looked as though Morgan executed a sinister telepathic attack, abruptly knocking out the five souls surrounding her.

"Morgan, what happened? Did you find the last teammate?" Louise asked over the loudspeaker.

"I..." Morgan gagged, vomit rising in her throat. The vivid memory of her recent kiss with the rapist flashed through Morgan's mind. Touching her tongue to his, convincing him of feigned desire. "...need to take a Silkwood shower. Sorry, I'll tell you everything in a bit," Morgan said in a rush, retreating to the living quarters.

The rest of the team woke up thirty minutes later. August, Louise, Trevor, and Tilly made sure everyone was comfortable. They had various supplies on hand just in case anyone got sick, needed water, or if there was a serious medical emergency.

Victoria patted her face down, running callous-tipped fingers along the skin of her temples, checking for wrinkles.

"You look beautiful as ever," Kyle said, rubbing the sleep out of his eyes.

Victoria laughed and ruffled Kyle's hair. "Thanks, and don't worry, your darling mug is intact."

"Morgan went to bathe immediately upon returning," Louise said.

"Great idea," Dorcha said. She got up on wobbly legs. "After the garden swallowed everyone else, we were in a gnarly sewer. I guess she made it through, 'cause I sure didn't. Excuse me." Dorcha headed straight for the showers.

"Someone please tell me we won't have to go back to Mother Nature's panic attack," Draven groaned, accepting Captain Tess's help to stand up.

* * *

Dorcha followed the trail of Morgan's clothes. She found Morgan facing a shower stream, her head lowered, and the stall curtain only partially closed. Water splashed Morgan's forehead on its way to dousing the rest of her naked body.

"Hey, you okay, buddy?" Dorcha called out.

Morgan didn't turn, but stuck out her left arm to give Dorcha the thumbs-up.

Dorcha left Morgan alone to recuperate. She chose a shower on the other side of the locker room to wash away the hallucinatory yet lingering sense of filth.

* * *

Morgan emerged from the locker room scrubbed clean. Her revived companions had relocated to the living room. The room was humming with excited discussion about their experiences. Morgan went into the kitchen, got a blue ice pack, and put it under her eye. Her facial expression was grim.

August handed her a joint and a lighter.

"Thank you," Morgan said. She sparked it, inhaled deeply, and passed it to Dorcha.

"Morgan, what's the ice pack for? Did you hit your head in the shower?" Victoria asked.

"Oh, I don't really need it," Morgan said while exhaling a cloud of smoke. "I got nailed in the face a few times during the episode, and the cold compress makes the memories somehow better."

"You're an odd bird, Martel," Victoria said. She leaned forward to snag the joint for a few puffs.

"No doubt about that," Morgan said. She was fascinated to watch Victoria smoke.

"What happened?" Louise asked.

"I almost got raped," Morgan said.

Morgan relayed the basement story to her companions. She finished with, "I can't tell you how glad I am we've trained so hard over the years. Worth every fucking sweaty second. I don't want to imagine what he would have done to me if I hadn't been able to defend myself."

"I'm impressed you pulled off a seduction feint to get the upper hand," August said.

"M-hmm," Victoria agreed.

"And gave that fucker what he deserved," Dorcha said.

"Let's start this from the beginning," August said.

"If you don't mind, I'll spin the tale," Victoria said. "Well done on the Ready Room hologram, that's exactly where we began the adventure." Victoria launched into an animated rendition of their UnderLife mission.

When she got to the part of the story where The Garden's rapid growth energy turned on them, Victoria said, "The power was irresistible. I knew it was killing me. I wanted to stop it, but a teeny-tiny part of me relished the consumption. That's all the permission The Garden needed to take me out."

"I'm confused. Was the scary guy who we were looking for?" Draven asked.

Dorcha shook her head. "I don't think so."

"The girl in the wardrobe," Kyle said.

"Yes," Louise agreed.

Captain Tess said, "We have to save her."

"Yes. We need to assume this situation is occurring right now," Trevor said. Trevor's fingers never slowed their dance across his personally assembled laptop.

"How are we supposed to find her?" Kyle asked. "Too bad the UnderLife episode couldn't have finished with a highlighted address or geographical coordinates."

"Everything needed to solve the mystery is here," Louise said. "We have to figure it out."

"Morgan," Mitchell said, "You didn't see anything while opening the wardrobe doors?"

"No. I only heard her whimpering. The shift occurred at the exact moment I freed her."

"How are you sure it was a little girl?"

"The pitch of her voice was too high to be adult. Definitely a kid, maybe a tween."

"Did the man or the girl have an accent?" Tilly asked.

"I couldn't tell with the girl," replied Morgan, concentrating hard on her memories. "There was a slight Midwestern lilt to the man's words."

"Concentrating on the Midwest first," Tilly typed to her husband from her matching custom laptop "Places with snow on the ground right now."

"Yes, Love," Trevor typed back.

The Vihzors sifted through a few sad abduction and disappearance cases. They found nothing conclusive. They widened their search to the whole United States and rummaged through global news feeds.

"Maybe no one knows she's missing yet," Victoria said.

"Describe the contents of the basement again," Captain Tess said.

Morgan repeated her description of the room. When she mentioned the cracked XI mirror, Draven interrupted.

"Cracked... How?" Draven asked while pacing around the room. "Can you tell what broke it? Did it get dropped or smashed?"

Morgan willed the details to surface in her memory, "Umm..."

"Focus, Morgan," Louise said, "Sit in the lotus position, close your eyes, and breathe."

Morgan slipped into meditation. She began to speak. "There was a circular wound on the mirror where all the fissures emanated from."

"The baseball bat," Captain Tess said.

The light bulb of an idea Draven cultivated lit up, "Did the etching look like a Viking in profile?"

"Yes," Morgan said, relaxing her posture. "How did you know?"

"In January 1977, Bud Grant's Minnesota Vikings lost Super Bowl XI to the Oakland Raiders. It was their fourth Super Bowl loss in eight years. After all, the crazy adventure started at a football field."

Mitchell whistled his approval for Draven's obscure football statistic. The others stared in amazement.

"What?" Draven smirked. "It's a fabulous game. Those men are hot."

Trevor confirmed Draven's pigskin trivia with a quick web search.

"Anyone who gets a mirror etching is one hell of a fan," Draven said.

"And most likely a local," August said. Trevor and Tilly's fingers blurred as their search focused on Minnesota.

"No shit," Victoria said. "Draven, remind me to tell the staff to start manufacturing a line of limited edition Victoria Shine mirror etchings."

Morgan grinned. "Can I pre-order now?"

Kyle patted Draven on the back. "Draven, I didn't realize you were so butch."

Draven laughed, "Does this mean you'll give me private Brazilian Jiu-Jitsu lessons?"

"I think Draven is already quite adept at transitioning into mount," Morgan said.

Kyle blushed.

Dorcha saved Kyle from floundering too long under Draven's devilish charm. "Maybe the nightmare Morgan stumbled into isn't happening now."

"Unconscious perpetual reliving of a horrific event?" Louise said.

"Highly possible," Mitchell said. "People's psyches have a difficult time letting go of extreme trauma."

"Found something!" Tilly announced. She reached in her pocket, pulled out a dark ball, and unfurled a computer cable. Tilly connected her laptop to the large flat screen TV. Electronic copy from a dozen newspaper articles scrolled across the screen. Tilly slowed the scroll and highlighted a particular article.

Headline of Thief River Falls Times - March 7th, 1977:
MIMI ESCAPES! POLICE ARREST KIDNAPPER!

"After twenty-two days of captivity, a brave and battered thirteen-year-old girl stumbles into Thief River Falls Police Station…"

"Mimi Winter! I remember her," August said. "Mom and Dad ratcheted up my martial arts training to an insane degree when that story broke. It was quite a demanding regimen for an eight year old."

"My dear, you knew what you were getting into when your soul chose to incarnate as our child," Louise said matter-of-factly.

Mitchell winked at his daughter. "We would have been hard on you no matter what, my love."

"This is sweet, guys," Kyle said. "But what happened to Mimi?"

Tilly put various photographs of Mimi on the flat screen. There were school pictures, evidence shots of her beaten and bruised body, and sketches of the girl testifying in court."

Trevor spoke, "Both of Mimi's parents were killed by a drunk driver when Mimi was a toddler. She was raised by her grandmother, Phyllis Winter. After Mimi escaped, the evidence she gave to the police led to the arrest of Roland Addanc, a 30-year old single man living in the area. At the time, people suspected that Roland had ties to the Addanc crime family, but it was never proven. Mimi and her grandmother started receiving written death threats right before the trial. The threats lasted for months. After the trial, the Attorney General granted the Winters entry into the witness relocation program."

"High profile case, smart move," Draven said. "Mimi already saved her own life, no thanks to the police. It'd be PR nightmare for the authorities if any more harm came to her."

"And the abducting rapist asshole?" Dorcha asked.

"Roland Addanc stood trial, got life in prison, and was brutally murdered two months into his sentence during a prison fight," Tilly said. "Many convicts feel they have free license to vent their rage on child rapists."

"Or The Family wanted to make sure he kept silent," Kyle said.

A sinister mug shot of Roland Addanc appeared on the screen.

Morgan gasped in revulsion, "That's him!"

The picture of Roland Addanc was replaced by a heartbreaking image of young Mimi Winter on the court steps surrounded by a media mob. Her eyes were set with a firm look of determination. Mimi looked exhausted.

Tilly continued, "Here's some news footage after Roland's

arraignment. He pled 'Not Guilty'. The judge let him out on four hundred thousand dollar bail."

Roland Addanc's leering face reappeared on the jumbo screen. He answered the reporters' questions by stating, "This is all a big misunderstanding. Mimi and I are in love. She's young, I know, and I'm waiting for her. Love conquers all restrictions. We had a minor lover's quarrel. She hurt herself to make me look like a common brute."

"Yikes," Kyle said.

Draven shrugged, "I'm just glad his fellow prisoners had their violent way with him."

Hovering over Trevor's shoulder, Mitchell laughed.

"What?" Louise asked.

"Guess who oversees Mimi's case for the U.S. Marshals office," Mitchell said.

Trevor said, "It says here is name is Supervisory Deputy Marshall Gareth Drake. Why is that funny?"

"You're kidding," Morgan said.

August froze.

Louise smiled and clapped her hands. "Marvelous! What WitSec field office does he work out of?"

There was a flurry of typing as the Vihzors raced to find the information.

"Wouldn't you know it? He's based out of the San Francisco office," Tilly said.

"Of course he is. This is perfect," Louise said.

August masked any visible reaction.

"What's going on? Who is Gareth Drake? I hate being left out," Victoria said.

Morgan filled the group in on what she knew about past events in New Orleans, and the spectacular coincidence decades in the making.

Victoria applauded the drama. "What a prodigious tale! I'm interested to hear how this plays out. Alas, I must take my leave. I've been ignoring important commitments of late which I must attend to. Good luck finding who you need to complete Current. Please let me know what happens."

"We will," Louise said. "Captain Tess, please prep the helicopter to fly our guests back home."

"Ma'am." Taylor left to carry out his orders.

"I'm going to bow out of this next venture," Draven said. "I need some alone time at home with my computer. Someone's got to play scribe here."

Tilly closed her laptop and stood up. "I'll go with you. Your technological defense measures will need to be upgraded."

Trevor nodded, "Don't want this story surfacing until its proper window of release."

"Understood," Draven said.

Victoria turned to Morgan, "Thank you for the thrilling ride. Happy hunting." Victoria enveloped Morgan in an affectionate hug. It meant the world to Morgan.

HugFest broke out all around as they bid farewell.

Victoria, Draven, August, Tilly, Dorcha, Kyle, and Morgan strolled to the cavern landing pad.

Along the way, Dorcha caught Morgan's eye. Dorcha knew Morgan was bummed out that Victoria wanted to withdraw.

Captain Tess refueled the Pave Hawk, and continued with pre-flight checks. He paused in his work to help Victoria, Draven, and Tilly board the aircraft.

Kyle didn't follow them. "I want to stay on and help find Mimi Winter AKA Who Knows?"

"I don't think including intense masculine energy is the wisest course of action," August said.

"Yeah, sorry guys, this is a chick quest," Morgan said.

Dorcha nodded.

Kyle said, "I guess Taylor and I will go... train. Joining your party sounds like so much more fun."

Captain Tess nodded. "I have security concerns about your mission..."

"Aw," Dorcha interrupted. "That's sweet." She squeezed their heavily muscled forearms. "As much as I enjoy your company, I think we'll be fine with Double-Oh-August and Genital Ninja Martel on the mission."

"We'll contact you if anything feels suspicious, Captain Tess," August said.

Captain Tess nodded.

"Please fly the others back to Los Angeles, and hold down the fort. I'll take care of our transportation to San Francisco."

* * *

August drove Dorcha and Morgan to a small private airfield about twenty miles away from the Mountain Compound. There, in a camouflaged hangar sat Mitchell Cannon's Bombardier Challenger 601 business jet. It was the same plane that had taken August away from New Orleans, and she found it fitting that it would be used to visit a man she had thought she would never see again face to face. Leave it to Fate's sense of humor that the three ladies Gareth Drake had met on that sad day were on their way to ask for his help twenty years later.

Despite the many lovers she'd enjoyed in her adult life, August had never forgotten the titillating encounter with the sexy Peace Officer turned Marshal.

From time to time, August had checked to see how Gareth had been doing personally and professionally. At twenty-seven he had married a fellow U.S. Marshal, Camille Harris. Unfortunately, Gareth had watched his wife go through a painful and fatal battle with pancreatic cancer.

When the elephant doors of the hanger opened, Morgan whistled in appreciation.

"Surprise, surprise, you guys have a private jet," Dorcha said.

"Let me guess, you can fly this as well," Morgan said to August.

"Mm-hmm," August winked at Morgan and Dorcha.

In less than an hour they had touched down at San Francisco International Airport, and were cruising north on Highway 101 in a rented black BMW Sports Activity Vehicle. Their destination: the Northern District of California U.S. Marshal's field office.

* * *

Gareth Drake was getting up from his desk to grab another cup of coffee when there was a knock on the door to his office.

"Come in," Gareth said.

August opened the door, and saw a handsome man with two day salt-and-pepper beard stubble. It matched his close-cropped hair. Gareth's whole physical demeanor slouched a bit with exhaustion. August's stomach fluttered as she ogled his athletic body in his tailored suit.

Gareth glanced up, expecting to see anyone but the person who was standing before him. His fatigue vanished instantly. His posture straightened, and a smile rivaling the glory of dawn breaking over the horizon lit up Gareth's face.

Gareth's once prominent southern accent had mellowed out, but a hint of the lilt was still there, "August Cannon, my God. Am I dreaming?"

"No," she said, she entered the room with her companions, and shut the door behind them.

Gareth throat constricted with emotion. He cleared it, willing himself to keep calm.

"And who are these lovely ladies with you?"

"You've met them before. Morgan Martel and Dorcha LeTour."

Gareth took a step back, and leaned on his desk for support. "Well look who got all grown up and more gorgeous since the last time I saw them." He hugged each of the women warmly, and then startled August by wrapping his arms around her for a lengthy embrace.

August eventually pulled away, a little embarrassed for holding on as long as she did. Gareth motioned for the women to make themselves comfortable. Morgan and Dorcha sat down next to each other on a broken-in brown leather couch they could tell sometimes doubled as a place to sleep. August pulled up a chair next to the couch, offering her a view of the door and of Gareth.

Gareth rolled his chair over, forcing himself to sit down even though he felt like doing wind sprints. "What can I do for you?" he asked, having a hard time keeping the giddiness out of his voice.

"We need to find Mimi Winter. It's our understanding you oversee her case."

"How did you…" Gareth cut himself off. He had a lot of questions for August, but asking her about how she knew about his connection to Mimi Winter was the least of them. "I've always been curious about what happened to you. A stone-cold mystery. You're way too interesting to stay off the grid for long, but somehow that's precisely what you did."

August shrugged, "Everyone has a talent."

"I need answers. Especially since access to WitSec details is highly illegal, and I know you're not a Federal Agent. Not only will they fire me if I tell you, I'll probably go to prison. So 'fess up. S'il vous plait, mon bel amour." (If it pleases you, my beautiful love.)

August smiled. Gareth's charm had matured to the edge of irresistibility.

The silence spurred Gareth on. "Darlin' if I give you the information you want, y'all gotta quid pro quo."

"Very well," August said.

Gareth turned to address Morgan and Dorcha, "Why does she have a life-long interest in you two? What do want with Mimi Winter?"

Morgan replied, "I travel to the Collective Unconscious, or UnderLife. I can transport other people there as well. It is our intention to assist people in healing themselves. We believe Mimi Winter can help us to calibrate a device designed to enhance my abilities."

Gareth's eyes narrowed like a shrewd poker player. Then he laughed and waved his hand. "Very funny, Morgan. Now what's the real reason?"

When none of them women joined him in the joke, Gareth stopped smiling. A puzzled expression lingered on his features.

August reached over to Gareth, putting a hand on his knee. "Where is Mimi now?"

Gareth paused. He was enjoying August's touch. August had been one of the most influential people in his life, and he had spent less than two days in her presence. Searching for August was what had gotten him interested in the Marshal Service in the first place. Camille's death had shattered Gareth's world, but he had rebuilt. Helping August would risk destroying everything stable in his life.

It's funny when life presents you with moments which define your loyalties, Gareth thought. He sighed, got out his cell phone, and made a call.

After a few moments Gareth slapped the phone closed and muttered "Typical."

"Did you just try to call Mimi?" Morgan asked.

"She's been Cynthia for many years now. She has a dangerous habit of turning off her cell phone, and letting the voicemail max out. I'll take you to her."

* * *

August drove. Gareth sat shotgun. He made little effort to hide scrutinizing August's every gesture, facial expression, and utterance. He navigated them northbound over the Golden Gate Bridge through thick traffic towards Marin County.

Morgan and Dorcha were quiet. They had never witnessed August around a man she found attractive, and they were fascinated by the subtle drama unfolding in front of them. The thoughtmosphere of the car was thick with telepathic traffic.

Very few actual words passed between Gareth and August other than driving directions. After an awkward half hour marked by stunted bursts of superficial conversation, Morgan and Dorcha assailed Gareth with personal questions. Gareth told them all about entering the Marshal Service, meeting Camille, falling in love, getting married, the discovery of her illness, fighting it, witnessing her passing, and having to find a way to keep on living without her. By the time they reached Sonoma, there was not a dry eye in the vehicle.

They cruised by one gorgeous vineyard estate after another. Morgan was so wrapped up in Gareth's life story that she barely noticed when they left the main highway around Kenwood. They traveled deeper into the foothills of northern California.

After twenty more minutes of twisting side roads, Gareth said, "That's it up ahead." August pulled the car over. They stopped in front of a simple, sturdy wooden gate. A green mailbox stood anchored on top of the gate post. Its red metal flag was up.

Gareth hopped out of the car to open the gate and check the mailbox. After August drove through the gate, Gareth closed it behind them and got back in the car.

An unseen dog barked twice.

A crow "Caah!"-ed while flying by. It circled on air currents above them and then headed deeper into the property.

Rocks crunched beneath the BMW's all-terrain tires as the vehicle rolled onto the long gravel driveway. The party lost sight of the gate when they plunged into a thicket of trees and around a bend. They drove through thriving orange, lime, and lemon groves. The trees infused the area with a bright citrus aroma.

After a mile of winding through the trees, the vegetation thinned. August parked their car next to a beat-up, thirty-plus year old dark green Ford Bronco.

August saw the crow sitting in the leafy side of an oak tree embracing a hundred-year-old house. The tree was encroaching on the corner of the house. Whoever built the house had not taken into account the robust growth of its leafy neighbor over the decades. The house had undergone extensive reconstruction to accommodate the growth of the mighty oak. The branches were very healthy, groomed of any dead leaves. An extensive vegetable garden peeked out from behind the southeast corner of the house. The entire area hummed with peaceful harmony. The air felt different, more humid and ripe, like it was about to rain.

Large white and red rose bushes lined the walkway up to the house.

A woman sat on the porch petting a purring male orange tabby cat. Flanking her were two big dogs, a Golden Retriever and a black Labrador. On a table next to her sat a full pitcher of ice cold lemonade on a tray with half a dozen glasses.

This must be Cynthia, Morgan thought.

Cynthia had a merry, cherubic face and long wavy dark-brown hair with glasses perched on top of her head. She was about five-foot-seven, with a stocky build and deeply tanned skin. Cynthia was dressed in well-worn denim overalls. She looked as though she spent the majority of her days working outside.

When they got closer, the cat got up, stretched, and jumped down from Cynthia's lap.

Cynthia stood up. She looked excited and a little nervous. Her well-disciplined dogs stood in place, panting and alert.

Cynthia was wearing a two-inch-long crystal cluster pendant. The pendant had been bonded with wire which looped around her neck. The minute the three women saw the pendant, they knew they had come to the right place.

"You don't seem startled by or wary of our arrival," Gareth said, reproaching Cynthia.

"My animal familiars would have warned me if there was any danger," Cynthia said.

Dorcha understood. Her cat Primo inspected anyone entering their home, and was very finicky about who he warmed up to.

Gareth asked, "Cynthia Sommers, have you been leaving your phone off and letting the mailbox max out again?"

"Yes sir," she said. "But I always check in on time, and I'd hit the panic button if anything went wrong."

August shot Gareth an annoyed look and said to Cynthia, "Why do I get the feeling you were expecting guests?"

The crow observing them from the house tree gave another "Caah!" Cynthia looked over and smiled at her feathered friend.

"Yesterday during the late afternoon, I was pulling weeds in the garden when I got incredibly dizzy. I felt so strange. Kept thinking of Voldemort... err...," Cynthia swallowed, "Roland Addanc. I went inside the house to meditate. I had just sat down, and suddenly I was in that wardrobe cell the first night he... violated me."

Cynthia looked at Morgan.

"Through the crack in the wood, I saw you! What you did to him. You were magnificent! Thank you!"

Morgan grinned.

Cynthia stepped forward, shook Morgan's hand vigorously, and pulled her into a big hug, "I can't believe you're really here. I mean, I hoped I would get to see you somehow, and... you're an angel!"

Cynthia released Morgan and continued, "My only regret when he died in prison was that I didn't get to see it myself. I was glad that the other prisoners and the rest of the world did not have to suffer his presence any longer. It's an absolute honor to meet you. How can I be of service to you?"

"Uh..." Morgan said.

"Oh, where are my manners? Please come in, beautiful ladies and good sir. Make yourself at home. Don't worry about the dogs. They only attack bad people. May I get you something to drink? There's lemonade, and I brewed some jasmine ice tea. What would you like?"

"Please," August said. "We'd love some. Tea sounds fantastic."

"Me too," Morgan said.

"I'll take lemonade," Dorcha said. She served herself.

"Pour one for me please," Gareth said.

Everyone got their drinks and went inside the house. August admired the way that the modifications on the house created an unplanned skylight. Cynthia had rigged an ingenious shutter system with a heavy weather-proof curtain which could be used to close the skylight, but which currently was wide open. A cool cross-breeze blew through the room as August said, "What a lovely home you have here."

"Thank you..."

"August Cannon. This is Dorcha LeTour, and Morgan Martel."

Cynthia said, "Morgan Martel, my hero."

August, Morgan, and Dorcha got comfortable on the gray and olive faux suede couches sitting perpendicular to each other in the living room. Gareth followed Cynthia into the kitchen. Several minutes later they returned with some snacks. Cynthia had a bowl of watermelon cubes speared with toothpicks, and a tan-and-green paste set in the center of a tray of fresh vegetables.

"This is artichoke pâté," Cynthia said.

"Cynthia is a strict vegan," Gareth said.

Morgan reached for a carrot stick and dipped it into the pate. "Yummy," she said in a voice muffled by food. Morgan reached for more pâté.

August said, "Your crystal pendant is beautiful, Cynthia. So colorful. Where did you get it?"

"Thank you! I made it. It's a protection charm."

August smiled, "Wonderful. Now, if Morgan doesn't mind, I'd like to tell you her story, and how she was able to meet you in such an unusual way."

Morgan nodded.

August went through the history of meeting Morgan, finding out about her ability, and supporting her growth over the years. August was happy that Gareth was finally hearing the whole story. Of course she omitted specific details of times and locations, but now Gareth would understand how serious they were about Morgan's abilities. August knew that Gareth would be thrilled to get an explanation of why she had fainted when she first met Morgan many years back in New Orleans.

"The majority of the populace is flailing around in the cosmic maelstrom, desperately striving to keep their heads above water," August said. "It's hard for them to perceive a grander scheme of things while they're sputtering and splashing about. We are planning to open up a whole new realm of healing, to help people to search for their soul's truth. Give them the tools and encouragement to self-correct."

Cynthia interrupted, asking Morgan, "Do you believe it was fated for us to meet?"

"All I know is we asked the Creative to lead us to our final team member, and UnderLife took us to you. I believe there is a greater plan at work, but I don't know most of the how's or why's. What I do know is that a monster resided in your UnderLife. Somehow you allowed me there to help you defeat it," Morgan said.

"How did I do anything? Through a crack in the wood I watched you kill him. I was helpless, as usual, in that damn wardrobe."

"Don't you see, Cynthia? Your psyche answered the call we put out. You guided us to you. Never forget that you are one tough cookie. Your growing garden defense system took out four intelligent, capable people. Dorcha and I barely made it through the garden, and then Dorcha was swallowed by the suffocating sewer that led to the heart of your darkness. You're the one who saved yourself by calling us to you. I just helped. By allowing me to play the hero and use my martial arts skills to defeat Roland Addanc, you gave yourself permission to live freely and to put your victimization to rest."

"It was amazing to witness what you did. I didn't know a woman could defend herself so well," Cynthia said.

"Thank God for muscle memory and excellent training."

"I want to learn," Cynthia said.

Morgan smiled, "And so you shall. Captain Tess is a magnificent instructor."

"I'm ashamed to realize I've held on so tightly to memories of that monster this whole time. It's like I had never escaped. The case-of-beer night you crawled in from the sewers was when Roland Addanc worked me over all night long. I lost my innocence, my virginity, and my sense of safety. Mimi Winter died that night. I didn't realize how much rage I've clung to. It's time to let it all go. The bastard is really dead now, thanks to your help. If you need anything, if I can help you, please let me know."

"Actually…" Morgan told Cynthia about Current, and their hopes that Cynthia would be able to identify and correct its flaw.

Cynthia said, "When do we leave?"

"As soon as possible," August said.

"I need to find someone trustworthy who will take care of the animals and water the garden."

The four women turned to look at Gareth simultaneously.

"Oh no," he said. "I've already broken several laws by taking you here. I can't just hand Cynthia over unsupervised. Also, I don't have time to house-sit. I have people to lead and a job to do."

"Consider this an essential part of that job." August sauntered up to Gareth, looped her arm in his, and guided him out of the front door for a private talk.

Morgan grinned, sipping her tea.

"He doesn't stand chance," Dorcha said. She giggled.

* * *

August led Gareth into the woods until they were out of earshot and visual range of the house. They argued every step of the way. Gareth stood firm. No way in hell was he going to let them ditch him and pull another disappearing act, especially not with someone who was his direct responsibility.

August was glad Gareth was putting up a strong fight. It gave her every excuse to do something she wanted to anyway. August pressed Gareth against the bark of a robust tree trunk. She reached her hands to either side of his head and kissed him so passionately that their knees buckled a bit, and they had to lean on each other for support.

"I can have one of my men come out here and watch the place," Gareth relented.

August shook her head, "That will raise suspicion. They'll want to know what you're doing, why you're leaving with her, and who the three mysterious ladies who showed up at your office are."

"Why do you need to be so secretive? What's this all about?"

"I know I'm asking for a world of trust from you. I promise to explain all the details later. I won't vanish on you again."

"Either I go with you or no deal."

August continued to ravage Gareth with kisses. It took a monumental effort from her to disengage from him. "Just give three me days," she panted, leaning forward to nibble his neck. "We'll be back before you know it."

Gareth's eyelids fluttered with pleasure. August's expert ministrations had dissolved all resistance. "One day," he growled.

August lifted her head. Their lips were a breath apart. Her eyes pierced his. "Thirty-six hours."

Gareth's right hand gripped August's ass with authority, forcing her hips into his. She grinded into his clothing-restrained erection. Gareth kissed August ferociously, assenting to her wishes. Their bodies made a promise to return to one another as soon as possible.

CHAPTER TWENTY-ONE
HERALD

Later that night, August, Morgan, Dorcha, and Cynthia arrived back at the Mountain Compound. Louise and Trevor greeted them, and suggested they rest while dinner was cooking. Cynthia insisted on seeing Current first.

The group went to Current. Cynthia climbed on the wooden benches, lay down in the center of the room underneath the crystal-encrusted canopy, and inspected the silver meditation disks on her hands and knees.

"This place is gorgeous," Cynthia said, "Unfortunately, the energy isn't fluttering. In order for Current to flow, there needs to be a physical manifestation of intention wiring it together. You need metal, a lot of it, primarily platinum and gold."

"How much is a lot?" August asked.

Cynthia said, "Do you have blueprints of this place I can look at? I need a more accurate sense of the dimensions in order to make a proper estimate."

"Yes, I'll go retrieve them," Trevor said and exited.

"You were headed in the right direction with these silver disks. To get the oomph you're looking for, the silver will need to be replaced by platinum, and the disks should be connected together by platinum wiring.

"Why platinum?" Dorcha asked.

"Platinum is one of Earth's most rare, precious, and pervasive metals. Tiny amounts are used in almost every type of technology. It can be found in cars, computers, fiber optics, fertilizers, glass, pharmaceuticals, fuel cells, and jewelry. Platinum offers a much bigger spiritual boost than silver. It's like comparing a space-bound rocket to a lit match."

Trevor returned with a long cardboard cylinder. He slid the plans out, unrolled them, and spread them out on the floor. Cynthia's correction made perfect sense. Trevor felt humbled that someone else had figured it out first, but he was elated that the conundrum would now be solved.

Cynthia studied the blueprints for a while. She asked for scratch paper, a pen, and a calculator. Cynthia scribbled notes and worked out a couple of equations. Then she drew a large spider web on several pieces of scratch paper, and held them over Current's blueprints, "You need to add gold wiring along this pattern beneath the onyx floor and among the ceiling crystals. Then you have to add gold disc shaped seats on the redwood bleachers which will also be connected by gold wiring. This is where new UnderLife travelers will sit. You're going to need at least eight pounds of platinum and twenty-two pounds of gold. However, once you finish it, this place is going to roar. Even people with no sensitivity to spiritual energy will be able to feel it. I hope you've got hefty security. This place is going make a Pharaoh's tomb look like chintzy decorating."

"I'll say," Morgan said.

Trevor consulted his laptop. "Platinum is at roughly $1800 per ounce, so eight pounds will cost $230,400. Gold is also at approximately $1800 per ounce, so twenty-two pounds will be $633,600. That's $864,000 just for raw materials. Total costs including construction will be in the millions."

Trevor looked at Louise and continued, "I don't know if we have enough in our coffers for a purchase of that magnitude right now."

Louise thought for a few moments. "We're going to need to throw a fundraiser."

Morgan laughed, "Yeah, right."

Louise smiled. "I'm not kidding. It's time to show a very select crowd the goods. For years we've been putting together a list of powerful people who would be receptive to supporting our UnderLife endeavors."

"Of course you have," Dorcha said.

"We're looking for candidates who are open-minded, altruistic, happy, successful, intelligent, adventurous, and wealthy."

* * *

Cynthia spent the remainder of her time at the Mountain Compound working with Trevor on the design for Current's upgrade. She enjoyed Louise's culinary talents and she got to know Morgan and Dorcha better. Cynthia volunteered to participate at the fundraiser for Current.

Later that evening, Captain Tess flew the Pave Hawk Helicopter to the Mountain Compound, picked up August and Cynthia, and took them back to Napa County Airport.

August got the keys to her rented Ford Mustang and escorted Cynthia home. They arrived twenty minutes before August's promised deadline. Gareth was waiting in the same spot on the porch where they had found Cynthia two days before. Cynthia's purring cat was snuggled on his lap.

Gareth and August made sure Cynthia was settled in before heading back to San Francisco.

They went to Gareth's house and it was two weeks before either of them returned to work.

* * *

While August and Gareth were enjoying a much deserved vacation, Louise, Trevor, Tilly, Kyle, Captain Tess, Draven, Morgan, and Dorcha met at the Skyscraper Space to hammer out the guest list and the agenda for the fundraiser. They invited Victoria, but she was busy. Victoria asked Draven to relay the bullet points from the powwow.

"Here's the list of our most favorable prospects." Louise handed out copies of the dossiers to everyone present. The thick document held a thorough biography of each person.

"Cool," Kyle said, "you included their astrological charts!"

Trevor smiled. "Yes, Son, for those with available birth information."

Draven scanned the document, shaking his head in bewilderment. "You sure don't do anything half-way. Everything is here: physical attributes, family, education, career achievements, assets, medical history, social circles, religious beliefs, political leanings, idiosyncrasies, and entertainment preferences. Hell, you even know that Neuroscientist Dr. Eileen Lombardo, MacArthur Fellowship winner, loves Ben & Jerry's Americone Ice Cream. You even know where she rented jet skis on a vacation to Kaua`i ten years ago."

"How many are in this packet?" Kyle asked.

"Seventy," Tilly said.

"Seventy?" Draven snorted. "That's a lot of people to impress with something which isn't fully operational."

Louise said, "We don't expect everyone to show. Many of these people won't want to be whisked away to a remote location for a vague sleepover which will include getting hit up for money. I'll be glad if half of the invitees decide to join us."

"Is that enough to generate the amount of cash we need?" Dorcha asked.

"It's an illustrious group. Check out the finances." Tilly said.

Dorcha flipped through a few of the packets, and her eyes bulged in their sockets. "Never mind," she said. In the packets, Dorcha came across the name of Kendrick Hawke. She nudged Morgan to show her. Kendrick Hawke was one of Victoria's noted lovers.

Draven skimmed through the profiles. "I think you're underestimating how impossible it is to get surgeons, athletes, stockbrokers, litigators, and... oh, and a Senator even, people who redefine busy, to drop everything and go camping inside a mountain led by a group they've never heard of before."

"The key is how we approach them," Louise said.

"In all honesty, this soirée is a contingency plan," Trevor said. "Up until recently we thought we'd be able to complete Current with our own resources."

"So how do we entice this illustrious bunch to hang out and throw money at us?" Draven asked.

"We use the profiles, and with the help of divination, we find out whatever in their lives is in need of healing. We declare our awareness of it, and we invite them to let us help them fix it," Louise said.

"Pinpoint pandering, I love it!"

"The more secretive and suspicious types are going to want to figure out how we got the intel on them," Captain Tess said.

"Excellent way for us to get even more attention from the people we're after. Bold discovery sure snared Victoria's curiosity," Draven said, "and she's notoriously difficult to pin down."

"I hate that Victoria went through all of those years believing you were dead, Draven," Morgan said.

"If it wasn't for you, Kitten, we'd both still be in the dark, and the lesser for it."

"Here, here!" Dorcha said. "What's the itinerary for the event? Who wants to bet Louise has it mapped out already?"

"Once our guests arrive, they shall be served hors d'œuvres and non-alcoholic drinks," Louise said. "We'll make the booze available after the seminars are completed. There will be an introduction speech explaining UnderLife, Current, and our mission. Each person will be pre-assigned to one of three guided seminars: I Ching led by Taylor, Astrology with Kyle, or Dorcha's Tarot Extravaganza. The three of you will give a media-supported presentation detailing your favored divination method. Our guests may then schedule private readings for the next few hours. While people are waiting for an appointment, there will be several activities going on, and guests may choose where to linger. I'll be creating crystal jewelry with people to strengthen, cleanse, and invigorate their chakras. Cynthia has volunteered to share her vegan cooking expertise with the culinary cats who want to learn, and we'll feed all who feel like grazing. There will be an open bar and an informal buffet dinner. We'll encourage everyone to socialize, digest the day, and pose their questions. Victoria, if she chooses to participate, will have free reign to play music and engage the crowd in the Living Quarters of the Mountain Compound. We hope she'll guide a session of Musical Healing, but that's up to Victoria. Draven will be our roving diplomat. We let this charming man loose to play with the populace."

Draven nodded his approval.

"What about me?" Morgan asked.

Tilly chuckled. "Go where your intuition leads you."

Louise continued, "In the morning after the slumber party, we'll serve breakfast, and there will be an auction for those who want to experience the inaugural run of the new Current. The top five bids win. Then we'll get everyone home safe and sound."

"Pimping out the ride, nice," Morgan said.

"How do we know who will be assigned to whom for the guided events?" Dorcha asked.

Trevor smiled, "Imagine if our public educational system could unlock the true potential of its students. My darling wife and I have created a structure and a curriculum based on the principles and use of Astrology, I Ching, and Tarot."

"We've been calling it AstroSchool," Tilly said.

"Yes, we intend to apply AstroSchool methods for arranging each guest's itinerary. Our four children and August were all raised in this manner, and look how well they turned out. All are distinguished, respected, and most importantly, happy."

Tilly continued, "By using AstroSchool principles, they were able to learn everything a top-ranked advanced placement student would, and so much more."

Trevor nodded. "The critical aspect of this system is its flexibility. AstroSchool adapts to the energy signature of the staff and the students. A minor adjustment can make a world of difference. For instance, Morgan is naturally a night owl. Despite her best efforts, the 8:00 AM elementary and high school start time hindered Morgan's academic performance."

"I can't tell you how many times I blamed narcolepsy for falling asleep in class," Morgan said.

* * *

Dr. Eileen Lombardo's patience had almost run out. Her wait time at Gate 31 of Detroit Metro Airport was crawling past the five hour mark. The snow outside was light enough that the airport remained open, but the delays were horrendous. Dr. Lombardo was afraid her hands would lock into claws if she spent any more time working on her laptop.

Dr. Lombardo decided to clean out her purse and briefcase. Gum wrappers, six month old receipts, and grocery lists sailed into the garbage. Dr. Lombardo unzipped an interior briefcase pouch and found a handful of forgotten mail.

A silver envelope caught Dr. Lombardo's attention.

Inside were three heavy sheets of royal purple paper. Dr. Lombardo unfolded them. They had an ornate border with an ivory damask pattern. In the top right corner of the first page, "37 of 70" was written in elegant white print.

Below, the page read: "Please join us on an overnight adventure. Vital assistance will be available to revolutionize your research on how emotional perception affects memory creation on a synaptic level. We will not ask you for money, despite needing four million dollars to complete our UnderLife project. This trip is offered with no strings attached. Consider it a gift for all your hard work. We want to share what we are doing with you. If this is something you find important, any support would be welcome. This invitation is for you alone: Please do not bring anyone who does not have an invitation. They will be refused entrance. We have selected a group of seventy esteemed peers for this experience. Enclosed are their names and an itinerary. A Security Day will precede the event where you, or a representative, are welcome to take a tour of the facility and review our safety measures. Please RSVP by the end of the month to secure your reservation. Thank you."

Dr. Lombardo scanned the list of names, and recognized many of them. She reached for her laptop to Google the rest of the group.

What a bizarre invitation, Dr. Lombardo thought. Whoever sent it had a lot of audacity to say they could revolutionize the work she'd spent the better part of her life chipping away at. Most likely a total scam, she thought. What could be so interesting to draw this list of all-stars from such an eclectic array of professions?

On the other hand, it would be good to get away for bit. After the debacle Detroit turned out to be, Dr. Lombardo needed a breather. She hoped Anne Rice had accepted the invitation. It'd be a thrill to meet her as well as many of the others. If these UnderLife people were telling the truth, that is.

* * *

Mountain Compound – Safety Day

There were twenty-two people on Safety Day's afternoon tour. The morning run had had twenty-eight guests, and it had gone off without a hitch. Overall, fifty out of the seventy people had accepted the Safety Day invitation. Sixteen guests arrived themselves to inspect the facilities, while the other thirty-four sent some type of representative.

"Make no mistake," Trevor said to the group as they entered Current's crystalline cavern. "This isn't an inert geological museum installation. Think of Current as an energy amplifier. However, Current still needs an imbedded network of gold and platinum wiring."

"Current's primary function is to facilitate UnderLife adventures. These are best described as a group shaman spirit walk led by Morgan Martel," Tilly said. "Morgan possesses a rare ability to travel our inner landscapes, to access the Akashic Records, to reveal past life incarnations, and to learn new ways to heal and solve problems."

"How?" asked Dr. Zerah Rowan, a twenty-five year old math prodigy.

"We're not quite sure," Trevor said. "How did you comprehend advanced calculus at ten years old, Dr. Rowan? The science of Morgan's ability is under investigation. Morgan will be here during the event to answer all of your questions."

* * *

Two Weeks Later
Mountain Compound – Green Room
An Hour Before The Fundraiser Welcome Brunch

August and Tilly had created a Green Room Lounge tucked away from the main living area. This private home base was decorated in a unique mix of Moroccan Opium Den Stoner's Paradise meets Gothic Vampire Bordello. A full hair and make-up station dominated one corner of the space. The Green Room exuded comfort. There was soothing music, soft, flattering lighting, a small gurgling water fountain, dark-green walls, gothic candle sconces, black-light posters of a moonlit silhouetted pirate ship and a pictorial chart of astrological sex positions.

Victoria, decked out in a sensual haute-couture suit, walked in on Dorcha, Draven, Morgan and Kyle curled up on the couches smoking joints.

Victoria's entrance caught Morgan in mid-toke. She coughed.

Victoria laughed, "It's no wonder you yank people into an alternate reality with how many psychotropic agents you puff through your system."

Morgan grinned and blew a few smoke rings.

Kyle said, "Actually, I think her extreme enjoyment of the herb helps keep Morgan's consciousness in Waking Reality."

Draven snagged the joint away from Morgan. "Or she's just a big ol' stoner."

"I vote for both," Dorcha said, giggling.

Draven offered Victoria the joint, but she declined. Victoria turned to leave. "Let's not get too red-eyed and silly. We've got a lot of heavy guns arriving. You need to impress them as professionals, not goofballs."

"Okay, Mom," Kyle said.

Victoria glowered at Kyle and cuffed him sharply upside the head on her way out of the room.

"Hey! I was just kidding."

* * *

Forty-four guests were bussed in from the Mountain Compound private airstrip. August took them on another quick tour of Current, and then she took them to the Living Quarters' main hall, which had been set up for brunch.

"Please help yourself. Let me know if you need anything. Bon appétit!" August said.

The esteemed crowd ate and continued their introductions and discussions.

As the meal concluded, Louise stepped up to a newly-built stage. From the Think Tank, Mitchell Cannon dimmed the lights and engaged an automated follow-spot. Louise approached the podium and said, "Good afternoon everyone. My name is Louise Cannon, Director of Operations for the UnderLife Project. Thank you for joining us for an exciting, entertaining, and educational twenty-four hours. For those of you who have not been here before, I hope you enjoyed the tour of our facilities."

She continued, "The essence of the UnderLife Project is about removing obstacles and letting go of the internal and external encumbrances which impede personal progress. In short, it's about self-correcting. Each of you was invited to be here because of the remarkable work you've already accomplished in this area. None of you would have been able to succeed in your chosen fields if you weren't already strong self-correctors.

"However, many people are trammeled by a major chakra imbalance. These imbalances create an immense amount of self-destructive behavior, which can make life an uphill climb.

"Even a mustard seed of doubt can ambush a great idea from ever being realized. The invitations you received are meant as a reminder, from a cosmic perspective, that everything we think, say, and do is an act of creation. We offer several methods of energy map reading to help you traverse the next step on your desired path.

"Without further ado, let me introduce our spiritual camp counselors for this evening."

Victoria, Morgan, Taylor, Kyle, Dorcha, and August joined Louise on the stage.

"You've already met my daughter August Cannon. The illustrious Victoria Shine has generously offered to share her musical talents with us. Dorcha LeTour, Kyle Vihzor, and Taylor Tess, the divination trio, are experts in Tarot, Astrology, and I Ching respectively. Morgan Martel is our

Primary UnderLife Guide. We'll discuss Morgan's roll further throughout the evening. Morgan is a pioneer in the burgeoning psychic awakening of the human race," Louise said.

"What is UnderLife?" asked a voice from the crowd.

"A revolutionary adventure to inner worlds," Kyle said.

Scattered laughter and murmured disbelief rippled through the crowd.

Victoria shot Louise a look. Louise handed her the microphone. "I know all of you either by reputation or experience. I respect your time. This is not bullshit. You are lucky to bear witness, and hopefully participate, in how humanity may heal itself. We can live in harmony with Earth, our home."

August stepped up. "Thank you Victoria, I agree. Based on AstroSchool, an educational system we're developing, the next portion of your time here has been pre-determined. I present the three paths of oracle guided by Dorcha, Kyle, and Taylor. Please consult the laminate handed to you upon arrival. Those with Tarot, please follow Dorcha LeTour. For Astrology, go with Kyle Vihzor, and the I Ching folks go with Taylor Tess."

Kyle brushed by Morgan on the way off the stage. He had a wild impulse to kiss her but he hesitated to intrude with his attraction. Kyle knew Morgan wasn't masturbating to his image. Morgan's rapt focus saw only Victoria. And who could blame her? Victoria had an amazing talent coupled with an energetic Royal Flush of Hearts. She defined attraction.

Kyle had been around Victoria his whole life. To him, she was family. He was acutely aware of Victoria's power. Victoria intimidated and exhilarated Kyle along with the rest of the world.

* * *

The guests left for their seminars. Victoria cruised into the kitchen in search of her band mates and food. Sure enough Drum and Bassie were eating, and from the sound of it, arguing. This came as no surprise to Victoria. Drum and Bassie were known for their periodic eruptions. Their slippery loyalty to each other was anchored by an ecstatic musical chemistry. They had abandoned their given names many years ago. Victoria had met Drum and Bassie while touring with Cuneo, and she adored their talents. Drum and Bassie's saving grace was that no matter how vicious, tear-stricken, or blissful their civilian relationship was, the one thing they both held sacred was music.

Drum pointed a fork laden with kale at Bassie. "You're giddy because that painter you love is here."

"Her art is amazing," Bassie said.

"You going to try to fuck her aren't you?"

"Oh c'mon, just because I enjoy someone's work doesn't mean I'm going to throw myself at them."

"She paints vaginas! I'm sure you'll volunteer for modeling with little to no provocation."

"Alright, settle down," Victoria said. "Bickering moratorium for the next twenty-four hours. I want sunshine and rainbows, ladies. This is an important gig. Everyone will have a good time. Capisce?"

"Aye aye, Captain," Drum and Bassie said in unison.

Victoria got a salad, a sandwich, and a hot tea from the buffet. She noticed how fit and crisply coordinated all of the caterers were. There always seemed to be at least one caterer lingering around with zero interest in food service. All the caterers were wearing high tech ear pieces. Either the Cannons and the Vihzors had pulled out all the stops by hiring elite staff, or Captain Tess's security detail was hiding in plain sight.

Victoria went to the Green Room to eat and warm up. She chose the Gibson Les Paul Standard from the four guitars she had brought. Victoria put headphones on, plugged into her portable mini-amp, and went through some chord progressions.

Victoria shifted into the guitar lines of the songs she considered playing later in the set. Victoria's eyelids fluttered closed, and her body moved to the beat.

When Victoria opened her eyes, Darian Vihzor was standing in front of her, flanked by sisters Jill and Vespa.

"Well, well, well. I spend a bit of time on the other side of our fair planet and look what you've gotten yourself into."

"Darian!" Victoria squealed. She abandoned the gear and scooped her best friend into a hug.

After a merciless squeeze and kisses on the cheek, they parted long enough to gather Vespa and Jill into their arms.

"I can't believe Mom and Dad managed to keep a mountain from us!" Jill said.

"Not all of us," Vespa said.

Darian gasped, "You... secret from me?"

"I knew only vague details until Kyle got involved. If either of you had been in town, I don't think we could have kept it from you."

"I should hope not," Darian said.

"How did the rest of the shoot go?" Victoria asked Darian.

"Fabulous. Sad. The usual nostalgia-release cocktail. I'm proud of the work. We'll see how it turns out."

"You two catch up. I'm going to watch the rest of the Tarot presentation," Vespa said.

"Astrology for me," Jill said as they left. "Check on our little brother."

Darian helped herself to Victoria's half eaten sandwich. "Do you mind if I hang out while you warm up?"

"I insist."

Victoria switched to an Eastman Uptown AR804 Acoustic Guitar. She hummed along while playing it.

Darian checked out the room. She smirked at the astrological poster of glowing anonymous figures fucking. Some were fucking quite athletically. She fetched a script from her bag and settled in on the couch to read.

Victoria did her best to concentrate, but Darian was managing to make reading an interesting thing to watch. It'd been months since they'd been in the same room.

"What's that?" Victoria asked.

"Love in Motion script for next season," Darian said without looking up.

"Oh," Victoria continued practicing, "Harmony in there?"

"M-hm."

Darian laughed at something on the page. Victoria glared at her.

What if Victoria were to say no? As much fun as she had had on Love in Motion, the hours were grueling. It left little time for music composition, or at least for brain-bleeding sessions of attempting to write. Darian would be hurt, but she'd get over it. What would they do? Rewrite the episode? Or maybe, gasp, recast Harmony Moore? Oh, hell no. That slutty scheming Australian vixen was Victoria's. Besides, Victoria hated the thought of someone else getting to torture Darian on screen. Who could be better than her best friend?

Victoria leaned over and grabbed at Darian's script. Darian anticipated this move and slipped it out of Victoria grip. "Hey, that's my copy! Don't worry, love, I brought yours along. Unless you don't want to play with us and you'd rather give the delicate writers heart attacks because they need to do a full rewrite? So cruel." Darian reached into her bag and pulled out a second Love In Motion script.

"Fuck you," Victoria said.

Darian laughed and handed the pages over. "That's what I like to hear."

Morgan barreled into the Green Room. "Oh! Hi. Sorry to interrupt." She began to back out.

"Nonsense, come in. I'm Darian," Darian got up to shake Morgan's hand.

"Yeah... I'm Morgan."

Victoria put the Love In Motion script into her gig bag, picked up the acoustic guitar, and played a mellow Spanish-sounding melody.

"Aha, the one I've been hearing so much about," Darian said to Morgan.

"You... You have?"

"Of course. You make quite an impression. I'm looking forward to my first UnderLife experience. Sounds like fun."

"For all of our sakes, I hope it is. Can I get either of you anything?"

Victoria shook her head and continued playing. She focused her eyes on the guitar's fretboard as her fingers danced through a difficult riff.

"No, we're good. Thanks," Darian said.

"Okay, see ya later," Morgan left, closing the door behind her.

"Bye." Darian watched Morgan go then turned to Victoria. "You didn't mention how in love she is with you."

"Touch up my make-up?"

"Fine, fine, you don't want to talk about it. Saddle up in the chair, missy."

* * *

Morgan didn't know if she was excited, terrified, or upset. Probably a bit of everything. Seeing Victoria Shine and Darian Vihzor in the same room made Morgan want to clap and cheer, "Wooo!"

When she was around her best friend, Victoria hadn't even looked at me, Morgan thought. What should I expect, kisses and professions of love? Eye contact is nice, though. I'm being selfish. Victoria is prepping to play. Calm down, Martel. What did Victoria tell Darian about me? Maybe nothing. Maybe Darian heard about me from Kyle, or Trevor, or Tilly. Morgan wished she could read Tarot and get some kind of explanation for everything. Too bad Dorcha was busy.

Morgan went to the Mountain Compound's basketball court, where Kyle was leading the Astrology Seminar.

Kyle was standing at a podium and punctuating his speech with a PowerPoint slide show on the large screen above and behind him, "We started today grouped with our fellow Sun Signs, then we explored Moon signs, and finally we saw the Rising Signs – our energy costumes, how we appear, and the final lens through which our personality radiates. Let's go back to our original Sun Sign companions."

Familiar with the procedure, the group rearranged themselves.

The projector's backdrop image defaulted to a Sun In Leo Collage of Neil Armstrong, Lucille Ball, Barack Obama, Bill Clinton, Madonna, Fidel Castro, Napoleon Bonaparte, Mata Hari, Jerry Garcia, Jack L. Warner, Carl Gustav Jung, Mae West, Coco Chanel, Robert Plant, Robert DeNiro, Amelia Earhart, Count Basie, and Lynda Carter dressed as Wonder Woman.

"I know I'm bombarding you with a lot of information today. Those unfamiliar with Astrology have been very patient and open minded, thank you. Astrological perspective allows us to discuss character flaws and understand Ego outbursts without anyone getting offended. The impersonal quality of symbolic reflection takes the sting out of a critical punch. This fosters peaceful fellowship and non-violent conflict resolution. The more we understand ourselves and learn how to self-correct gracefully the closer we all get to achieving World Peace."

The crowd applauded Kyle's earnest speech.

"Thank you. Our next segment today is Libran Lures and Loves. It is my pleasure to introduce one of my favorite mixed martial arts training partners and one of my chief spiritual advisors, Morgan Martel. Don't be fooled by that smile, folks, she's a vicious fighter."

Morgan sat down in one of the two comfortable chairs angled to face the crowd. "Thank you Kyle, you sure know how to make a girl feel dainty and ladylike."

"You're definitely a lady, my friend, but I'd be hard pressed to assign the word dainty to any aspect of your character. Now, let's get right to it, give us your Big Three."

"Ah, yes. I am a Libra, The Scales, the only sign not human or animal. We're Cardinal Air, ruled by Venus, and represent justice, beauty, partnership, and balance. The latter is a state I rarely find myself in."

"You're being modest, fitting for the sign of charm. Please continue."

"My Moon is in Leo and I have Pisces Rising. This makes me an emotional cat with fickle tastes. It gives me fantastic empathy if my emotions are engaged, and it helps me to be a courageous healer. At least, that's what Kyle's been telling me."

"Stop being coy, Morgan." Kyle played to the audience. "She knows it's all true." His attention swung back to Morgan, "How about the houses of your Big Three?"

Morgan racked her brain for the answer. "Uhm, I know you've told me, but I don't remember."

"Your Leo Moon is in the Sixth House, the house of Virgo. It's no surprise that you couldn't hold on to a job for more than three months before becoming a Shaman-In-Training. I'm surprised you forgot your Sun Sign is in the Eighth House the house of Scorpio. This house rules sex, death, legacies, and the occult. You're familiar with Scorpios, aren't you, Morgan?"

"Oh yes."

"What religion, if any, do you practice?"

"Personally I'm all about pantheistic spirituality, but I have a deep respect for anyone following a path of Love and Light. Between Astrology, I Ching, Tarot, the Mayan Calendar, and crystals I'd say I'm on the Choose Your Own Adventure Spiritual Path."

"Morgan's Pisces Rising makes her a natural healer. I believe this helps her to bend perceptions of reality for herself and for others, and to travel underneath Waking Life into the collective unconscious. The places we go in the collective unconscious is what we call UnderLife. Thank you, Morgan and our wonderful audience!"

When the applause died down, Kyle said to the guests, "I release you from my clutches. Even though I'd rather tie you all down and pontificate on astrology for the next three hours, I'll restrain myself. Louise is having an on-going crystal healing workshop. Check it out and help create a personal talisman. Cynthia is doing the same thing with her vegan culinary skills. Whatever your food preferences are, I'll bet Cynthia can delight your palate. If anyone wants a private in-depth Astrology reading from me, Tarot by Dorcha, or I Ching with Taylor, sign up and we'll find you when it's time. Victoria Shine is performing later, and if you've never seen her live before, this is a treat you don't want to miss. Go explore, eat, and the free bar is now open. Enjoy!"

* * *

Victoria slipped into the room where Dorcha was reading tarot. She sweet-talked her way into jumping the queue while the staff located the next person on the list to be read. Dorcha was entranced by the cards in front of her, and she didn't notice Victoria. It appeared to Victoria that Dorcha was taking a break to do a reading on herself.

"What are you reading on?" Victoria asked.

"Nothing." Dorcha gathered the Tarot cards together. "It's dumb, a silly inappropriate crush."

"Those are my favorite kind," Victoria said, and sat across the table from Dorcha. "You know Kyle has no clue how hot you are for him."

"But..."

"Be bold, lady. Kyle thinks you're too cool to have such a paralyzing loving focus. He's young, programmed to be ultra-chivalrous, and he's used to being around women who demand what they want. Scratch the kitty behind the ears, tell him how pretty he is, and you'll have him purring before you know it."

"Eh, easy for you to say," Dorcha said.

"You mind doing a one card reading for me?"

"You mean a general reading using one placement and five cards?"

"Yeah, yeah, whatevah."

Dorcha shuffled the Druid Craft deck and fanned it out. "Specific intention helps to focus the cards, and that dress looks fantastic on you."

"Bravo! I love correction wrapped in compliment. It's infinitely more appetizing. So I should be focusing on something right now?"

"No, we've established this is a general reading. Just let your thoughts flow as they will. The cards will take it from there."

Dorcha shuffled and fanned the 5 decks, and Victoria selected one card from each.

General one card spread for Victoria using the Druid Craft, Faeries' Oracle, Gendron, Tao, and Vampire Tarot decks.

> Druid: 4 of Swords @
> Faeries: #26 – O! That Gnome
> Gendron: #17 – The Star @
> Tao: #25 - Innocence
> Vampires: 8 of Pentacles

"Overall, it says to keep an open mind, follow the rules, beware of random disappointment or pessimism, or of bringing up old wounds."

"Check. Let's do another one on my best focal point for tonight."

"Certainly."

Victoria's best focal point for tonight using the Druid Craft, Faeries' Oracle, Gendron, Tao, and Vampire Tarot decks.

> Druid: #1 – The Magician @
> Faeries: #64 – Gawtcha @
> Gendron: Ace of Pentacles
> Tao: #29 – The Abysmal
> Vampires: Ace of Wands

"Hexagram 29 from the Tao Oracle I Ching is water over water, The Abysmal. Flaws in our character are like cracks in the earth. Filling them is scary, disorienting, and dangerous. Your emotions are the water, and it's as though you're caught in an oceanic riptide. Struggling only makes it worse. You have to ride it out. This is the spiritual weather you are stuck in tonight, and fighting the cosmic flow is stagnating and dangerous. Let events take their course. Forcing issues now will only create more problems."

"Thanks, Dorcha, I appreciate it." They hugged. "Time for me to go sing and shake it." Victoria winked and departed.

* * *

The audience buzzed with excitement in the cavernous main hall of the Living Quarters. After brunch, the staff had transformed the hall into a sultry nightclub atmosphere with tables and chairs. Servers waded through the crowd with drinks and food.

As promised, the day had been unique, enlightening, and entertaining.

The private readings went on twice as long as anticipated because nearly everyone got all three readings.

Kendrick Hawke had brought a lavish flower bouquet for Victoria. He placed it on the cocktail table in front of him.

The room didn't have a formal backstage, so Victoria was unable to make her usual dramatic entrance. Instead, Victoria Shine just walked into the hall with Darian Vihzor. Cheers and applause erupted for both women. Darian joined Vespa, Jill, and Draven at the table next to Morgan, Kyle and Dorcha.

Victoria looked molten sexy hot in a Ja'Mei original from her upcoming Rock Star line. Morgan felt Victoria's allure pouring, burning, melting and hardening. Glancing around the room, Morgan knew she wasn't alone in how she felt about Victoria.

Victoria had studied every guest's dossier. She read in between the lines and was able to know much more about these people's lives than they would have felt comfortable telling a therapist. Passionate, intelligent ambition was driving most of them towards excellence, but everyone was snagged in the love department.

Victoria stepped up to her Yamaha S90 ES electronic keyboard and coaxed out the first notes and chords of "Left".

Drum and Bassie, who were already waiting on stage, slid seamlessly into the song. As Victoria dropped her defenses with each passing note, it became apparent that "Left" was the lifeline out of a pit of despair from losing her first great love.

When the song ended and the applause waned, Victoria sighed and said, "We used to have so much fun together."

The band kicked into "Lure", a Virtuoso smash hit. It'd taken years for Victoria to develop the manual dexterity to play Cuneo's compositions, but now she made it look easy.

"Lure" illustrated Victoria's point perfectly. The more you tried to force love to do your bidding, the more nimbly it slipped away.

Morgan slid into an unexpected micro-UnderLife moment. Watching Victoria on stage, Morgan could see a web of energy expanding from Victoria out over the audience. It was the same type of energy web Morgan had encountered at the Akashic Records, when learning about her mother's latent telekinesis. Morgan marveled at how the energy web danced with the song, creating dazzling power bursts. The energy rained down on the audience, splashing everyone with pure glee. The sonic communion was invigorating everyone's chi. It was an amazing sight to behold.

The audience sat spellbound while Victoria bounced around doing Harmony Moore hits, Virtuoso jams and ballads, and the occasional cover. Each song brought the audience into further intimacy with Victoria and her band mates. Drum and Bassie were having a ball. They couldn't keep silly grins off of their faces.

Victoria stalked around the stage with her dress shimmering and her sweat beading on her luscious skin. She alternated between playing the guitar, piano, and just focusing on singing her heart out. Victoria held court like a true queen.

Morgan's vision snapped back to normal at the crash of breaking glass. The musicians pretended they didn't notice and continued playing. A few heads turned to the commotion in the back of the hall.

The accident had been caused by Chad, Kendrick Hawke's personal assistant. Chad had bustled into the room as if the sky were falling and had collided with one of the servers. Chad had the distinction of being the fundraiser's only uninvited guest. Kendrick had shown up with Chad at the Mountain Compound knowing full well it wasn't allowed. After Kendrick had put on a display of charm, bullying, and name-dropping, Chad was begrudgingly allowed to stay. Chad took himself way too seriously, and he had been a miffed douche-nozzle all day, especially with Kendrick out of ear shot. Even on his best days, Chad was a vicious little man, but his loyalty, cleverness, and work ethic made Hawke like him. Kendrick affectionately called Chad "Smithers" behind his back.

Chad wound his way through the crowd towards his employer who was sitting near the front of the stage.

"Sir…" Chad said.

"Not now," Kendrick whispered.

"But Sir…"

"Can't you see I'm busy?"

"Yes, but…"

"Go away."

"The Italians, Sir," Chad got louder. "The deal is on but they insist on speaking to you personally."

"Shhhh!!" said several annoyed guests.

"It can wait," Kendrick said.

"I'm just…"

"Later."

"Now! Sorry… It must be now or it's off. You can do fuzzy playtime later, half a billion is at stake!"

Victoria's gesture cut the song short. Her predator eyes locked in on Chad. Victoria hated it when people failed to understand that performers on stage could hear nearby audience members. Chad was banking on the idea that his status as devoted employee should trump Victoria's status as lover, but Victoria was no ordinary roll in the hay.

Victoria threw a look over her shoulder at Drum and Bassie and snapped her fingers. They immediately dipped into a slow, sexy, jazzy version of a PJ Harvey cover.

Victoria sang, "Who the fuck do you think you are? Get out of my hair. Who the fuck do you think you are comin' round here?"

The audience laughed and clapped their approval.

"... Who the fuck? Who the fuck? Who the fuck do you think you are? Get your comb out of there, coming out my hair. I'm not like other girls, you can't straighten my curls. I'm not like other girls. You can't straighten my curls. Who the fuck you tryin' to be? Get your dog a way from me! What the fuck you doing in there...?"

Morgan couldn't get enough of the musical dressing down Victoria was giving Chad and Kendrick. Then the energy web vision filled Morgan's sight again, and she gasped.

The walls were crawling, rippling, and pulsing with power. All the energy rivulets of the web were flowing towards Victoria. Before there had been raw harmonious communion, but now Victoria was only giving back a sliver of what she was getting from those around her.

"...Get your dirty fingers outta my hair...!"

Victoria's inner control freak was driving her. She was keeping the audience transfixed, mesmerized, and docile.

"... Who? Who? Who? Who? Fuck! Fuck! Fuck! You ..."

The Victoria Shine persona was now standing on stage. The open, flowing, unadulterated personal Victoria was no longer there. To her horror, Morgan realized Victoria was siphoning energy from the crowd.

"... I'm free. You'll see. I'm me. You'll see. Who?"

Victoria got a standing ovation. Everybody roared. Morgan stepped up to the foot of the stage, into Victoria's limelight, and shook her head no. In response, Victoria stepped over to the guitar rack, picked up her Gibson Les Paul Standard, and smiled to Drum and Bassie. Drum ignited them into a fast-paced version of "Supervixen" by Garbage.

Victoria wailed on the opening guitar riff. The band paused, and then continued jamming. Victoria focused on Kendrick. "Come down to my house. Stick a stone in your mouth. You can always pull out if you like it too much." Victoria's gaze shifted to Morgan. "Make a whole new religion. A falling star that you cannot live without, and I'll feed your obsession, there'll be nothing but this thing that you'll never doubt." Victoria scanned the room, oozing seduction. "A hit is hard to resist. And I never miss. I can take you out with just a flick of my wrist. Make a whole new religion. A falling star that you cannot live without, and I'll feed your obsessions, there is nothing but this thing that you'll never doubt. This thing that you'll never doubt. And I'll feed your obsession. The falling star that you cannot live without. I will be your religion. This thing you'll never doubt. You're not the only one. You're not the only one. Bow down to me, bow down to me. Bow down to me, bow down..."

* * *

Morgan and Victoria found themselves in a modern kitchen with the roof and half of the walls ripped off. They were in a house built on a mesa, at the edge of a cliff. Eerie permanent dusk gave the place a creepy apocalyptic feel. A storm raged in the distance, and lightning scorched the sky. There were pots and pans on the stove and a bundle of utensils standing upright in a small clay pot on the counter next to a wooden butcher block knife set. The silverware gleamed from half opened drawers, and there were glasses and mugs on the shelves.

"Why did we shift into UnderLife?" Victoria asked.

"This concert is supposed to be interactive," Morgan said.

"What do you mean? The audience is completely involved."

"Yes, as spectators, but that's not the point. We're here to support their self-discovery. It's a musical healing seminar for everyone, not just a feast for you. You've got them worshipping you, not working on themselves. You're draining them, feeding off of their devotion, exhausting them when you should be exhilarating them. It's a mis-take."

"You did this on purpose? How dare you! You did this out of jealousy. Fucking come clean."

Morgan wavered. Of course she was jealous of Kendrick, but this wasn't about him. Morgan knew Victoria had overstepped her bounds. The night was about touching and enriching everyone.

"This needs to stop," Morgan said.

"What? No. Why?"

"It's time to."

"We just had a breakthrough. Things are going great. Why would I want to stop?" Victoria asked.

"Yes, we did and it was awesome, until Chad showed up and disrupted the flow. You need to retreat now before your Ego continues to feed on them."

"Like you're feeding on me by trying to control me? Who gives you the right? How dare you monitor me! The audience is fine. I know how far my fans can go, thank you very much. They love it!"

"Your fans?"

"Yeah, and you're one of them. Musical genius, was it? I'll decide what to play and when my set is done."

"You're making a mistake. This isn't about you!"

"Fuck off!" Victoria turned to walk away from Morgan.

"Oh no you don't," Morgan grabbed Victoria's shoulder. Victoria wheeled around and slapped Morgan across the face with her left hand.

Morgan took the blow without reacting.

Victoria followed up with a rapid right jab, hitting Morgan square on the nose.

Morgan's eyes began to water. She staggered back and sprawled into the counter, knocking the wooden knife block onto the ground. The blades scattered on the kitchen floor.

Victoria picked up a nearby frying pan and swung at Morgan's head.

Morgan high-blocked the blow. She hit Victoria's wrists hard enough to knock the frying pan out of her hands. Morgan rushed forward and wrapped her arms around Victoria's waist. Morgan locked her left hand around her own right wrist, putting Victoria in a double underhook clinch hold.

Victoria tried to push Morgan away, but she couldn't. She punched Morgan again, but they were too close together. In this position, Victoria's punches were painful, but not injuring.

Morgan made sure they had room to fall, and then she executed a body fold takedown. Morgan stepped forward as they toppled over to lessen the impact. Morgan landed on top of Victoria and mounted her. Morgan dropped her weight on Victoria's torso to gain positional control. Morgan's ample breasts were smashed into Victoria's face.

"Really?" Victoria growled.

Morgan chuckled. It felt embarrassing, but it was the proper technique. Morgan couldn't let Victoria get away from her. Who knew how much damage Victoria would inflict before Morgan subdued her?

Victoria was a clever and natural fighter. She realized Morgan was doing her best not to inflict pain. Victoria held no such qualms. The bitch was pissing Victoria off. Victoria knew she couldn't do any lasting physical damage in UnderLife, so she decided to put a beating on Morgan without any twinge of guilt. Morgan had crossed the line restraining her. Unacceptable. Fuck That!

Morgan was surprised at how freakishly strong Victoria was for her size. Morgan knew that ordinarily Victoria would be able to make her submit with just a glance, but the event was too important. +

Morgan thanked the heavens that Victoria didn't have any real jiu-jitsu training. Morgan was a blue belt, and she had only just begun to hone her grappling skills.

Morgan gave Victoria a bit of breathing room, hoping she was ready for a truce.

Victoria held her hands up. Morgan made the mistake of relaxing. Victoria reached for a knife on the floor and struck. The blade sliced a two inch bloody gash across Morgan's left cheek. Morgan put a hand to her face, stunned by the attack. Victoria bucked her hips, threw Morgan off-balance, and reversed their position.

Morgan locked up her legs around Victoria's waist, putting her into full guard. Morgan grabbed Victoria's knife-wielding right wrist and forced it across her body. Morgan took the blade out of Victoria's hand and tossed it out of reach. Morgan held onto Victoria's wrist.

Victoria figured Morgan was going to put her in an arm bar like she had done with Roland Addanc. Victoria pulled away from Morgan to stand up.

Blood was trickling down Morgan's face. She grabbed the back of Victoria's head and held her down long enough to open her guard. Morgan thrust her hips and legs up in the air and locked them around Victoria's body once more. Morgan put her right leg over Victoria's left shoulder, and her left leg compressed Victoria's knife arm into her own neck. Morgan hooked her ankles around each other.

Victoria punched Morgan with her free hand, and did her best to wrestle out of the position.

Morgan continued to hold Victoria's head down. At the first opportunity, Morgan readjusted her right leg to wrap even more securely around Victoria's neck. Morgan moved her left hand to her right shin, and snapped her left leg over her right ankle, putting Victoria into the signature Gracie Jiu-Jitsu Triangle Choke.

Morgan squeezed her thighs, flexed her hips, and pressed Victoria's head down. Victoria could still breathe normally, but Morgan was compressing her carotid artery, cutting off the flow of blood to her brain. Dark spots appeared across Victoria's vision, and she slid towards unconsciousness.

Victoria tried to roll out of the hold, which only made it worse. Morgan kept the triangle choke locked. She positioned herself on top, adding her full weight to the constrictive grip.

Victoria's eyes fluttered closed and she stopped struggling. Morgan waited a couple of beats. She unfurled her legs and slid her body back down into the mount position. Morgan watched Victoria warily.

Sure enough, Victoria's eyelids snapped open.

"Get off of me!" Victoria yelled.

"Only if you promise not to hit me with anything, and we talk this out," Morgan said.

Victoria began to struggle again. Every time Victoria tried to roll Morgan, Morgan propped her hand on the ground and used her opposite leg to anchor on Victoria's. Morgan drove her hips into Victoria, keeping her pinned down. Morgan took a few glancing shots from Victoria, as Victoria batted at Morgan in exhausted frustration.

"Alright, we'll talk!" Victoria said.

Morgan released Victoria. Victoria mumbled, "For now."

Morgan brought a sleeve up to her blood-smeared face. The wound on her cheek was oozing. Morgan asked, "Why are you acting like this? I'm your friend. You know I'm right about the audience. Vampirism is beneath you. Can't you see that?"

"You don't know what you're talking about."

"Then explain it to me. You said you knew why you were blocked while we were in the UnderLife forest. Tell me."

"No."

"Please. It's obviously torturing you."

"Maybe I deserve to suffer for what I did."

"What did you do?"

Victoria shook her head. "No, you'll tell everyone."

"I promise I won't tell a soul."

Victoria was silent for a minute before saying, "I killed him."

"Who? Cuneo?"

"No. Our baby."

"You had a child?"

"After Cuneo committed suicide I found out I was pregnant. I hated him for giving up. We had the world at our feet. I became consumed by the idea Cuneo's child would inherit his father's weakness for life, so I aborted our kid. I refuse to raise a quitter."

Morgan said, "I can see why you've been so secretive. The tabloids would have had a field day. Your creative block is a giant ball of grief and self-reproach."

"And disgust for not being more careful in the first place. You think I'm a coward for not having his baby," Victoria said.

"On the contrary, I respect that it was your choice to make. I probably would have done the same thing. I can't imagine how angry and upset you must have been at Cuneo for leaving you. But just because you decided not to have his kid doesn't mean your songwriting should be crippled for life." Morgan said.

"Maybe I just wanted to curse Cuneo by making sure his progeny never got to taste the breath of life. Or maybe I don't want anyone to be more important to me than I am."

Both women paused. Victoria said, "Well? Wasn't that the big lesson I was supposed to learn? Why haven't we transitioned back to Waking Life?"

"I don't know," Morgan said.

Nothing happened. Victoria stood and dusted herself off. She grinned at Morgan, turned, and sprinted towards the cliff edge.

"Victoria! No! Don't!"

Victoria leapt into empty space while screaming "WOO HOO!" She vanished from Morgan's sight, plummeting into the chasm.

The exhilarated yell morphed into a terrified cackle as Victoria descended.

Morgan's body was rooted in place with shock. She winced at the
abrupt silence.

* * *

Victoria lost consciousness and fell off the stage.
Morgan lunged forward and broke Victoria's fall with her own body.
The momentum carried both of them into a cocktail table which smashed
flat on impact.
The audience cried out in surprise and alarm. Drum and Bassie
faltered and went silent.
Victoria recovered consciousness in Morgan's arms a minute later.
"Hi there," Morgan said, brushing strands of disheveled hair out of
Victoria's face.
Victoria groped for her microphone, found it next to them, and from
the floor purred to the audience, "You all got me so excited I fainted."
The crowd cheered in relief.
"I'm gonna hand you over to Drum and Bassie to play for a bit. See
you soon."
Victoria's band mates took the cue and glided into a mellow beat.
Drum and Bassie pretended like the recent theatrics were all part of the
show, and pulled the audience's focus to them.
Victoria and Morgan slowly stood up. Kendrick said, "You could have
been badly hurt if Morgan didn't catch you."
"That's a generous recollection," Morgan said. She rubbed her left hip
and shoulder which had taken the brunt of the impact.
Kendrick moved forward to help Victoria, "Darling I am so sor…"
"I'm fine. Just going to take a break," Victoria shrugged off
Kendrick's hands. "Go answer your call."
Victoria gave a reassuring smile to the worried faces around her. She
retreated from the room, and gestured with a slight nod of her head for
Morgan to follow.

* * *

Victoria locked the Green Room door behind them.
Morgan and Victoria sprawled out onto the thick shag carpet.
Flickering firelight was coming from the ornate gothic sconces on the walls.
Morgan sat up. She watched Victoria, excited to be alone with her. As
usual, Morgan was overwhelmed by an impulse to pounce on top of
Victoria and smother her with kisses. The memory flashes of their recent
fight only intensified Morgan's desire to pleasure Victoria. Instead, Morgan
just allowed herself to imagine such a delicious endeavor. She continued to

watch Victoria's lithe frame stretching out on the rug in a languid, cat-like fashion.

Victoria stopped stretching, and crawled over to Morgan. Victoria let her body slide onto Morgan's lap. Morgan cradled Victoria.

They gazed into each other's eyes. Morgan bathed Victoria in a patient, loving gaze, as if she were enthralled by the greatest work of art ever created. Morgan would have been content to spend the rest of her days in this moment. She was more turned on by simply holding Victoria than she had ever been in her life.

Victoria felt immersed in Morgan's gentle embrace. Morgan's microscopic attention could only be coming from someone head over heels in love. Victoria felt safe and a bit sad. Feeling safe was an exceptional and startling experience for Victoria. She knew Morgan would follow her to the depths of hell if she asked. It was all tinged with an undercurrent of melancholy for Victoria.

Victoria wished she could love as easily and completely as Morgan did. Victoria cared for Morgan and felt very protective of Morgan, notwithstanding the recent attempt to kick the living shit out of her. Victoria knew Morgan spent every waking moment writhing over her desire for Victoria. She was sure Morgan dreamt every night of kisses and caresses that Morgan would never be allowed to express.

Victoria felt herself bracing with restraint to naturally respond to Morgan's palpable lust. It was an unusual experience for Victoria. Normally she made it a rule to sexually investigate people who intrigued her, but this time Victoria wasn't sure if her interest would go the moment she came. She was afraid of ruining one of her most fascinating friendships with sex.

Victoria believed their friendship had the resiliency and loyalty to overcome a doomed affair, but why risk it for something which sounded scary rather than scintillating?

Victoria doubted that Morgan had the sexual prowess and passion to please her properly. It would be disastrous if she gave Morgan permission and was met with a fumbling or tentative touch.

When it came to sex, Victoria wanted to be eaten alive. She wanted to be consumed by copulation, left sated and smiling from a championship fuck where nothing else existed but pleasure with her partner. If the experience yielded anything less than this, Victoria knew it would evaporate any hope for further romance.

Victoria didn't want to lose the friend she loathed to admit was becoming an essential part of her life. Morgan always provided Victoria with a devilishly delicious perspective. Morgan chose to be an adamant advocate for the happiness of humanity. She was convinced that Victoria had the power to help lead people into a more harmonious and satisfying way of life.

Victoria wanted to believe Morgan's lofty statements, but a part of her always felt this idealism was bullshit, and it was all about Morgan wanting to fuck her. Morgan's prolific vision was a ploy of lust, and would disintegrate like a sugar cube under the hot stream of rejection, making one of Victoria's nightmarish fantasies come true.

The fears did not stop there. Victoria also entertained the ugly notion that a sexual experience with Morgan would reinforce Morgan's romantic feelings for Victoria. Morgan would have no awareness of Victoria's discontent and dismay. She would think that the sex was permission to continue the courtship. Victoria's growing disgust would make Morgan intolerable to be around, forcing Victoria to walk away from her friend.

Morgan watched Victoria's essay of expression. Morgan split her time between Victoria's oceanic eyes and her voluptuous lips. In Morgan's dreams they were always the softest lips she would ever have the fortune of tasting.

Victoria watched herself being examined by Morgan. Morgan always looked as if she were waiting for the permission to ravage Victoria to her carnal content. This put Victoria on the defensive. She was more than a little angry that she had to feel on her guard around someone she had never demonstrated any physical interest in.

This was the point where Victoria usually started to feel uncomfortable, but as Morgan watched her with rapt, silent attention, Victoria began to relax. Victoria's relaxation made her aware of Morgan in a new way. Victoria could feel Morgan's naked lust. The clamor of intellectual warnings in Victoria's head became a singular static which was fading with each passing moment she allowed Morgan to hold her tenderly.

Victoria reached up and caressed Morgan's unharmed cheek. Then she snaked her arm around Morgan's neck and pulled her down for a kiss.

The only warning Morgan had gotten was the spark of fire igniting Victoria's eyes. There was no denying, even if she wanted to, Victoria's strength. A smile barely had time to reach the corners of Morgan's mouth before it met the velvety moist texture of Victoria's lips.

The kissing was exquisite. Victoria's fingers made their way through Morgan's hair and gripped the nape of her neck. She locked Morgan into the embrace. Joy cascaded through their bodies.

Morgan's thoughts were obliterated by Victoria's kisses. Morgan would have been hard pressed to know her own name at this point. Her lips trembled as her long asked-for wish was being fulfilled. Morgan was embarrassed that the overwhelming excitement was making her shake. Morgan pulled back slightly to search Victoria's eyes for some sense of help or direction. Victoria smiled and drew Morgan back in for more kisses. All of the specific and the nebulous fears Victoria had about Morgan, or about the future of their relationship, were washed away in the tide of rising pleasure.

When Morgan's lips quivered again and the sheepish look returned, Victoria loosened her grip on Morgan's neck. She pushed Morgan back on the carpet and laid her full body on top of Morgan. She punctuated the maneuver with a kiss so bold that it eradicated all fighting against the deluge of bliss.

Their hands explored each other with finesse and familiarity. Morgan stroked Victoria's muscular back and firm ass, massaging her as they kissed. A fine sheen of sweat developed on both of their bodies as their legs entwined and they writhed together. It became a top priority to remove the barriers of clothing, but they kept getting interrupted by kissing.

Things were about to get a whole lot more naked when a yell echoed down the outside hallway. Moments later, the door to Green Room burst open. Captain Tess spoke in a rush, "Apologies. Morgan, Victoria, we have problem."

CHAPTER TWENTY-TWO
HUMAN FAMILY

If the sexy scene Captain Tess stumbled into surprised him, it did not register on his face. Captain Tess looked as though he were interrupting a board meeting.

Morgan extricated herself from Victoria's luscious neck and helped her to stand up.

"What is it, Taylor?" Victoria murmured. She was stunned and embarrassed at having been caught with Morgan.

"Follow me." Captain Tess spun on his heel and left the room.

Victoria's eyes drifted down Morgan's body. She slithered Morgan into an embrace, hands roaming Morgan's back. "Such a pity we have to go back to work," Victoria whispered into Morgan's ear. She kissed her on the jaw, disengaged, and exited.

Morgan shivered in frustrated pleasure and followed after Victoria and Captain Tess.

Captain Tess took them to the Think Tank where an entire wall of computer screens was set up with views of every room in the compound. Mitchell Cannon was sitting at the helm dressed in a black suit and sporting a bushy Einstein-style moustache.

Victoria scanned the monitors and chuckled. "Wow, some of these overachievers know how to party. It looks like Burning Man meets Mardi Gras. Is that a keg on the basketball court?"

Morgan's eye's narrowed at one of the screens. "How about the coke moguls in the bathroom? Where are August and Louise?"

Mitchell pointed to the security feeds on his right.

The camera showed August and Louise sitting in the crystal workshop listening to and counseling a weepy Dr. Eileen Lombardo.

UnderLife

Victoria saw Mitchell's reflection on the screen in front of him and bit her lower lip to keep from laughing at his moustache. Victoria searched the panels for views of the Green Room, but she couldn't see any.

Kyle knocked on the door and entered. "Did anyone notice some of our guests tripping balls out there? Morgan, are we doing drug therapy now?"

Morgan said, "We certainly had no plan to, Kyle. Okay, we'll figure out how this happened as we go. I'll bet the majority of these people haven't taken a lot of drugs before and we don't want anyone to have a meltdown because no one was taking care of them. Our top priority is to be as Fonzie as possible and figure out what everyone has taken so we can make sure they have a good time. Last thing we need is this bunch on a bad trip. Captain Tess, do you know where my medical marijuana stash is?"

"Of course. I'm on my way," Captain Tess said.

"The weed will help everyone to calm down. I'll go smoke with the guests, for bonding purposes, obviously."

"And so you can get stony baloney," Victoria said.

"Well… yes."

Mitchell focused a camera at Drum and Bassie boogying on the dance floor. "Are they on something?"

Victoria stepped closer to the screen for a better look. "Shit I don't know, probably. Those bitches have done everything under the sun together. One week they're organic, the next, chemical. It's hard to tell with professional partiers. It's lucky for me that music is their strongest addiction. I'll take care of them."

As Victoria left Morgan heard her grumbling, "This better not be Austin all over again."

* * *

Victoria danced her way through the crowd to her band mates. "Hey, c'mere!"

"Victoria!" They yelled in unison. Drum and Bassie bounded over, and followed Victoria away from the thumping speakers.

Victoria wheeled on them. "You gave E to everyone?"

Drum and Bassie leaned back at the outburst, smiling involuntarily.

"I can't believe you dosed them and didn't tell me!"

"You said you wanted to make sure everyone had a good time," Drum said.

"So we did," Bassie finished without an ounce of remorse.

"Did you bring an entire pharmacy with you? How did you manage to get everyone rolling?"

"All we did was spike a couple cases of water bottles. We're not the only ones holding," Drum said.

"Yeah there's a bunch of yayo and dolls floating around this party," Bassie said.

Victoria looked up into a nearby security camera. "Good luck stopping this avalanche," Victoria said for the benefit of anyone watching the feed. She started dancing with Drum and Bassie.

* * *

August and Louise entered the Think Tank. Everyone filled them in on the situation. Louise said, "That explains a lot," then turned to her daughter. "Want to go pick some pockets with me?"

"I love our tender moments together," August said.

"Shall we?" Louise asked.

August nodded and led the way out of the room.

Dorcha passed by them in the doorway, "Hey guys, what's going on out there? Has anyone seen Draven?"

Mitchell answered, "He's in closed negotiations with one of our guests."

"Sounds like he's getting some action to me," Kyle said and laughed.

Morgan said, "If we handle this properly, we'll host a wonderful night not soon forgotten. Security knows how to keep an eye on everyone without hindering their good time. However, our guards' primary objective is to protect us from external threats, not to act as bouncers at a rave. It's up to us take care of loose ends and details."

"We'll handle the remaining water bottles," Dorcha said, putting her arm around Kyle's back at the waist. Kyle nodded and they left.

* * *

Morgan watched August and Louise waiting around the corner from the hallway leading to a private bathroom. Moments later, Pro, a skinny fellow barely out of his teens, exited the latrine. In cyberspace Pro was a God. Unfortunately, in person the young and wealthy computer genius's social skills were underdeveloped and atrophied. Pro's solution was to bring an eight ball of synthetic self-esteem to the party.

August unbuttoned a couple of rack-freeing buttons on her blouse.

"Try not to give the kid a heart attack," Louise whispered and turned the corner.

August leaned against the wall and reapplied her lipstick.

"Pro! Just the artist I was looking for," Louise said.

Pro loved the way Louise referred to writing code as art. If only his parents understood how peaceful and creative programming made him feel.

The UnderLife Project's invitation to Pro had consisted of a compact disc and a letter claiming they knew how to take Pro's work to a whole new level. "Give it two weeks. We promise you'll see results." The disc contained a program composed in ravishing code which offered a complex and detailed regimen designed to alert and encourage Pro to sleep, eat, exercise, bathe, and relax.

At first he found the program annoying and a hindrance to his craft, but his curiosity and ambitious nature made him stick to it. Pro's usual plan of coding until being ready to pass out from exhaustion, hunger, or the funk coming off of his unwashed flesh had fed into an illusion of productivity. However, after the two trial weeks had passed, Pro had to admit that he had noticed a marked improvement in every facet of his life.

"How can I help you, Louise?" Pro asked.

"Please forgive my naiveté, but I wanted to ask you about…"

The rest of Louise's fabricated geeky computer question was drowned in a flood of hormones as August stepped into his line of sight. She looked radiant. August sauntered down the hall as if every breath of air she took was a bit of a turn on. She pretended to ignore Pro gawking at her, then brushed by and accidentally bumped into him.

"Pardon me," August said, purring.

"Hi," Pro squeaked out, unaware that agile fingers from both women were stealing his cocaine.

* * *

Kyle and Dorcha had no trouble finding the Ecstasy-laced water bottles. There were three bottles left.

"Should we?" Dorcha asked.

"My whole family is scattered around here," Kyle said.

"Is that a no?"

"Just stating facts."

"Oh." Dorcha downed a spiked water bottle, "Whoops."

"Dorcha!" Kyle opened a bottle and chugged a dose. "Can't let you roll away from me."

* * *

Victoria snuck up on Darian, who was holding court in the dining area. Dorcha was regaling half a dozen party goers with acting anecdotes.

"Hey, twinkle toes, get your dancing shoes on," Victoria said.

Victoria grinned when Darian jumped a bit at her sudden appearance.

"We're doing the routine in twenty," Victoria said.

"The one from home? You're joking," Darian said.

"Get the girls. Harmony wants go-go dancers."
"Of course she does, that whore. Alright, see you in the spotlight."
"Sparkle."

* * *

August and Louise pick-pocketed the remaining few individuals who had taken it upon themselves to bring their own party favors. To delay and mollify the inevitable shock of losing their stash, the servers took special care of each formerly drug holding guest with cocktails, water, appetizers, and orders to fulfill any reasonable request.

* * *

Darian found Vespa and Jill Vihzor with Cynthia Sommers. They were sampling all of Cynthia's culinary creations.
"Vespa, Jill, how sharp are you on the dance routine from home?"
Jill shimmied and busted out a few moves. "You mean this?"
"You got it, woman. Let's go show it off," Darian said.
"Cool!" Jill said.
Vespa blanched.
"Vespa, c'mon," Darian said.
Vespa remained rooted in place. "Oh God, no."
"Sister. Yes. Now," Jill said, half-hugging half-wrestling Vespa out of the kitchen.
On orders from Victoria, Drum and Bassie met the Vihzor sisters in the Green Room to help them prepare.
Darian's make-up design for the trio was slap-dash, dramatic, and bathed in glitter.
Bassie dug a few hooker-short sequined dresses out of their gig bags for the ladies.
The Vihzor sisters dazzled.

* * *

Outside the door to the Green Room, Victoria glanced at a ceiling camera. She scooped up an empty wine glass from a nearby table and winged it into the wall. The sight and sound of shattering glass brought a feral smile to Victoria's lips. She kicked open the door to the main room and strode out into a thumping dance hall.
The moment Morgan saw the signature lip gloss, heavy smoky eye make-up, fake eye-lashes, and wig she, knew Victoria Shine had let loose Harmony Moore.

Morgan grinned. "I..."

"Go," Mitchell said.

* * *

Up at the third floor balcony of the Living Quarters overlooking the dance party downstairs, Kyle and Dorcha were lounging on a bench and talking up a storm. They passed a one-hitter back and forth. Their plan was to puff and dish, and then roll and dance.

"Well, it's no secret to anyone who Morgan wants," Kyle said.

"You've known Victoria for a long time," Dorcha said.

"My entire life. Don't think that gives me any special insight into her world. Fourth sister Victoria is just as mysterious as she seems to the public, more so even. She's awesome, scary, and impossible to ignore."

"Scorpio."

"Yep, walking proof. All traits exponentially magnified with a conjunct Scorpio moon and Kitty rising. Darian has her sun in Scorpio too, but Victoria makes Darian's razor-sharp intellect and emotional theatrics seem like gentle rain compared to Victoria's deluge of raw power. They get each other and care for each so beautifully that it set the bar high on what I consider a best friend," Kyle said.

"Do you think Morgan has a chance with Victoria?" Dorcha asked.

"Too soon to tell... Victoria continues to interact with Morgan and participate in UnderLife adventures. Home girl doesn't linger without at least some interest. What does the Tarot say?"

"That is has been a long time since anyone has surprised the hell out of Victoria."

"Here here!"

At that moment Morgan ran by.

"Morgan what is it?" Dorcha asked.

"Hhh..." Morgan panted, barely slowing her pace, giddy with excitement, "Har... Harmony Moore."

* * *

Flanked by a trio of dazzling and agile Vihzor sisters, Victoria opened her Harmony Moore set with Kylie Minogue's "Aphrodite", "Can you feel me on your stereo? Can you feel me on your stereo? Can you feel me on your stereo? Can you feel me on your stereo? This song lets you in, gonna get back down and up again. I got you on my side. It's just a roller ride. It's the truth, it's a fact, I was gone and now I'm back, yeah can you feel me on your stereo? ..."

Surrounded by her confident and capable sisters, Vespa's nerves began to settle. The four women rocked the well-practiced number they had been fooling around with privately for years. What the women lacked in polish, technique, and training, they made up for with electrifying enthusiasm. Throughout the song, Victoria as Harmony would alternate between beckoning and dancing with the Vihzors and dramatically shunning and upstaging them.

"…Can you feel me on your stereo? I got soul, you can check, in my heart, in my head. I got spirit you can feel. Did you think I wasn't real? I'm going back and forth and forth and back. Can you feel me on your stereo? Can you feel me on your stereo? I'm fierce and I'm feeling mighty I'm a golden girl, I'm an Aphrodite. Alright? Alright yeah yeah yeah! I'm fierce and I'm feeling mighty. Don't you mess with me, you don't wanna fight me. Alright? Alright yeah yeah yeah! Here's what I do when I know what I can do I let you into my world, with mouth to mouth and kiss to kiss oh oh oh. Can you feel me on your stereo? Can you feel me on your stereo? You sure you can take me in? Coz this is where the fun begins. I'm gonna feel your heart stop in my hands. I'm going back and forth and forth and back oh oh oh. Can you feel me on your stereo? Can you feel me on your stereo? I'm fierce and I'm feeling mighty I'm a golden girl, I'm an Aphrodite. Alright? Alright yeah yeah yeah! I'm fierce and I'm feeling mighty. Don't you mess with me, you don't wanna fight me. Alright? Alright yeah yeah yeah! You know that I'm magical, I am the original. I am the only one to make you feel this way. The moment that you kiss me, you know that you'll miss me. I am the only one…"

The crowd roared its approval. Victoria finished "Aphrodite" and plunged into her next song, the title track to Harmony's Harem.

* * *

Harmony Moore was a triumph. Victoria launched her entire sonic arsenal at the crowd and got everyone dancing themselves into happy exhaustion.

Morgan couldn't wait to congratulate Victoria on a stunning performance. She rushed to the makeshift backstage hallway, and halted in her tracks when she found Victoria with Kendrick. Kendrick was standing snuggled close to Victoria. His fingers played up and down the curve of Victoria's hip while he whispered in her ear.

A bolt of jealousy sucker-punched Morgan's Ego. She smiled, did her best to ignore the searing pain, and shifted into kill-with-kindness mode.

Kendrick watched Morgan's approach and smiled. "And here's our favorite psychopomp now. Thank you for a fascinating day I won't soon forget."

"I'm glad you enjoyed it," Morgan said.

Kendrick stepped towards Morgan, and shook her hand in a strong grip. He turned and strode by Victoria, "Think about it," Kendrick said and walked away.

Victoria grabbed a water bottle sitting in a nearby ice chest. She inspected it thoroughly before beginning to drink. Morgan took in the view of Victoria's strong and supple body in her stylish concert dress and lost the ability to connect two thoughts together.

Victoria's skin was glistening with sweat. She ran a chilled finger along the plunging neck line of Morgan's blouse. Morgan's breath caught in her throat. She was rocked by the bolts of pleasure being elicited from Victoria grazing the naked swell of her breasts. "Did you enjoy the show?" Victoria asked.

Morgan swallowed, "Thrilling" was all she managed to whisper before they were interrupted by the explosive entrance of the Vihzor sisters.

"VICTORIA!!!" The Vihzor sisters yelled in unison. They pounced on Victoria, sweeping up Morgan into their massive group hug in the process.

"That was so much fun!" Jill said.

"I needed that," Darian said.

"Thank you!" Vespa said.

"Sexy bitches!! You rocked it! Let's go stake our claim on one of the rooms upstairs before they're all taken," Victoria said.

"Yay slumber party! I already scoped the joint and know just the place. Follow me," Jill said.

Jill took them to an intimate room with a half dozen single beds spaced around a community closet, nightstands, and an adjoining bathroom.

A loud and silly nighttime grooming ritual commenced. Morgan could barely keep up with the rampant banter of the four soul sisters. Vespa was kind enough to explain what she could to Morgan. Morgan marveled at how the serious, stoic scientist was a total goof ball around the ladies.

"Victoria, will you sing us a lullaby?" Jill asked.

"How old are you?" Darian asked.

"C'mon, don't tease me. I love her voice."

"Yes, please, Victoria," Vespa said.

"How can I argue against the cutest go-go dancers in the mountain range?" Victoria asked.

Victoria hummed while making a show of tucking everyone in. Saving Morgan for last, Victoria curled up next to her. The tune evolved into a wordless melody which Victoria sang while stroking and running her fingers through Morgan's hair. Savoring every touch and sensation, Morgan drifted away and fell asleep.

* * *

Kyle and Dorcha were tucked away in the Mountain Compound's library. They had split the remaining Ecstasy-laced water bottle during Victoria's Harmony Moore set. Afterwards, they grabbed some sleeping bags and decided to camp out away from everyone else.

"I heard Taylor agreed to be your chief strategist for your first mixed martial arts fight. How's it going?" Dorcha asked.

"Wonderful! I'm learning a ton from the world class coaches and training partners he has me working with. Captain Tess designed a gnarly workout schedule and got all OCD about evaluating my strengths and weaknesses. I can't wait to put everything together in the Octagon."

"I hope we can get a hold of the birth time on your opponent so you can run his chart and study hid strengths and weaknesses, energy-wise. Consider Tarot at your disposal."

"Fantastic, thank you," Kyle said.

"After going up against Genital Ninja in the demon-filled spaceship UnderLife arena, your first bout should be easy."

"We'll see." Kyle's head tilted to the side a bit in appreciation. "You really are beautiful, and don't think it's the drugs talking. I've always thought so."

"What? I stopped listening after the word beautiful."

Kyle picked up Dorcha's hand and massaged it. Dorcha barely understood Kyle when he asked, "Are there Tarot cards which have Astrological correspondences?"

"Planetary or the signs?" Dorcha asked.

"You're such a flirt."

What's he doing? Dorcha thought. Shut up, woman, Dorcha's libido replied, I'll kill you if you screw this up!

"Yeah, some decks come astrologically-coded, but even when they don't both systems are based on universal archetypes," Dorcha said.

"That's hot."

"Yeah, it's fascinating how it all interc…"

Kyle kissed Dorcha.

* * *

Morgan woke with a start. How long had she been out? Where was Victoria?

Looking around, Morgan saw Vespa, Darian, and Jill Vihzor passed out on the other beds.

Morgan rubbed her eyes and sat up gingerly. She was sore from the multiple contusions she had earned by flattening a cocktail table in a valiant attempt at chivalry. Morgan stretched the kinks out of her muscles and went looking for Victoria.

Morgan checked the Living Quarters, Current, and Green Room. Then she headed towards the elevator nearest to the ground level entrance. After twisting and turning through several hallways, Morgan saw Victoria hugging August. Victoria's favorite guitar case and gig bag were at their feet.

"You're leaving?" Morgan asked. August stepped away.

"Yes, with Kendrick," Victoria said.

"You are… But…" Morgan's eyes welled up with tears.

"Aw, Morgan," Victoria stepped closer. "You can't have me that easily. Where's the fun?"

"Easy? Is this a game to you?"

"If it's going to hurt too much to play with me, I strongly suggest sprinting in the opposite direction. Let me go. I understand how unfair my rules are."

"I'm afraid it's a permanent, hard-wired attraction. Maybe if you smelled, looked, acted, felt, and tasted different it might change something for me, but I wouldn't count on it. Besides, why trifle, when your human perfection is so enthralling to witness and enjoy?"

Victoria kissed Morgan and said, "We'll play hide and seek later if you're up to it."

"Why can't we play found and loving it?" Morgan asked.

"You'll have to find me first," Victoria said, and left.

Morgan watched her walk away. When Victoria turned the corner and out of sight, Morgan's body flexed instinctively to follow her. Before Morgan could move, a hand gripped her shoulder from behind. It was August.

"It's better if you let her go," August said.

"I don't want to," Morgan said.

"Victoria has made no obligations to work with us beyond tonight. We should be grateful. Her presence has been pivotal in making this fundraiser a resounding success. If the early bids are any indication of what the rest of the group intends to contribute tomorrow morning, we will have more than enough money to finish the modifications on Current."

Morgan gave a weak smile. "This isn't fair! After what happened… she leaves with him?" Morgan asked.

"Honey, when it comes to love and sexual attraction fair rarely makes an appearance. Victoria told you what she wants. Something within her is resisting. Victoria challenged you with an invitation to explore why. You should be elated to get further license from someone so private. Don't let your lust blind you to the opportunity at your feet."

"I can help Victoria so much more if we're around each other. I already miss her terribly."

"You've done everything you can do. The best way to influence Victoria Shine is to take care of yourself and to continue your work. Keep in mind, when your wish is fulfilled, all of the pain and frustration will melt away. It will fade like a bad dream. Let this carry you through. These difficulties are transitory. Don't worry, you're in Victoria's thoughts, and you will hear from her again. Steady your heart and walk your path. Now it's time to learn something in between."

"I can't believe I made the same mistake with Victoria as I did with Balthazar. Just when I assumed they would understand my behavior is when the relationship was at its most vulnerable to ending."

"This isn't an ending. It's only a reprieve."

"Maybe not. Victoria broke through her creative block."

"What happened?"

"Last night Victoria sang Vespa, Darian, Jill, and me a wonderful melody she made up on the spot. I know her music well enough to recognize the seed of a new song when I hear it."

"That's wonderful!"

"Victoria doesn't need my help any more. She took off with Kendrick."

Morgan buried the rest of the story about Victoria's secret abortion deep in her psyche. Even if she never saw Victoria again, betraying her trust was out of the question. If August suspected Morgan was hiding the whole truth, she did not let on or pressure for more details.

"Don't sell yourself short. Victoria cares about you. Be patient. Go get some rest."

* * *

Sheer exhaustion took over Morgan and she fell asleep back in the dorm room.

Vespa and Jill roused Morgan late the next morning to prepare for the sleepover fiesta's finale: an auction for seats to Current's inaugural run. Morgan was interested to see who among the esteemed guests were willing to support and participate in The UnderLife Project. Morgan showered and dressed and wandered into the kitchen looking for something to eat. In the kitchen she found Draven. "Draven! Where have you been?" Morgan asked.

"Oh… around," Draven said while pouring himself a glass of orange juice.

"Having sex all night with someone you just met?" Morgan said and sat down next to him.

"More like a lengthy reunion with an old friend," Draven said. He was about to elaborate when Darian and Dorcha joined them.

"Breakfast in Florence," Darian said.

"Florence, Italy?" Dorcha said.

"Yeah, I'm jealous," Darian caught Morgan's gaze. "Victoria will be back in a couple of weeks for Love In Motion rehearsals."

"Cool," Dorcha said.

"Dorcha, mind doing some Tarot for me?" Darian asked.

"Sure! Right this way."

Dorcha gripped Morgan's shoulder on the way out.

"Let's go smoke a bowl," Draven said.

Morgan hugged Draven. "Absolutely."

* * *

The guests had a casual brunch. Then they gathered at the basketball-court-turned-auction house to submit their bids for the UnderLife Inaugural Mission. There were five seats available.

Louise played an impromptu video from Victoria on a large screen. Victoria said, "I had a lovely and memorable evening with you all. Thank you for coming. To those courageous enough for the adventure, I highly recommend UnderLife. It's definitely worth it to pony up some cash for the ride of your life." Victoria blew a kiss and the recording ended.

Seeing Victoria on the screen donkey-kicked Morgan in the gut. It was all she could do not to run from the room crying. Morgan managed to keep her composure long enough to field some questions before the bidding.

"Is UnderLife like the Matrix where you can load up stylish outfits, gain abilities, and pull off dramatic acrobatic fight scenes?"

"In my experience people generally keep the same skill sets and appearance they have in Waking Life, but there are many dramatic things I've seen and participated in UnderLife which can only be described as magical. Physics are more malleable in UnderLife. There can be an infinite variety of settings, characters, and creatures. It largely depends on the archetypal spiritual architecture of the people involved. It's a hike into collective unconscious. Every adventure is a deliberate creation. Think of UnderLife as a spiritual lesson seminar where personal conundrums manifest themselves for investigation. I believe our higher selves, operating in conjunction with the Cosmos, determine the specifics of UnderLife scenarios."

The crowd buzzed with excitement. Morgan held up her hand and continued, "Please understand. I've endured many horrific nightmares best forgotten during forays into UnderLife. There are many heavens and hells in Under and Waking Life. Spiritual lessons use all available resources to disseminate their truths. Be warned, this is not a vacation."

The interest in the mission was overwhelming. Louise announced that due to the high number of bids, they would also be auctioning off a second five-seat mission, as well as spots on the wait list, in case someone lost their nerve or couldn't otherwise participate.

This announcement caused the bidding for the First Mission to soar even higher. The guests were an enthusiastic and competitive bunch and nobody wanted to have to hear about the mission from someone else.

The rest of the auction was a haze for Morgan. Next thing she knew, the last guests were departing, and she was sitting in between Dorcha and Draven on a front row bench at Current.

"You two made out all night. I think it's safe to say he likes you," Morgan said.

"We were rolling." Dorcha glanced over her shoulder to make sure Kyle's attention was fully occupied by his sisters. "They don't call it Ecstasy for nuthin'."

"What do the cards say?"

"I haven't really had a chance to…"

Louise walked in with a triumphant smile and applauded the group. "Congratulations everyone! Your tremendous efforts made last night an absolute triumph! We have more than enough money to complete Current. Everyone performed impressively. It has been an honor. Now, please take some well-earned rest. You are welcome to stay here and relax, or Captain Tess and his capable staff will take you wherever you want to go. Thank you."

* * *

Three Weeks Later
On the set of Love In Motion
Hollywood, California

Victoria Shine sucked in as much oxygen as her lungs could handle and exhaled forcefully   …7:52, 7:53, 7:54…

Victoria stared at the digital timer. It took all of her focus to control her breathing and not pant. Victoria was holding a perpendicular wall-sit position by the sheer tenacity of will. Her legs trembled with effort.

Victoria drove her legs back against the wall as though she were trying to topple her trailer. Sweat dripped on a towel lying underneath her.

…8:03, 8:04, 8:05…

A production assistant knocked on the door. "They're ready for you."

"Thanks, Janelle," Victoria said and slid to the floor. Victoria rubbed her quads, stood up, and shook out her gooey leg muscles. Victoria typed 8:08 minutes in the Excel Wall Sit Tab of her exercise spreadsheet, hit save, closed the laptop, and exited the trailer.

Victoria scanned her script while walking towards set. They were shooting a scene in the bedroom of Darian's character, Agatha Moore.

Christina the make-up artist hovered around Victoria doing touch-ups. Victoria envisioned where Harmony Moore was the moment before she would enter the room for the scene they were shooting. Victoria pictured a steamy sexual tryst, and let the image sink in.

"First team into places," Greta the 1st A.D. commanded. "Last looks... On a bell!"

A school bell ring echoed around the lot, and the red bulbs next to the studio doors lit up. "Picture is up! Quiet on the set!... Roll sound."

"Sound speed," Zane the production sound mixer said.

"Roll camera," Greta said.

"Speed," George the camera operator said.

The clapperboard slid into frame. "Marker!" Bobby the clapper said, and slapped the board shut.

"A-a-and... Action!" Jeffrey the director said.

Agatha Moore (Darian) walked into her bedroom. "What are you doing? Is that my dress?"

"Eh, yeah, thinking about borrowing it for a bit, mate," Harmony Moore (Victoria) said.

"Last time you borrowed my clothing it came back with all of the buttons ripped off."

In the script there was a smash cut to Billy Slater as Gavin Dolmo making out with Harmony and slowly unbuttoning her blouse. Impatient, Harmony batted his hands away and tore it open. The buttons were still airborne as Gavin pounced on Harmony.

"That top was poorly designed for an active lifestyle," Harmony said.

"Where were you earlier?" Agatha asked.

"Out confirming a hunch."

Agatha paused. She knew her half-sister's penchant for crippling honesty. Agatha hated it when Harmony would give a vague response. Agatha's eyes zeroed in on the dress Harmony was holding.

"About what?" Agatha asked.

"Your boyfriend."

"What hunch?" Agatha grabbed the red dress, "I thought I left this at Varro's place. How? Did... Did you fuck him?"

Harmony stared at Agatha, gave a non-chalant shrug, and went to turn away.

Agatha advanced and got into Harmony's face.

"Why did you do that? Of all the men and you have to have him? Why?"

Harmony didn't answer.

"Do you hate me? Tell me, you conniving bitch!"

"Varro doesn't deserve you. He's not good enough. If he really cared about you he'd have kept his grubby hands off of me."

"If you really cared about me you'd stop sabotaging my life."

"Sabotage? Me? You're dreaming. I always have your best interests at heart."

"Right, real believable."

"I did it because you were so dazzled by him. Nothing else would expose the giant sleazy tosser lurking underneath."

"A generous hate fuck on my behalf? How thoughtful, you shouldn't have. How ever shall I repay such a kindness?"

"Agatha, you'd be handing Varro half of everything you own soon if I hadn't stepped in. You're too idealistic and naïve to sign a bloody Pre-Nup."

"Who knew your ravenous vadge had an altruistic side?"

"Please don't go buying any of Varro's bullshit that this was a hapless mistake. He'll screw you over any chance he gets."

"That's rich coming from you. You know, you're a real piece of work. God help the next person you actually have feelings for. How will anyone survive the vicious vetting?"

"Any lover worth keeping will see through the smoke and mirrors," Harmony said.

"Yes I am sure there are plenty of masochists out there who would love your attention," Agatha said.

"Cut!" Jeffrey the director said. "Victoria, I love the adlib at the end, but can we get that again with the original line so we have options later?"

"Of course," Victoria said.

Amanda the script supervisor slid onto stage next to Victoria. "The line is, 'Any partner who lasts can take it.'"

"Thanks, Amanda."

"Alright everyone," Greta called out, "we're going again. Back to one."

* * *

Mountain Compound
Current 2.0 Test Run

Morgan exited the helicopter with her duffel bag and backpack. Overhead, the giant steel doors slid closed. Morgan barely noticed her surroundings. Before today, every flight to the Mountain Compound had been an adrenaline infusion en route to untold adventure, and now it felt like an extended commute to work. During the landing, Morgan accidentally offended fellow passenger Trevor by referring to the impressive landing bay he had designed as The Garage.

Morgan's enthusiasm was dampened by Victoria's absence. Morgan would have loved to share this moment with her. Morgan was happy for the resurgence of Victoria's creativity, but it scared her in equal measure. Morgan thought that Victoria probably thought of her as some sort of an avant-garde creative therapist she fooled around with on a whim at a crazy party. Another anecdote to toss onto the mountain of sexual encounters and unique gatherings.

To fight feeling depressed, Morgan consulted the I Ching during the trip and got Hexagram 33: Retreat. It helped. By backing away from the steady barrage of fear, desire, and self-reproach, Morgan was able to submit her traitorous impulses.

Morgan started to walk towards Current. Dorcha sidled up next to her. They shared a brooding silence. Dorcha felt that Kyle had been doing a polite job of keeping her at arm's length since the fundraiser. The Tarot kept telling Dorcha to chill out, but Dorcha couldn't help thinking that Kyle's hesitation hiccups were showing a graceful disinterest.

Kyle and Draven fell into step behind the women. Kyle looked at Dorcha. She looked back at him. They obviously liked each other, Kyle thought, but they were tripping over their respective cartography skills. Kyle read up on Dorcha's chart. It was dominated by Capricorn and Pisces, which made typically confident Kyle feel self-conscious and intimidated. Dorcha was serious, intelligent, and a gifted psychic. If he chose to pursue her further, Kyle had to be certain of his intentions. Unfortunately his real feelings were obscured by a paralyzing haze of lust and doubt.

They rode the elevator to Current. Kyle turned to Morgan and said, "Darian said Victoria is practically living on set this season. Victoria made a deal with the studio to be able to stay overnight to compose."

Draven decided to share some intel on his sister with Morgan, hoping it would cheer her up. "Last time we talked Victoria told me about being inspired by a radical shift in her creative perspective, and she planned on burrowing into the writing cave to capitalize on it as much as possible."

"Thanks, guys," Morgan said.

August, Louise, Trevor, Tilly, Cynthia, Taylor, and Mitchell met the group outside the closed doors of Current.

"Ladies and Gentlemen, are you ready to test Current 2.0?" August asked.

"Before we start," Draven said. "I'm curious about what is lurking inside the psyches of our elders. How do you all manage not to get sucked into UnderLife like the rest of us?"

"Is it some sort of spy thing?" Kyle asked.

"We've spent years developing our psychic defense systems," Louise said.

"Fine by me," Morgan said. "I'm sure even a decade's worth of training would leave me sorely unprepared to face your dark sides."

"Indeed," Mitchell Cannon said. "Now let's get this show on the road." Mitchell hit a series of buttons on a wall panel next to him and the doors of Current whooshed open.

Cynthia quivered. "Does anyone else feel Current humming?"

"Mm-hmm," Kyle said, and everyone laughed.

"Maybe this isn't a good idea," Draven said. "What if I get transported into my worst nightmare?"

"Being straight?" Dorcha asked.

"Oh God, I didn't even think of that. How awful!"

"Don't worry, Draven. We've got your back," Captain Tess said.

"Despite that sounding enticing and vaguely sexual, I'd be much more reassured if y'all had any clue about what we're getting ourselves into. Where's my divination report?" Draven asked.

Dorcha went first with her Tarot analysis. "We're going through some kind of difficult emotional initiation, and the key is to withdraw in time or regret it. The Vampire deck Two of Wands says 'Insuperable limits, the prison of one's own conquests, regret.' Maybe it means this attempt won't work? Or we're in for a rough ride."

"That's just great," Draven said.

Captain Tess went next. "Great Power is involved. Hexagram Thirty-Four: Taming Power of the Great. This is an important challenge."

"I agree," Kyle said. "Our karma during this mission demands we pay special attention to integrity and truth. This can protect us. Fear or Ego based behavior from one will hurt all."

"I concur with my colleagues," Louise said. "Keep a firm grasp on your attitudes. You have the opportunity to release a clog of entrenched negativity. Don't miss it."

"Alright, I guess we're as prepared as we can be," Draven said. "Why are you people so intent on stalling? Let's go on an adventure!"

* * *

The team again awakened in UnderLife to find themselves sitting on couches in a circle. The elongated oval-shaped Room Of Many Doors appeared almost the same as before. Kylie Minogue's "Come Into My World" was playing on an invisible sound system. There was a movie theater popcorn machine sitting on one side of the room, and a one hundred square-foot squishy white membrane-like sheet hanging on the other side of the room. Everyone did a mental head count and realized Morgan was missing.

Captain Tess made a twirling motion with his finger. Everyone began to examine the Room Of Many Doors.

The industrial-sized popcorn machine started popping a batch of corn on its own. As they searched the room for an unlocked door, buttery delicious popcorn frothed forth and piled in the transparent bin.

All of the doors were either locked or sealed closed.

"Looks like we're trapped in here," Cynthia said.

"I wonder where Morgan is," Dorcha said.

The membrane-screen flickered to life like an old television set and projected where Morgan had landed.

* * *

Morgan found herself in the moonlit courtyard of a medieval villa. There were torches placed around the area. An impressive stone fireplace framed an equally captivating fire. There were two chaise lounges covered in soft furs facing each other in front of the warm blaze.

Morgan sat on one of the lounges, and across from her was Victoria. Victoria swooned and sank back onto the animal furs. Victoria pulled at the collar of her loose blouse. Underneath the skin, it rippled, pulsing. A fleshy mass began to grow from the place where her left shoulder and her neck met. It developed infantile monstrous features which more and more horrifically resembled Victoria as it continued to form. The form opened a mouth with jagged fanged baby teeth, and it snarled a high pitched mew. Morgan didn't even flinch. The second head was no big deal.

"Victoria?" Morgan asked.

Eyes wide, Victoria nodded. She opened her mouth to speak, but no sound came out.

"What is it?"

Terrified, Victoria tried to speak again, but couldn't

Morgan asked, "Are you feeling okay? Maybe you need to rest." Morgan touched Victoria's right shoulder.

"Help me," Victoria whispered in a plaintive, desperate voice.

"Oh my God! What the fuck is that!" Morgan screamed.

The grotesque creature bared its sharp mini teeth and snarled with a mew-like growl.

Victoria's real head looked panicked and nauseous as the evil abomination continued to manifest.

Before Morgan could think of what to do, her fist sailed towards the horrid thing. Morgan's knuckles smashed into its face. Morgan grabbed it by the nub ears, went on healer instinct, and cried out, "I call in the Archangel Michael for protection! I call in the Archangel Raphael for healing! I call my spirit guides to help me purge this pestilence!"

Morgan pulled on the abomination with all of her might. She couldn't allow another second to pass of the parasite gaining strength from Victoria.

It struggled to stay attached and it hissed curses at Morgan in an ugly unknown language.

Light started to form around the edges of the creature.

Morgan could feel it loosening its hold ever so slightly.

"Be Gone Foul Demon!" Morgan cried out, wresting it from Victoria's body.

The thing squealed in pain and frustration. Morgan smashed it onto the stone floor. She stomped on it until it was a grey, oozing, foul smelling pulp. Morgan took a blazing torch out of its sconce, kicked the abomination to a safe distance, and walked over and incinerated the remains.

Morgan was feeling exposed and easily out-flanked by whatever else might be lurking in this UnderLife Realm. She threw Victoria's arm over her shoulder and helped her to her feet. Victoria leaned against Morgan while they walked. The possession and exorcism had left her exhausted. As Morgan and Victoria were moving inside the house and into a bedroom, they heard the shrill cry of another one of those creatures in the distance.

"Please rest. I'm going to take care of this," Morgan said.

Victoria nodded.

Morgan ran towards the sound of the monster's yell. She processed the recent fight for clues about her enemy. The creature was somehow casting the illusion that its growth was normal. The head looked like an ugly bastardization of Victoria, like a physical representation of her shadow side, her Ego.

In this UnderLife Realm, subjugation of the Ego was a fight against demonic possession. Morgan searched for the leaders of this Ego Head Plague. She figured that if she could defeat them, it would be the key to their freedom.

Morgan had no idea where the rest of her companions were. She hoped were safe, and she kept a keen eye out for them while she searched for more abominations.

Minutes later Morgan found the leaders. It wasn't too difficult. They were on the hunt as well. Morgan and the abominations entered on opposite sides of another cobblestone courtyard facing each other.

The demons had taken over two large men. One was a bulky brute dressed in green leather armor. The other man was taller, thinner, and was wearing matching blue leather armor. The hosts' eyes were closed, their mouths twisted in agony. Their normal heads were ashen, withered, and radically aged. The second evil heads were fully developed. The men were armed with stilettos.

The Green clad abomination raised his dagger and charged Morgan, screaming in rage. Morgan put her hands up and crouched into a defensive stance. The creature lunged, intent on stabbing Morgan in the heart. Morgan advanced diagonally towards the man, slipped the strike, grabbed his wrist with her right hand, and smashed her left elbow onto his forearm. Morgan peeled the stiletto out of its hand. Hissing, the creature swung a hook counter punch at Morgan's head. Morgan ducked, crouching her body like a coiling snake. She sprang forward and put her full weight behind the thrusting blade. Morgan impaled the abomination in its larynx. The force of the blow plunged the weapon to its hilt, nearly severing the evil head clear off. Green pus-like blood gushed from the wound while the creature writhed in its death throes.

The Blue Leader pounced on Morgan, sinking its fanged teeth deep into her neck. Morgan swung her left arm back hard, and elbowed it square in the face, smashing its elongated nose. The creature howled and disengaged.

Morgan extracted the blade from the Green Leader's neck. She spun, feet pivoting, hips fully engaged, and sunk the dagger into the Blue monster's belly. It roared, staggering back.

Morgan went to finish it off, and instead stumbled to her knees in searing agony from the wound on her neck.

The Blue creature turned and ran, doubled over, clutching its wound.

The pain was excruciating. Morgan had been infected by the Evil Head plague. She felt the evil creature festering. It started to grow out of the wound on her neck.

Morgan called out for help, "Jesus! Buddha! Allah! Krishna! Pele! All the Gods of Mount Olympus! All the Faeries in the land!"

It wasn't enough. Morgan felt incredibly faint as the evil doppelganger began to feed off of her life force. Morgan had precious little time to defend herself.

Much to her surprise, Morgan grabbed the thing and said, "The Power of Christ compels you!" Morgan wrestled the terrifying parasite out of her neck while periodically invoking any help she could think of. Morgan was happy that the various deity archetypes had given her a template of perfect love to ground and anchor her chi.

A thought sprinted through Morgan's mind. Balthazar would love to know how strongly he had influenced Morgan for the visualization of Christ-consciousness to become such a powerful personal symbol.

After finally eradicating her demon, terrible fatigue washed over Morgan, but she could only rest for a handful seconds before going to search for the Blue Leader. If it got away, it would infect more people.

* * *

Morgan muttered, "Nasty bugger," before realizing she was out of

UnderLife, fully conscious, and back at Current.

The team was staring at Morgan.

"Where the hell did you guys go? I could've used some help."

"You mean from the second evil heads? I'll say," Kyle said.

"You saw it?"

Captain Tess answered, "We were trapped in the Room Of Many Doors. We were watching your adventure on a screen like a movie."

"Yeah, we watched you kick demonic ass!" Dorcha gave Morgan a high-five.

"Was that really Victoria in there with you?" Draven asked.

"I don't know. You'd have to ask her." Morgan rubbed her neck, exhausted by the creepy ordeal.

Cynthia said to Kyle, "I can't believe you ate the popcorn! It could have been seasoned with cockroach eggs for all you know."

"What, it was delicious," Kyle said.

"No way! Y'all got popcorn?" Morgan's cell phone rang. "Who is 213-284-5908?"

Draven laughed, "Victoria!"

Morgan answered the phone, "Hello?"

"What the fuck was that?"

"I don't know… second evil head?"

"Fuck That! Cut it out."

"I…"

Victoria hung up.

* * *

Two Weeks Later
Mountain Compound – Current Green Room
UnderLife: First Mission

"Mom!" Kyle whined, "Jill is still fuming about not being allowed to participate in the First Mission."

"It's not fair!!" Jill hopped up and down in frustration.

"Sweetie, we're just concerned about how your passion for extreme physical challenges will manifest in UnderLife," Tilly said.

"No one knows what will happen. I'll be good, I promise. I can help."

"What were you doing two days after last month's big wave surfing contest?"

"Rock climbing. What? So?"

Morgan put a hand on Jill's shoulder, "Your UnderLife is a black diamond run and I am still biting it on the bunny slopes. I'm not quite ready for you, darlin'. Soon."

"When? The next mission?"

"After I spend several hundred more hours at the gym."

"Okay, bunny, get cracking and train up quick. I hate being left out."

"Tweakers would have a hard time keeping up with you, Jill," Dorcha said.

Kyle laughed. Jill huffed in frustration and left the room as Louise was entering it.

Louise asked Tilly, "Did you go over the seating assignments with everyone?"

Tilly nodded.

Louise addressed the room, "I am sure each of you have committed your respective initiate's dossier to memory. Remember: Assess, Acknowledge, Assist. People have a tendency to be consciously cooperative but unconsciously guarded. Gauge their receptivity to your efforts, and be careful about when it wanes. This isn't about helping to solve all of a person's problems at once. Respect limitations and focus on the situation at hand. Your role is to be a guide. Do not force your will on them. There is no shame in a timely retreat."

"Gotcha, the Obi-Wan routine," Kyle said.

"Hopefully minus the Anakin debacle," Dorcha said.

"Your psyches better not conjure up nerdy space creatures," Captain Tess said.

"I won't, if you can keep from unleashing any rabbit assassins," Kyle said.

"Is it okay if I take a Xanax?" Draven asked.

"Can I bring my cat?" Cynthia asked.

"No," Morgan said. "But I think we should smoke a fat bowl."

"Do whatever you need to prepare. Curtain's up in five minutes," Louise said.

* * *

August ushered the new five UnderLife guests into Current. She directed them each to sit on a gold disc imbedded in the redwood bench in front of their assigned guide. The group marveled at Current. It was a masterpiece of technology married to tools of nature's magic. It was no wonder where the money had gone. There were now six platinum meditation disks in the center of the onyx floor. Each was surrounded by a ring of amethyst crystals. Matching gold meditation discs were spaced evenly on tiers of redwood benches. The surrounding cavern walls now held a vast mélange of amber, citrine, rose quartz, aquamarine, and sapphire stones. Clear quartz crystals studded the sealing, and the entire structure was wired together by gold.

"If everything goes according to plan," August said, "collectively you ıl initiate an UnderLife Episode via guided meditation in Current, and you will transition to our UnderLife Room Of Many Doors. A hologram of this oval shaped room will be projected through Current to harmonize the group's intentions during the meditation. Once in the Room Of Many Doors, you and your assigned guide shall find a door to enter and see what lies within."

Kyle Vihzor entered Current while August was speaking, followed by Captain Taylor Tess, Dorcha LeTour, Cynthia Sommers, and Draven Powers. They headed towards the ring of platinum discs in the center of chamber.

"What happens if things don't go according to plan?" Dr. Eileen Lombardo asked.

"Then we improvise."

"Do I get my money back if this doesn't work?" Hsu Suzuki asked.

"Yes, if you wish." August said. "As far as we've been able to determine, a successful UnderLife Mission ends with an instantaneous transition back into Waking Life." August stood at the door to Current, ready to exit the room. She didn't dare to be in there after Morgan had entered.

"And an unsuccessful one?" Hsu Suzuki asked, despite knowing the answer.

"We went through this, Sir." August Cannon exited. Morgan Martel walked into Current, and the door closed behind her.

"You get to taste what death feels like," Victoria Shine said.

Morgan gasped, frozen in shock. Victoria was sitting comfortably, across from Draven on a gold disc.

"Morgan, please take your seat," Louise's voice instructed over the sound system. Morgan complied and settled onto her disc.

The lights dimmed everywhere except beneath the amethyst crystals in the floor, projecting a star pattern of purple lights around the entire chamber. The group murmured their delight.

Morgan stared at Victoria in the dim light and saw something she'd never seen from her before. Victoria was nervous. Their eyes met, and Morgan couldn't help but smile.

Victoria had been caught vulnerable, again, by Morgan. This was usually a punishable offense in Victoria's book, but instead Victoria laughed, shook her head, and winked at Morgan.

"Assume the lotus," Louise said.

Everyone adjusted to sit in their best version of the cross-legged, meditative lotus position.

The UnderLife freshmen audience was mesmerized. They kept stock still, eagerly ready for the tantalizing adventure they had been promised.

Morgan smiled. It was one of those perfect moments in life when she got to touch cosmic awareness, feeling in complete harmony with an unfathomable Life Plan. The Streaming Moment where possibility lived.

Morgan's excited breathing echoed throughout the whole room, through the perfect acoustic stadium design which was centered upon her exact location. Anticipation and adrenaline rippled through everyone present.

The hologram of the Ready Of Many Doors flickered to life. Louise's melodic voice resonated throughout the chamber, backed by a meticulous soundtrack of nature sounds.

Morgan and her companions slipped into meditation like weary bodies in a warm bath. Their breath calmed and started to take on a slow, steady rate. Soon they were in unison...

ABOUT THE AUTHOR

Jocelyn Romero was born in San Francisco, California on January 7, 1977 at 12:22 PM (for all those Astrologers out there). After spending a wild freshman year at Tulane University in New Orleans, Jocelyn graduated with a BA in Theatre from Arizona State University. As a daily user and champion of Tarot, Astrology, and I Ching, she's developed a strong belief these tools can be used by anyone as non-denominational spiritual maps. Jocelyn's primary ambition has always been to forge an acting career, but Tarot, Astrology, and I Ching said the path to that goal required writing *UnderLife* first. Jocelyn resides in West Hollywood, California with her two cats, Primo and Dolores.